Charlotte Street

Charlotte Street

Juliette Mead

SIMON & SCHUSTER
A VIACOM COMPANY

First published in Great Britain by Simon & Schuster UK Ltd, 1999
A Viacom company

The right of Juliette Mead to be identified as author of this work has been
asserted by her in accordance with sections 77 and 78 of the Copyright,
Designs and Patents Act, 1988.
Words by Bob Dylan taken from the song 'The Times They Are A-Changin'' by kind
permission Sony/ATV Music Publishing

1 3 5 7 9 10 8 6 4 2

Simon & Schuster UK Ltd
Africa House
64–78 Kingsway
London WC2B 6AH

Simon & Schuster Australia
Sydney

A CIP catalogue record for this book is available from the British Library.

ISBN 0-684-86034-1

Typeset in 12/15pt Berkeley by SX Composing DTP, Rayleigh, Essex
Printed and bound in Great Britain by
Butler & Tanner Ltd, Frome and London

For my aunt and godmother, Helen Pehrson,
with love as ever from JH

Acknowledgements

I am an enormous admirer of certain contemporary chefs mentioned in this novel: Rowley Leigh, Simon Hopkinson and Jeremy Lee, all London based, and two American culinary giants: Alice Waters and Richard Olney, all of whom are inspired writers as well as cooks. I would far rather read them and eat in their restaurants than cook for myself.

Friends and family, as always, have made a great contribution: my parents, Tina Jenkins, Janos and Jenny Nyiri, Georgina Brown and James Runcie gave their generous advice plus a few anecdotes. Liz Sherman, Norma Farrelly and Steve Lay were invaluable for their authoritative input on food, restaurants and all culinary matters. Certain younger friends, aged between nine months and fifteen years, contributed unwittingly to the novel and I did not ask their permission – nor will I name them! Suffice it to say that any examples of shockingly bad behaviour were provided by my own children. I would especially like to pay tribute to the early gastronomic and descriptive gifts of my seven-year-old son, who tasted oysters for the first time at Christmas and uttered the sublime summary judgement: "Yes. Rather nice. Just like snot."

And finally, thanks to two consummate professionals, Clare Ledingham of Simon & Schuster and Carole Blake of Blake Friedmann. Ah, girls : what can I say? Another big thank you.

Frontispiece

Two bedroom first-floor flat with easterly aspect above shop in popular Charlotte Street, the heart of fashionable Fitzrovia. Kitchen, bathroom, spacious sitting room (24′ x 18′) with parquet floors and near full-length windows. Generous storage space and built-in wardrobes. In need of minor refurbishment. Long lease available, competitively priced for rapid sale. This ideal investment or *pied-à-terre* is well located for all local amenities of Oxford Street, Soho and the West End.

Prologue

The best stories are the ones that make you laugh and cry. Enrico told this story several times, and it generally made people laugh. It used to make him cry. Lucy would get him to repeat it while he sliced paper-thin rashers of pancetta, or scooped the glistening balls of creamy buffalo mozzarella, which always reminded her of putti's bottoms, from the vat behind the counter of the deli.

It had started around half past eleven on a Tuesday morning in late spring. Charlotte Street is never quiet, but this incident occurred after the late breakfasters had departed, and before the lunchtime rush, so there can't have been too many people around. The sound of a door slamming alerted Enrico and the regulars sitting outside the café opposite to a commotion across the road. A young woman emerged from the street door of number 53, cursed as she pulled the clamping authorization off the windscreen of a battered Nissan Micra and wrestled with the key in the car door.

Thirty seconds later, the first-floor sash window was thrown up and a male head and shoulders emerged. 'You want to go, Izzy?' the man shouted. 'Fine, bloody well go.' The whole street heard him, although the blonde woman did not acknowledge him in any way. He disappeared, and the six or seven spectators returned to their cappuccinos, smiling in uneasy collusion at this glimpse into the private life of strangers. No longer closely observed by anyone except Enrico, the woman briefly rested her forehead on the steering-wheel. She put the key in the ignition; the engine turned over half-heartedly and cut out. She tried again.

The man reappeared at the window and shouted, 'Seeing you're going, you can take all your bloody crap with you . . .' A shower of black – skirts, dresses, shirts – tumbled from the first floor, some falling on the pavement, some on the bonnet of the car below. Again his head ducked inside. The young woman wound down her window and looked up, squinting into the sunlight. Another burst from above, this time scattering clothes ranging from darkest aubergine through every shade of red to the palest pink. The third downpour – splashes of green – brought Enrico, a white apron tied tightly round his impressive stomach, out of the Italian delicatessen below the flat. He glanced up at the window, shrugged sympathetically at the woman in the car and began to collect the clothes from the pavement and street.

Several people in sleek suits had stopped to watch the spectacle. A couple paused at the entrance to the restaurant Elena's L'Etoile. A clamper van that had been prowling menacingly down the street slowed to a halt. The blonde emerged from her car and opened the boot. Without saying a word to each other, she and Enrico began to toss clothes randomly in.

The man in the flat leaned his elbows on the window-sill as he watched them with a smug expression. 'So much for your bloody colour co-ordination now,' he yelled, hands cupped around his mouth. 'Poor baby. All your blacks mixed up with the yellows . . . If you had any idea how much your sodding fanatical colour-coordinated wardrobe has pissed me off, your sodding anal neurosis about keeping everything in the right sodding space on the right sodding hanger. Hang on!'

2

The woman flinched, and turned to face the deli owner. She held out her hand. 'I'm sorry about this, Enrico,' she murmured. 'It's so . . . uncivilized.'

'You will see, he loves you.'

'He used to.' Socks, stockings, knickers and bras in various pastel shades fluttered around them like wedding confetti, and they stooped to their work again. The woman would not allow herself to meet the eyes of the strangers watching her, but a blush crept slowly up her neck and over her pale cheeks. When the window slammed down she went back to her car and lifted a hand in salute to Enrico. Holding up one finger, he shouted, 'Aspetta, Signorina!' rushed into the shop and returned with an enormous salami, which he thrust through the driver's window. The woman smiled her thanks.

Enrico watched until the car had turned the bend at the bottom of the street and vanished from sight. 'Eh! Nell'amore c'é sempre un nocciola d'amarezza,' he had observed sadly to himself, and he translated the expression later, for Lucy, when he recounted the story: 'There is always a kernel of sadness in love.' He then returned to bottling sun-dried tomatoes.

Less than one week later a sales board appeared outside the first-floor flat.

'Ah, Signora,' Enrico would often say to Lucy, in the early days when he called her simply Signora rather than Signora Epstein, or Lucy, 'Ah, Signora, I could have wept till I cried. C'é sempre un nocciola d'amarezza . . .'

After twenty years in London, Enrico's English idiom still left something to be desired, but in time she learned exactly what he meant.

Chapter One

It was the kind of day that assumes greater importance in retrospect, memory distilling the limpid blue sky, the intermingled scents of the sea air, the bouillabaisse, and the cool fruit of the wine into a sort of abstract symbol of well-being.

Richard Olney

How can I be a good, wise, morally grounded, spiritually sound wife and mother, Lucy thought, squinting at the clouds that scudded above her, and still crave pure linen sheets? It was a problem that increasingly vexed her: how to balance the mundane desires of her family life with her more cerebral goals, to be able to say that chaos over the breakfast table was *in itself* a thing of joy. She was certain that whoever it was, the Dalai Lama or some other great visionary, who had said, 'The purpose of life is to be happy,' had not intended to include the expansion of her linen closet in the message. I am happy. Blissfully, she reminded herself. She had everything she had ever wanted, except freedom from craving linen sheets. Her friend Constance Purcell had linen sheets coming out of her ears. Sod it, Lucy thought. It was too beautiful a day to waste thinking about sin, and even if she was guilty of avarice, and yes, OK, envy too, she was innocent of the other five.

Except maybe gluttony. Every now and then she came a cropper over gluttony.

Like many happily married people, Lucy Epstein lived emotionally at the narrow margin that falters between unconscious contentment and vague frustration. It had taken a good three years of married life for love's bright young dream to lose its lustre and the first inklings of discontent to take hold, but after nine years of marriage Lucy was wise enough to know that the frustration she occasionally felt was commonplace, and could not be attributed to her marriage. Let alone to her husband.

That afternoon was one of those times when Lucy felt as close to pure contentment as she ever came. She now regarded the three, nearly four years she had spent as an independent single career woman – a management consultant, no less – as quite utterly joyless. Hindsight did not blind her to the degree that she felt it had been a waste of time. She had enjoyed self-esteem, professional recognition, the camaraderie of colleagues, and a high degree of intellectual stimulation, as well as financial reward. These combined did not compete with the unadulterated pleasure of lying flat on her back, bare feet in the grass of a Dorset meadow with a stream running by, and her three children gambolling happily around her.

Earlier that day Lucy hadn't been happy at all: she had been pumped up with righteous indignation. She had been to the supermarket with all three children, as well as, most unusually, her husband. Mark detested shopping but had volunteered to entertain nine-month-old Abigail in the café while she did a marathon shop with the two older ones. As Lucy and Charlie returned to their car, some way ahead of Mark and the girls, Lucy spotted a small boy charging a trolley repeatedly into the boot of a car parked a few spaces away from their own. She had intervened impulsively like an avenging angel. 'Hey – what do you think you're doing?' she had shouted, snatching the child by the hood of his sweatshirt. 'Is that your car?'

The child had not replied, but kicked the tarmac sulkily.

'You really mustn't treat other people's property like that.' Lucy held the boy's arm firmly as he tried to ram the trolley again.

'Oi! Get your hands off my kid!' A tank of a man approached from nowhere and confronted Lucy, as Mark and the two girls drew near.

'Look, I'm very sorry,' Lucy began, 'but your child was damaging that car.'

'Your car, is it?' The father snarled.

'No, but –'

'Fuck off, then, and leave my kid alone. I don't need the likes of you butting your big nose into what my kid does.'

'Oh, really?' Lucy had demanded, feeling nervous but sounding haughty.

'Come on, Luce, get in the car and let's go,' Mark had urged. A pacifist but not a coward, he stood between Lucy and the stranger.

'Let me ask you just one question.' Lucy, standing with her arms akimbo, leaned around Mark. 'If your child was about to be run over by a car, because you weren't watching him, would you want me to butt my big nose in then?'

Mark had hustled his wife and children into the car while the father shouted abuse and damned Lucy and all her sort to hell several times over. Lucy was still breathing heavily as she fastened her seatbelt. 'Well?' she'd demanded of Mark. 'Was I wrong?'

'No, darling, you were perfectly right. But nobody likes being told how to look after their children, or criticized for not doing it. You may have an obligation to protect a stranger's life, but you can't tell them how to live it.'

The incident that morning had been unpleasant, but the leisurely afternoon picnic had more than compensated. Lucy allowed herself a degree of complacency as she watched her own perfect and delightful children. Children were happy so long as they had clear boundaries, she told herself, and unlimited attention. And that was why she had decided to stop work: to enjoy them and give them all the attention they needed. It had meant they had significantly less money, but that had been an exchange both she and Mark were willing to make for their children. And if occasionally her darlings filled her with feelings that fell a little short of pure delight, then all she had to do was spend some time in the company of other people's children to know that hers were exemplary. Lucy did not adhere to the 'manners maketh man' principle, and her children, particularly Grace, could often be a handful; what she was inclined to label bad behaviour in other people's children she identified as strength of character in her own. Lucy could not be condemned for this hypocrisy: bias is an essential part of the maternal job. She was a happy mother, as well as a devoted one, as she inhaled the clean, country air deeply, and looked up at the late spring sky.

'Charlie, what do you think that one looks like?' she asked her son.

'I don't know. It just looks like a cloud.' Charlie was a grave child, and took his time before volunteering opinions. At eight he had already developed a considered approach to life, and scrunched up one eye as he studied the cloud. 'It could be the Abominable Snowman, a Yeti. Or,' he added, with the glint of mischief that Lucy loved in his eyes, 'it could be Mrs Hetherington, when she's leaning over our desk, being really cross and blowing smoke out of her nose.'

His mother laughed. 'It looks so white and fluffy, it couldn't be cross at all . . . Anyway, is Mrs Hetherington ever cross with you?'

'Not with me, but you should see her yelling at Howie.'

Lucy stroked the head of the dozing baby tumbled across her

lap. 'I've always liked Howie when he comes over.'

'He's OK. Only none of the teachers think so.'

'Where's Grace?' Lucy craned her neck to look for her daughter, who was piling mud from the edge of the river bank on to her lap. 'Gracie, darling, don't do that . . .' Lucy lay back again, enjoying the gentle warmth of the afternoon sun on her face. 'Grace,' she called lazily, 'come over here and tell us what you think the clouds look like.'

Grace didn't see anything at all in the clouds. Once she stood up, all she saw was a lot of mud on her pretty dress, and it displeased her.

With little Abigail slumped across her stomach and chest, Lucy coaxed her two older children to lie in the crook of each arm and study the sky. 'Let's pretend there's nothing but us in the whole wide world,' she told them. 'That everything up there belongs to us.'

'The sky's the same colour as my dress!' Grace shouted excitedly.

'It's not brown, Grace, and your dress is now. Your dress is horrible.'

'Shhh . . . Grace is right. OK. The whole sky is your dress, Grace. And the river is Charlie's wide smile.' Lucy was rewarded by her son beaming broadly.

'And the white clouds are Abby's nappies,' Charlie finished. 'Before she poops in them.'

It was a perfect moment in Lucy's life: surrounded by her three beautiful children, after a lazy picnic by the river, in sunshine that heralded a glorious summer. She cradled the baby and rose to her feet. 'So, my darlings, shall we head home and make your daddy stop work?'

Constance Purcell was far too busy organizing her children's return to boarding-school after the Easter holidays to have time for lazy afternoon picnics. A large trunk occupied the centre of each of their bedrooms. That morning each trunk had been surrounded by piles of neatly folded and name-taped clothes, but by noon they were almost ready to go. It was easy packing for Luke: provided he had all his sports kit in order, he rarely asked for anything else and was supremely unconcerned by the notion of mufti. Francesca was a different fish altogether.

Now she threw herself face down on her bed and covered her head with a pillow. 'I can't take the same jeans back, Mum, I just can't. You don't have a clue. Nobody's wearing bootleg any more . . . Hardly anyone's wearing jeans at all. I have to get a pair of combat trousers.'

'I simply don't have time for this now, Chessie. You might have said something when we were in town yesterday.' Connie's foot tapped the carpet in irritation.

'You don't have time for anything when it comes to me,' her sixteen-year-old daughter whined pitifully. 'You have plenty of time for the restaurant, and anything else you care about.'

Constance pursed her lips and placed the final pile of her daughter's clothes on the top of the trunk. 'You've had all holiday to work out what you need, Chess, and you can't expect –'

Francesca sat up suddenly. 'Are you taking us back to school or is Dad?'

'Dad. We have the Epsteins coming to dinner.'

'Then if we drove through Cirencester, Dad could stop and I could dash in and buy some combats.'

'Oh for God's sake, Francesca! If you can con your father into stopping, that's fine by me. But you'll have to leave almost immediately, and I don't even know if Dad's home yet –'

Francesca had already flown off the bed and was racing downstairs to wrap her father round her little finger. Her mother

sat on the trunk and clipped the locks down. In a couple of hours'
time, her house would be her own again, and not the playground
of overactive adolescent hormones. She sighed heavily as she took
a final look around the room. When she spotted Francesca's diary
on her bedside table she stifled the desire to flip through it and
slipped it along with the teddy bear into her daughter's suitcase.

'Mum?' Luke stood tentatively in the doorway. He had learned
to gauge his mother's mood carefully. When she smiled at him and
patted the bed next to her, he sat down and leaned gently against
her. 'Dad says we have to leave right away.'

'Blame your sister. She has some vital bit of shopping.'

'Mum . . . I don't much feel like going back to school.'

'Why not, darling?' Constance ran her fingers through his mop
of hair. 'You're in the first eleven next term, and you're brilliant at
cricket.'

'I'm just OK, that's all. I'm not brilliant at anything.'

'That's not true. You're brilliant at just about everything, and I
won't tolerate that sort of modesty in a child of mine,' she teased
him, elbowing him playfully in the ribs.

'I dunno. It's just, you know . . . All such a bore.' His words may
have been inarticulate, but his widely spaced grey eyes beneath the
fall of dark hair that he habitually flicked off his forehead gazed at
her with a look that said clearly, 'Look, I'm not all that thrilled
about going back, but I'm not going to make a fuss. I'd just like to
know, from time to time, that you care.'

Constance studied his face before taking it between her cool,
practical hands and kissing him. She yearned to tell him he could
unpack and stay at home with her for another week or two – a
year, if he liked – but she understood that he had reached a stage
of needing her and needing not to need her, while knowing that
she needed him. 'You'll be just fine. I'm the one you should be
worried about. What will I do without you? Right, Muscleman. As

11

soon as your father comes up, you two can load the car up with the trunks. It'll be the exeat weekend before you know it. You can bring Spig home with you, if you want.' She ruffled his hair, and just as quickly smoothed it back into place as she heard her husband's slow, heavy tread on the stairs.

They lived, these two couples, and conducted conventional family lives, in a time when all the buzz was of restructuring the concept of the family. Perhaps they were behind the times, or perhaps they were ahead of them; it was certainly a time when many women no longer felt comfortable existing solely as wives, mothers, daughters and friends, yet the dedicated performance of all these roles continued to be expected of them. The Epsteins and Purcells may have had varying private traditions and practices, but they shared a common experience, and a casual perusal of their respective photo collections would have been more striking for their similarity than their differences. In each collection a visitor would find a snapshot of children huddled, heads bent, in a circle on a beach, examining some fascinating object that the camera could not see; a man, standing a little self-consciously, perhaps holding an umbrella, before an important-looking edifice; a baby with chocolate all over its hands and face; a laughing woman in a hat, her hand up to stop it blowing off, whether she was attending a wedding, or a garden party, or even the funeral of a distant and unlamented relative now long forgotten. A photo of the Eiffel Tower. A lake with a boat on it. A Christmas tree. These scenes were absolutely uniform and common, although the four adults who had taken all those photographs to record their family memories could not have been more fundamentally dissimilar.

In common with many women with small children, Lucy Epstein's life was busy, but her role was at least clear-cut: chief nurturer of her husband and children, responsible for their welfare and the general maintenance of the household. That evening she took one quick look at the new baby-sitter and what she had brought in tow – her even newer, rather hairy boyfriend, a six-pack of lager and a video – and contemplated cancelling their dinner engagement. She asked the couple to wait in the kitchen while she consulted her husband who was 'dressing' for dinner – in other words lying flat on his back on their bed and not bothering to change – with their neighbours Constance and Julian Purcell.

'Connie won't mind if we bottle out,' she proposed, after giving a thumbnail sketch of Frankenstein and his bride below, 'not on a Tuesday night. It's only a kitchen supper, after all.'

'That's a joke! Constance detests people who cancel at the last minute. Constance detests people who do *anything* at the last minute. The kids will be fine. A couple of cans of lager never hurt anyone.'

'Six, Mark. Six cans.'

'Between two of them,' he replied reassuringly. 'Don't judge a book by its cover, Luce. I'm sure they're fine.'

'I don't care what they look like – they just don't look that responsible, that's all.'

'Give the girl Connie's number and relax. We've barely been out in three weeks, and I refuse to live a hermit's life because we have kids. Hang loose, Luce. You know you only raised the doubt to show what a responsible mother you are. You have no intention of cancelling.'

A man who has been married to a woman for close on ten years can land a hammer unerringly on the spot most guaranteed to annoy her, but Mark Epstein also had a gift for making perfect remarks. He had a knack for saying the right thing at exactly the right moment, a sort of conversational stitch in time to save nine. That was one of the reasons why Lucy had fallen in love with him

13

in the first place. They had met in the late 1980s at Corney & Barrow, where Mark had been working as a wine agent. Lucy was then a rising analyst at a firm of management consultants and had been called in to pitch for the Corney & Barrow job. Mark had nothing to do with the marketing or financial end of things, but he kept barging into the room and hanging about, feigning fascination with the subtleties of push-pull strategies, segmentation criteria and billing rates. Without ever directly looking at him, Lucy had weighed him up. He was undeniably attractive, albeit a little too edgy for her taste, wiry and thin, and very dark, whereas up till then Lucy had been attracted to big strong blond types. Through a combination of boyish charm and dogged persistence he had persuaded the young consultant to have a drink with him, so she could 'talk him through' the latest concepts on balanced score-card performance measurements and the Government's proposals for changes in VAT regulations. He took her to a private wine club, all dark heavy woods and sombre upholstery, and during the first lull in the conversation – Lucy was quite accustomed to lulls in management-consulting conversations, particularly when they concerned accounting – Mark had stared hard at the striped wallpaper and announced, 'We should have something like that in our flat when we're married.' She'd only known him about twenty minutes. He said it so bluntly, yet without looking at her, that for a moment she thought she had misheard. Then she laughed. It was all a question of timing. Everything is. They fell in love, and it was the right time for both of them. They knew nothing about marriage, but were engaged six months later, and even after ten years of married life he hadn't lost his touch.

Their circumstances had changed a great deal during those intervening years. An unplanned but nonetheless welcomed pregnancy had brought them Charlie, and Charlie had turned them overnight into a family. For three years Lucy continued to work, going through the familiar stages of extending her maternity leave without pay, then returning full-time to find that she could not stand to be away from the baby all day, finally negotiating part-time employment, which meant that she earned half her full-time salary and did three quarters of her original job, often working late into the night from the tiny third bedroom of their Fulham maisonette. When Lucy conceived a second time they took the opportunity to change their lives radically, pulling up roots to head westwards. It had taken the best part of the pregnancy for the Epsteins to organize their exodus from London; originally intending to keep within forty-five minutes of London, they had finally settled over two hours away in a ramshackle farmhouse in a small Dorset hamlet.

The first months had been difficult to say the least. Charlie, then a toddler, had tricked them into thinking that all babies were compliant, biddable creatures that gave joy and asked for nothing but love in return. The arrival of Grace, coinciding with the move as well as Mark's setting up as an independent wine dealer in the West Country, brought havoc to the household. Mark was preoccupied with starting up the business; Lucy was terrified that his commercial timing was misguided; the arrival of a sibling caused Charlie to metamorphose from angel to demon, and Grace herself began a seven-month-long bout of what the health visitor euphemistically called 'a touch of colic'.

It had taken the Epsteins longer to settle in Dorset than they had expected, but this was no bad thing. The distance between Fulham and rural life was far greater than the road map suggested, and the journey required a greater psychological leap than most London-leavers assume. The Epsteins had leaped nervously, but landed with a firm footing. In time, Grace had carved her place in the family and Charlie had stopped asking when they were going to return her to the hospital. Mark's business, Epstein & Rose, named after the grandfather who had fortuitously died and left him the first year's running costs, was stable if not booming, and provided sufficient security after three years to allow them to feel that it was time to add another member to their brood. Mark had named his second daughter after poring over a book of babies' names. He'd pointed out that after the Teutonic Charles and Greek Grace it was high time they had a Hebrew name. Besides, Abigail meant 'father rejoiced' and that was certainly true: unlike some men, Mark Epstein adored babies. He had formed a solid bond with Charlie, now approaching his eighth birthday, but relations with four-year-old Grace were at best turbulent. Mark was inclined to wallow in the brief stage of parental omnipotence that only babies allow.

That Tuesday evening the Epsteins compromised by taking Abigail with them to dinner at the Purcells', in the illogical yet under-standable reasoning that more harm could befall the most recent addition to their family than the more established members. It took about twenty minutes to drive to the Purcells' house; it lay three villages away from their own, but they referred to Constance and Julian as their neighbours, and their closest friends. Mark speculated happily on what Constance would give them for dinner. She was more than a good cook: she was a professional one. Like the Epsteins – and perhaps this similarity lay at the root of their friendship – the Purcells had also left London although, their marriage and their children being older, they had preceded the Epsteins by some four or so years. The two couples had met in church on Christmas Eve when Lucy and Mark had taken Charlie and the infant Grace to Midnight Mass. Julian had read the lesson and after the service, when Lucy found herself standing next to him in the queue to greet the vicar, she had complimented him on his reading. An invitation to lunch had followed, and barely a week had passed since without the two families getting together in one form or another.

The friendship had been conducted at breakneck speed, which would have made people in London suspicious but seemed acceptable in the country. After all, the two couples had much in common, having abandoned their old friends in search of a higher quality of life and in the certainty that those London relationships were stale, only to find that what they most missed were the like-minded people they had been so willing to leave behind. As far as the Epsteins were concerned, and the Purcells appeared to endorse this impression, it was very hard to find a foothold in the local social whirl. They did not fit in with the Dorset born-and-bred families who retained a healthy suspicion of outsiders, and although Mark, Julian and Constance had their work to occupy them, Lucy found herself in limbo, unwilling to resign herself to village jumble sales when she had followed a supposedly high-flying career, yet all too aware that to the rest of the world she appeared to be sitting on her arse doing nothing but disciplining her children, and that rather ineffectually. She had confessed as much to Constance the first time they'd talked.

'Oh, don't worry about that. Don't ever worry what people down here think. That's the joy of living in Dorset – you don't have to *be* anything.'

Lucy paused. Constance was right: no one expected her to be anything except herself, and that was half the problem. 'I haven't even got the right wardrobe,' she'd joked. 'No tweed jackets, no gardening cords . . .'

'As far as we're concerned it makes no difference if you wear Armani or Oxfam. We're not *Country Living* people.'

'Country living?'

'*Country Living* couples – you know, the magazine. All those couples who've gone way, *way* beyond stencilling and liming and are deep into compost bins and organic fertilizers.' Humour had rippled through Constance's voice. 'The woman wears stonking great hiking boots and a scratchy grey jumper her "partner" has cast off. She makes trugs out of the dead wood she's foraged in her garden and talks earnestly about setting up her own cottage industry. He was an architect, but abandoned a successful urban practice to learn how to lay drystone walls.' Constance had warmed to her theme. 'Their herbaceous borders are stuffed with potatoes and brassicas. They don't make fudge brownies for their children, they make disgusting things called "market piglets" – probably with wholemeal flour.' She had laughed. 'God, I sound bitchy. I can imagine what they'd say about me. Anyway, that's not us, and it never will be.'

At the time, in those first few months in her new role as rural mother and châtelaine, Lucy wondered how she would have described herself in magazine terms. Not a *Country Living* person – not yet, and never would be, having heard Constance's parody. Certainly not a *Harper's & Queen* person, although a lifetime ago, in her fancy-free youth, she'd considered herself a hybrid *H&Q/Tatler/Vanity Fair* Woman. Now she felt more Waitrose in-house mag, outwardly struggling to be *Elle Decoration* Woman, and inwardly yearning to reach the elevated status of *New Yorker* Woman.

'So what are you? I mean, do you work, or what?' Lucy had asked curiously, looking around Constance's pristine kitchen.

'I'm a cook,' she had stated briskly. 'A chef, in my moments of deluded grandeur. I run a restaurant near here, only open at weekends but we do all right. It's called the Lonely Falcon.'

'The people who sold us our house raved about it, said it was the only place to eat around here.'

Constance had barked with laughter. 'That's not very flattering – coming first in a race with one entrant.'

Lucy had blushed, and corrected herself. 'No, they said the food was fantastic.'

'That's nice. Actually, they didn't come that often. Well, that's what I do, at weekends at least. Julian's an architect – mainly restoration work, a lot for the National Trust. I'd call him *Architectural Heritage* with a top dressing of Sotheby's catalogues. And I'm . . . I'm . . .' she mused, 'I'm the Saturday *FT* Weekend Section. How To Spend It.'

'Not Sainsbury's? Not Delia Smith, then?' Lucy had asked, with a teasing smile.

'That isn't even funny,' Constance had replied, with a broad grin. 'And I hoped we were going to be *such* good friends.'

'At least you *do* something,' Lucy had grumbled. 'My husband does something, your husband does something, I don't do anything any more.'

And Constance had given her a strange but sympathetic look, and poured her a glass of wine. 'You have a baby and a three-year-old. You've just moved house. That's enough for anyone, man or woman. I didn't do anything until we got the children into their maximum security units.'

'What?'

'Boarding-school. Your time will come.' Over my dead body, Lucy had thought, but wisely kept it to herself.

Constance's then fledgling restaurant near Blandford Forum had gone from strength to strength, and the Lonely Falcon was now open from Thursday evening through to Sunday lunch. In the near desert of West Country dining she had created a small but increasingly respected oasis. She had become one of Mark Epstein's key clients, and they spent many happy hours sampling new discoveries together.

In the car driving to the Purcells', Mark told his wife about the order Constance had just placed for the restaurant. 'Business must be good – she's building up an excellent cellar. I hope we're having the lamb in balsamic.'

'What?'

'I hope Connie's cooked her leg of lamb in balsamic,' Mark repeated, as he turned down the drive to the Purcells' house. 'I could eat that till the cows come home. Or should that be sheep?'

'Did you bring any wine?' Lucy wrestled to get Abigail's car seat out of the back without waking her. She was an unpredictable baby: some nights she could sleep through her sister using her as a trampoline; others she would wake at the drop of a pin.

'In the nappy-bag. I brought a couple of bottles of a rather unusual Muscat. I wonder if Connie will have done that rhubarb and Wensleydale thing . . . It would go down a treat with that.'

'I don't know why you don't just move in with Connie and have an orgy.' With the heavy nappy-bag over one arm and the car seat over the other, Lucy had only her eyes free to use. She did her best to plead with them. '*Please* don't let's spend the whole night talking about food and wine again. It is possible to have too much of a good thing, you know.'

Mark took the handle of the baby seat and swung it a little too vigorously. 'Not of the best things. Not of Connie's lamb, or Puligny Montrachet on a summer evening, or a mighty burgundy in front of the fire. And never, my beloved, enough of you . . .'

Chapter Two

Onion, the apple of the earth, is able to emit such scents as women meeting their lovers do. Hot bacon dripping, the lover of the onion, keeps asking sizzlingly from the top of the stove: why was I born? The onion then passionately explains everything . . .

Gyula Krúdy

After kissing Julian and settling Abigail upstairs, Lucy headed for Constance's domain, a huge hyperspace kitchen where Constance adapted old recipes and experimented with new ones during the week. Unlike the Epsteins' shambolic home, the Purcells' was a monument to good taste coupled with idiosyncratic flair – a partnership that pretty much summed up the Purcells themselves. Julian, with his portly build, greying hair and mild manners embodied solidity and kind consideration. Constance reminded Lucy of a latterday Coco Chanel, not only because she was inclined to wear black and white, and had an Eastern slant about her eyes, but also because she contrived to keep her short black hair slicked behind her ears without any evidence of hair stuff to glue it in place. She had maintained a lean, gymnast's body without ever taking exercise and without any unfeminine muscles showing except in her strong hands. Constance was several years senior to Lucy, and Julian some ten years older than his wife, but the Purcells often made Lucy feel unfit and sweaty, as if she'd just sprinted round the corner late for class and hadn't had time to brush her teeth, let alone her hair. Despite this unhappy comparison, Lucy liked Constance a great deal but, then, Lucy liked most people; more significantly, she admired her.

Lucy did not make the mistake of offering to help. Amateur assistance was not something Constance accepted gracefully, and Lucy knew perfectly well that every food item that could be prepared in advance would have been prepped and coached until it was word-perfect and panting to perform. Constance was gazing intently out of the window with a glass of wine in one hand and a cigarette in the other. She had recently banned her staff from smoking anywhere in the restaurant, let alone the kitchen. In his habitually logical way, Julian had responded by banning cigarettes from the house. Constance had retaliated by banning Julian from the kitchen.

'Hello, Luce. Got a drink?' Constance peered through her business-like half-moon glasses at the patchwork quilt of her herb garden. Most women approaching forty would have been buried rather than spotted in half-moon glasses, but they made her look younger than she was, and very chic. 'D'you have any idea why my sage won't grow there? I've given it perfect Mediterranean conditions, and the thing keeps dying on me.'

Lucy obligingly stood beside her at the window and observed the suicidal plant. 'I could tell you how to nurture a flourishing crop of bindweed, but I'm not much cop at anything else.'

'Stuff the garden. Who wants to be self-sufficient when it's so glorious being utterly dependent?'

This made Lucy smile – the notion of Constance being utterly dependent on anything was farcical.

'I'm afraid we had to bring Abby with us. Dodgy babysitter.'

'That's fine, so long as she doesn't make me broody. I'm in such a bate about the restaurant I'm actually considering having another baby. Can you believe that? Me, of all people.' Constance widened her extraordinary light blue eyes and shivered. She confided that the restaurant was not going well or, rather, not going as well as Julian thought it should be going, given how much time and money had been sunk into it. The recurrent problem seemed to be staff, the difficulty of recruiting local ones who were any good, or foreign ones who stayed beyond three months. 'Everyone who's good wants to be in London. I spend at least half my time training, and as soon as they're up to speed, they bugger off. Honestly, I just don't know if it's worth all the grief. Not at this stage in my life. I'm nearly forty, Luce, d'you realize that? *Forty*, and still working my rear off for the satisfaction of a poxy little country restaurant where half the clientele want bangers and mash, and the other half want something out of the sodding *River Café Cookbook* at a third of the price they charge in London.'

'Can't you find some local gem who does everything and will stay with you for life?' Lucy suggested.

'That sort of person escorted the dodo off the Ark. Anyway, they couldn't cope with my standards.'

'What is it exactly that you expect your staff to do?' Lucy was toying with the idea of offering her own services, part time. It might be quite fun, assuming Constance could teach her to cook.

'It would be a lot quicker to list what I *don't* expect them to do. I'm a tyrannical megalomaniac.' Constance called a spade a spade, especially when the spade in question was herself. 'No. I've decided. I'll give it another six months, and if business doesn't pick up I'm going to dump it.'

'Mark says it's booming.'

'Oh, it's going OK, I suppose. It was just a bad week last week.'

'You're too hard on yourself. Anyway you'd go mad without the restaurant.'

'Not if I had something else to keep me busy.' Constance smiled suggestively, lit another cigarette and inhaled slowly.

'You're not serious about having another baby?'

Constance exhaled at force through her nose. 'No – maybe something else, though.'

'What? You're not getting a pet?' Lucy knew how much Constance hated animals: she barely set foot in their house without complaining about their Labrador. The knowing, mischievous expression on Constance's face provoked her. 'What?'

'Just a different preoccupation.'

'Such as?'

'Such as . . .' Constance drawled, rolling her eyes dramatically '. . . a lover.'

'You're joking!' Lucy grinned gamely. Although Constance wasn't much of a comic she loved to shock, and it seemed the appropriate response. 'As if you'd honestly say that with Julian sitting next door.'

'I am perfectly serious. Don't pretend you've never thought about it, Luce. Every woman does. It isn't as if I actually want one, not *want* one as such, it's just that now-or-never thing, timing, you know what I mean? Biological clock.' Lucy had always thought the biological clock referred only to getting pregnant, but if Constance wanted to put a new spin on it, she was prepared to listen. 'I met Julian when I was twenty-four and he was thirty-four. In the past fifteen years I haven't so much as snogged another man, and sometimes I wonder, am I going to die like this, only Julian's lips on mine from twenty-five to ninety?'

'You'll be lucky to live till ninety, smoking like that.'

'Will I? Would it be lucky, I mean? I just have the feeling it's now or never. A lover by forty or bust. I mean, really, Lucy, whatever I had is fading fast. Why not make the most of it before it disappears completely – before I disappear completely?'

Lucy put her arm around Constance's narrow shoulders and squeezed. 'It's not one of the more convincing justifications I've heard for infidelity. If you said you were going to stop smoking by forty, or become a triathlete, fine, but isn't it a bit, oh, *cold-blooded*, to say "I'm going to take a lover before I hit the big four-oh"?'

'Wait till you get there. You're only thirty-five. Salad days, still.'

'If only. Tell you what: I'll come and work for you as an unpaid skivvy, so you have to keep the restaurant going and are too busy to get wandering eyes. It's the least I can do to preserve your marriage.'

It had never crossed Lucy's mind to have an affair. She barely had time to cope with the one man she had and loved, and besides, what on earth would anyone have an affair *for*? All that effort, and courtship and game-playing – for *what*? Connie was just talking for effect. Lucy watched her set out two perfectly golden tarts, one crammed with melting onions and the other with caramelized leeks; a tray of tiny baked potatoes stuffed with pecorino and sun-dried tomatoes; finally a parsley salad with finely chopped red onions, anchovy, capers and generous curls of Parmesan.

Connie gazed into the pot in which she had cooked the onions to a syrupy, viscous melt, scooped out a fingerful and sucked it. She breathed in slowly, inhaling the scented vapour with her eyes closed. 'I love onions.'

'Umm. Me too,' Lucy agreed.

'No, you don't love onions the way I love onions,' her hostess corrected, shooting Lucy a piercing look, as if they were rivals discussing claims to a man. Lucy sometimes thought Connie was a little mad when it came to food. 'I *love* them,' Constance continued. 'I adore them. They're like sex. Better.' She shook her head, a tiny little shake to clear the fantasies from her mind.

'Mark will be gutted,' Lucy said mildly, and added, just in case Connie thought she was offering her husband as a sexual distraction, 'He's been pining for your lamb in balsamic.'

'Then he can come into the restaurant and pay for it. No one else does. Personally, I've decided to go vegetarian.'

'You're joking!' Lucy said again.

'Only until I've got rid of my tummy.' Connie patted her stomach, as flat as a glassy lake. 'I can't catch a lover with a great fat belly, can I?'

'Con, how can you even joke about having an affair? You and Julian are happy, aren't you?'

'Of course we are.'

'Then why jeopardize that?'

'Oh, Lucy, you can be so bloody serious sometimes. I'm not talking about anything major, I'm just fantasizing about a fling. I'd just like to know if I can still *do* it, you know, turn some poor sod mad with lust. Maybe I can't any longer. For years I've been certain I could have any man if I wanted him, and now I don't know any more. The older you get, the more your currency is devalued – or you've got the wrong currency altogether.' Constance finished dressing the salad, laughing. 'After forty it's like going on holiday to Italy and finding you've only got francs in your pocket. Maybe one final fling would get all that out of my system.'

'What if you can't get *him* out of your system?' Lucy nibbled a bit of crust that had broken off the tart.

'I wouldn't pick that kind of man.'

'And what if the man you pick says thanks, but no thanks?'

Constance smiled. 'They never say no. Believe me.'

God, Lucy thought, that complete self-assurance. How many affairs has she had already? Five? Ten? 'But what if they did?' she pressed, still smiling but genuinely curious. 'What if they said, "I'm sorry, you're too old, or too fat, or just not attractive enough?" What on earth would you do then?'

Constance arched her eyebrows meaningfully and carried the plates through.

To Lucy's relief, the conversation over dinner did not revolve around the gastronomic or viticultural. For a while the four talked idly about general matters – their children, the proposed local bypass, who would take over the organic dairy when Bill Marshall retired, the appalling train service to Waterloo, escalating prices at the local garden centre, why there were no foreign films at the local cinema and back to their children. So much for *New Yorker* Woman, let alone *The Economist* Woman.

Finally Julian put his fingers together and cleared his throat to signal a major announcement. 'There's something we wanted to discuss with you two.'

'Fire away.' Mark refilled the glasses, turning to Constance. 'I'm so glad you took a couple of cases of this for yourself. Did you see the write-up in *The Times* last Sunday? He may be a small producer, but the –'

'Mark? If I may . . .' Julian inclined his head and waited for Mark to pause respectfully.

Julian could be such a pompous fart, if a dear pompous fart, Lucy thought, trying to contemplate him objectively. If Constance was serious about something extramarital, she could occasionally understand the temptation. 'Constance and I wondered how often you two went up to London.'

It seemed such a complete *non sequitur* that both the Epsteins were flummoxed into silence, an unusual condition for Mark, particularly when he'd had a bottle and a half of wine all to himself. They spoke together.

'Well, I don't get the chance apart from the odd –' Lucy started.

'I'm there quite often, once a week or so, you know, buying, seeing contacts . . .' Mark shrugged.

'Precisely,' Julian said smoothly. 'Once a week, more if you could. And where do you stay in town?'

'With Mark's brother Josh . . . the Lansdowne club occasionally.'

Lucy waved a hand vaguely. 'It's very good value for country members. Sometimes we stay with my sister, if we're together – honestly, we're not there very often.'

'Constance hates staying in other people's houses,' Julian said. 'For some peculiar reason she can't abide using somebody else's bathroom, with the result that whenever we do go up to town, Muggins here has to drive back.'

Lucy shook her head. 'That's not a problem for us.'

'Hang on a minute, Lucy!' Mark raised a hand in protest. 'I ought to get into London more often – you're always moaning you want to too. We've just never been organized enough about it.'

Constance leaned across the table, pressing her arms to her side so that Mark was treated to a full frontal of her small but undeniably attractive cleavage. 'But, Mark, that's the whole point. Being organized, not having to take clothes and a toothbrush every time. If it was easy, we'd all go whenever it suited us. Besides, it's mind-numbing being here all the time. I need to eat in state-of-the-art restaurants, get inspired by different influences – I want to feel excited, feel fresh, try new things, not be middle-aged before my time, get some outside input . . .'

Lucy arched one eyebrow expertly, a trick inspired by Roger Moore that had taken her months in front of the mirror to perfect when she was a schoolgirl and considered it the height of worldly sophistication, and which had become a habit she couldn't shake, like so many of the habits acquired in childhood. These days, she felt it might be her only trick – her Unique Selling Point, as Mark had called it when he'd completed the Running Your Own Business Seminar at Cranfield.

'. . . in *culinary* terms,' Constance finished pointedly, for Lucy's benefit.

'Connie and I,' Julian continued, in a voice like melted butter, 'Connie and I were wondering, theoretically, if there might not be a mutual benefit, perhaps, both economic and practical . . .' They waited, all leaning forward, slightly impatient. 'Of course, it would have to be calculated on the basis of shared interest, a partnership, and equitable understanding on every level . . .'

Constance was the first to snap. He was her husband, after all: she had to put up with his ponderous style more than anyone else, and knowing that it stemmed more from tactful hesitancy than real pomposity, she found it easier to interrupt. 'Julian is trying to ask you if you would like to buy a London flat with us.'

'What?' Mark gawped, his mouth full of the rhubarb and Wensleydale pudding he had craved.

'Julian and I have been thinking about buying a *pied-à-terre*. We looked into it, and it makes more sense financially to buy a two-bedroom flat than a studio or one bedroom.'

All at once Julian became succinct. It was clearly something he and Constance had discussed several times. 'We couldn't use a larger place enough to justify buying it outright – one or two nights a week, either together or alone, never at weekends, because of the Falcon. You two could use it one or two nights a week, and any weekend you wanted.'

Constance's bright eyes shone with conviction. 'Don't you see how sensible it is? We go halves on everything. We have it Mondays and Tuesdays, you have it Wednesdays and Thursdays, weekends and holidays *ad hoc*. It's perfect. You must agree. It's so obvious I can't believe I didn't think of it years ago.'

Lucy tried to fork a stray piece of rhubarb. She could have made a pretty good stab at why the idea had so suddenly sprung to Constance's mind, but held her tongue and listened to her husband answer sensibly. 'Look, it's a fantastic idea theoretically but it doesn't make sense,' Mark stated firmly. 'You have money, we don't. We don't have any spare capital at all. It's all tied up in the house and the business.'

'You could, perhaps, buy the flat in the name of Epstein & Rose, as a company property, thereby having tax-deductible status on the whole of the mortgage, say fifty per cent of the purchase price.' Julian swirled his wine. He and Constance had had plenty of time to think through the details from everyone's viewpoint. 'We could provide the fifty per cent cash deposit, you could make the mortgage payments. We divide running costs, rental income if we ever choose to let it, profits if and when we decided to sell. We could even have some sort of a nominal share in the business to represent our interest, perhaps. It should be perfectly easy to account for, don't you agree, Lucy? You're our resident financial expert.'

'In *theory*, if we bought it in the company name, we could deduct all mortgage interest for tax purposes,' Lucy agreed. 'But then there'd be a question of capital gains when we sold. Or we could just let it to the company. I don't know how we'd structure your ownership – I'd have to look into it, it's so long since I've dealt with anything like that.'

'Oh God, who cares about the technicalities?' Constance exploded with exasperation. 'We're *friends*. We trust each other. We could work all that out.'

Lucy shook her head. 'No. This is purely academic. We can't do it. We can't afford it.'

'Lucy.' Constance closed her eyes. 'Stop thinking so hard and just imagine it. A two-bedroom flat in London. We can do it up any way we want. A bolthole. A delicious retreat where we can pretend we don't have domestic responsibilities, don't even have children. We can be urban, free. Keep our marriages young.'

Both Julian and Mark grinned broadly. Lucy's face set into a stubborn frown. 'I wouldn't have the chance to get to London at all, not with the kids and everything.'

'Maybe we could get an au pair . . . You know, I'm beginning to think it's a brilliant idea!' Mark leaned forward enthusiastically. 'Think how many times you've complained about being stuck in the sticks, Luce. So, one night a week you go up to town and live it up – see old friends, do an evening course, whatever you like. We'll sort out the money somehow. Maybe, if we had a flat, you could go back to work a little, do some freelance consulting, work for your old mates. Anything. I'm on.'

'Me too,' Constance breathed, lighting a cigarette in premature celebration and oblivious to her husband's momentarily pained expression.

'It's the logical solution to our problems,' Julian concluded.

'Absolutely,' Mark concurred.

'I wasn't aware that we *had* any problems,' Lucy hissed at him, 'apart from pretty significant financial ones.' If they had been alone, Lucy would have torn a strip off Mark for even contemplating the idea. They could not possibly afford it with any degree of security, yet he was suddenly willing to throw caution to the winds and gamble on the future of his business, the future of interest rates, as well as the future of their relationship with the Purcells. He was acting like one of his own children spotting a new toy.

'Think,' Constance grabbed Lucy's hand, knowing at once that it was Lucy and only Lucy who needed to be persuaded, and tossing in an unfair appeal to Lucy's selfless instincts, 'about how much it would help the restaurant. You said you'd do anything to help the restaurant. I could hire you to work with me. That would help pay for the flat.'

'Uh . . .' What could she say? She was tired of being the former consultant, the sensible one, tired of being a killjoy. Certain as she was that it was pure fantasy, Lucy could hardly pour cold water on it when they were all so eager, so keen, so convinced, so . . . pissed. It would be forgotten by tomorrow. She made a tiny gesture of compromise. 'How much money are we talking about?'

'We can put down up to a hundred thousand in cash.' Julian had the grace to colour slightly when Mark whistled. 'We'd be prepared to co-sign your mortgage for up to another hundred K, if that made things easier for you.'

'No, that's far too much,' Lucy said flatly, in a maternal brook-no-nonsense tone. 'We could only consider it at all at a much lower level, and I mean *consider* it. No way could we spend more than a hundred and fifty thousand in total. Otherwise it's a farce. Anyway, I don't know what co-signing would do to the corporate tax-relief status.' The tax status didn't concern her at all, except that it provided an easy wall to retreat behind. In the morning, Lucy was sure, everyone would think better of it. It would be one of those moments of sober realization when you blush and feel a bit queasy, in the cold light of day, and realize how pissed you must have been the night before to have spouted such nonsense, and then wonder what greater and further nonsense you have conveniently forgotten. In the morning, Constance would phone up no doubt, sound embarrassed, laugh, and say, 'My God, did we really agree to all that? How much wine did we drink?'

'Lucy, Lucy, Lucy . . . You know you'll find a way of working out the technicalities on a little mortgage. You're so good at working things out.' Mark patted her shoulder. That would have been a good moment for one of his wonderful remarks, but he didn't offer one, and his wife saw red.

'That little mortgage will cost us at least seven hundred a month. How d'you think we're going to fund that, Mark, plus an au pair?'

'Through the company.'

'Dream on.'

'Children, children,' Constance laid both palms flat on the table, 'it's just an idea, something to mull over, not to fight about. I *know* we can make it work. There's no sense in Julian and me doing it alone – we couldn't justify it. And if, say, for a year or two, Julian and I bear more than half of the financial burden, so what? It will all come out in the wash.'

For a couple of minutes, looking at the others, Lucy felt completely enraged. Julian had his arms folded across his chest, sleepy eyelids half closed; Mark was aquiver with excitement, like a trainee gun dog confronted by his first pheasant; Constance was cool and composed as she left the table only to return with a bottle of champagne. They were all so certain that they were right.

'The only obstacle is your wife's indecision.' Constance passed the bottle to Mark who rose to his feet. 'I say we toast the deal.'

'Since when did prudence become "indecision"?' Lucy murmured to herself as Mark popped the cork.

The cork hit Abigail's hair trigger, and as her ear-splitting screams reached the terrace, Mark stared at Lucy. 'So, darling, are you really telling me it wouldn't do you, and me, and *us*, a world of good to be able to get away from all *that*,' he jerked his thumb upwards at the bedroom window whence Abigail's bawling emanated, 'just once in a while?' He let the thought sink in, then rose to collect his daughter.

And so she capitulated, on the understanding that all details – tax, financial, personal and practical – had yet to be resolved; in Lucy's experience, this generally meant it would all come to nothing. That was how it happened, how it began. Lucy was the innocent party. It really didn't have anything to do with her. It would never have crossed her mind if she hadn't been bullied into the whole thing. She didn't even feel a flicker of excitement about it.

Chapter Three

In my vague state of emotional torment I decided that I wanted to be loved, and looked about me . . . I studied my own heart and tastes and could not discover any definite preferences.

Benjamin Constant, *Adolphe*

The next morning Constance rose early to phone her children's former nanny, Helen, explaining that some friends had a sudden crisis, and could she look after one adorable baby for the day? Over breakfast she fired questions at Julian, checking that he had certain dates in the diary and other chores in hand.

'Right. Now, you won't forget to order another load of manure?'

'I wouldn't dream of it.'

'And book my car in for a service?'

'Consider it done.'

'And you'll call Lewis for me?'

'The very second I've swallowed this mouthful.'

'Good.' Constance stared at the newspaper that faced her. 'Oh, by the way, darling, I'm vaguely considering the idea of taking a lover.'

'Mm-hmm . . . Anyone specific in mind?'

'No, it's just that I already mentioned it to Lucy, so I thought I should tell you.'

'How very civil of you, darling,' Julian acknowledged, lost in the editorial. Constance pushed the paper aside and kissed him fiercely on the mouth. Twenty minutes later, shortly after nine, she had collected Helen and arrived unannounced at the Epsteins, where Lucy was struggling to feed Abigail.

'Helen's come to look after Abby for you,' Constance announced brightly, ignoring Lucy's bleats that she simply couldn't just drop everything on the spur of the moment, 'and we're off to London to look at flats.' Mark emerged from his office in the barn and volunteered to keep an eye on the home front and collect Charlie and Grace after school, and although Lucy didn't like the idea, partly because she'd promised Grace they'd go swimming after school and partly because it was a complete waste of time, she dropped everything – on the spur of the moment – and climbed into Constance's car.

Constance was clever. She didn't discuss flats at all. All the way down the motorway she discussed their respective children, and told Lucy not to worry about Charlie and Grace's constant bickering. Her own strategy, she explained, was to ignore all fluctuations in family relations unless physical violence was about to occur, at which point she locked them all in separate rooms – Julian included. Anyway, she asserted, before Lucy knew it they'd all be grown up enough to handle their own fights, and as they grew up parenting became primarily a question of running a tight ship. Constance endeavoured to keep three steps ahead of everybody else in the family, so that when the wail went up, 'You haven't bought me new cricket trousers/regulation Mac/squash racquet,' she could silently produce it, already neatly labelled with name and house. Lucy could only marvel at this degree of organizational supremacy: it always seemed to be three weeks into the summer term before she managed to find the old or buy the new swimming briefs, by which time Charlie had been well and truly humiliated by having to wear his Lion King trunks when everybody else in the school pool sported neat black Speedos. Outwardly Lucy marvelled, but inwardly she doubted that Constance's organizational skills contributed much to her children's well-being. The rights and wrongs of parenting remained something of a no man's land between these two mothers.

When they had parked outside an estate agent near the British Museum, Constance laid her arms on the roof of the car and looked at Lucy gravely. 'I know you think you're being bullied, but you're not. This is only to see what's around. I called this agent because I liked the idea of being in Soho, at least the West End – just so we know we're really in the heart of town. And it's easy to reach from Waterloo. If we ever actually go through with it, and you and Mark want to be in Notting Hill or Hampstead or somewhere, that's fine by us. He's going to show us three flats around here, and then we'll go have a boozy lunch. Or *you* can have a boozy lunch, and I'll drive home. Lunch will be on me.'

Lucy silently welcomed the fact that Constance was directing the search at the smartest parts of town, precisely the area where they had the least chance of finding anything Constance would settle for. 'OK, but I –'

Constance held up her hand imperiously. 'Let's look first, and talk later. They'll probably all be vile.'

Lucy resolved not to like anything, and certainly didn't take to the estate agent. She had forgotten what they could be like. When the Epsteins moved to Dorset, she had rather admired the middle-aged, gentlemanly agent who showed them around the lovely houses they couldn't afford and the less lovely ones they could. When Mark swooned over half a million pounds of bricks and mortar nestling in the Sherborne valley, and Lucy had patted him on the back and said that it was way out of their range, Martin Baker had seemed positively relieved. 'A noose round your necks, that would have been . . . and such an ugly extension. I'm sure the roof's dodgy too.' He didn't seem to care if they bought anything or not. He seemed much more interested in discussing wine with Mark, and advising them what breed of dog they should buy when they were finally settled, advocating Labradors first and Jack Russells a close second.

The agent Constance had selected was a different type altogether. He was Australian, which might have been a plus but Dominic had worked so hard at removing any trace of essential Antipodean integrity from his persona that you would have sworn he was English born and bred. He had all the cocky oiliness of the native breed of estate agent. As soon as the two women sat down he grinned at them like a shark and said, 'So, ladies, I just want to make sure your intentions are serious. The market's very hot, you know what I mean? It's important we know your situation so we're not wasting anyone's time . . .'

Constance cocked her head on one side. 'I assure you we're not wasting *your* time,' she said silkily.

'It's just if you need to talk to our mortgage department first, see what you can aff–'

Constance's stare silenced him, and he rustled the papers on his desk. 'Are you looking to buy now? Selling first? Stuck in a chain?'

'We're looking to buy right now. In cash. No chain.' Constance stretched across his desk and laid her left hand on a pile of property descriptions, so that all three carats of her large diamond engagement ring glittered under Dominic's gaze. 'We *are* pressed for time, so perhaps . . .'

Dominic was far from stupid. 'Right you are. I've got three places lined up in the hundred and fifty, hundred and seventy K bracket. We already took an offer on one of them this morning, so if you're interested you'd have to move sharp. Shall we, ladies?'

Constance gagged as he preceded them out of the office.

The first flat was a two-bedroom first-floor conversion in a building round the corner from the agency in Little Russell Street. 'Very convenient for the British Museum,' as Dominic pointed out. Constance asked him how often he popped into the museum, but he replied sharply that, business being as buoyant as it was, he didn't have time for popping in anywhere. It was a heartless place, despite its tasteful decoration, and Lucy's heart soared. The last thing she wanted was to see a flat she actually liked. They politely poked around, which didn't take long.

'Not much of this quality on the market.' Dominic pressed himself helpfully against the wall so the women could squeeze past into the minute kitchen. 'You won't find many places with period features.'

Constance and Lucy looked quickly at each other, and back to the agent. He nodded at the gas-flame fire in the sitting room.

'I see what you mean,' Constance mused. 'Luce? What do you think?'

'Well, it's not quite what I had in mind, not quite . . .'

'No, not quite.'

'That's all right. You wouldn't have been able to move fast enough to get it.' Dominic sniffed and looked at his watch.

The second flat, 'a peach', in Dominic's opinion, was on the fourth floor of a small modern block in Poland Street. 'I'd think of this as more of a younger person's flat, if you know what I mean, Soho and all that.' He had the nerve to wink at them as they went up in a lift the size of a shoebox. Lucy didn't actually witness the wink, as her nose was pressed so tightly against his pinstripe breast pocket that she could smell the sweat underpinning his cologne, but Constance assured her later that he had, actually, winked. The flat was barely larger than the lift.

'Clever use of space, don't you think?' Dominic picked the skin around his fingernails nonchalantly.

'For a very small, *younger* person, yes . . .' Constance observed sarcastically. 'Tell me, once you manage to squeeze yourself into the bathroom, is it possible to close the door, or is it an open-plan idea?'

Lucy studied the particulars while they sniped at each other.

'A lot of our clients like the minimalist look. It suits an upbeat, urban lifestyle.'

'No. I just don't like it. Sorry.'

'I'm glad about that, Con,' Lucy observed. 'Did you see the service charges? Nearly two thousand quid a year.'

'That's because it's a portered block, so you have security and the benefit of the lift, of course. I don't want to be rude, ladies,' Dominic ventured, clearly itching to be precisely that, 'but if you're looking for space in this area, you're going to have to rethink your price bracket. You said on the phone a two-bed in W1 or WC1. You get what you pay for. Perhaps you'd be happier looking in Pimlico, or south of the river?'

Constance was twitching, although the flat left precious little room for physical movement.

'Wasn't there a third flat?'

The agent sighed long-sufferingly. 'There's a place we've just listed. I haven't seen it yet myself, but we can hop in a cab and have a look. It's not in a prime area, and it's above a shop, so you don't have any of the amenities of a purpose-built flat, but then you don't get the service charges either. I'll have to warn you that there's some refurbishment needed . . .'

As the taxi pulled down Charlotte Street Constance brightened up. 'I know, Luce! We'll go to Bertorelli's for lunch. At least the day won't be a complete waste of time.'

'You ladies pop into town for lunch often, then?' Dominic asked suspiciously.

'We like to, as often as we can. It makes such a nice change from the pinochle afternoons at the retirement home. We always look at a few flats beforehand, just to pass the time.'

Constance had a way of being rude that attracted people; she was the sort of woman who was far sexier when angry than when she tried to be friendly. Instead of bridling, Dominic grinned at her appreciatively, and she rewarded him with a sultry glance from beneath her lashes. At the door of number 53 he struggled with a ringful of keys, trying several in the lock. A burly, aproned Italian came out of the delicatessen next door and recommended they simultaneously tug the doorknob towards them, turn the key and deliver a hefty kick to the bottom of the door, advice the agent dismissed with a maximum display of disdain. The Italian folded his arms across his chest and watched from the shop doorway. When Dominic had finally wrestled the door open he emitted a full four-syllable cry of 'Jee-sus Ker-ist'. A narrow flight of shoddily carpeted stairs ran up in front of them, with crates of mineral water taking up most of the floor space and salamis of different lengths hanging randomly from the banister rails.

The Italian appeared from an inner hall doorway and shrugged. 'The door sticks. Most people come in through the shop.' He turned to go back into the deli. 'The last owner let us keep stuff here. A very nice man and lady, the last owners. Very kind. Huh,' he grunted, shaking his head sadly, 'a *good* couple.'

Dominic led the way upstairs. 'He's got to be in breach of the lease ten times. I assure you, he's not allowed to use the common parts like this.'

'It adds a certain aroma, though, doesn't it? Garlic. I can smell fennel too . . .' Constance inhaled deeply.

'We can get that all sorted out.' Dominic pulled out another set of keys labelled 53B. 'Okay, ladies. Last stop before your pensioners' lunch.' This time Lucy saw the wink.

When the door swung open they stood on the threshold of a largish room full of light. Three arched sash windows, nearly floor-to-ceiling and each with an empty window box, looked out on to Charlotte Street. Watery sunlight splashed across the pale wooden floors. At one end of the room there was a small archway leading on to a narrow galley kitchen. There was no fireplace; the walls were a murky white; the kitchen units looked as if a DIY incompetent had quickly banged together some chipboard before losing interest, and some plates had been left in the kitchen sink for at least a couple of weeks by the look of them. A full ashtray sat starkly on the living-room floor. Opposite the windows another arch led on to a tiny hallway, with a bathroom and two bedrooms leading off it. The bathroom suite was avocado green, and two damp, grimy towels remained on the cracked grey linoleum floor. The bedrooms were far from spacious, and made smaller by bulky built-in wardrobes.

'Like I said, it needs complete refurbishment. This is what I'd call very inefficient use of space.' Dominic kicked at the skirting-board recriminatingly. 'Jeez, some people just don't care, do they? Don't even make an effort.' Constance struggled to open the central sash window, bending low to pull it up from the floor. The agent leaped to assist her, and the noise of traffic from the street joined them. She lit a cigarette and leaned against the frame while Dominic retrenched. 'I'm not saying you couldn't do something with it. It has plenty of –'

'Potential.' Constance finished. 'I love the location. The flat doesn't do much for me, though these shutters are rather nice. But the smell . . .'

'Any decent builder could do stuff to this place so you wouldn't even recognize it. And when I get hold of the shop lease you can bet your bottom dollar we'll get rid of the smell. Probably get the Eyetie evicted.'

'I *like* the smell,' Constance corrected severely. 'And the deli. It's the best thing about it.'

Lucy didn't listen to them. She walked back to the bedrooms. The floor of one had the same pale boards, the other was covered in industrial-style fraying sisal. When she closed the door behind her she bent to pick up a Polaroid photograph, heavily creased, of a young woman sitting on top of a packed crate, surrounded by suitcases and raising a glass of wine to whoever held the camera. The blonde woman was vaguely familiar: there was something in the stubborn tilt of her chin, something in the direct gaze that reminded Lucy of – herself. She let the curling snapshot drop back to the floor. The sisal was pristine where the double bed had been, grubby and stained everywhere else. On the window-sill she saw a tumbler of dead flower stalks, the surrounding petals turned papery, the water long since evaporated. Otherwise there was nothing in the room. All of a sudden she felt light-headed and sat down on the floor. 'Luce?' Constance called. 'Luce? Have you seen enough?' Constance's kitten heels tip-tapped across the parquet towards the bedroom and Lucy looked up as she opened the door. Dominic stood behind her.

'Lucy! Are you all right?'

'I'm fine. I felt queasy, that's all. There was nothing to sit on,' she explained redundantly.

'Are you sure you're all right?' Constance squatted down next to her friend and lowered her voice to a whisper. 'You're not pregnant, are you?'

'No, I'm absolutely fine.'

'You're probably hungry. God – this carpet would have to go.' Constance pulled up the edge; it gave way easily for a few inches, revealing bare boards underneath. 'Hmm. Shall we push off and see if we can get a table at Bertorelli's?'

'Can you get rid of Dominic for a minute?' Lucy whispered back, now that the agent had returned to the living room. 'I just want to look around on my own for a bit.'

'There's not that much to see, is there? I'll go down to the deli and drag him with me. I'd like to see what they've got. You sit still for two minutes and then come and find us.'

Lucy sat still until she heard the front door shut, then went back into the sitting room. She stood in the middle of the dusty, vacant space, holding her breath, frightened to move. Does it sound ridiculous to say that she fell in love right then, in love and in lust with a few empty rooms? She had never cared much about buildings. Mark had been openly annoyed by how little interest she had taken in the houses they looked at in Dorset: Lucy would have been equally content with any of three of them. Her requirements for a home were modest: enough bedrooms, a potential playroom near the kitchen, and a garden that did not front a dangerous road. That was all, and she had never lost the sense that she was lucky to have that. Now, as she looked at the tall, unpretentious windows, the glorious honey-yellow wooden floor, and the pair of raw open gashes in the shabby walls where the wall lights had been brutally ripped out, she felt like a trembling teenager. Lucy faltered her way back to the down-trodden bathroom, swooning at the intimate privacy of it all. If, *if*, she could just find a way of having it, she knew it would always be her flat, never really Constance's or Julian's or Mark's; just hers. It was sleeping now, in hibernation, but it was waiting for her, ready to whisper her name. She felt that she had never wanted anything so badly in her life. The flat had cast her, if you like, into a near-erotic trance.

She had stepped into it feeling tired and brow-beaten, middle-aged and hassled, and resolutely unattractive. She had felt vaguely envious of Constance's certainty, the tight grip her friend had on

44

life, compared to the rather loose and accidental one that she herself employed. Then Lucy looked into the cracked bathroom mirror and saw someone else, someone she had quite forgotten. She floated out into a world that made no demands of her at all, that was quite happy just to let her hang out, that did not value certainty above accident. Her head swam with the bustle, the anonymity, the laid-back charm, the mix and the meld, the warp and the woof – the warp and the *woof*? Mark would think she'd gone mad if he had been able to hear the thoughts that were floating around her head. She thought she was more than a little flipped herself. So there it was: a door had opened and let her see a different woman looking back from the empty bathroom mirror above the avocado basin. It was not that she wanted to be shot of Dorset, not that she didn't love her life there, adore her kids, dote on her husband, but suddenly she had had a glimpse of an old Lucy, or perhaps a brand new one, she didn't know which, and the chance of a tiny sanctuary where she could keep the two Lucys quite separate.

She could be the perfect mother at home, and in London she could go to see old French movies, in the middle of the afternoon, even, and sit and drink four cappuccinos in a row without feeling lazy; she could look at paintings that she needn't even pretend to like in art galleries she didn't yet know. She could experiment with recipes she'd never dared try, and serve a meal without ketchup. She could drink a bottle of wine alone in the comforting, warm embrace of a darkening room; watch the comings and goings in Charlotte Street; befriend the deli owner and try a glass of grappa with him; walk around London with absolutely no purpose at all. She could even – yes, this is how hard she fell, because this is what love is all about, a madness that makes the craziest things desirable, that turns everyone upside down and shakes them so hard their brains rattle and bang and can't function at all – she could even imagine herself finding sensual pleasure in cleaning that neglected and abandoned flat. She could see herself hand-polishing those floorboards and scrubbing the grimy window-panes until they gleamed back with pure love and gratitude. Her. Lucy. Lucy, who hadn't willingly picked up a duster in six years. She loved that flat so badly she wanted to clean it from top to toe that very day. She would have licked it clean.

'Luce?' Constance looked at her oddly when Lucy joined her in the deli. The Italian man was holding out a chunk of cheese on the end of a knife. Dominic was outside the shop on his mobile phone. 'Lucy, this is Enrico. Enrico, my good friend Lucy Epstein. Are you quite *sure* you're feeling all right?'

'I feel absolutely wonderful' she replied brightly. Lucy wasn't going to tell Constance what had happened, not Constance, not anyone; it was too private, and far too illicit. 'Shall we go and have lunch?'

Constance was concentrating on the cheese. '*That*,' she said, shuddering with pleasure, 'is absolutely divine. We'll be back.'

Oh, yes, you just bet we will, Lucy said to herself, and stepped out on to Charlotte Street in Constance's slipstream.

Chapter Four

*The real manace in dealing with a five year old is that in no time
at all you begin to sound like a five year old.*

Jean Kerr

During an indulgent lunch upstairs at Bertorelli's, Constance
flirted with every male within an eight-foot radius of the
table, from the young boy who brought round a basket of assorted
breads to the vintage waiter who brought coffee. Lucy had to
admire her: all that willpower and energy packed as densely as
sardines – or as Constance, outrageous food snob that she was,
might have put it, packed like a box of salted anchovies. When she
asked what Lucy thought of the flats they'd seen Lucy was non-
committal. She couldn't stand any competition; far better to deny
the attraction than have Constance steal it from under her nose.

'For us, the only question is financial. The flat itself is almost
irrelevant.' If only that were true, she thought.

'Oh, Lucy! You wait, we'll find something you fall in love with
and you'll stop being such a cautious goody-goody.'

'I am not a goody-goody,' Lucy retorted crossly.

'Oh, yes, you are.' She held Lucy in her gaze, and Lucy couldn't
outstare her. 'All that crap about being so shocked that I might just

consider an affair. It's not as if I told you I'd launched a full-blown raid on all British men between the ages of eighteen and sixty.'

'Why stop at sixty? Why not start at fourteen and go on until they croak?' Lucy was still smarting. 'And why restrict your campaign to the British Isles?'

'It was a *joke*. Besides, if you were really shocked by the notion of an affair, then you are the most extraordinary prig. And if you weren't, then you're a hypocrite. You can't convince me that you have never, ever, even for the briefest moment, thought about being attracted to another man, or a man being attracted to you. You're very pretty.'

'Meaning women who aren't are the only ones who are faithful?' Lucy snapped. She *was* pretty. Even in her least self-confident moments, Lucy knew that she was pretty. But she also knew that she was not striking in the way that Constance was – not a woman who caused men to jump slightly, as if startled, when she came into a room. Lucy's charm was soft and fuzzy around the edges, more Fragonard than Constance's sharp-edged photographic beauty. 'I don't think about it,' Lucy continued firmly, secretly pleased Constance had praised her looks and trying not to show it. There aren't many women who praise a girlfriend's appearance with sincerity, and those who do generally have confidence in their own looks before they can be generous. This was certainly true of Constance. 'That doesn't make me a prig. I'm not being judgemental –'

'Oh, that's a laugh.'

'It's just that I don't understand you. If you said you'd fallen madly in love, I'd understand – at least, I'd try to. But to be so *deliberate*, to say, "It sounds like an interesting idea so I'll give it a whirl . . ."'

Constance tossed her neat head so that her chin-length black hair swung in a perfect arc and dropped back into place. 'Call yourself a mate! I can't describe one impetuous whim without you reading the Riot Act.' She leaned half-way across the table, in the intimate manner she had with men and women alike. 'Look, I'm just a bit stale, that's all. Life's too bloody serious and too bloody dull. Maybe I need a new project. Maybe I'm menopausal. Anyway, I didn't mean anything by it.'

'The thing is,' with every word Lucy knew she sounded more like a senior prefect, but she had to know: the flat was too important to have anything mess it up, 'if we *did* go ahead and buy a flat together, I'd feel a bit uncomfortable if I thought there was anything . . . *going on.*'

Constance smiled ironically. 'Anything Going On?' she repeated, in a cut-glass voice. 'You mean, you don't think it should be my "love nest"? You and Mark wouldn't like to find a stranger's boxers in the laundry basket? I promise you, Luce, that if I ever do have an affair, Julian will be the very first to know.'

'Before the lucky man?'

'Lord, yes. I wouldn't dream of having an affair without discussing it with Julian.'

'I don't understand your marriage at all. You're either mad, or taking the piss.'

'Lucy, sometimes you make me feel twenty years older than you – which I don't appreciate. Nobody ever understands somebody else's marriage from the outside – it's hard enough to understand it from the inside. And better not to try.' She took Lucy's hand from the table and gave it a little shake. 'Look, if it makes you feel better, we can draw up a contract saying that if any one of us bonks somebody other than their spouse, without prior spousal permission, they get kicked out of the flat and forfeit all financial interests. How about that? Would that let you sleep easily?'

'There's no need to be sarcastic.' Lucy said huffily. 'It was a perfectly valid point.'

So she had been teasing. That was one of the problems with Constance: it was so hard to tell when she was serious. Except when she was talking about food. After she'd signed the tab she said to the waiter, 'Tell the chef it was very good, but that the tuna was overcooked, OK? Not inedibly, but just enough to disappoint.' Now that time she was in absolutely one hundred per cent deadly earnest.

Back at Lucy's house early that evening they found Charlie sulking up an apple tree and Mark in the kitchen engaged in the opening skirmishes of a battle with Grace. Constance's former nanny was holding wide-eyed Abigail on her hip, and looking as if she were longing to grab her coat, be paid and get the hell out of there. In fact, she looked as if she'd be willing to pay good money to get the hell out of there. Mark had already opened a bottle of wine, at twenty past six, and Constance accepted a glass and sat back to referee the fray. Grace was still warming up, but her mind was sufficiently concentrated on the imminent battle with her father not to pay much attention to her mother's arrival home: she was keeping her mother in reserve. At two her advanced manipulative skills had been noted, but by her fourth birthday she had honed them into something quite extraordinary. If you weren't the pitiable object of her attention, you could only sit back and gawp in admiration.

Grace was perched, stark naked, on the edge of the kitchen table. 'I want some milk in a bott,' she said, in a level voice, ominous only in its quiet precision.

Constance observed Mark's response with detached curiosity; Lucy watched with sympathy.

'No, darling, you're a big girl now. *Big* girls drink milk out of mugs.'

'I want some milk in a bott,' Grace repeated, menace creeping in.

'In a mug,' Mark asserted cheerily, with naïve self-assurance.

'But I *want* a bott . . . I want a *bott*.' The pitch was still soft, but the whine was developing, her voice rising further and further into the roof of the mouth and heading nosewards. Mark took a mug out of the cupboard and Grace silently watched him fill it with milk and hold it out to her before her heels started drumming the kitchen chair.

'Not *that* mug! Not *that* mug!' The wail escalated. Constance held her hands over her ears. 'I want the pink mug! I want the pink mug! I want the *pink* mug! I want the –'

'For pity's sake, give her the *pink* mug!' Constance cried.

While Mark started looking in the cupboard, Lucy rushed to the dishwasher, found a pink mug, rinsed it out and tipped the milk in, just as Grace's ear-splitting soprano hit notes that threatened the windows: 'I WANT THE PINK MUG WITH THE *TEDDIES* ON IT! I WANT THE PINK MUG WITH THE TEDDIES ON IT! THE TEDDIES, THE TEDDIES –'

Mark snatched the Care Bear mug from the draining-board, sloshed the rest of the bottle of milk in it and slammed it down on the kitchen table. Grace stared at it wordlessly for five beats, then slowly raised the big innocent eyes she had inherited from her mother and resumed the low-pitch, whispered whine: 'I don't want milk. I want 'bena.'

Mark put his face inches in front of hers. 'You asked for milk, darling. Everyone heard you. There are witnesses. You specifically asked for milk.'

The bottom lip trembled. The baby blues screwed up tight, and the mouth opened to bare a full set of pearls. Grace drew a deep breath and yelled, 'I want 'BENA! I WANT 'BENA!'

Constance and Mark scrambled for the kitchen door in unseemly haste, clutching their glasses. There was a crush at the doorway when the nanny joined them, Abigail clutched to her breast. Lucy picked up the now bawling Grace and cradled her against her shoulder, murmuring softly, and swaying rhythmically from side to side. When the others had closed the door behind them, she tipped the milk down the sink and refilled the mug with Ribena, all the time whispering, 'It's all right, darling, I understand, it's all right . . .' until Grace's jagged crying had been reduced to the odd sniffle. So much for establishing clear boundaries. Lucy deposited Grace in front of the video next to Helen and Abigail, asked Helen very politely to hang on for another thirty minutes, and went outside.

Constance had collapsed in a garden chair and was fanning herself. 'Christ, it's even hotter than it was this afternoon. So when are you two going to call the au pair emergency help-line number?' She looked at the Epsteins expectantly.

'I already have, actually, to say we might be in the market for someone. Gracie's just . . . tired. And hot,' Mark finished lamely.

'No, she's not. *You*'re tired and hot. She's got the upper hand.'

'It's fine by me if they have the upper hand every now and then,' Lucy acknowledged as she joined them. 'Sometimes you just have to stop the thing escalating.'

'I'm sorry I ran out screaming, Luce,' Mark said, shame-faced. 'It's a big no-no in the rule book.'

'It beats slugging her. Who gives a toss about rules, anyway?' Lucy stood behind him, massaging his shoulders.

'Sometimes it makes you want to sink to your knees and weep with the sheer hell and sweat and stress and shame of it.' Mark gulped at his wine. 'I mean, what gives them the right to behave like that?'

'*You* do, we all do, us poor dog-tired parents.' Constance helped herself to another glass. 'Parents worry so much about damaging their kids' fragile little egos, but they're the ones who do the serious abuse. We've been through it. You two are just at the most physically tiring stage.'

'Come, on, Con, I don't believe Chessie or Luke ever got the better of you!'

For a moment, Constance looked wounded by Lucy's implication, and Lucy regretted the comment. Constance shrugged. 'After you two left last night, Julian and I were talking about Francesca being so stroppy all the time, and wondering whether we'd made a mistake sending her to board. Julian said that it was all too late anyway, the damage was done. He said it was like my smoking – by the time you realize there might be a problem, it's too late and there's no point worrying about it.' She dismissed her refusal to stop smoking lightly. In truth, Julian was far more concerned by damage to his wife's lungs than any psychological damage that he may or may not have inflicted on his children. She smiled suddenly. 'You know, I can't help admiring Gracie. I wonder how Julian would react if I lay on the floor screaming, "I want to go to Bibendum for dinner! I want to go to *Bibendum* for dinner!"?'

'You've got a point,' Lucy agreed enthusiastically. 'All that dogged insistence, that wonderful force of repetition. You have to envy it. We must have had it once and our parents whipped it out of us, or we lost the knack somewhere along the line. From now on, I'm going to behave exactly as Gracie does.'

'Me, too,' Constance vowed.

Mark put his head in his hands. 'Heaven help me now. Sweet Jesus, help me.'

Lucy flung her arms wide. 'Tonight I intend to strip naked, stand on the kitchen table and yell at the top of my lungs, "I want a Dries van Noten cocktail suit! I want a Dries van Noten cocktail suit!" until I've worn you down into exhausted acquiescence.'

Mark leered comically at his wife. 'Tell you what, if you do it stark naked on the kitchen table, I might just buy you that suit . . . I'd make you keep it up for quite a while first, though. Say an hour or two.'

'Luce, darling, you've missed the subtler points of Gracie's performance.' Constance lit a cigarette. 'You're a rank outsider, and Grace is a pro. Didn't you notice she didn't start off by saying what she really wanted? She started off with the impossible – a bott – which meant that you ended up giving her precisely what she really wanted. The pink mug with the teddies on it.'

'So I should scream for Dior couture, to end up with Dries van Noten off-the-peg?'

'That's the idea. You've got a long way to go, but you're learning,' Constance comforted.

Mark gazed pensively at the candy-floss clouds chasing each other across the orchard. 'Just let me get one thing clear: at this point are you still standing on the kitchen table buck naked?'

'In your dreams.' Lucy took a sip of wine. 'The problem is, I could never keep it up. Grace can repeat the same phrase fifteen times. Thirty, probably. I've never been able to endure it past fifteen. Once I insisted she finished her cereal before we left the kitchen table. I caved in after an hour.'

Constance resumed her regular paean to British boarding-schools, but as Mark and Lucy were both adamant that they were not a good thing, and privately rather disapproved of the Purcells for sending their children away, Mark changed the subject quickly. 'So, you two, how was the flat hunt? Any joy?'

'We met a prick of an agent, and saw three flats, but your wife wasn't impressed. Do you mind if I chain-smoke? I've got to get my fix in before I go home.' Constance didn't wait for permission.

'Lucy's never impressed when it comes to houses. Sometimes I think she'd have been just as happy with a kennel. Or a cardboard box.'

Lucy thought she would be quite happy with a cardboard box, so long as it was moored in Charlotte Street. Perhaps she should stand naked on the table and yell 'I want fifty-three B Charlotte Street! I WANT FIFTY THREE B CHARLOTTE STREET!' But she was learning from Grace and Constance, from both of them, to hold her cards closer to her chest. 'Actually, you're wrong, Con. I did quite like one of them.'

'You did?' Constance echoed in surprise.

'Yes . . .' Lucy spoke slowly, as if she couldn't remember which, but it would come to her in time. 'I sort of liked the one above the deli. Where we had lunch.'

'Charlotte Street? Hey, I'm amazed. I thought if you'd liked any of them it would have been the one near the British Museum. Well, Charlotte Street's fine by me.' Constance began to rifle through her bag looking for the details, and passed them to Mark. 'It would need complete gutting, of course.'

Lucy's blood ran cold. Constance was so damn efficient at gutting things, animate and other. 'Not gutting,' she said in a rush. 'Painting, perhaps, but not gutting.'

'The floors were decent. Other than that it would have to be gutted,' Constance insisted.

'Then maybe it's not a good idea . . .' Mark looked from one to the other.

Constance shrugged. 'OK, perhaps we wouldn't have to gut it, but it certainly needs a new kitchen. And bathroom.' The twist she gave to the simple word 'bathroom' left Lucy in no doubt over Constance's feelings towards the avocado suite. 'The location's ideal.'

'A hundred and forty-five grand. Looks cheap.' Mark glanced up from the sales particulars as Lucy audibly choked. Seventy-five thousand wasn't going to be cheap. *Fifty* thousand wasn't going to be cheap. If this had been her suggestion, rather than Constance's, if she had said casually, 'Why don't we splash out on a flat for a hundred and fifty grand?' he would have had her sectioned into a mental asylum on the spot. With Constance, everything was suddenly achievable.

'Wouldn't that be amazing, though? If we'd found our flat on the first trip? It would be like a sign from God.' Constance stood up. 'Or a nudge from Barnard Marcus at least. I'm going to talk to Julian tonight – right now. We should all go back immediately, seeing Lucy's so keen.'

'I'm not "so keen",' Lucy corrected. 'I said I quite liked it.'

'Quite liked is good enough for me. I thought it was going to take *months* to persuade you. I'm off to rescue Helen. D'you want me to ask her if she'll come back tomorrow so we can go for a second look?'

'I'm on,' Mark agreed gamely.

'OK. See you tomorrow, fellow landlords!' and Constance swept back through the kitchen and out, taking the profoundly relieved Helen with her.

While Mark was in the shower Lucy lay on the bedroom floor in her underwear doing sit-ups. This was not a nightly occurrence: she had talked frequently about getting rid of her tummy ever since Abigail had been born, but there was a great chasm between talking about it and regular exercise. After five half-hearted attempts she put her arms behind her head and rested, her feet on the floor and her knees bent and tilted slightly to the right. She craned her neck to peer down the length of her body. Not that bad, she thought, not that bad for a mother of three the wrong side of thirty.

'Hey, Mark!' she called to the bathroom. 'Hurry up and come here!'

'What's up?' Mark emerged, rubbing his hair with a towel.

'Look,' Lucy hissed – more strenuous speech made the bulge reappear. 'In this position my tummy vanishes.'

'You are utterly ridiculous, darling.' Mark held out his hand to help her up. 'For a moment I thought you'd slipped a disc.'

'I thought you'd be impressed.'

'You don't have to contort yourself into peculiar positions to impress me, sweetheart. I like you just as you are.'

'I like me skinny. I might have to spend the rest of my life flat on my back. Flat on my back, but skinny.'

'That's not skinny, Luce. That's just basic gravity. Nice effect, though.'

In bed later, Mark rolled over as if accidentally, and gently pulled up her nightgown. Mark and Lucy had always had an active sexual relationship. Lucy was puzzled by those of her married girlfriends who said they didn't have sex any longer. For the Epsteins it was no big deal, but it was no big deal precisely because it happened regularly enough, and was good enough, for Lucy at least, and Mark had never complained. When they had first met at Corney & Barrow Lucy did not look at him and feel, 'Phwoar, I'll have some of *that*', which she had occasionally felt about previous boyfriends. She was attracted to Mark because he was funny and sweet and genuine, and she had known at once that he was fundamentally a good man. She did not initially have high expectations of sex with him. Her secret suspicion was that really sexy men who knew how to make love didn't have a clue about how to live lovingly, and nice men who made perfect husbands probably didn't have a clue about rampant, all-out sex. In fact, Mark and Lucy had had plenty of rampant, all-out sex for several years, and it was only after Grace's arrival that their marital sex life had settled down into an every second- or third-night basis. It had always been good, often better than good, and always loving and unfraught, which suited Lucy down to the ground. Fraught was something she just didn't deal well with at all. And rampant? Well, she simply hoped that by the time their children were old enough to allow their parents the chance for rampant sex, she and Mark wouldn't be too old to enjoy it.

Lucy didn't like change: as she often said of herself, 'Show me a rut and I'll climb straight in and start running up the curtains and plumping the cushions.' She knew all about keeping the home fires burning, gently smouldering at least, and all about the risks of sexual monotony, monogamy's twin brother, but it had never been an issue. There were times when she thought, My God, I've just been moaning and whimpering like an animal, only to find herself, ten minutes later, fighting over the duvet or arguing with Mark why her mother should come to stay for yet another weekend. The rational side of Lucy believed it was near impossible for ferocious sexual passion to survive parenthood: it could survive monogamous marriage perfectly well, it could even flourish in certain exclusive environments. She'd seen couples who could not keep their hands off each other long after they had waved their tenth anniversary farewell. But passion could not co-exist, except in very short, sharp spurts, with the long-haul stamina required by the raising of children.

The man who looked at his tired wife at midday, spotted baby sick on her dressing-gown, unwashed hair and a bottle of head-lice ointment clutched in her hand, yet still saw Ursula Andress stepping from the sea, that man had to be either a lunatic or a highly talented actor with a great deal to gain from the performance. Every parent had experienced those nights when the children were finally safely in bed and they were just *starting* to feel human and adult again, before the bedroom door creaked open to admit a little figure who stood behind the husband's shoulder bleating, 'Why haven't you got your 'jamas on, Daddy?' Three Postman Pat stories later – two, if it was Thomas the Tank Engine, because the saint who could stomach three Thomas stories in a row did not exist – when the intruder was back in bed with Barney or Tinky-Winky or some other much-loved television character, 'Daddy' was either snoring deeply, lost in *PC World* or watching the football, while passion had limped away whimpering to lick its wounds somewhere in the dark. Passion, Lucy reasoned, could not tolerate interruption or interference from anyone or anything – not children, not work, not domesticity. Passion blossomed in luxury hotels, trans-European couchettes and shabby bedsits, and shrivelled when it was asked to cohabit with playrooms, laundry rooms and bank managers' offices. Fortunately for Lucy, and unlike Constance Purcell, she was not hung up on pure passion. She thought it overrated, and would have elected sexual compatibility and contented family life every time.

They made love, and afterwards rolled to their separate sides of the bed in that happy post-coital state when it was OK not to talk and there was no need to worry about being apart because perfect intimacy had just been demonstrated. Lucy hugged the duvet around her, her back turned to Mark, listening to his breathing slow as the thought 'I want fifty-three B Charlotte Street. I want fifty-three B Charlotte Street . . .' pulsed through her head.

'I know what you're thinking,' he said suddenly.

'You do?'

'Yep. You're thinking you don't want to be rail roaded by Constance and Co. into buying that flat.' He stretched to rub her back in a reassuring way. 'I know you hate being shoved into things. If you think it's a bad idea, or you don't want to share with the Purcells, or we can't afford it, or if you just hate the flat, then I'm with you all the way. We won't do it. OK?'

Was he saying *he* didn't want to do it? Branding her as a killjoy so that he could now wriggle out of it? 'You're saying you don't want to do it,' she replied tentatively, while thinking, Please, God,

I don't care how, just please, God . . .

'I'm dead keen. It would suit me down to the ground to have somewhere to stay. And a bit more flexibility, work-wise.' His hand was now stroking her hair. 'I just want you to know you're the boss.'

'Let's sleep on it, OK?'

His voice grew slower and drowsy. 'I can't imagine what it would be like having somewhere to go where we could be alone – no kids, no babysitters, no toys, no nappies, no animals . . . Just the two of us alone again.'

And passion. The two of them and passion: that's what he was saying. It was Mark's gentle way of acknowledging that their lives were a trifle short on passion and privacy, if not short on sex itself, and a flat in London would change all that.

'We'll see.' She shuffled closer to him and held his hand briefly against her cheek. When she released it it slid limply down on to her breast: he was nearly asleep.

'Talking of animals,' Mark yawned, 'did you remember to worm the cat?'

Chapter Five

Never cook slavishly, rigidly following a recipe and thoughtlessly adhering to the measurements it gives. Recipes, as formulas, are almost always approximations anyway . . . Trust your intuition and your own taste.

Alice Waters

The three of them stood outside Fratelli Camisa the following afternoon waiting for Dominic. Constance was inside sampling salamis. Mark was staring up at the roof, interrogating Julian about evidence of subsidence and struggling to look attentive when Julian replied at considerable length. It was the sort of summer day that made you wonder if you were dreaming, whether it was physically possible that this sweltering, steaming, blistering heatwave had struck England. The windows on the top floor of number 53 were open, and the walls seemed to gasp in and out, as if the very building was on the point of swooning in the heat. Lucy leaned against the front door trying to look as if she were not watching a young couple across the street. The girl was in white Lycra leggings and a bare midriff top that displayed a glittering array of chained belly-button jewellery; the man was neck to toe in black leather, tight as a sausage skin, without a bike in sight. She coiled around him, lifting one leg high as if she intended to mount him, purring and writhing like a hungry cat. Almost reluctantly, he chucked the cigarette he had been chewing on to the street, filled his hands with her muscular buttocks and began to snog her. In broad daylight. On the street. Such displays were a rare sight in Dorset villages. Lucy half expected him to peel off her top and chuck it into the street with the fag end, but after a while they began to walk in a peculiar fashion, a sort of crab-like three-legged race, lurching down Charlotte Street with hands deep in each other's back pockets, mouths still joined. When Dominic arrived, striding briskly past the couple without a glance, he took one look at Julian's Jermyn Street-suited bulk and decided he was the boss. Perhaps it wasn't the clothes: perhaps it was the scattering of grey through Julian's hair that lent him instant credibility. Whichever, it did the trick for Dominic.

Lucy didn't look at the flat very much that time; she didn't need to and, besides, there was hardly room for the five of them to move about. Constance joined her at the elegant arched windows.

'Still like it?'

'Mm-hmm.'

'So what would you do with it?'

'*Do* with it?' Lucy repeated. Lucy had applied the same two-stage decorating philosophy to the two flats and one house she had ever called her own up until then. She either kept it exactly as the previous occupant had left it, or she did it up exactly as her mother had decorated her house.

'Yes, *do* with it. Modern minimalist or traditional Georgian bachelor? Provençal colour or feng shui?' Lucy didn't want to do anything with it: she just wanted to be in it. Luckily, Constance wasn't waiting for an answer. 'We rip out the kitchen right away – I couldn't bring myself to cook an *egg* in that.' She shuddered. 'We need steel cupboards, a La Fournière range . . .' Dominic slid up behind her, bobbing and nodding like a wooden marionette, all but genuflecting. 'Maybe sand-blasted glass for the unit fronts. I wonder where we can hide a sound system. I can't stand all that hi-fi crap being on display.'

'Marrakech,' Lucy murmured inaudibly. She fantasized about a Morocco-meets-Uzbekistan den, draped, tented, dark red kelims, a vast white bed billowing with mosquito netting, huge, gold-tasselled wall hangings, tribal cushions slumped around the floor, a samovar in one corner, an elaborately brass-studded chest in another. The Sheik of Araby, your love belongs to me . . . Rudolph Valentino coming in off the steppes. Men with high cheekbones, sallow skin and natural black eyeliner. The red of dried blood, filigree plasterwork, sumptuous, lavish, and utterly disordered. Everything contained in one room, abundance for abundance sake; like a tent, nomadic yet introspective. Something enchanted, a little dangerous – the essence of inshallah: if God is willing.

Constance was in a very different world. 'It could be classic Mediterranean. Maybe we take our starting point from the deli?' she pondered. She prowled the sitting room elaborating on her plans with Dominic pattering behind her heels, his ears flapping as Julian ruminated about damp. 'Window boxes crammed with lavender and thyme; bare plaster walls . . . That's an idea – bare glazed plaster. Med blue, sun-dried-tomato red . . .'

'No structural problems that I can see, only superficial damp. Not that we can get away without a full survey.' Julian poked and prodded, tapped and banged his way over the flat in a way that reminded Lucy of an offensively tactless gynaecologist. She winced in sympathy for the flat when he said, 'I know a bloke I can call in to give it a real going-over. I'd like to know when the exterior was last redecorated.'

'Oh, yes, of course,' Dominic cooed, lapsing into Australian in his eagerness. 'No worries.'

'Can't assume anything at all about the wiring, might be pre-historic.'

'Ooh, no, no, no, I doubt that . . .' Julian's eyebrows twitched at the agent who had the grace to look away and fiddle with his mobile phone.

'Window-frames will need to be replaced sooner rather than later. I wonder about the noise – we could consider some type of double-glazing.'

'No!' Lucy yelped impulsively. 'I mean, not necessarily. It's just that it's so quiet in Dorset. It's the contrast. If we're here, surely we want to know that we're really in city? Hear everything?'

'You wait and see how you feel when you're trying to sleep at midnight and a passel of drunken louts tip out of the pub. Did you see the Irish place on the next corner? You know what that means, don't you?' Julian's voice was heavy with significance. What? Lucy thought wildly. Open-air limerick concerts? Celtic harps? Leprechauns? Why should an Irish restaurant be more worrying than the Portuguese one virtually next door? Fado sessions and wild port quaffing . . .

Dominic became conspiratorial. 'Now there *is* a place that we should be listing officially early next month – Fitzroy Square, much quieter. The tenant's still there, but as a personal favour I might be able to get you in today for a sneak peek.' His index finger hovered over the green button on his phone.

'No, Julian's quite right.' Lucy put her hand on the agent's arm to stop him. 'We'll look into double-glazing. That makes the most sense.' They were standing in an irregular circle and Lucy feared Dominic might stretch out his long arms and embrace all of them simultaneously in a congratulatory love-hug.

'So?' Connie said expectantly. 'Seen enough?'

'We need to discuss it.' Julian and Mark nodded at each other.

The agent's eyes narrowed with cunning. 'I feel obliged to warn you I am expecting another offer this afternoon. There's been *significant* traffic through this flat, a *great* deal of interest. If you are considering an offer, I would have to advise you that speed is of the essence . . .'

Lucy looked at Mark with her eyes wide with longing, but he and the others were already following Dominic out of the flat, leaving her terrified they would lose it.

They didn't. They made an offer later that week, at the asking price, which was accepted at once. Lucy spent several weeks at the computer working out finances, checking mortgage rates and settling the technicalities of joint ownership, sweating that they would be gazumped, not trusting Dominic an inch, and praying. By putting their share of the flat into the company name the Epsteins managed to borrow £75,000 at a rate Mark considered reasonable and Lucy considered just short of usurious. The Purcells were putting up the balance in cash, plus some to cover the essential refurbishment costs. It wasn't going to be easy to meet the second mortgage, but Lucy was willing to hack their domestic budget to pieces. She deleted her theoretical clothes allowance entirely, and axed what she mentally allocated to the apocryphal annual-holiday-without-the-kids budget. She sacrificed with one swift blow her dreams of a pony or two for the children, which had never seriously been on the agenda, in exchange for sporadic visits to the riding school in the distant future. She could easily spend less on food, simply by saying she and Mark would eat a lot more vegetables and rice, and banning supermarket pizzas: it would be healthier, and anyway, she reasoned, after a month or two living above the deli she'd be able to knock up her own pizza dough by some sort of miraculous osmosis.

Two weeks before completion they drew up a set of ground rules over two bottles of champagne. The rules began:

(1) No children to be allowed in the flat without express permission from each of the four named occupants, such permission not to be unreasonably withheld, but such permission not to be requested except in highly unusual circumstances.

Given her budgetary constraints on the child care front, Lucy wasn't too happy with this one, but let it rest. If she had to take the children up with her, she could always twist Constance into agreeing. She thought it perfectly absurd that she was also meant to ask permission from Julian and Mark, but rules, all rules, were theoretical, and could be relaxed in practice.

(4) Monday and Tuesday nights to be officially for the use of the Purcells or their named representatives above the age of 21. Wednesday and Thursday nights to be officially for the use of the Epsteins or their named representatives above the age of 21. Alterations to official weekly schedule to be agreed in advance by all parties. Use on Fridays, weekends and holiday periods by prior negotiation, with the understanding that any and all use should be equitable.

Again, there was considerable debate over that one. They agreed that none of them would want the flat at Christmas, but they might all want it at New Year. Julian felt that as they would be unable to use the flat at weekends, thanks to Constance's restaurant, then they should perhaps have first call at periods when the restaurant was closed. After going back and forth on this, they decided that as it was only June, they had plenty of time to play it by ear.

(6) The flat to be left clean on the departure of respective user; if not, each of the two parties, Purcell and Epstein, undertake to hire someone to clean the flat for two hours on their day of departure. Laundering of bed-linen, dishcloths, towels, etc., to be the responsibility of each user.

Lucy certainly wasn't planning to hire anyone: their budget was already stretched as thin as gossamer, and just as fragile. By the sixth rule, Lucy was beginning to wonder if they shouldn't specify exactly what punishment should be meted out to the unfortunate who left a dirty plate in the sink – hanging? There was something to be said for Constance's painstaking efficiency, but not that much.

(10) Basic food supplies to be regarded as communal – tea, coffee, eggs, bread, butter etc. – but must be replaced as they run low by whichever of the named parties has run afore-mentioned basic supplies low.

This triggered another round of heated debate. None of them wanted to have fridge shelves labelled 'Purcell' and 'Epstein': communal dwelling at their age should not result in a return to student meanness. On the other hand, Constance stated quite fairly that if she had prepared a ratatouille terrine on a Tuesday she did not particularly want Mark to scoff it on Wednesday because he couldn't be bothered to get himself a takeaway. Mark retorted that he didn't particularly want Julian piling into his stocks of Brouilly, if it came to that. Lucy pointed out that Mark could no longer afford to drink Brouilly, so the issue wouldn't arise. They finally agreed that enough had been said on the subject for them all to be considerate and not have to discuss it further.

(13) Telephone and all other utility bills, overhead costs, ground rent, service charges to be divided equally between the four parties.

At this point Lucy queried why they kept saying 'the four parties' rather than 'the two parties', seeing that she didn't have a separate account or source of income, but Julian assured her that it was better that way, 'in case of unforeseen future events'. When she asked what those might be, he waved vaguely.

(18) Above all, each named party signatory to this agreement will respect the well-being, privacy, rights and entitlements of the other three named parties. In the event that one or more of the named parties wishes to dispose of the flat, the remaining named parties, be they one, two, or three, will be granted a three-month period to buy out the would-be seller's share at a fair market price, subject to third-party consultation.

'I think there are far too many parties in all this.' Lucy giggled, quite light-headed by this stage in the proceedings. 'And I don't think it will stand up in court.'

'I don't think *you* could stand up in court if it comes to that,' her husband said discourteously. 'Bottom line, we're friends. We don't need any more lawyers involved, we've already got two sets of the bastards. These are simply the ground rules. Everybody agreed?'

Constance added one last clause:

(19) The four named parties to hold regular meetings (at least quarterly) at which any issues on the management of 53B Charlotte Street may be raised. Any dispute or disagreement over the use of the flat to be settled by open discussion between all four parties and subsequent vote; in the event that agreement

cannot be reached, the casting vote shall be given by an outside arbitrator without bias to any party.

They signed; they embraced; they opened a third bottle and Julian proposed a toast to 53B Charlotte Street. It did occur to Lucy that they had omitted Constance's clause about no extramarital bonking in the flat, but whether this was an oversight or not on Constance's part she couldn't be sure. So long as she didn't do anything right under their noses, Lucy didn't think she'd care anyway, and clause 19 would enable her to bring it up ('in open discussion') if the need ever arose.

Mark and Lucy didn't tell the children until the flat was well and truly theirs. Lucy had imagined that they would be excited, but Charlie was immediately wise to the implications.

'So?' he responded bluntly to the news in the garden one summer evening. 'So what? This is our house.'

'Darling, this will always be our home, but isn't it exciting for all of us to have a place in London too?'

'It just means you and Dad will go off to London and leave us with a baby-sitter. What's good about that?'

Lucy pulled his resistant eight-year-old body on to her lap. 'Because we can do all sorts of lovely things there . . . In the holidays I can take you to London all by yourself, and we can go to museums, and science displays . . . You can go and see Father Christmas.'

'I don't believe in Father Christmas.'

'Don't be silly, darling, of course you do,' his mother soothed. 'Don't you remember my telling you that when I was about your age I actually *saw* Father Christmas? In the flesh?'

'You weren't telling the truth, Mum, you can't have been. I read something in a book. It said the boy was really disappointed when he realized that Father Christmas was a myth.'

While Lucy ummed and aahed and stalled for time by asking which book, specifically, and then in what context, before suggesting various explanations why a writer might have told such a heinous lie, Charlie looked at her glumly. 'Anyway, Mum, last Easter I saw you and Dad hiding the eggs, so I know there's no Easter Bunny. Last time my tooth fell out you forgot to leave money under my pillow, and when I said the Tooth Fairy hadn't come, you said I'd made a mistake and next time I went up to my room there was a pound there. I know it wasn't there when I woke up.'

'Maybe the Tooth Fairy was running late?' Lucy suggested feebly, while Mark gave her a superior look over the top of Charlie's downcast head. Good mothers never allowed the Tooth Fairy to oversleep.

'You made the Tooth Fairy up. I know.'

'Even if you were right about the Tooth Fairy –'

'And the Easter Bunny.'

'– and the Easter Bunny, which I don't think you are,' she jollied him along, miserably guilty for snuffing out the feeble flame of his childhood innocence, 'that doesn't necessarily mean there's no Father Christmas.'

'He doesn't exist.' Charlie said stubbornly. 'I'm not a baby, Mum. Everyone at school knows it's something parents make up.'

Mark leaned forward and took both Charlie's hands. 'Who was it at school who told you that there was no such thing as Father Christmas?'

'Howie.'

'Isn't Howie the one who's always in trouble? Doesn't he get demerits all the time?'

'Yup. He got three last week.' Charlie's eyes brightened. He enjoyed reporting on the scurrilous behaviour of his classmates.

'*Three.* In *one* week.'

'Well, I don't know Howie's parents, but you know how Father Christmas only brings presents to children who've been good all year?'

'I 'spose.'

'Maybe Father Christmas doesn't visit Howie, and maybe Howie's parents feel so sorry for him, and love him so much, that they buy him presents anyway, and tell him there's no such thing as Father Christmas, so he won't feel hurt or upset.'

'Then how's he going to learn not to be naughty?' Charlie was half-way there.

'Maybe his parents hope he'll learn to be good by himself. Maybe parents are more forgiving than Father Christmas.'

'Yeah. Maybe.' Charlie wriggled his bony bottom off Lucy's lap and ran to meet Grace, who was bustling her way busily across the garden towards them. 'Gracie, Gracie, you smelly little girl, we've got a flat in London!'

'Nice work,' Lucy complimented her husband. 'That might just hold him for one more year, though God knows what he's going to say to Howie tomorrow morning.'

Mark looked aghast. 'What? Are you telling me that there really *is* no such thing as Father Christmas? Bloody *hell*.'

Oh, she loved him, really she did. If Constance had had a husband like hers, rather than serious, stolid Julian, she wouldn't be worrying about never kissing another man in her life. She'd be thanking her lucky stars. Lucy imagined herself and Mark, sitting on the floor of the barely furnished flat – My God, maybe even that time next week! – eating blood oranges, drinking hot, sweet espresso, then climbing back into the cradle of a big unmade bed and making love for the rest of the morning. One slight hitch: they didn't have a bed as yet, but she was going to try to sort that out before they took possession. *Possession!*

71

'I do love you, Mark, I really do.' Lucy smiled at him as Mark picked up Grace who was complaining incoherently about Charlie. 'Darling? Do you think Connie's beautiful?' She'd asked him before, normally to trick him into admitting he thought she herself was too fat, and his various answers had never satisfied her. This time it did.

'She's incredibly attractive, but I wouldn't say beautiful, not to me anyway. She's too scary.' Mark ran his hands through his daughter's hair as he talked.

'Meaning?'

'She has too much pent-up energy. She's . . . *coiled* all the time. Too complete. She swallows you up. She's got a great body, and she's smart and sassy and sexy . . . But scary sexy, not beautiful sexy.'

'That's interesting. Do you think she could pull a man if she wanted to?'

'She's already done it.'

'Not Julian. Another man.'

'Now, what have you two women been talking about?'

Lucy laughed. 'Oh, nothing. She never said anything.' By this Lucy confirmed that Constance had, in fact, said more than something. 'Just that she was scared of turning forty, that it would all be over.'

Mark was genuinely puzzled. 'What would be all over?'

'Oh, you know, love, sex, romance, grand passion . . .' Lucy waved her hand airily.

'It depends what she's looking for. If Connie wanted grand passion, then I doubt it would be all over in Connie's case.'

'And mine?'

Mark smiled lovingly at his pretty blonde wife, then, when she quirked one eyebrow suggestively, threw her a *pas devant les enfants* expression, and said briskly, 'It was all over for you when you were about twenty-four, all over the day I walked into that presentation, picked you off the shelf and dusted you off. You've got no chance of another man.'

'Thanks.'

'I'd kill him first. Then you.'

'You're a prince.'

'Any time. Whose turn is it to do Abigail?'

'Yours. It's your turn to put them all to bed,' Lucy said, with a quick grin, and left him in the garden with the kids before he had time to work out that it was her turn.

Lucy thought frequently about her children, generally where she was going wrong with them, and less often what she was doing right. Having drawn up the rules for co-ownership of the flat, it occurred to her that perhaps she and Mark should have done the same before they had kids – decided on a set of ground rules. They had a haphazard, rule-of-thumb code they had attempted to embed in Charlie's psyche: never be unkind; be especially kind to the shy, the lonely, the weak and the sad, and to new boys and girls; never lie; don't cheat or steal; be polite to grown-ups; be gentle to animals; never call anyone fat and never call anyone stupid. The problem was there were plenty of fat and stupid people around, and Charlie struggled to come up with a way of describing them. The books he read were full of nice and nasty people, beauties and monsters. One of his favourites suggested that no one is born ugly, but each mean or ugly thought a person has makes the person grow uglier and uglier. Charlie had taken to examining himself in the mirror whenever he said something nasty, looking for immediate transformation; Lucy had started doing it herself, sometimes.

One of the main reasons behind the Epsteins' removal to the country was to escape the pressure of competitive parenting: they did not approve of violin classes for two-year-olds, football coaching at the Chelsea ground, no less, for the under-fives, or toddler preparation for advanced calculus, but lacked the courage and security to walk to the beat of a different parental drum in London. Even in the comparative safety of Dorset, sports day was looming large, and they would once again have to navigate the treacherous waters that swelled around the notion that winning wasn't everything, all that mattered was playing the game. Charlie, old enough to put the finger on Father Christmas, old enough to understand the notion of God just as well as his parents apparently did, and doubt Him just as much as they privately did, was quite certain that winning was the only thing. This made sports day post-mortems particularly bloody.

At that time, just before they took possession of Charlotte Street, Lucy had no real concerns about her family life. She'd read the books, watched countless documentaries, and felt in her heart that she was, as the phrase had it, a 'good enough' parent. She did not know what it really meant. If she had the tiniest grumble it was that between Abigail all morning, Abigail and Grace all afternoon, Abigail, Grace and Charlie all evening and Mark all night, there wasn't much left for her – or even *of* her. Mark at least had the odd indulgent afternoon painting in the garage; he always seemed refreshed by it, and it was incontrovertibly his place. If she could get to London just one night a week, she thought, maybe even one night a fortnight, without throwing the family routine into uproar, then she could nurture a little bit of her original self back to health.

Even before marriage, Lucy had never dwelt on the accumulation of possessions. That she owned – disregarding the mortgage – a large farmhouse in Dorset, and was the proud new (joint) owner of a London flat – disregarding a second mortgage – meant little to her. The ultimate reward in life, for Lucy, had always been marriage to a loving husband and healthy, happy children. To have achieved those things without penalty, except for the gradual erosion of her youth and waistline, was something to be grateful for. And if she occasionally felt a little personally overlooked . . . well, a degree of casual conjugal neglect was to be expected after nearly ten years of marriage. Count your blessings, she'd tell herself sternly as she waited in the supermarket queue. Most people would give their eye teeth for what you have, as she waited in the school car park. For absolutely no explicable reason at all, the grace she had learned at school haunted her increasingly: 'For what we are about to receive, may the Lord make us truly thankful . . .'

Chapter Six

Keeping separate a good deal is a wise plan in crises – and being both free – and expecting little: neither gratitude, nor attentions, nor love, nor justice, nor anything you may set your heart on. Love-interest, adoration and all that kind of thing is usually a failure – complete – someone comes by and upsets your pail of milk in the end . . . Hundreds of wives go through a phase of disillusion – it is really a pity to have any ideals in the first place.

Letter from Emma Hardy to a friend

Looking back over those summer months, it all happened in a flash, certainly for Constance. Lucy felt that the weeks passed painfully slowly. She resented not getting everything in the flat absolutely perfect on day one. It took a brief eight weeks between making the offer to getting the keys, and some of the credit for that belonged to Dominic, who by the end of it all had become a friend, at least of the Purcells. On completion Constance sent him a bottle of champagne and a large bunch of flowers, which Lucy thought was going a bit far, but as Constance didn't ask the Epsteins to chip in she didn't complain.

There was a hiatus between the longing to have it, then the actual having it when Lucy hadn't sorted out quite what she wanted to do with it. The first week of ownership she had to stay at home as both Grace and Abigail were laid low by colds, Mark was busy and she could not bring herself to leave them with a stranger. The childcare problem was still unresolved by the second week, so Mark took a day off with the children and Lucy rushed off alone. Initially she had welcomed the idea of being alone in her flat for the first time, but the reality was oddly disappointing: the expectation had been so much more exciting than the reality. Constance and Julian had come up with the movers two days before, and handed Lucy her own set of keys on the Wednesday morning. When Lucy examined the flat she knew why they'd looked so satisfied; the kitchen had been gutted and the fitters were already at work. The drawing room was pristine white; Lucy's precious gashes in the walls were gone. A large squashy sofa was pushed against one wall, and a simple wooden table with eight chairs extended from the arch of the kitchen into the reception room. On it Constance had placed a vase crammed with overblown white peonies; at the other end there was a pile of white plates, six goblets and some cutlery.

'We had to buy a few things, Luce,' Constance said breezily when Lucy arrived. 'I can't eat out of takeaway containers. If you don't like them we'll choose something else together. I left a note for you on the table about who's coming when to do what. Call me if anything doesn't make sense . . .'

'It all looks great,' Lucy mumbled, as Constance had proudly shown her their bedroom, and suggested Lucy use it until she had found a bed of her own.

She had liked the flat more before they'd mucked about with it. Lucy was reminded of a bizarre anecdote Constance had told her about a type of Hungarian dumpling: they were called 'pinched' dumplings and, according to Constance, a truly discerning diner could tell exactly whose fingers had pinched off the dough – the cook left a permanent imprint. Already Constance's fingerprints were all over the flat. Lucy had even been deprived of her passionate need to clean the flat. The kitchen was a building site, the living room spotless, barring the builders' dust, the Purcell bedroom was immaculate and there was no point touching the bathroom as Constance's note warned it would effectively be dynamited at nine the following morning. She spent the day at auctions and ended up blowing her rainy-day emergency fund of £1,500 – inherited from a godmother she hadn't seen since she was twelve years old – on a low Indian bed from an overpriced shop at the bottom of King's Road. Even at that price they wouldn't deliver it until the following week. By the time Lucy returned home Enrico's deli had closed, so she couldn't select her supper and dine in front of the window looking down on the street. The telephone wasn't connected and she'd left her mobile behind, so she couldn't call Mark or anyone else. She didn't have the will to go out to see a movie by herself. She bought a kebab from the Tottenham Court Road and ate it quickly and without any pleasure, then had a bath. Constance was right about everything: the colour was nauseating, the enamel scratchy and soiled, and a few tears slid pathetically into the tepid water around her. She left for Dorset as soon as the builders arrived on Thursday morning. Driving home Lucy wondered if Constance's quest to find a lover might end in equal disappointment – all so raw and raunchy on first meeting, only to find illusions stripped away as perfunctorily as the lining paper.

A few weeks later the analogy no longer suggested itself. Their search for au pairs had not been fruitful. They had received three 'family letters' from would-be au pairs, of which Mark's favourite had been the Russian who wrote: 'My real father is died. My stepfather is a computer. I am thirty-six but I am not looking to that and am in a strong state of enthusiasm.' Meanwhile, they had had the good fortune to discover Amy, a twenty-two-year-old who lived five miles away from them and was looking for part-time work before starting her training as a midwife. Best of all, she was willing to sleep over one night a week as well as coming in two mornings and two afternoons to help Lucy with Abigail or the school run. For the first time, Mark and Lucy would be able to stay in Charlotte Street together. On the train journey to Waterloo they laid elaborate plans for their inaugural visit, mainly at Lucy's suggestion. She arranged to meet Mark at a bar down the road from the flat that evening, and spent the whole day putting finishing touches to their bedroom. The bed had finally arrived and was perfect. She had draped it in sari silks from Columbia Road market, begged one of the builders to fix a hook centrally on the ceiling and hung swathes of the finest mosquito netting around it.

That afternoon she purchased two kelim cushions from Liberty's, with price tags so enormous that she had swallowed hard as she handed over her credit card, and lugged them by bus all the way back to Charlotte Street. Enrico supplied ciabatta, cheese and cold meats, the neighbourhood Oddbins made the wine choice easy, and Constance's super-modern little fridge chilled it to perfection. She'd moved the white peonies into the Purcells' bedroom and replaced them with vivid ranunculi in every shade of red through orange and yellow. She put candles in the bathroom, incense in her bedroom and Bach on the CD player Julian had donated. Constance had already supplied a chrome citrus-juicer, a coffee-grinder and a 'real' Italian espresso machine. Coffee beans were in the freezer (it took Lucy an age to find them) milk in the fridge, croissants for breakfast in the bread-bin. And yes: she'd bought six large blood oranges and arranged them on a pale shallow bowl that matched the honey-coloured wood of the floorboards. The romantic ambience was perfect. So attentive was she to the flat that she barely had time to look in the mirror before rushing out to keep her rendezvous with her husband. She was determined to get there before him and let the scene play out properly. The carefully orchestrated scenario went like this: Lucy would be sitting at the bar, on her own, with a bottle of champagne and a single flute glass, or possibly a vodka martini. The bar, she imagined, would be nearly empty. Mark would come in, look around and ask if the stool next to her was taken, and she would respond with a Lauren Bacall shrug, letting a curtain of blonde hair fall in a sweep over one eye, before giving him the cold shoulder. But he would persist, as Bogart would have, and then . . .

Lucy hit her first problem when she arrived at the bar to find it two deep in eager advertising types. She elbowed her way through the throng to order a drink, but her nerve failed at asking for a bottle of Veuve Clicquot and one glass, so she was forced into the martini option. One of the men offered her his stool, but she still felt like a prat sipping a powerful cocktail in the middle of a group of men ten years younger than her. She fished the olive out of the glass and waited for Mark. She ordered a second martini, forgetting to tell the guy to hold the olive. A man sitting with his back to her swivelled round on his stool, flicked his eyes over her and said, 'Hi. D'you work around here?'

'I'm waiting for someone.' The words blurted out an instant before she could think that this was not something Lauren Bacall would ever have said, on or off the set. She went downhill fast. 'I don't work, actually. I don't even live around here.'

'Oh.' He half turned back to his friends, but she couldn't let him get away: if she wasn't going to be alone at the bar, she ought to be talking to someone, being chatted up, for Mark's benefit.

Lucy nervously tapped the stranger on the shoulder. 'So, do *you* work around here?'

'Excuse me?'

'Do you work around here?'

'Yeah. Just down the road.'

'Do you enjoy it?'

'It's a job. So what are you doing here?'

Lucy shrugged, dumbstruck. It felt like a lifetime since she had had a conversation with a man she didn't know and with whom she had no purpose in having a conversation. 'Oh, just hanging out.' She winced inwardly, praying, Please, God, let Lauren Bacall not be able to hear me now . . . Should she mention that she had three children, in the faint hope that he'd look surprised and say, 'You don't look old enough to have three children'? No. She took another sip of her martini, which turned into a slurp that dribbled down her chin, and searched in vain for a napkin; she had to use the back of her hand.

'Luce – sorry I'm late –' Mark was working his way through the crowd. He wasn't meant to say her name; he wasn't even meant to *know* it.

'Oh, hello,' she breathed huskily, her voice catching in her throat as she tried not to laugh. 'I didn't expect to bump into you, of all people. This is . . .' She gestured towards her new friend. The man gave her an odd look, climbed off the bar stool and told his colleagues he was off to meet his girlfriend.

Mark sat down heavily. 'No champagne, then?' He ordered a beer. 'Bloody hell, what a day it's been. First they don't deliver at all, then three shipments arrive at once . . .'

'Mark.' Lucy pretended to glare at him. 'That was not in the script. You are meant to be a mysterious man encountering a beautiful woman in a strange bar for the first time. I don't think you would start discussing your delivery problems, do you?'

'Sorry. I forgot. The bar's certainly strange. Ahem. What's a nice girl like you doing in a place like this?' As Lucy collapsed into giggles, Mark shrugged sheepishly. 'I can't do it, Luce, I'm sorry. I'd love to indulge your fantasies, but I'm a lousy actor. I know you're my wife, and I'm incredibly glad you're my wife and not some wacko barfly. I want to talk to *you*. Like two adult, married people in their mid-thirties, who've left the children at home for once. And then have something to eat and go to the flat and sleep. Can we do that?'

Lucy agreed willingly. She was not cut out to be Lauren Bacall having an erotic encounter. Not tall enough for starters. 'Let's. The guy next to me thought I was raving mad. So, did you bawl out the shippers?'

When they eventually went back to the flat it was better than Lucy had planned. Mark was enchanted. They drank far too much, made love on those golden floorboards as well as in the drifty Moorish bed, and Lucy knew that buying the flat was the best thing that could have happened to their marriage. The next morning they were eating blood oranges in bed and getting the juice all over the new sheets when the doorbell rang and a carpenter turned up to put shelves in the sitting room. Constance hadn't left a note about him, but Lucy didn't care a bit. She left Mark to his meetings, had a chat with Enrico in the deli – that was the first time he told her the story about the young couple who had preceded them in 53B – and drove home without a care in the world, longing to see her children, even to take the two older ones to the dentist. How many times in her life does a mother honestly look forward to that? It must have been love, to combine the dental drill with such a feeling of euphoria . . . As Enrico said so mournfully, 'Nell'amore, c'é sempre un nocciola d'amarezza . . .'

Over the four or so years that they had known each other, Lucy had never felt close to Julian Purcell. They saw each other all the time, of course, and Mark liked him, and they did boy things together, straddling the barbecue, for instance, or lethargically watching football from time to time, each feigning a casual interest in the game for the other's benefit. Lucy was certainly fond of Julian, it was impossible not to be, but they were not close. He was a good man, and an intelligent man, and he was no trouble, if that could be said without belittling him; he was one of those husbands who simply don't get in the way. He went along with pretty much anything Constance suggested, and did nothing to upset the equilibrium. Lucy could not feel close to him because she had no idea what went on in his head. This did not seem to bother Mark. The two men had tacitly agreed to be friends because it was not worth resisting when their wives were so close; this seemed to Lucy a common phenomenon in couples' relationships. Men were capable not only of smothering dislike but even of forming friendships as long as their women loved each other; women rarely possessed that adaptability. Lucy could not decide whether this made women more intractable than men, or more genuine.

As for Constance's children, again Lucy's feelings were divided, this time against her own sex. Fourteen-year-old Luke was a natural charmer, a rare achievement in the book of anyone who knows adolescent boys. Facially he had inherited his mother's delicate, feline bone structure but with a more masculine cast, and he shared her thick dark hair and wide-set eyes. Francesca Purcell, known as Chessie, was an altogether different kettle of fish, if just as good-looking. Rising seventeen, she coupled a permanently morose expression with a waspish tongue, and her moods ran the gamut from petulance to bored superiority with nothing pleasant in between. Lucy couldn't understand how Constance put up with her, yet Constance quixotically seemed to favour her daughter over her son. Lucy, in a Charlotte Street-inspired surge of spousal devotion, heard the latest when she called Constance to ask her how to cook a steak.

'A steak? Even *you* must have made steak before.'

'Of course I have, but never successfully. Mark loves steak. I thought I'd call you before I cremate another cow.'

'There's nothing to it.'

'So tell me the nothing, blow by blow.'

'Right,' Constance began. 'Have you bought them already?'

'Nope. I'm waiting till you tell me where to go. I want it to be perfect.'

'Go to Jack Hall's in Sturminster. He'll give you organic beef, and at least he hangs it properly. Ask for prime rib. Get them to cut it *at least* an inch thick. Personally I prefer rump, for the flavour, but it's trickier in the way it behaves. You should go for prime rib, or eye of rib.' Lucy scribbled down the rapid-fire instructions. 'Leave them to rest at room temperature, not in the fridge. Rub in freshly ground black pepper, wait a minute and then *press*, gently but firmly, sea salt on both sides –'

'You see? It's not nothing, all this rubbing and gentle but firm pressing.'

'It sounds like sex, doesn't it?' Constance laughed. 'Julian's idea of sex, anyway. Remember to do the pepper before the salt – the pepper won't hold if you salt it first. And, for God's sake, use your hands: press it down firmly with your fingers. People don't touch food nearly enough . . .' Constance chuckled throatily.

Press it down firmly . . . Lucy noted.

'Fry them – have you got a really heavy pan? – in a mixture of butter and the tiniest drop of oil. You should use all butter, but if you do you must clarify it – and make sure it's really hot before you put the steak in. Fry them for three to four minutes, and whatever you do resist the temptation to touch it or you won't get the right effect.'

Resist the temptation . . . Lucy scrawled.

'The outside is just as important as the inside, remember that.

85

You want a scorched, crusty outside. Pallid grey stuff is just out – bin it. Then flip it over. Two to three minutes on the other side, and you *must* let it relax for five minutes before serving. Don't worry about it losing heat.'

Must let it relax . . . Don't worry . . . Lucy wrote.

'You know something?' Constance chuckled again. 'That is *exactly* Julian's recipe for sex. Talking of sex, you'll never guess what Chessie said to me last night. They're both home for the weekend, so I had Lewis take over in the restaurant Friday night, you know, so we could do some "quality" family time all together. Chessie came into the kitchen, supposedly to help me but all she wanted was to con me into giving her my Galliano bustier and my ancient Biba skirt to take back to school. I told her they still fitted, thanks to years of utter self-denial, and that they were the most flattering clothes I had.'

Lucy agreed with this. Constance could pass for being in her late twenties in that outfit: she'd stopped a couple of Dorset parties stone-dead. 'Go on,' she urged.

'Chess sniffed, you know, that really patronizing sniff, and said, "Mum, you can't believe anyone is ever going to fancy you again, not at your age." She said I was sick if I wanted anyone to. I suggested her father might just, and she looked like someone was holding dog shit under her nose and told me not to be disgusting. I thought, OK, here's the moment for the big sex talk.'

'Chessie's a bit old for that, isn't she?'

'Not the birds-and-bees stuff, the mother-to-daughter, long-term emotional-relationship stuff. I pointed out that sexual desire didn't grind to a halt when you hit thirty, and she looked at me with absolute horror and said, "Don't tell me you and Dad *still do it?*"' Constance's laughter rippled down the line. 'When I admitted that yes, occasionally, once in a blue moon, we still managed to get it together, despite the rheumatism, she told me I was a really sad

86

person. That's what she said – a *sad* person, that it was sad to be thinking like that at my age.'

'Don't. I can already hear Gracie calling me sad in ten years' time.'

'You can bank on it. But then I started thinking, What if it's true? What if I *am* sick?'

'To have sex with your husband?'

'Well, to think about sex and being fanciable.'

'You're not sick. All women think about it. They ought to.'

'You don't,' Constance said accusingly.

'Oh, yes, I do,' Lucy replied, 'I have my moments. I think of being fanciable plenty. I just don't fancy anyone except Mark.'

Lucy believed Francesca Purcell had been allowed to grow up far too fast, but then she and Constance had never seen eye to eye on child-rearing. Constance firmly believed that children suffered from too much attention, just as certain plants can suffer from too richly fed a soil. She'd often shake her head as she watched Lucy racing towards Charlie or Grace when they fell or cried, and Lucy knew what she was thinking, that children, even more than adults, needed to go unwatched and unmonitored to develop themselves, and that it was a mistake to be poised there, waiting to unravel every knotty problem they came across just like you were untying their shoelaces for them. In a way Lucy agreed with this; they disagreed only about the timing. Constance thought that the earlier you shoved children in the general direction of independence the better; Lucy believed you needed to keep a very close eye on them until they were genuinely mature, and she wasn't prepared to fix the age at which that happened. It might not be until they were well into their twenties.

'How is Grace going to learn to look where she's going, if you never let her fall?' Constance had asked just the previous week, as

Lucy grabbed her daughter at the top of the stone steps. 'Kids *have* to hurt themselves. They have to feel pain and remember what caused it or they won't be safe when you're not there holding their hand.'

'Oh, that's a great system!' Lucy retorted, her hands flung up in exasperation. 'So when Grace says, "Mummy, is the fire hot?" I should say, "Stick your hand in and find out for yourself?"'

'Have you noticed any serious burns on my children? It isn't enough to warn them it hurts, Lucy. They have to know it hurts for themselves. That's the basic lesson of survival. You've got to let them fall off the wall once or twice.'

'Or run in front of a car?'

'You're deliberately missing the point. You don't let them run under a car because once they were dead they wouldn't benefit from the experience, right? How did you learn not to run out in traffic?'

'From my mother telling me not to.'

'I bet she didn't say, "No, no, sweetie, don't play with the cars, poppet." I bet she gave you a colossal crack on the rear and it hurt like hell. What you remembered was the pain. And *that*'s what stopped you doing it a second time. That's what little kids have memories for, Lucy, so they can remember stuff that will keep them alive until they've got kids of their own. If we didn't have our heads full of bad memories that stopped us doing dangerous stuff, we'd be running around as helpless and vulnerable as, as – well, as Abby is right now.' And Constance had pointed to the naked baby lying on her play mat in the sun, and then back to Lucy's wounded expression. 'Oh, look, Luce, I'm not saying you're a bad mother, I know you're fantastic, the best, and how much you love your children . . .'

It took years and years to weave the safety-net that would save her children when they crashed, Lucy thought, and besides, she was incapable of standing back and looking away and 'leaving them to their own resourcefulness' – a phrase Constance used a great deal. Chessie's brand of resourcefulness was not something Lucy sought for her own children, and if the price was being labelled a neurotic cosseting mother, then she was willing to pay it for several more years to come. Besides, she told herself, being there wasn't just to prevent them hurting themselves: it was also to give them the confidence of her attention. Both Charlie, and now Grace, and in a couple of years Abigail, would go about the business of jumping off a step or spinning like a top saying, 'Watch me, Mummy! Watch this!' and she was determined to be there, rewarding even the most humble new achievement with her unbridled pride.

Over the steaks that night Lucy recounted Chessie's disgust at her parents' sexual relations, and Mark and Lucy followed the natural path that led them towards their own offspring, until they found themselves talking about Charlie's understanding of sex. Lucy had frequently if casually chatted to Charlie about where babies came from, not wanting to make a big thing about it, but wanting him to hear the news from her rather than one of his playmates. When Lucy talked about babies, and how once a man and a woman loved each other and decided that they wanted to spend their lives together, they might decide to start a family, Charlie showed little interest in the subject, although he appeared to listen politely while carrying on with his computer game. Mark assured her he'd already done his bit, gone through the nuts and bolts. The next morning Lucy was determined to bring the subject up lightly, just to check how much had sunk in, and did so while Charlie was preparing the food for his rabbit.

'Darling, you know how Daddy and I have talked to you about where babies come from?'

'Mu-umm!' He groaned. 'I'm not a baby! I know all about mating and reproduction from the telly.'

Lucy sighed. David Attenborough had a great deal to answer for. 'I know you're not a baby, you're very grown-up. That's precisely why I feel I can talk to you like this. I just want to be sure you understand.' Lucy toyed with the idea of sketching two figures, male and female, but she was not a good draughtsman, and she was certain her attempts at drawing a penis would only give them both a fit of the giggles. 'So you know that the man, I mean, you, and Daddy, and all boys, have a special part of their body that women don't have, a special part . . .'

'Willies. Is that what you mean?'

'Yes, darling, willies, or you can say penis, if you like. Most grown-ups call it a penis.'

'Boys have balls too.'

'Yes, of course, balls too. And women have a special part of their bodies as well.'

'Bosoms.'

'Yes, women have much larger breasts than men –'

'Daddy says men don't have breasts at all, they have manly chests.'

'That's fine, but women have larger breasts so that they can feed their babies milk that they make inside them,' Lucy continued, 'and they also have another special part of their bodies –'

'Yes, Mum.' Charlie rolled his eyes. 'Their fannies.'

'That's right, fannies, or you can also say vaginas, a special part that you can't see . . .'

Charlie looked up over the rabbit food he was measuring, his face a mixture of curiosity and bewilderment. Oh, God, Lucy thought, bloody typical. Mark didn't really tell him anything about women . . . 'But, Mum, if you can't see it, how do you know it's there?'

Lucy was caught off-guard. 'That doesn't matter – I mean, you just know it's there, because it is. You feel it.'

'Though you can't see it?'

'That's right.'

'So it's like God?'

Lucy chewed her lip to stop smiling. 'Charlie, darling, it's not quite like that. I mean, you can see it, it's just that it's inside the body, not hanging outside.'

'I know that. Otherwise, if they all stuck out, how could the penis fit into it and let the sperm go in? It wouldn't work.'

Lucy smiled broadly. 'Exactly. And you know how grown-up men and women make love, sometimes to have children?'

'Mum, I know all that stuff already. Can I go feed Thumper? He'll starve.'

'In a minute. Daddy and I –'

'It's OK. I know you and Dad did that stuff ages ago, three times . . .'

'Three times?'

He looked at her as if she were stupid and held up three fingers to make things simpler for her. 'Me, Gracie, Abby. Three.'

'But, Charlie, dearest, do you understand that sometimes grown-ups make love just for fun?'

'For fun?' He seemed puzzled, and then his blue eyes darkened and opened wide. 'You mean, you and Dad do it *here*? At home?'

Lucy nodded. 'Once or twice,' she replied feebly, but Charlie had forgotten all about Thumper and shot off towards the orchard to find Grace.

Chapter Seven

*An inconstant woman, tho' she has no chance to be very happy,
can never be very unhappy.*

John Gay

Lucy was slowly rediscovering various old friends on her
weekly visits to London, some former work or college
friends, some going even further back than that, to schooldays.
Old friends were far better than new friends, because she did not
have to explain who or what she was in relation to other people
and places. When she had first stopped work in London, she
had dreaded parties, for the simple reason that meeting a
stranger would prompt the question 'What do you do?' and she
would say quickly, 'I'm a consultant, but I'm not actually
working at the moment.' Sometimes she was tempted to say,
'Do? Well, I do the *Times* crossword in about six minutes flat,
and guess what? I can manage the laundry in under half an
hour,' but she never went that far. In Dorset new acquaintances
asked, 'Where do you live?' so that they could pinpoint her
village and house and thereby her status, or 'Which are your
children?' if she met them at school, or the worst of all, 'Who is
your husband, and what does *he* do?' Occasionally she'd arrange

a lunch in London with an old friend, even dinner if Mark was free to come up.

Now that the autumn term had started, and Lucy only had Abigail to deal with, she was finding that time lay quite heavily on her hands when Amy was there. Spurred on by the financial burden of the flat, and the emotional benefit of Amy's immediate popularity with the children, Lucy began to consider looking for some part-time work, or perhaps taking a course, to prepare herself for the time when she no longer had any babies and had no reason to stay at home. In the meantime she wallowed in 53B on her weekly jaunts. Mark was rarely able to come with her. Lucy had imagined that they would always go up together, but despite Mark's conviction that a London flat would revolutionize his way of working, it seemed to have had little effect. He was always prepared to come, but she was the one who wanted to go, not him, and it seemed foolish to drag him away from work without reason. Lucy became accustomed to having some time alone each week, or at least every other week. If Mark was not around, she often arranged to go up on a Wednesday and join Constance for lunch, and would then take over the flat as Constance left it. They had the occasional minor dispute about things they had each sneaked into Charlotte Street: Constance took a dim view of the Arabic star lamp Lucy had hung in the entrance hall, as well as the wok she had stuffed into the back of a kitchen cupboard. Lucy objected to the metal blinds that had appeared in the bathroom. Once they had voiced their gripes, they were content to let them rest as they were. They were close enough friends for the initial sparks of a row to fizzle out quickly, just as they did in their marriages.

One Wednesday, Lucy was waiting for Constance in Elena's L'Etoile. Generally the two women snacked on something from the deli, in an effort on Lucy's part to save money and on Constance's to preserve her waistline, but that day they had agreed to splash out. Lucy loved the photographs all over the walls, and the cavernous way the restaurant wandered further and further back, like stepping through the belly of a whale. Constance burst in twenty minutes late and by her standards dishevelled. By Lucy's standards she looked pretty good, but their standards were a world apart.

'Luce – help! *Absolute*. One *hundred* per *cent*. Disaster.' Constance pulled her cigarettes out of her bag and ordered a gin and tonic – most unlike Constance – before she explained, 'Julian's coming.'

'Here? To lunch? That's fine by me.'

'No, not *here*, here. He's on his way to London. Now.'

'So?' Lucy asked, thinking how happy she'd be if Mark did the same. 'So?'

Constance shook her head urgently, and flapped a hand. 'So he's not meant to be here. It's not what we arranged. He just phoned me on the mobile. He's been in Scotland since Sunday night.'

Lucy wasn't sure if Constance was on the point of cancelling their lunch date or if there was some genuine family crisis. 'And?'

'And now he's just called me at the flat. So he knows I'm in London.'

'You *are* in London. Am I being thick? I just don't understand what the problem –'

'He doesn't know I was in London last night. When he left on Sunday I told him I wasn't coming to town this week. So when he called, and there I was, he said, "Great, because I'm about to pull into King's Cross."'

'So great. You get to go home together.' Lucy studied the menu for a moment then looked up. 'Does he want you to meet his train or something?'

'Christ, Lucy, you can be obtuse when you want to be.'

95

Constance closed her eyes and swallowed hard. 'He thinks I'm staying at the flat tonight.'

'But it's a Wednesday. Wednesdays and Thursdays are our nights.'

'I *know* it's a Wednesday. I had no intention of staying in the flat. I intended to go home after lunch. But how do I explain what I'm doing in London at lunchtime if I wasn't in London last night? Which I wasn't.'

'Weren't you?'

'Oh, *God*, of course I was. But I told Julian I wasn't. I told him I'd come up this morning to stay tonight.'

'Why?'

'That doesn't matter. I just did. What am I supposed to be doing here now?'

'Having lunch with me?' Lucy asked, with false naïveté. She had an inkling of what Constance was about to ask.

'I told him we'd swapped. I said you'd let me have Wednesday night.'

'Can't you just say that seeing he's home you'd rather go back to Dorset?'

'It's too late for that, I've told too many lies. You have to let us have the flat tonight. You have to help me out.'

'Connie, I don't have to do –'

'Please. Please, Lucy.' Lucy had never seen her so flustered. Come to think of it, she couldn't remember when Constance had ever asked her for a favour. She was intrigued to know why she had lied when the truth was so innocent – if the truth were innocent . . .

'Well, does it matter if I'm there too?'

'It wouldn't make sense. I told him we'd swapped.'

'But why did you tell him that? I've got Amy staying late specifically. If I cancel I'll just have to go home and pay her anyway. Besides, I have an appointment at nine tomorrow morning.'

'What kind of appointment?'

'A hair appointment, actually.' Constance put her head in her hands. 'Look, Connie, I just don't think it's fair –'

'Maybe you could be there too if it's sort of a surprise. I could tell him you called up at the last minute and apologized but said you simply had to come – a sudden change of schedule, some crisis at home.'

'Bloody hell, Con, if I do this at all, and I am not saying I'm going to, I don't see why I should have to apologize to Julian and look like a moron. What am I meant to do, be some sort of sodding gooseberry all night?'

'Well, what were you going to do anyway?' Constance wheedled. 'Weren't you planning to go out?'

'No, actually. I had a bloody awful night with Abby last night, and Grace had nightmares, and I was planning to settle down in some peace and quiet and look through the literature courses on the City syllabus. And that's exactly what I'm going to do.'

'Lucy. Have I ever asked you to do anything for me?'

'Plenty,' Lucy bluffed.

She became beseeching, a new, and rather intriguing, Constance. She could have wrapped Joe Stalin round her little finger if she'd wanted to, if it would have served some specific purpose. 'I'll do anything for you. I'll have all your kids for a weekend. I'll buy you the most wonderful present. Lunch is on me. Have the lobster.'

'I am not open to bribery.' Lucy had already decided to agree.

'Anything, Luce, you have to help me.'

'I want to know why you lied. What happened that you couldn't tell Julian?'

'It's not serious. It's completely stupid. It's just that Julian and I have a pact about not lying to each other, and if he finds out I told him this silly, utterly pointless lie about not being in London last night, he'll think there's some big reason, something I'm hiding, and there just isn't.'

'There isn't?' Lucy echoed, arching her eyebrows and feeling entitled to be arch.

'No. I'll tell you all about it, I promise. Just say you'll be on my side here.'

'Just this once, Connie, just this once. But you have to have all my children for a whole week. In February. And you buy me a present. And I will have the lobster. *And* you and Julian go out tonight, if you want to. I'm not budging from the sofa.'

'Deal. Thank God.' Constance picked up the menu.

'So? What were you up to last night?'

Constance did not tell Lucy all about it. She told Lucy very little about it, and if Lucy had been thinking sensibly, which one tends not to with close friends, she might have been suspicious whether Constance would tell her anything when she had lied so impulsively and so needlessly to her husband. Once she had convinced Lucy to support her lie, Constance didn't *need* to tell her any more than the bare facts. All she was prepared to say was this: that she had met someone she was interested in, but that everything was absolutely above board and legit; she was not having an affair. The 'man' had not set foot in the flat the night before, although she had come to London in order to meet him. They had just had dinner. He was not a threat; he was simply a friend. He understood her work. She would definitely tell Julian all about him this weekend, and next time she came to London she intended to introduce them to each other. She simply hadn't wanted to explain it all to Julian on the phone while he was in Scotland, and the lie had popped out of her mouth before she had had a chance to think of the repercussions. That was it. The lie was very, very tiny, and bleached-bone white. It wasn't really a lie at all, more of an accidental slip. If, and this was a very large if, *if* she ever found herself tempted to consider a more involved relationship with this man, Julian would definitely know all about it.

Lucy didn't believe a word of it. She asked who he was, how they'd originally met, and what he did, but Constance was too bright. She pursed her lips, laid the fingertips of each hand on the edge of the white tablecloth, then waved the questions aside as if her nerves were too frail to risk further discussion. They had lunch in the literal media feeding frenzy that hits Charlotte Street between noon and four in the afternoon. Lucy let Constance pay the bill, and told her she'd be back at the flat around seven.

That afternoon Lucy met her younger sister, Dash. Their father had nicknamed her Dash, and very apt it was – she never stood still for a second. Most people had forgotten her real name – Jemima – or had never known it. The sisters' relationship had improved significantly since Lucy had acquired the share in Charlotte Street. Until then, Lucy had always felt like a visiting country cousin, sitting like a lump and watching Dash flit about between work (she was a researcher at the School of Slavonic Studies), home (Chiswick) and her partner (Greg, currently assistant director at the Young Vic). The sisters had been sworn enemies as children: it had taken Lucy a long time to come to terms with having a rival for her parents' time and affection. Their parents had many times recounted the story of finding Lucy, aged eight, gathering yew berries in their neighbour's garden, alternately squashing one, and putting the next carefully in her pocket. When lectured about their toxicity, Lucy had looked contemptuously at her mother, and said, 'I *know* that. I'm pretending the squishy ones are Dash's eyeballs, and I'm keeping the rest for her tea.' The girls had progressed to lukewarm friendship when teenagers, then slowly and unintentionally drifted apart. Dash felt Lucy had slumped into complacent narcoleptic domesticity, as she put it, and needed regular shaking about, plus an occasional kick up the backside. But Lucy's ownership of Charlotte Street let Dash believe her older sister was finally heading in the right direction, i.e., Dash's direction, and Dash's first pregnancy let Lucy believe that Dash was facing in hers, and between the two, they found themselves spending more time together and having more in common.

Dash was having a rare afternoon off work after an obstetric scan. Lucy told her sister all about her strange session with Constance, and saw Dash's brow furrow. Dash had long professed an intellectual dismissal of the legal state of marriage but she was passionately committed to fidelity, except that she called it monogamy, which is quite a different thing.

'I know her type. She's already screwing the socks off someone.'

'You've never even met her, Dash. You *can't* know her type.'

'I don't have to have met her to know her type.' Dash sniffed. 'She's the type that nabs a rich man when she's young, gets having his kids out of the way, buys her country pile with his money, reinvents herself then preys on other women's men.' Dash nodded aggressively. 'I know her type only too well.'

'You're ridiculous.' Lucy wondered where on earth her little sister found such certainty in her own judgement. 'Besides, Julian isn't that rich.'

'Oh, *puh*-lease . . . Talk about establishment fat cats.' As far as Dash was concerned, anyone who owned one suit, let alone four or five, was an establishment fat cat.

'Connie never "reinvented" herself, she's always been exactly what she is today. And she's not preying on anyone.'

'If you're not suspicious, then why did you bother telling me about it?' Dash sat back on the sofa, confident she'd hit the winning blow.

Lucy had to admit she was curious but she was still willing to give Constance the benefit of the doubt. 'Connie may be bored, I'll give you that. She may have been tempted into an evening's innocent flirting, or something, but she's too busy to have an affair. She simply hasn't got time.'

Dash leaned close to her sister and stared deep into her eyes; the two sets were remarkably similar. 'What's happened to you, Luce? Why don't you wake up and – what's the phrase? – smell the coffee? You don't understand anything about men and women. You don't understand diddly – squat. Since when was flirting ever innocent? And no woman is ever "too busy" to have an affair. No woman is too busy to find the time to do *anything* she wants *so long as she wants it enough*. Over sixty per cent, Lucy – sixty per cent – of men in monogamous relationships have affairs. Who do you think they're having them with? No man, not even the best – not even my darling Greg, not even dear, sweet Mark – *ever* turns down an affair with an already encumbered woman.'

'By already encumbered I suppose you mean married?'

'Of course. They're safe. They don't carry the risk unmarried women have that they might just want to hold on to you when the affair's over. Married women are the perfect no-strings bonks.'

Lucy rose to her feet, dismissing her sister's comments. 'If we're going to see this movie, we better make a move.'

'OK, but just mark my words,' Dash said darkly.

In the cinema they clutched each other's hands and sniffled through *Les Enfants du Paradis*. Afterwards Lucy would have liked to go for a drink and talk about pregnancy and babies, but Dash was eager to go home and catch Greg before he went to the theatre. Lucy was left with an hour to kill before she could turn up apologetically at her own flat on her own contractually allocated night. She took the tube home and was struck by the fact that she didn't have anyone, not one single friend, male or female, whom she could call up on the spur of the moment and say, 'Fancy a quick drink?' Most of her working friends would either still be at work or have other plans; most of her non-working friends, the London full-time mothers, would have their hands full in the early evening dealing with their children. Whatever she'd gained by having children (yes, three beautiful, precious babes, as her own mother would say, to whom she ought to be happy to dedicate the rest of her life) she'd shed an awful lot along the way. She dawdled slowly, reached the flat with half an hour still to kill, and found Enrico locking up the deli. Feeling brazen, Lucy asked him if he'd like to have a drink with her. He looked surprised but pleased, and they went into the pub opposite.

Enrico described the young couple who had lived there before, and how blissfully happy they had seemed until the day the man had dumped his girlfriend's clothes into the street. Again he repeated that aphorism, 'Nell'amore c'é sempre un nocciola d'amarezza', and Lucy nodded sagely, with a suitably wistful expression. Then he said a strange thing. He said that he knew her friend very well. 'Constance?' Lucy had asked. 'Mrs Purcell?' and he had tapped the side of his Roman nose and confirmed, 'Costanza.'

Good Christ. It all fell into place – the delicacies in the fridge, her saying she'd spent the evening with a 'friend', perfectly innocently, who understood what she was about. Doubtless they had discussed their mutual interests over the . . . salamis. Enrico wasn't the obvious candidate for an illicit liaison: he was a big man, with a paunch that could have passed for four-month gestation, bushy eyebrows with long grey hairs shooting out of them above doggy brown eyes, but the more Lucy studied him the more plausible it seemed. After all, except for one being so obviously Italian, and the other so obviously British, Enrico and Julian were a lot alike. Enrico was gentler; he had a sentimental soul, you knew that from the way he talked about their predecessors in 53B, and he was clearly a romantic, but it was possible that Constance had settled on a Mediterranean version of her own husband to reach the spots that Julian didn't.

'She is a lady of – passion.' Enrico confirmed Lucy's suspicions. 'Talking to her is like . . .'

'Like?' Lucy prompted. *Like making love?*

'When I speak with her, I feel I talk with my partner. I speak with my – how do you say it? My friend of the heart.'

'Soul-mate,' Lucy corrected. 'How nice for you both. I know she feels exactly the same about you.' Enrico beamed. 'Have you met her husband? Julian?'

'No. I hope soon. I have met *your* husband. He is very nice. We talk about wine.'

So there it was: he talked to Mark about wine; he talked to Lucy about Constance; and he talked to Constance about the soul.

Constance had a rare ability that Lucy had recognized early on in their friendship. She never lost her footing, wherever she was, whatever she was doing. People talk about others landing on their feet, but that was a quite different skill. Constance Purcell simply never tripped up, even when she wasn't looking. She was never exposed in such a way that she had to recover her balance. It was tempting to associate this characteristic with nasty people, mean, self-centred people, but that was unfair. People who never fall off the plank could be as nice or nasty as people who did; they were simply surer-footed. Seeing Constance and Julian in the flat a little later, this talent was demonstrated. Constance didn't bat an eyelid. She was in the kitchen when Lucy entered the flat; Julian put down his newspaper to greet her. 'Ah, Lucy! I hear we

103

are to have the unexpected pleasure of your company this evening.'

'Yes, well,' she stumbled, 'it was all a bit confusing at the last minute.'

'Julian, don't rub it in,' Constance said smoothly, handing Lucy a glass of wine before pecking her cheek, acting as if they'd last met over her rose-bushes in Dorset. 'I told Luce it was perfectly fine for her to be here if she needed to be. Don't make her uncomfortable about it.'

When Lucy sat down next to him Julian tweaked her cheek affectionately. 'I find it rather endearing that you're so scatty, Lucy. Constance told me about your desperate phone call.'

'Oh, *good*. I'm glad she explained everything. I'd hate to have to go through it all again. So you know why I'm here, do you?'

'Some mix-up at the hair salon?'

Salon. Only Julian could use a word like salon, Lucy thought. 'That's right, yes.'

'At least I know what to buy you for Christmas.' Julian pulled an electronic diary out of his jacket and waved it in front of her. 'One of these.'

'Now *that* would revolutionize my life,' Lucy said emphatically. 'Do you have one, Connie?'

'No, darling, I keep it all up here.' She tapped her temple. 'Will you join us for dinner, Luce? There's plenty . . . I didn't know if you had any plans.'

'I simply can't remember. Brain like a sieve, you know.' Lucy joined Constance in the kitchen, and dug her elbow in her ribs. 'I just had a drink with Enrico.'

'Really?' Constance's light blue eyes opened wide with surprise. 'How on earth did that happen?'

'I asked him. So as not to barge in on you and hubs.'

'How tactful of you. Isn't he a darling?' Not a flicker. Not a single flicker of guilt or apology, only her normal smile. 'So, are you in for dinner? You'll never guess who's coming round.'

'Don't tell me. Enrico?'

'No. Dominic. It was a last-minute thing. You do remember Dominic?'

Chapter Eight

*Life has taught us that love does not consist in gazing at each other
but in looking outward together in the same direction.*

Antoine de Saint-Exupery

A few weeks later Dash and Lucy had a brief but flaming
telephone row about the nature of marriage. Neither sister
could remember later quite why the subject arose, but the taste of
it lingered in their mouths like sour milk for some time later. Dash
reiterated her opinion that marriage was an antiquated and
redundant concept, and because Lucy was in a bad mood, having
been up half the night with Abigail, she retorted that it was
definitely redundant in Dash's case because Greg wasn't offering it.
Dash had hung up on her. Lucy felt both righteously indignant
and guilty; after all, Dash was five months pregnant and clearly
longing for Greg to propose while banging on about how artificial
the whole marital set-up was. But Lucy had other justifications for
being cross, besides the perpetual broken nights, which Dash
could not have known about.

Amy, the Epsteins' new part-time super-nanny, was being so
full-time super that none of the children seemed to want to spend
any time at all with their mother. Their first question at breakfast

would be whether Amy was taking them to school; the second would be whether Amy was picking them up. This was exactly the sort of loving child-care Lucy had been looking for ever since they had moved to Dorset, but now she'd found it she didn't like it a bit.

Mark, or rather Epstein & Rose, had been written up in the Saturday *FT*, not once but twice, once in the Running Your Own Business feature and once in the wine section. Inquiries were flooding in, business was soon to be booming, Mark said, rubbing his hands in expectation, and he had impulsively – in Lucy's opinion – responded by hiring a full-time assistant. This again was exactly what they had been hoping for ever since they'd moved to Dorset, and did Lucy like it? Not a bit. As a wise man once said, and as Lucy was wise enough to acknowledge, there are only two tragedies in life: not getting what you want, and getting what you want. The fact that Mark's new full-time assistant was an athletic young brunette called Samantha, who had worked for Adnams in Suffolk before nobly moving to Dorset to be closer to her elderly parents, the fact that she maintained the most picture-postcard perfect sixteenth-century cottage not three miles from the front door of Manor Farm, the fact that she was calm, cool, business-like and perfectly suited to the job, the fact that she had persuaded Mark that the best marketing strategy was to concentrate on the West Country with the aim of local market domination, the fact that from the moment she joined, she was closeted with Mark for ten hours a day in the office in the barn next door, none of these points had anything to do with Lucy's flash of bad temper towards her sister. Not a thing. Nor that Samantha had told Mark that very morning, and Mark had passed the comment on to his wife, that she was certain the next time he was featured in the *FT* it would be in the Lunch With the *FT* interview. None of these things could possibly bother her. Lucy was perhaps justifiably annoyed that it had taken Mark two weeks to comment on her new highlights and haircut, and even then he'd only asked how much it had set him back – set *him* back, mind you, but that was a triviality. No, her justification for bad temper had deeper roots. Having obtained the perfect flat, and all that was necessary to enjoy her reclaimed liberty, she simply didn't know what to do with it. She had expected the faint niggling sensation of hunger, of something that was missing, if she didn't quite know what, to be instantaneously satisfied by the mere possession of the flat itself. Instead she found herself much the same, if significantly poorer. Seeing that Amy was more than happy to be left in sole charge of the children, Lucy popped over to see Constance. She never got round to spelling out her real frustrations.

'I've just had an almighty row with my little sister,' Lucy opened, leaning against a kitchen counter.

'What about?' It was early Friday afternoon, and Constance was in the kitchen. She hadn't seemed wildly enthusiastic about the impromptu visit: she was experimenting with different game recipes and had to leave shortly for the restaurant.

'The normal sibling row – i.e., everything and nothing. Marriage. Commitment. Fidelity.'

'You don't need to tell me who was for and who was against, Miss Goody-Two-Shoes.'

'Oh, for Christ's sake. Sometimes I think I should just go out and bonk someone and announce it in the local paper so that everyone will get off my case about being a boring little prude.'

'That would certainly liven up the conversation at the village harvest festival,' Constance agreed.

'Connie, if I promise not to criticize you or ever say anything to anyone, would you just tell me something? Are you having an affair?' Constance continued to disembowel a pheasant with intense concentration. Lucy had seen her being 'sensitive'. She'd seen her near orgasmic over scents and sights, euphoric over the sheer shape of a tomato, or the texture of a lump of unrefined brown sugar, but she could gut a fish or eviscerate a bird with the speed and efficient cold-blooded brutality of a lioness. Constance picked up a larding needle and avoided both looking at Lucy and replying. Lucy persisted: 'That man – the one you went to London to meet.'

'What about him?'

'Are you having an affair with him or not?'

'Are you asking out of concern for me or for Julian?' Constance asked haughtily. 'Or is this purely a salacious query?'

'Are you?'

'Whom could I possibly be having an affair with?'

Lucy studied her. She could have been having an affair with the Prime Minister for all Lucy knew. 'Enrico,' Lucy hazarded.

Constance smiled as if she knew a secret, injecting fat near the pheasant's rear. 'Is that your best offer?'

'Dominic, then.'

'You were there when we had dinner. Did my behaviour suggest we were having an affair?' She turned to face Lucy, the larding needle pointing dangerously close.

'You were very friendly to him.'

'I'm very friendly to everyone, haven't you noticed? I like him. I like Enrico, too. Very much. But I haven't had dinner with either of them – not alone. Pass me that pancetta, could you?' She wrapped it around the pheasant, and examined the label on a bottle of Italian white wine before adding pointedly, 'I also happen to like Julian.'

'Connie, if we're friends, I think you could tell me a little bit more . . .'

'We *are* friends and I've told you enough. I've told you that I've met someone I'm quite interested in. That's all it is right now, interest. If it becomes anything more, you will be the third – no, I suppose the fourth person to know. God knows why you want to.'

'Because I don't understand!' Lucy said insistently. 'I want to know. What the sod is marriage for, what is it about, if it's not about fidelity? Faithfulness?'

'It's about all sorts of things – stability, security, companionship.' Constance said the words quietly, her voice dipping low. 'Lord, Lucy, I do love you: you're *quaint*. You must be the last woman on earth who gives meaningless labels such importance. They're just words. Faithful and fidelity: what a double-act. Personally, fidelity always makes me think of Fidel Castro, and faithful reminds me of a smelly old dog.'

'There's no reason to be nasty!' Lucy bridled.

Constance looked at her curiously before leading her over to a chair and giving her a cup of coffee. 'I'm not at all sure why you're asking, but I'll tell you what I think marriage is about. I think marriages can either be bad, a mistake from the out, in which case you need to erase them as quickly and permanently as possible. Or, like mine, and yours, and basically most of them, they're good ones. If they're good, then the marriage is not over and decided at the altar, not by a long shot. That's simply the beginning of a long, long road, Land's End to John O' Groats. You have no idea when you marry the man – and it's not just the flesh and blood, you understand, but the whole package, who he is, what he is, where he comes from, what he wants from life – you have no idea of all of that, and you can't slice off the bits you don't like, you have to stick with the entire package. And you have no idea whether the road is going to be straight and easy, or very bumpy.'

'And yours and Julian's?'

'Has been a bit bumpy at times.' Constance acknowledged with a shrug. 'We coasted the first stretch. I suppose we had lots of time for each other then, and lots of energy. Then maybe we changed our minds about where we were heading.'

'But you do still love him, Connie?'

'I don't think love is a box you're in or out of,' Constance said pensively. 'I'm not sure it's a good idea to think about it like that at all. I guess I think of it as just a general direction. We're still pointing the right way, but our speed's slowed down.'

'And what's the final destination?'

'That's the big question, darling, isn't it? Look at it like this. There's the great long thoroughfare of marriage, right?' Constance picked up a pencil and started to draw on the back of one of her summer menus. 'And there are all these little turn-offs, slip-roads, and some are dead ends, and some lead back to the main road, and some lead God alone knows where. Some are signposted, some aren't. You just have to choose carefully. It isn't about blind faith, or freaks of fate, right? Everything is achievable, and everything is avoidable.' She had drawn a road map, and began to embellish it. 'There are roundabouts, and traffic lights, and stop signs. "Decrease speed – roadworks ahead": maybe that's children. And then there are lay-bys, where you just stop for a bit, change the oil, change a wheel, call the AA, maybe . . .'

Lucy grabbed the pencil and drew two heavy lines across the marital motorway. 'And what about this? What about if you come to a bloody great intersection? Hm? What then? Do you go right or left?'

'You go straight over, you twit. If in doubt, do nowt, as our West Country friends would say.' Constance smiled.

'I thought that was a Yorkshire saying.'

'Is it?' As they both gazed thoughtfully at the map, Constance added, 'Unless it's a T-junction.'

'So why would anyone bother with the slip-roads and lay-bys?'

'Pit-stop. For a breather. You know it's a diversion, you know you've got to get back on track, but it's better than nothing, isn't it? Better than ceaseless toil, slogging year after year down the M1.'

She reached out and touched Lucy's hair in an uncharacteristically tender gesture.

'Con, is this your way of telling me you're having an affair?' Lucy asked again.

'No. Maybe there's a lay-by up ahead. I don't know yet if I want to stop or not. Sometimes you get the urge to do something dramatic, drive off the road crazily, maybe just to check if your husband's awake. I don't know.' She yawned, scrunched up the menu and returned to the pheasant.

'You'd have made a good teacher.'

'I'd be a crap teacher, Lucy. Absolute crap. Teachers have to be confident of what they're teaching, and I'm not. The only thing I might be able to teach you is how to cook – if it can be taught. That's the only thing I know anything about at all.'

That was the moment when Lucy decided that she would support Constance whatever she did, and that Constance's secrets would be her secrets, and that friendship should be stronger than rules. Right or wrong, and Lucy did think that a lot of what she said made sense – at least for Constance, if not for Lucy herself – Constance was her friend, and she loved her.

By the time Lucy got home Amy had gone, leaving a note to say that Grace had outgrown her shoes, and would Lucy like her to take Grace shopping to buy some new ones? Would I hell, Lucy thought petulantly: Go have your own children. Mark was in the garden with Grace on his lap trying to thread a daisy chain, a most frustrating task for a four-year-old, and there was the blessèd Samantha entertaining Charlie. 'Isn't she a dream?' Mark asked rhetorically, and echoed the Russian au pair's letter: '"She puts me in a strong state of enthusiasm."'

'That's a novel way of putting it.' Lucy looked at Samantha in the orchard. She was sitting next to Charlie on a limb of the apple tree, swinging her long, bronzed legs, and they were deep in conversation. 'Hasn't she got a home to go to?'

Mark threw his wife a critical look. 'You should be grateful, not sarcastic. She volunteered to stay till you came home, so I could spend a bit of time with Grace. She's not paid to do that, you know.'

'Since when does she have the right to decide if my children have enough quality time or not? Since when does she have the right to criticize how I raise the children?'

'All I said was, it's not what I pay her to do.'

'How would I know what she's paid to do? She's your employee, nothing to do with me.'

'For Christ's sake, Lucy, pack it in and stop being a bitch.'

'Am I allowed to ask where Abby is?'

'She's asleep.'

'Oh, great.' Lucy slumped back in the lounger and covered her eyes with one hand. 'So she'll be up until ten tonight – or she'll wake at ten and stay up till four in the morning. And I guess it will be me who's up with her, just like it has been the last few nights.'

Mark, normally slow to anger, pulled his lips into a thin line. 'It was your choice. If you disappear in the afternoon and leave the kids to Amy, then all you can expect is that she'll try to keep them busy. She took them swimming. Abby fell asleep in the car on the way home, so I told Amy to put her in her cot.'

'How considerate. Thanks very much. But I don't hear you offering to stay up with her tonight.'

'For God's sake. The kids had a great time, thanks to Amy and Samantha. You should be grateful. I don't know why you're in such a bad mood, but don't take it out on me – it's nothing to do with me. And if you get up for the kids when I don't, that's only because I'm earning our living, remember?'

Now here is the essence of marital rows. Whatever the experts say, they are not about money, or sex, or domestic routines – who does more housework, or spends more time with the kids, who takes the garbage out, who pays the bills, who sacrifices their career, willingly or otherwise. The big ones, the arguments that suddenly combust and consume everything around them, simply concern what one person assumes the other is privately thinking about them. They ignite when what one suspects the other is thinking is exactly what they most dislike in themselves. Mark was thinking about the business, and what a poor job he was making of providing for his family. He was also convinced that Lucy resented the time he spent painting in the garage when he could have been working harder; he often felt a degree of guilt that his time and energy were only partly at the disposal of his wife and family whereas hers were absorbed by them. He would have liked to tell her this, to say how appreciative he was, and how much he admired the way she nurtured and raised their children, but the tilt of her jaw prohibited him. Lucy knew exactly what Mark was thinking: he was thinking that she was going to pieces and falling apart, neglecting her children, easily replaced in their affections by others, and resentful of the very people who were caring for her children, behaving like a baby herself – bottom line, scoring zero as a mother. He had given her love, support, companionship, freedom, even a flat in London, and still she wasn't happy. She wanted to tell him that she didn't know what was wrong with her, why she couldn't just be happy when he had given her everything she wanted, but the thin line of his mouth prevented her from talking to him. As she looked at him, the vague suspicion that he only loved her when she was behaving nicely and predictably grew like a tumour. Grace and Charlie's frequent accusations were understandable, however much she denied them – when they were horrid, she didn't love them, and right now Mark didn't love her. And so, blaming Mark, Lucy did something she hadn't done in all her married life. She withdrew completely.

She stood up abruptly and said, 'Fine. So you earn the money and I handle everything else? Well, I'm tired of being in charge day in day out, and oh-so-predictable. Why don't you ask Samantha to stay on and help you deal with the children tonight? The five of you can have dinner together. I'm going to bed.'

'You're worse than Grace. It's always got to be exactly your way, hasn't it, Lucy? Can't you just grow up?' Mark rubbed his eyes wearily. When he took his hand away, they looked simply sad, as if he had wiped his anger away with his palm.

'Grace isn't spoilt. Grace needs attention and recognition and, amazingly, so do I. I'd really like to know what you'd do without me, Mark – I suppose you'd cope just fine, so long as you had Amy and Samantha to help, you wouldn't need me at all.'

'What's got into you, Luce? Is this some kind of jealousy or what?'

'You tell me.' Lucy was trembling with anger, but also with fear. She knew perfectly well, *even at the time*, that her reaction was absurd but she didn't know how to reverse. She was left with the desire to provoke Mark into an emotion equally fierce, in the hope that he would rescue the situation. She crossed her arms over her chest. 'Tell me. If I wasn't here, and you had Samantha and Amy at your beck and call, which one would you rather sleep with?'

'You're totally ridiculous. I'd rather sleep with you, but not when you're behaving like a mad woman. Frankly, that leaves me cold.'

At once Lucy went inside, for a few minutes unable to get her breath. The fight had been of her own making and had been worse than any row in their marriage. She had no intention of sleeping in the same bed as him when she could be in London within two hours – by ten at the latest. She'd have a chance to patch things up with Dash, and see if she felt like coming home on Saturday night or not, which would depend on Mark's reaction. A Saturday alone

116

with the kids would let him know exactly how far she lived up to her responsibilities. She went into Abigail's room and felt an overwhelming surge of mixed emotions as she looked at her sleeping baby: devotion; remorse; her baby's innocence; the desire for a dramatic gesture. Lucy was prepared to sacrifice Charlie and Grace on this marital pyre for twenty-four hours, but not her babe. She threw some Babygros into a hold-all, grabbed the changing bag, which the infuriatingly irreproachable Amy had stocked meticulously, and gathered up Abigail. When she was lifted from the warmth of her bed, the little girl's lips made the sweetest *moue* before falling back into deep slumber. She could dream away on the drive to London, her mother thought, and then the two of them could sit up all night watching old movies on the tiny telly in the flat. Lucy came downstairs to find Mark standing in the hall.

'What are you doing?' he asked flatly.

'Going to the flat.'

'Sit down, Luce. Talk to me, please. I don't understand . . .' For a second she wanted to hand Abigail over and fall into his arms weeping. Then she heard a heavy sigh of resignation before he said, 'You can't seriously do this. You cannot behave like this, there's no excuse.'

'Just watch me, Mark. I'm sure Samantha will be delighted to help you with Grace and Charlie. You can call me on the mobile in a crisis, but Abby's the only tricky one and she'll be with me. You should be grateful.'

He stood watching from the doorway as she drove away.

After less than fifteen miles Lucy bitterly regretted her impulsive walkout, but there was no way she could turn round, crawl back, baby under arm, to walk in on her husband and his assistant sitting down to supper with her children. Lucy had committed herself, however rashly. If Mark wanted her back, if he loved her *at all*, she argued to herself, he had only to call her on the mobile, which was on her lap the whole way to London. She checked it at least five times to make sure the battery was fully charged and the signal receiving. 'Bloody hell,' she shouted, after fifty miles, why didn't he call? One gentle word, the most hesitant apology, and she would have turned the car round and headed for home. She shed a few tears; she called herself stupid; she also blamed Mark as she waited in vain for the mobile to ring.

At five past ten Lucy pulled up in front of 53B and was rewarded for the first time with a parking space right outside the flat. She struggled with the front door, holding Abigail, who had now woken up and was wailing, under one arm, and gave the bottom of the door a hefty kick as she put her shoulder to it. Abigail slumped against her neck while Lucy walked up the flight of stairs, longing to be back in her bed in Dorset, back with her husband beside her and her children all safe in their beds, cursing herself for being a fool. When she opened the flat door she was confused by a faint green glow in the living room. She switched on the star lantern that Connie loathed, and twinkly white glints of light flitted across the ceiling.

'God – who the hell's that?' a male voice groaned. Lucy froze in the doorway. 'Constance?' A shape loomed up from the sofa and Lucy clutched Abigail more tightly, making her yelp, and stepped backwards on to the landing. The man half rose and half fell off the sofa, cursing. 'Oh, *shit*. Turn the proper bloody light on, for God's sake, whoever you are.'

Shifting her keys between her fingers so that one, the sharpest, jutted out below her palm, Lucy nervously switched on the chic wall lights Constance had installed a few weeks earlier and stared at the stranger who stood rubbing his eyes in the middle of her living room. There was a near-empty bottle of wine, one glass and a full ashtray next to a laptop computer on the coffee table; the last was responsible for the eerie light. Abigail wailed again, and Lucy shifted her on to her other hip, her secret weapon now trapped under the baby's bottom as she stroked her head with her free hand. Only then did the man smile at her.

'That's better. At least I can see who I'm talking to.' He saw a flustered blonde clutching an infant protectively to her breast, and glaring at him with suspicious blue eyes. 'You must be the flatmate.' He yawned, and stretched languorously. 'What time is it?'

'About ten.' Lucy stood in the hall, poised for flight.

'Bugger. I must have fallen asleep. I lay down for a moment or two, but that was hours ago.' He strolled casually back to the table and tipped the dregs of the wine into his glass. 'Oh, excuse me. Won't you join me? There's plenty more in the fridge.'

'I know there is.' Lucy stepped into the room briskly and dumped the nappy-bag, hold-all, muslin cloth and her handbag on the sofa, before settling Abby down beside them. 'It's my wine.'

'Course it is. Sorry again. I'll replace it, I promise. Shall I open a bottle anyway?'

Hands on hips, she confronted him. 'Would you mind telling me who you are and what you are doing in my flat?'

'Would you mind not yelling at me? My head. I feel like I've been run over.'

'If that were true it would at least explain what you're doing staying in my flat, but you don't look injured to me.'

'Do calm down, whatever your name is. I'm not "staying" in your flat. I borrowed it briefly – with Constance's permission.' He moved into the kitchen, which only took a couple of steps, and studied the fridge before selecting a bottle of Sauvignon and taking a second glass out of the cupboard. 'May I? Come on. You look shagged out. You know you'd like a glass. Don't deny yourself just to make me feel a shit. I feel bad already – bad enough for both of us.'

There are moments in life, maybe when you're feeling particularly tired, or stressed, or not altogether there, when you do things that don't seem real; it is as if they are happening in a dream. That was how Lucy recalled her first few dates with Mark. She saw them like that; rather otherworldly, as if she and Mark weren't the two characters concerned, as if they were merely scenes from a film she'd seen a long time ago, and only dimly remembered. They had a ghostly air, those images, because they only existed in memory, and perhaps only in hers. Lucy felt the same thing that night, in the present, without the diffusion of memory: that she knew it couldn't really be her, sitting on the sofa, with Abigail on her lap, drinking wine with that big stranger, chatting together as if they'd known each other all their lives. And in a way, she *wasn't* sitting on the sofa: she was drifting around in a dreamy place while an unknown man flirted with her, while he watched her stroking her baby's soft head. And he did flirt – that wasn't in doubt; his hooded eyes fairly bristled with flirtation. Everything else was in doubt – she didn't even think to ask his name.

'So Connie said you could stay here?'

'Connie?' He smiled. 'Not exactly. Not in so many words.' He sighed. 'I phoned her and asked her if I could borrow the flat briefly.' She looked at him steadily, bouncing Abigail softly on her lap and waiting for an explanation, which he promptly gave. 'I'm not selling myself very well, am I? OK. I'm a journalist. I review restaurants. I met Constance – can't imagine anyone calling her Connie –' He laughed abruptly. 'Anyway, to cut a long story short, I first met her at a restaurant opening years ago, and then we bumped into each other last month. Today I was absolutely up shit creek.' He kept topping up her glass and Lucy kept slurping it. 'I'd got pissed over lunch down the road with a colleague – drank too much because the food was so bad – and found myself stranded with a flat battery on my laptop and barely two hours to file my copy. I remembered Constance had a place near here, called her up and begged her to lend me a power point for an hour or so. The bloke in the deli gave me the keys. And the rest, as they say, is history. I had no idea anyone would walk in and catch me – *in flagrante*. Constance said the flat was always empty on Fridays.'

'It normally is.' Abigail, at her most obliging, fell asleep again. 'I'll just put my baby to bed.'

He stood up with her, Constance's restaurant critic, and shadowed Lucy into her bedroom, standing behind her as she bent to bolster Abigail with pillows so that she couldn't roll off the bed. As Lucy straightened up she felt his warm breath on the back of her neck and snapped her head up so sharply that she knocked him in the mouth. Her hand flew to the back of her head as he fingered his bottom lip. There was a momentary embarrassed pause before a rush of apologies.

'I'm sorry – did I hurt you? I didn't realize you were so close.'

'No, I'm sorry – I didn't mean to crowd you. Are you OK?' He grinned, still rubbing his mouth, his lip already swelling. 'No blood spilt. I just wanted a better look at your babe. What is it?'

Lucy smiled. Any woman, even blindfolded, would have known Abigail was a girl. '*It's* a girl.'

'She's beautiful.'

'All babies are beautiful when they're asleep.'

'Not that beautiful.' Lucy felt a fluttery rush of pride as she rearranged the mosquito netting around the bed. 'This is a fantastic bedroom,' he drawled. She felt faintly embarrassed by it – the blatant, phoney sensuality of it, all that drapery and hackneyed exoticism. Ten million miles away from Marrakech.

'Well, bedrooms matter, don't they?' Lucy murmured, chewing a fingernail. God knew how long it had been since she'd stood in any bedroom, let alone one as unsubtle as this, with a man other than Mark. Except for the man who had come to take up the sisal and quote on restoring the floorboards. He didn't really count.

'They matter a great deal . . .' he agreed gravely without a hint of a smile.

She heard herself say nervously, 'Do you know, at least half the people on *Desert Island Discs* choose their bed or duvet, or something bedroomy as their luxury?'

'What would *you* choose as your luxury?' His arm was stretched across the doorway so that she had to duck under it to get out.

'Oh, God. I don't know. A computer? Something practical, I suppose.' She was dying to have a pee, absolutely dying, and paused by the bathroom door, but he was so close to her she found herself unable to say it or to squeeze past him.

'Somehow I don't see you choosing anything practical. You don't look the organized type. A bed, yes – or a case of champagne . . .'

Lucy wrapped her arms tightly around herself. 'That would be too obvious. My husband's a wine dealer.'

'Ah-ha! *That* explains the well-stocked fridge. Talking of which, shall we?' He raised one questioning eyebrow, just the way she did.

'Why not? Go ahead and help yourself.'

As he moved to the kitchen Lucy slipped into the bathroom. She sat on the loo thinking, So this is Constance's maybe lay-by lover . . . How could she ever have suspected Dominic, let alone Enrico? This man was perfect for Constance, as he called her. He looked the right age, around forty; he was huge, but didn't have the slack waistline and collapsing chin – or should that be slack chin and collapsing waistline – that Julian carried so casually. He looked fit, and bold, and more than happy in his skin, like a Russian hussar. And there was clearly a meeting of the minds and appetites; similarity of taste went a long way, no doubt, towards fanning ardour. Lucy imagined her uninvited guest and Constance discussing the relative merits of wild rocket and sorrel before leaping into bed. There was the faintest thread of threat coiled about him, yet there was a boyishness too, a casualness that Constance would certainly find irresistible. Lucy studied herself in the mirror and grimaced. Messy hair, deathly pale, no lipstick, scared blue eyes stretched wide. She hadn't brought her bag in with her or she could have done something about it, not that there was any cause to look her best for Constance's lover. Besides, even if he meant nothing to her, she wouldn't want any man to think that she'd put on makeup for *his* benefit, and if she'd gone into the bathroom without any and come back plastered in it – Lucy splashed cold water on her face and scrubbed it hard with Constance's face towel. Constance had a thing about her towels: no one, not even Julian, was allowed to touch them. They were shell pink, and as soft as thistledown. If she thought anyone had used them to wipe their greasy mitts let alone less appealing body parts she would have thrown them out.

Lucy came back out and curled up at the far end of the sofa, tucking her feet under her so that nothing would be too close to him. From the opposite end he stretched to pass her a glass.

'Is she your first baby?'

'Abby? No, she's my third. And last.'

'What a pity. You obviously have a knack for it.'

'Do you have children?' she asked, not quite able to acknowledge the compliment.

'Me? I don't have anything at all. Not a wife, not a child, not brothers, nor sisters, nothing but me.'

'You must have parents.' Lucy addressed her wine-glass.

'I did. They're dead.'

'I'm sorry.'

'Don't be. My mother died when I was quite young; my father died about ten years ago. I am as you see me – unencumbered.' This was a concept Lucy found absolutely impossible to understand. Single, she could grasp. Footloose and fancy-free. But to have nothing and no one? She still had both her parents, and she loved them, plus Mark, whom she adored, plus the children, likewise, plus Mark's mother, plus Dash, plus Greg, whom she thought of as a brother-in-law whether he welcomed it or not, plus her eagerly awaited niece or nephew, plus Mark's nieces and nephews and two brothers and one sister-in-law, plus, plus, plus, all loved . . . So many people connected her, integrated her: family, family-in-law, friends, even friends of friends. She was silent as she contemplated complete isolation. He smiled at her again, green eyes twinkling. 'What a big heart you have.'

'I'm sorry?'

'You looked so sad just then, pitying my lonely state. I like women who look sad: they're normally so much more interesting than happy women.'

'Oh, I wasn't thinking that at all. I'm sure you're not lonely – not with your job. You must meet thousands of people, all the time.'

'I meet waitresses and foodies.'

'Like Constance?'

He laughed loudly, with easy confidence, showing all his teeth. 'Constance isn't a foodie.'

'She isn't?'

'No. She's something on a far grander scale, and earthier, too. I would call Constance a "food*euse*" . . .' He dragged the word out languorously, with his eyes closed, so that Lucy could not mistake what he intended by it. 'Do you know her well? Have you noticed that when she talks about garlic she'll never imply your common or garden garlic, she'll say, Rose de Lautrec, and assume you are familiar with the variety?' For a moment Lucy thought he was poking fun at Constance, but then he shook his head and looked grave. 'She's far too professional, too dedicated, too *sensual* to be a mere foodie.'

'I see what you mean.' Lucy did: he meant he was besotted by her, and who wouldn't be? Elegant, masterful, mistressful Constance. These two had already embarked on far more than platonic friendship. She stood up abruptly. 'Look, I hate to break up the party, but Abby's going to be up at the crack of dawn, if not earlier, and I have a busy day tomorrow.' She grabbed both half-full glasses, pressing the bottle to her bosom and went into the kitchen, calling over her shoulder, 'Did you manage to do your review in time? Get everything you needed?' He didn't reply, so she was obliged to peer around the edge of the arch back into the sitting room. He looked at her exactly the way Charlie sometimes looked at her, when she told him off for some minor misdemeanour: wounded, but righteous. Abruptly he stood to pack up his computer. He held out the ashtray tentatively, and she took it from him and emptied it.

'I'm sorry I overstayed my welcome – not that you welcomed me in the first place.'

'It's not like that . . . We share the flat. If Connie – if Constance says you can use it, that's absolutely OK by me.'

'I hope I'll see you again, Constance's flatmate.'

Lucy opened her mouth to speak, swallowed hard, and sighed. 'I'm not here that much, and never on a Friday so I doubt we'll meet. I'm only here now – to take Abby to the specialist.' She scowled, cross with herself. She had no need to justify her presence, or tell him anything at all, yet she heard herself elaborate. 'To the paediatrician.'

'She looks the picture of health. She's not sick, is she?'

'No. Not at all.'

He picked up his cigarettes and slipped them in his jacket pocket. He hadn't touched them since she'd arrived, but Lucy imagined the critic and Constance smoking up a storm together. It was twenty years since she'd felt excluded from the schoolyard élite by dint of not being a smoker. *Goody-goody. Teacher's Pet. Coward.* Hoisting his computer case over his shoulder, he held out a hand. 'It's been very nice talking to you, Constance's flatmate.'

'Lucy.'

'I hope I do see you again, Lucy. Very much. Perhaps you could come with me, when I review a restaurant? I'm always looking for interesting people to take to lunch.'

'Oh, you've got the wrong idea. I'm not interesting at all.'

He smiled. He found something about her distinctly amusing; more than that, refreshing. She was quite unlike the ambitious young women he normally met, and he enjoyed the way she volleyed back every compliment he paid her in rebuttal. Having not really intended to press her to a lunch engagement, he found himself determined to arrange one. 'Any day you like. Whenever you're next in town.'

Her hand was somehow in his. He seemed simply vast – bigger than the doorway, bigger than the flat itself, broader than the forehead of God. 'Maybe.' Lucy pulled her hand back a little too anxiously.

'It's Steven, by the way. Steven Armitage.' As he left he bent swiftly and dropped a friendly kiss on her cheek. When she heard the street door slam she gingerly touched the spot where he had kissed her. By the time she had climbed into bed and pulled Abigail up close, it seemed to Lucy that he hadn't really flirted at all: he had simply been polite in a potentially embarrassing situation. An hour later, as she paced the living room with a cross, hungry baby, waiting for the milk to cool, Lucy decided that she was far too long married to recognize the difference between flirting and simple good manners.

Chapter Nine

In her first passion woman loves her lover. In all the others all she loves is love.

Byron

Lucy felt as if she'd barely slept, whether because of Abigail's wriggling and squirming and wide-awake, toothless beaming or her own unsettling dreams, she didn't know. Either Abigail tugging softly at her hair or a dream woke her well before the telephone rang at eight the next morning.

'Darling? It's me,' Mark said. 'Are you OK?'

'We're fine . . . Apart from the fact that Abby has a lunatic for a mother. I'm so sorry, Mark.'

'I upset you. I didn't mean to, but I realize I did.' He paused, and Lucy held her breath until she heard him say, 'I never mean to upset you, darling, not for the world. I missed you so much last night – we all did. I don't know what we would do without you.'

'You'll never have to do without me,' she said in a rush. 'I've been an idiot. I wish I could say it was PMT, but I can't. I'm sorry. I missed you too.'

'Would you please come home?'

'I'm on my way. I just want to have a quick look in the shops while I'm here and see if I can get the children some winter clothes – can we afford a tiny bit of shopping?'

'Get whatever you like, but put it on credit. Let's pray our bank balance looks better by the time the bills come in. Hurry home, my darling, but have fun.'

After taking Abigail to Selfridges and spending a small fortune on new clothes the children didn't quite need, as well as presents for Charlie and Grace so they wouldn't think she'd walked out on them for nothing, and stopping to buy Mark a copy of a book he'd been talking about so that he wouldn't feel left out, then picking up a little Victorian stick-pin from a shop around the corner from the flat as a thank-you gift for Amy, and going back with gritted teeth to buy a second one for Samantha, thereby managing to spend about two hundred pounds that they could ill afford in the space of two hours, Lucy drove home. When she arrived Mark told her she looked like death, and ought to take a nap, and although she didn't feel tired she wanted to acknowledge his solicitousness and agreed meekly. She didn't nap as such: Grace kept barging in saying, 'Mummy, get up! It's not bedtime!' over and over, and when Lucy heard Abigail crying, and Mark's voice becomingly increasingly strained as he attempted to soothe her, she rose to help. Mark made her a cup of tea, and it was apparent that the fight of the previous night was going to be one of those that they left in cold storage before discussing it, if it was ever discussed at all.

'Connie called this morning.'

'You didn't tell her I'd gone mental, did you?'

'Of course not. She and Julian are going to pop over with the children for a drink this evening. Julian's taking them skating while Con's working.' He saw Lucy smile. 'We can put them off, if you like.'

'No, that's fine – I was just imagining the sight of Julian skating.'

'He might be very good for all we know.'

'He'd be absurd.' They laughed together.

'They think it's time for a Charlotte Street management meeting. I don't have anything to raise, Luce, do you?'

Lucy was changing Abigail's nappy on the kitchen table, something she knew would have made Constance retch and call the hygiene police had she been present. Lucy did it all the more defiantly. 'No. I think everything's just as we thought it would be.' Except for Steven Armitage. 'Mark?'

'Yes, beloved?'

Bang. It was that easy. If he had said, 'Yes?' with any discernible trace of irritation or impatience, however faint, if he'd even said, 'Yes, Luce?', if he had sighed, if he had ignored her, if he had grunted, she might have replied very differently. But by calling her 'beloved' he erased every bad thought and feeling she'd ever had about him. 'I love you, Mark. I'm . . . you know. I'm really sorry about last night. Can we go to London together next week? See a movie? Have dinner with Dash and Greg? Do something?'

He took her in his arms and nuzzled her ear. 'You bring the oranges, I'll bring the martinis.'

When Constance and Julian arrived, in two cars, with their delightful son and difficult daughter in tow, Mark took them all into the orchard to enjoy what they agreed was going to be the swan-song of that Indian summer. Constance was wearing a perfectly Constance outfit: cropped black jacket, white shirt, stretched-wool slim pants. Once in the restaurant, Lucy knew, she'd change jackets for her surgical white, buttoned-up-to-the-neck job. So *noli me tangere*; so knowingly erotic. For a split second Lucy envied her. Mark busied himself as bartender. 'Chessie?' he asked. 'What can I get you, sweetie?'

'I'd love a gin and tonic, Mark.'

'She'll have a Coke, thank you very much.' Julian eyed his daughter lugubriously.

'*Diet* Coke, if I must.' Chessie pouted, crossing her legs and dangling one platform sandal off the end of her toes.

'Luke?'

'Nothing, thanks. Maybe I'll hang out with Charlie for a bit.'

Mark went inside to get the drinks, Julian trailing behind in the hope of a chance to check the cricket scores. Boys one, girls *nul point*, Lucy thought grimly, wondering again how Constance stomached her daughter. Grace seemed to sense this too, for she stopped flitting from one adult to another, like a bee buzzing from flower to flower, and bounded up to Constance. She climbed on to her lap and held Constance's face firmly between her two small hands.

'My daddy says you're sexy.'

Connie laughed and gave Grace a hug. 'Does he? That's very kind of him.'

'Grace darling, come here. Don't climb all over Constance like that.' Lucy reached out her arms to Grace, but her daughter wouldn't be prised away and studied Constance more seriously.

'He said you're scary sexy.' The little girl spoke without interpretation; she was merely reporting a fact.

'Is that a nice thing to be? I wouldn't like to be just scary . . .' Constance was still smiling; in fact, she looked delighted.

'Daddy says,' Grace continued, enjoying her audience, 'Daddy says you're scary sexy, but not beautiful sexy –'

'That's enough, Grace!' Lucy barked. 'Go inside and get some crisps.'

Constance was now wearing a quizzical smile. Francesca, seizing a golden opportunity, leaned towards her mother. 'Out of the mouths of babes, huh, Mum? I mean, I can't see you as sexy at all, myself, but assuming some people might, it would definitely be scary sexy rather than beautiful sexy.'

Constance gave her a Medusa look. 'Go and help Mark with the drinks, Francesca. Or maybe you could take Grace up to her room and play Barbies with her?'

'Why should I listen to what you say?' Francesca examined her green fingernails.

Lucy watched Constance brace herself. 'Because I'm your mother.'

'That's not a good enough reason.'

'OK,' Constance replied tolerantly – too tolerantly, in Lucy's opinion, 'you're right. You should listen to me because I've been around a lot longer than you, and I might have learned something that might just save you a mistake or two.'

Her daughter weighed up how far she could go, pushing the boundaries of civility out that bit further every time. 'I don't see why I should respect your experience –'

'Chessie, please,' Lucy interrupted, with more tension in her voice than the two protagonists evidenced. 'This is my home, and we're trying to have a pleasant evening with your parents. If you're bored, you're welcome to turn on the television.'

But Constance opted for public confrontation. 'Why not, Chessie? Why shouldn't you respect my experience?'

'Well,' again a sly glance towards Lucy, and then eyes back to the sky, 'let's face it, Mum, what have you achieved in your life to date, actually? What have you actually ever *done*?'

'I've cooked.' Constance was visibly ruffled. 'Professionally. Under some respected chefs. And I'm running a pretty decent kitchen almost single-handedly.'

'Cooking.' Her daughter sniffed. 'So what? Women have been doing that for dog's years. You're not even on the telly. Anyway, it's hardly what you'd call a meaningful career, is it?'

'Chessie, you have no idea how unusual your mother is,' Lucy

133

began, and finished lamely, 'and you shouldn't speak to her like that anyway.'

'I've raised a family.' Constance was leaning forward, her face inches from her daughter's.

Francesca drew back with a smile that was simultaneously smug and nervous. 'Ditto my previous comment.'

At that moment Mark and Julian reappeared with a tray of drinks and crisps. Julian looked startled as he heard his wife say fiercely, 'At least I'm a happy and fulfilled person, which is more than a lot of people can say. And I've never consciously done anyone any harm.'

Francesca rolled her eyes and threw her hair back. 'Or any good. But even if that were true, so what? So what, Mother? It's not like you were in the government, or had invented a cure for cancer, or anything. I mean, God, you're forty. If you were going to do anything important, you'd have done it by now. Surely.'

'How dare you speak to your mother —' Julian looked furious; Constance looked relaxed.

'I'm not forty. Yet,' she interrupted. 'And I don't really see any need to justify myself to you anyway.'

'So why are you trying so hard to do it? Look, Mum, don't get me wrong, I just feel sorry for you,' Francesca said sulkily, glancing quickly at her father. 'I mean, what are you going to have on your scorecard? Just cooking and having kids, and it's not like you were a single mum or anything amazing.'

'Francesca . . .' Julian's warning tone provoked a deepening scowl from his daughter. Francesca was sharpening her claws on her mother simply because she had no better place to do it: it was an instinctive exercise, just as a domestic cat keeps its claws free of cuticle, without the sense to realize it has evolved and been civilized well beyond its hunting years.

Constance took a sip of wine before saying, 'I'll be back late

134

tonight, and in the restaurant early in the morning. Your father's taking you back to school tomorrow night. I may not see you.' Shrug. Lucy would have slapped the girl. She would also have expected Constance to do the same. 'I made you each a cake to take back to school.'

'God, Mum, I'm not a baby any more. You're trying to make me get fat.'

'OK, I'll give them both to Luke, then. Are you intending to come home next weekend? The restaurant's closed.' Shrug. 'I'll take that as a no. In that case, Daddy and I may go away for the weekend, if we don't have to babysit you.'

'Suit yourself.'

'That is exactly what I intend to do.' As her daughter rose languidly from her chair and sauntered off towards the orchard, Constance cursed under her breath and muttered, 'Bloody ingrate.' Then she flicked her hair back behind her ears, and smiled her brightest smile. 'I'm sorry, you guys. That must have been excruciating to listen to. Call it a preparatory course in ritual parental humiliation by teenagers.'

'I've a bloody good mind to take her back home and send her straight to bed, horrid little child.'

Constance shook her head slightly at Julian's comment. 'Don't. It was nothing to do with you. We'd already started the row in the car coming over, and I'll handle it. Just remember she's still our baby, and she's upset.' She turned to Lucy. 'Dear Luce, I *am* sorry. I know how much you hate scenes like that.'

'Don't be silly. I'd just like to clout her one.'

'It's fine. She's even right, in some ways . . .'

When all the children rejoined them, Luke presented his mother with an apple from the orchard. She weighed it thoughtfully in her hand. 'I remember when I used to peel apples just to toss the skin over my shoulder and see the initial of the man

I would marry.' She winked at her husband. 'Luckily, it can almost always look like a J. Do you and your friends ever do that, Chess?'

'No, Mum,' Francesca replied, in an attempt at a sophisticated drawl. 'What we do is peel potatoes. They're much harder to do in one piece. Then you get to see the initial of the first person you're going to shag.' She moved away immediately: she was brave enough to say it, but not brave enough to face the repercussions.

'Francesca! You've gone too far this time!' Julian bellowed after her. 'Come back here and apologize this minute!'

Constance waved her hand. 'Oh, leave it, Julian, do, she's trying to be tough. She only says it to shock.'

'Not much doubt which side of the family she takes after, then, is there?' Mark observed, with a broad grin. '*That* apple didn't fall far from the tree . . .'

Constance downed the contents of her glass in one swallow. 'You're right, Mark. I wanted to talk about the flat, but I've got to dash. Don't wait up for me, darling, and enjoy the skating. Push her over for me, discreetly, if you get the chance.' She pecked her husband on the cheek.

Julian and the children left half an hour later. As she was leaving, Francesca turned to Lucy and said, 'You know what, Mrs Epstein?' She had always called her by her first name, never Mrs Epstein, so Lucy understood that she did this to underline the yawning generational chasm between them. 'I'm not going to get married, not ever.'

And instead of saying, 'You haven't a clue what you're talking about, you snotty little twerp', which was what she wanted to say, Lucy smiled at her, and said pleasantly, 'Oh, you're far too young to decide that, Chessie darling. Wait a year or two longer before you make up your mind.' Francesca gave Lucy a look generally reserved for incontinent animals, and Lucy prayed to God that Constance and her restaurant critic were having an affair of Anna

Karenina proportions, wild enough to justify Constance abandoning her miserable daughter and running away to Paris.

Mark opened a bottle of wine as Lucy flipped through the index of an Italian cookbook. Abigail, her internal clock shattered by the excitement of a night flight to the bright lights of London, had crashed out yet again.

'Have we still got those aubergines?' she asked hopefully.

'Dunno . . . They'd been hanging around a while. I might have chucked them.'

'Mum?' Charlie stood on one leg. 'What do you call a donkey with –'

'Scrap the aubergines. I haven't got any basil anyway.' Lucy, delighted to scale down her ambitions, flipped to the pasta section as Charlie tugged her sleeve. 'We've got plenty of bacon, haven't we?'

'None. We had bacon sarnies last night.'

'What do you call a donkey with three –'

Lucy tossed the cookbook on the table. 'I don't know why I'm thinking Italian at all if we haven't got any basil. I wish someone would write a cookbook called *What to Cook When You've Only Got Crap in the Fridge*.'

'Mum, you told us we weren't ever allowed to say crap.'

'So don't say it, Charlie. How about chicken stir-fry?'

'That's fine, whatever you feel like. Or we could get a takeaway.'

'Mark, we are on an economy drive, remember?'

'Dad, what do you call a donkey with three legs?'

'God, I hope our kids don't turn out like Chessie. Maybe it's just a girl thing. I can't imagine Charlie ever being so rude . . .' Lucy took some chicken breasts out of the fridge and began to slice them. 'Connie says you should always let meat come to room temperature before you slice it.'

Mark was leafing through the cookbook. 'Can't see that it makes any difference to the chicken once it's dead.'

'Dad, *Dad*, what do you call a donkey –'

Lucy's head was buried in the fridge. 'Things are looking up! We've got coriander, we've got peppers, and beansprouts . . .' When she emerged triumphantly she saw Charlie leaving the kitchen, shoulders slumped. Both parents followed him, calling, 'Charlie, sweetheart, what *do* you call a donkey with three legs? Charlie? Charles darling . . .' A door slammed upstairs.

'I'll go,' Lucy said firmly.

'No, you carry on with dinner, and I'll go up and see him.'

'No. You cook. I shouldn't have gone off like that last night – I'm a crap mother. *I'll* go up and see him.'

Charlie was on his computer shooting aliens. He did not look up when Lucy put her hand on his shoulder, but his spine stiffened.

'Sweetheart, I know you're cross with us –'

'I'm not cross with Dad. I'm cross with you.'

'I see. Would you tell me why?'

'Don't you know?' Charlie shrugged away from her hand.

'Is it because I took Abby to London last night?'

'You didn't even say goodbye.'

'I know. That was very wrong of me, and I'm sorry. I was in a bad mood, and I was being selfish and thoughtless. It didn't have anything to do with you. Charlie, look at me, darling.'

'Sometimes I think you don't love me at all.' Her little boy twisted round and looked straight at Lucy, into her stupefied stare. His eyes were red and puffy, bee-stung. 'Sometimes I think you don't even like me.'

Lucy's hands flew to her cheeks. *Oh, my God, what have I done? How could he think that? How could he?* Lucy knelt down by her son. 'Charlie, listen to me. There is nothing, *nothing* on earth more precious to me than you are, you must believe that. Being your mother is the most important thing in my life. I'm so sorry I went away last night, if it made you think I didn't care about you.' He shook his head and swung back to the computer. 'You know, even though adults are always telling you what to do, and how to behave, they don't always behave very well themselves. I didn't, anyway.'

'Dad stayed with us.'

'I know, darling, and that's why I knew you'd be safe.'

'So why didn't you think Abby would be safe?' Charlie said resentfully. 'You took her.'

'Charlie, Abby is still a baby. That doesn't mean I don't love you just as much as I love her, and Gracie . . . Would you stop that a minute and talk to me?'

'I don't want to talk about it any more.'

Lucy bit her lip and tried to smile. 'Darling, the suspense is killing me. I can't stand not knowing. What *do* you call a donkey with three legs?'

'Doesn't matter.'

'It does to me. Please. I won't be able to sleep tonight if you don't tell me.'

'It's stupid, anyway.'

'You call the donkey Stupid? Poor donkey.'

'*No*, Mum.' A ghost of a smile flitted across his pale face. 'I mean the joke's stupid.'

'I like stupid jokes best of all.'

'OK.' He groaned. 'You call him Wonky.'

Lucy smiled and hugged her son. 'That's *brilliant*. Wonky. D'you want to go down and tell Daddy?'

'Nope.'

'Mind if I do?' Lucy rose to her feet as Abigail began crying next door. 'Supper will be ready in ten minutes.'

'I hate stir-fry. It makes me sick.'

'But it's stir-fry with noodles.'

'Stir-fry with noodles is the kind I hate most of all.'

'Tell you what, come down with me now and choose something you'd really like.'

The Epsteins enjoyed a normal family supper. The parents tried to coax the children into eating a properly balanced meal and trying the unknown, and the children ate exactly what they wanted to eat and refused to touch the unfamiliar. After their nightly routine lecture about having fruit for pudding, Charlie, Grace and Mark had Cornettos, while Abigail smeared mashed banana around her face, less than half of it getting into her mouth. Lucy, who wanted a Cornetto, was hoist by her own petard into having two small handfuls of grapes and a third glass of wine. This, Mark suggested charitably, constituted the recommended five daily helpings of fruit.

Mark took the older children to bed while Lucy bathed Abigail and asked herself whether she was, indeed, a crap mother. Like most mothers, in her heart of hearts Lucy believed she was a pretty good one, not a great one, but a tiny bit better than average. It struck her that every mother probably thought she was a tiny bit better than average, and it stood to reason that a good half of them had to be at least a tiny bit worse than average. Many aspects of parenting did not thrill her. No sane woman could genuinely enjoy the excretion side of the business – the drool, snotty noses, bloody knees, baby sick trickling into her ear and down the back of her neck in bed at night, the steam rising from an 'accident' in bed. These could not be termed enjoyable, but they were easily survivable, and they passed. Nobody liked the permanent state of exhaustion that resulted from regularly disturbed nights. Nor the belligerent side of the business, the 'No, I won't wear that/eat that/do that' scenario that Grace had embarked on far earlier than

Lucy remembered Charlie doing. This went hand in hand with the 'I want' stage, ricocheting like a shuttlecock between possession and rejection from 'I want to sleep in your bed' to 'I want you to go away'. Finally there was the point Lucy had reached with Charlie, the long-haul stage where the only thing more worrying than a child's confidences was the child's withdrawal of them. Half the things Charlie said now had a subtext: I don't want to tell you what's wrong (but, believe me, something's very, very wrong); You don't understand me (only Daddy/my best mate/Granny does); and, worst of all, I am Unhappy (and yes, it *is* your fault.)

By eight, Charlie had passed through the years when his parents had to be fearful of his swallowing sleeping pills, falling out of the window or drowning in a shallow paddling-pool, but the demands he made of them as parents were more onerous than the ever-watchfulness necessitated by his younger siblings. Lucy increasingly found herself asking Mark, sometimes wordlessly, 'Do you think he's all right?' to which Mark would reply, 'He's just fine, let him be.' Letting him be was the most difficult thing of all. Letting him be assumed that the safety-net she had woven for him over the preceding years was secure: too much was at stake if it wasn't. '*Look:*' Mark would say patiently on those afternoons when Charlie came home from school sullen and silent and refusing to talk, 'Worrying about it now won't do any good. It's semi-deliberate – he wants you to worry; he wants to be certain that you care, and know that he can upset you. You're putty in his hands; I wish you would be in mine,' Mark would say with a grin, stroking her hair. This was no comfort to Lucy, however well intended. She wanted to be a plugged-in parent, with fully joined-up thinking on all aspects of her family's well-being. She wanted the umbilical cord to stay in place for ever and ever, yet she also wanted some complete existence without her children. She worried about them most of the time. Feminine idealism is a strange fish; women are inclined to set the fence so high for themselves, that it is almost impossible for them not to fall short. They appoint icons of feminine perfection from the public arena – celebrities, princesses, actresses – then have mixed feelings of disillusionment and relief when their icons crash and are exposed as ordinary mortals. The burden of creating the perfect home environment is generally self-imposed, as it was in Lucy's case; this did not stop her from berating herself for failure one minute, and privately blaming her husband for giving her the responsibility the next.

'Charlie's fine,' Mark said when he rejoined her in the kitchen. 'He even read Gracie her favourite bedtime story.'

'Which?' Lucy asked, with a smile. '*Winnie and the Poo*?'

'*The Wind and the Widows*. D'you want a whisky?' He poured Scotch into her empty wine-glass without waiting for her reply, and they sat opposite each other across the scrubbed-pine kitchen table. 'Charlie was pretty upset you weren't around last night.'

'I know. He made that very clear,' Lucy replied quietly. 'Were you?'

'I wasn't upset that you flew off the handle. Charlie was upset. I admit I was a little annoyed at first, mainly because I couldn't understand what made you lose your rag.' Mark fingered the stem of his glass. Lucy felt the blood rushing to her cheeks, and kept her eyes on his hand while she waited for him to continue. 'Charlie's anxious about lots of things. Maybe we should both spend more time at home.'

'Are you saying I should spend more time at home? Are you pissed off that I'm using the flat, and enjoying it? It was your idea, remember.'

'I'm glad you have something else to do, to keep you occupied –'

'Oh? You think I need a hobby? Maybe I should take up macramé?' Sarcasm, Lucy's preferred defensive weapon, did not alleviate her rising guilt.

'Lucy, please. I'm delighted you enjoy the flat, and I don't belittle your interests. After all, my painting is nothing more than a hobby, I know that . . .' He looked at her with soft, Labrador eyes. 'I just don't think you should use the flat to run away to, or to beat me over the head because you have some idiotic paranoia about Samantha. I can understand why you were pissed off, but Charlie and Grace can't be expected to.'

'Do you?' Lucy whispered. 'Do you really understand why I was pissed off?"

Mark sighed. 'Not really. I wish you'd explain it. Frankly, last night I just felt bloody relieved I didn't have to sit down and have a row with you. I was glad you went. Then this morning I missed you and wanted you to come home. I don't understand what I've done to annoy you. What's going on?'

'I don't know.' The pain had started behind her eyes as she drove home from London with her tail tucked between her legs. It had shot back and forth between her eyeballs and the back of her head like a ping-pong ball, before working its way through her jaw and up through her teeth, setting each one so on edge she felt like pulling them out. She wished she could hit the reverse button and erase the whole of the past twenty-four hours. There wasn't really anything the matter; he hadn't done anything that she could feel worked up about; she was not jealous of Samantha. She looked at Mark, his face tired and drawn, his brows ever so slightly furrowed, and knew that she had to make a decision – to tell him everything, a little bit, or nothing at all, and if she settled, as she knew she would, on the little bit, she had to decide whether the little bit should be close enough to the truth to worry him, or far enough away to make him happy. How could she tell Mark that what was wrong was that when she had looked in the bathroom mirror of the flat that morning – and the night before, while Steven Armitage had been sitting in their living room waiting for her – she

143

had not recognized the woman who had looked back at her? She had known who it was in the mirror, but she thought it was somebody very different from herself. How could she tell her husband that? Lucy took Mark's hand across the table. 'I've been feeling really low, but I don't know why. Just pissed off and useless. Old. Invisible. Irrelevant. I honestly don't know what's got into me. I don't know if I'm bored and ought to go back to work, or if that's just another way of running away. I feel like nothing's ever going to happen in my life again – nothing new or exciting, no wild adventures. I know you think I'm spoiled, that I've just got too much for my own good. I'm sorry. I keep reminding myself I have everything I ever wanted – more, even. I love you, and I adore the children –'

'I know you do. So do they.'

'But sometimes I think, so what? I don't know who I am, Mark. I feel more and more dislikeable every day. I can't expect anyone to like me.'

'Oh, stop feeling sorry for yourself, Luce! You've got too much free time on your hands if you can bother about whether or not you're dislikeable.' At her bleak expression he felt remorse, and added, 'Besides, everyone does like you. They can't help it.'

Lucy smiled wanly. 'Sometimes I don't know if you like me, let alone love me.' Only after she had made the statement did Lucy realize she was echoing Charlie.

Mark smiled then, his eyes creasing up in the way she loved, and he squeezed her fingers and brought them to his lips. 'I'll always love you, Lucy. You mean everything to me. You do know that, don't you?'

She thought he did, she at least believed he thought that he did; but whether that was enough was a different matter.

Chapter Ten

Cabbage has developed a lingering reputation as a common-place,
even coarse food, but it is worthy of the most refined preparations.
At the restaurant we serve it with foie gras and caviar.

Alice Waters

Julian Purcell greatly admired his wife. Before he married her
he had presented his sceptical mother, who was quite
convinced that Constance would ruin him, with a string of
reasons why she would make him the perfect wife. Julian's
superficial reasons for selecting her were precisely the same as his
mother's for fearing her. The young Constance was beautiful,
talented and had ten times Julian's ambition. She had a near-
ruthless efficiency that complemented his mathematical leanings;
each and every line of her was clean – Palladian, he had told his
mother as she questioned him. Constance positively crackled
with energy, and Julian, who knew he was inclined to be
indolent, drew strength off her as easily as he warmed himself
before a fire. He did not inform his mother of the one supreme
asset that his intended possessed, the one characteristic that
made him certain she was the one and only woman for him:
unlike every other woman of his acquaintance, his mother

included, Constance knew men and did not expect too much from them. This pragmatism allowed Julian the confidence that he would always be able to give her more than she expected, rather than disappoint her with his shortcomings. He saw this at once, although he would no more have admitted it to Constance – let alone his mother – than he would have stripped off and streaked along the Mall.

Fond of likening people to buildings, if not always in a flattering manner, Julian privately aligned his wife with the great cathedral of Léon, a masterpiece of engineering, seemingly constructed almost entirely of glass yet strong as hewn granite. Elegant, precise, multi-faceted and soaring. As he lay in bed surreptitiously watching her moving about their bedroom, he thought that the years, far from softening her edges, had sharpened them: she was stronger and cleaner now than ever before. And like a building that has become a home, the longer he observed her the more he found to cherish. Julian had floated slowly and safely into the harbour of middle age. He knew he had docked, because he increasingly found himself calmly acknowledging that there were things in life, great journeys and adventures, triumphs and experiences that he was never going to have. The certainty that he would never leap on to a train, destination unknown, or gallop beside the Indian Ocean on an Arab stallion caused him not the slightest regret. Women are said to spend half their youth thinking about the simply wonderful things that are going to happen to them: the glorious dresses they will wear, the fairy-tale palaces they will furnish, the handsome princes they will kiss . . . It is not surprising that after all those years of fantasizing they spend the second half of their lives morbidly dwelling on what has *not* happened to them – and isn't going to happen. The same should surely be true for men, that for some forty-odd years their heads are consecutively occupied by visions of match-winning goals, slavishly devoted super-models and expanding business empires, only to find in their forties that all these have slipped quietly out of their reach. Yet at forty-nine, Julian Purcell experienced no such discontent.

Constance was sitting in her robe at the dressing-table. He could see her reflection in the mirror, but she was neither looking at him nor aware of being watched. She was fingering her hair, fussing over some errant strands that would not for once behave as ordered; then fiddling with her earrings, licking her lips before biting them sharply, examining herself in the mirror, turning her chin two inches first one way and then the next. Julian observed her critical examination with pleasure; her complete detachment from him and the world; her complete self-absorption. This was his favourite time of the day; Constance's precise morning routine reassured him that nothing would go amiss. She suddenly caught his eyes in the mirror and stared at him, leaning close to the glass. It was a moment of intense communication between the two, the reaffirmation of their partnership.

'Julian?' She spoke softly, and he closed his eyes. 'Are you really awake?'

'Almost.'

She moved to the bed and sat down next to him. 'How do you feel about halloumi?'

'It's all Greek to me.'

'Stop it.'

'All right.' He smiled slightly. 'In what context?'

'A warm salad. Griddled halloumi, a little chorizo, a few chopped olives . . . Maybe dried chilli flakes.'

'On?'

Constance pouted. 'Frisée? Rocket, if I scrap the chilli . . .'

'It could work. Try it out.'

'I can't get the autumn menu right. It's too flat. It's too . . . I don't know what. Too God-awful uninspired.'

'The halloumi sounds good to me.'

'Have I the guts to go for broke with the menu? I'm thinking of everything dripping with oil, positively *slick* with it. Maybe cassoulet. Goose fat popping on the surface . . .'

Her eyes flashed as she spoke, but she was no longer addressing him; she had moved away in body and spirit, and was now subjecting her wardrobe to intense scrutiny. He put his head back on the pillow: Julian found his wife's restlessness faintly tiring. He never rose from bed himself until she left the room, conscious that his meandering would annoy her. As he bathed, Julian considered alternative methods of underpinning the front portico of a house he had recently taken on without coming to any conclusion about it, then pondered a good ten minutes over which trousers to wear. Thirty minutes later he made it downstairs just in time to kiss Constance goodbye before prising the Sunday papers off Luke.

'Dad? Mum said just now she was thinking of having plastic surgery.'

'Did she indeed? Where's your sister?'

'Still in bed. She's been avoiding Mum since last night – you know, the stuff she said at the Epsteins'.'

'Then she isn't a complete idiot.'

'She can't help narking Mum. Everyone at school goes on about how amazing our mum is, what a looker, and it just pisses Chess off. You don't think she'd really go and do it, do you?'

'Do what?'

'Have a face-lift.'

'No. She was probably pulling your leg.'

'There are some mothers at school who've been done: they look disgusting. All mad, staring eyes and stupid, fixed grins, you know. Why do women do it?'

'God alone knows why women do half the things they do. That's something you'll just have to accept, Luke.'

'I think Mum looks great. Given that she's getting on and all.'

'You should have told her that.'

'I did.' Luke grinned broadly. 'That's when she started talking about having a face-lift.'

'In that case she was probably saying it to provoke you.'

'She did that all right.' Julian looked at his son over the newspaper. ''Cos then I said, "It's not worth it, Granny, put your hair-net back on."'

Julian laughed. 'What a pity Chessie missed that. She would have loved it.'

Luke poured himself a third bowl of cornflakes. 'If Chess had been in the room,' he confided, 'I wouldn't have said it.'

Julian looked appreciatively at his son: Luke was shaping up into something to be proud of. 'Was Mum in a good mood when she left?'

'Pretty good, yes, except she kept rattling on about halloumi and soufflés and truffle custard. What *is* truffle custard? A chocolate pud?'

'That is for your mother to know, and mere mortals like you and me to marvel at.' Julian reached out for Constance's homemade apricot jam. It was ambrosial, syrupy with honeyed fruit, scented with elderflower, and blessed with nutty fragments of apricot kernels. Julian wanted to spoon it straight out of the jar and into his mouth, but he did not allow himself the indulgence. He took a perverse pleasure in self-denial.

Constance pulled her car up to the back of the restaurant and slammed on the brakes. Six boxes of vegetables were sitting on the doorstep, as she had known they would be; had they not been there, she would have reversed the car, driven seven miles further down the road to her organic supplier and ripped out his guts with her bare hands. He had never yet let her down and, in consideration of this, Constance paid him well over the market rate. If she had been asked to name the greatest of all human virtues, she would have been torn between reliability and consistency. These mattered more to her than honour, integrity or courage; they embodied honour, integrity and courage. She had approximately half an hour on her own in the restaurant before the reliability of her staff would be tested; she did not quite trust any of her three regular helpers the way she trusted her suppliers.

Constance loved being alone in her restaurant, and particularly appreciated the peace and calm order of the place on Sunday mornings. It had taken the place of church for her – or filled the place where church had never been. It had not passed her notice that even the word service they used so constantly – lunch service, dinner service – had a religious parallel. Food was both her religion and her philosophy. It embraced concepts of heaven and hell, morality and perfection. She had been fascinated by the chemistry of food since childhood, wanting to discover precisely why juices should run clear when the chicken was properly cooked, and exactly what happened to the blood. This metamorphosis was far more intriguing, far more magical, to the young Constance than lectures on the sex life of the newt, or lighting strips of magnesium ribbon had been. She read cookbooks as literature, and contrasted theories on browning meat – did it seal in the juices, or did heat begin the taste fusion? Always she tested things for herself. Twenty years on, she still took enormous pleasure in the mystical union of air and egg white, how the simple addition of air could convert white albumen from a weird, underground snot-like slime to an ethereal, foaming pillow of meringue. Only one rule was set in stone: the simpler the basic ingredient, the more magical its properties, and the more she respected it and observed its natural laws. Salt could not dissolve in oil, and she would no more add salt after oil to a dressing than she would toss a lighted match into her petrol tank. Gelatine entranced her: she could contemplate cubes of glossy, trembling, amber jellied beef consommé as others might admire Michelangelo's *Pietà*. The humble egg was the holiest of all shape-shifters – from the orange yolk spilling out of a lightly boiled one, through mayonnaise and other emulsions all the way to soufflé – but sugar also possessed enviable properties. Eggs, sugar, oils: these three were the incarnations of Connie's trinity.

On the drive over she had run through her menu several times. Once she had laid out the ingredients she had little to worry about, and used her solitude to think through the issues of the week that she had not allowed herself to dwell on. That morning, as she unpacked the boxes, giving each vegetable a cursory examination before setting it on the prep table, she was thinking about Francesca. Constance worried about her daughter in a way that she never worried about Luke. She did not worry about him because she knew that he had a good head and a kind heart, and a man did not need much more than that to succeed well enough. She knew that Francesca had an equally good head and kind heart, however much she tried to prove the opposite, but she worried that her daughter was too easily influenced. Francesca had hit a point in her life where every sinew of her body struggled towards the attainment of style; nothing else mattered beyond being deemed cool, and although Constance identified only too closely with her, and had herself gone through a particularly nasty stage at the same age, she wished to spare her daughter the wasted time and effort. She unfolded the chamois bag that held her knives and sharpened them one by one, first on a rectangular stone before defining the edges on a steel. By the time she reached the paring knife she had decided to take Francesca to Paris and let her run riot just for the hell of it, because there were times when a young woman needed to run riot. She then turned her thoughts to her husband. She was recalling with amusement Julian's phlegmatic reception of the news that she was contemplating an affair, when Lewis arrived.

Lewis called himself her *chef de partie*, which, given the Falcon's regular front and back staff of four, was something of an embroidery. Constance overlooked his delusions of grandeur because he was a hard worker and a quick learner, if not one hundred per cent reliable. After catering college Lewis had worked in two pub restaurants before joining Constance at the Lonely Falcon, and although he grumbled about his hours he did not grumble loudly, and although he talked of leaving for London, he was highly unlikely to leave his girlfriend, who was firmly rooted in the rich Dorset soil, so he put up with Constance's irascibility as she put up with his sloppy timekeeping.

That morning, Lewis wore a self-satisfied grin as he chirruped, 'Morning, Chef.'

'Lewis, if I've told you once I've told you a thousand times. Call me Constance.'

'Right you are, Chef.'

'What are you looking so smug about?'

From behind his back Lewis revealed a platter covered with a tea-cloth; he removed it with a flourish to reveal ten little scraps of what resembled green twine skewered on toothpicks. 'This.' He bowed over his creation. Constance approached warily, picked one up, examined it, and popped it in her mouth. Lewis waited. 'Well? They should be piping hot . . .'

Constance sampled another. 'Lewis, I hate to admit it, but somewhere in that useless lump you call your body you have a streak of genius.' She took his cheeks firmly between her hands and kissed him on the mouth.

Lewis blushed. 'I was thinking about what you said last night about needing sharper flavours in autumn. I was experimenting with your Parmesan fritters –'

'Experimenting with *my* Parmesan fritters?' Constance echoed threateningly.

'Just trying out some ideas, adding smoked paprika, shredded anchovy, a little sage. None of them worked.'

'Of course they didn't, you berk. How many times have I told you not to mess with things when they're right? Parmesan fritters – come on, it's nearly ten thirty, get cracking – don't need embellishment.'

'You're right. But I had all those sage leaves, and slivers of anchovy, so I rolled it up, stuck a toothpick through it and dropped it in the hot fat. Hey presto!'

'I wish we had a separate bar. A plate of these, served with a gin and tonic or two . . .' She sighed wistfully. 'It would be like Lennon and McCartney.'

'Like springtime and Paris.'

'Like tomato and basil.'

'Like Romeo and Juliet.'

'Don't get carried away, Lewis, it's only a canapé.' He looked crestfallen, and she punched him on the shoulder. 'A bloody *good* canapé. A slap in the face to a set of tastebuds, and that's what you want – something that sings.'

'I was so excited I got up early to make you some more.'

'That, Lewis, is the joy of cooking, that moment of creation. That's when you get to be God. And after you've been God, you get to worship your own work. It's the only thing I know where every single part of the process is sublime.' She winked at him slowly. 'It's better than sex.' The thought that flashed across Lewis's mind – that he would willingly trade a couple of future inspired creations to go to bed with Constance – was too outrageous and altogether too terrifying to contemplate further. 'Get on with the veg. We've got twenty-seven covers booked.'

When the phone rang on the kitchen extension, Constance snatched it, uncertain whether she wanted it to be someone cancelling a booking or making a new one.

'Constance? I just wanted a brief word . . .'

'Uh-huh.' Connie cradled the phone against her shoulder, glaring at Lewis and using her free hand to point to the vegetables while she waited for Julian to get to the point. She lost patience quickly. 'Yep. Look, we're running behind here.'

'I simply wanted to say that if you have ever seriously considered, for even the most fleeting moment, letting anyone loose with a knife around your face, I'd be obliged if you would dismiss the idea.'

'What *are* you waffling about, Julian?'

'Luke said you'd mentioned something about a face-lift.'

Constance smiled. 'I thought it might be a nice present for my fortieth. Any objections?'

'Many, not least that it would be an act of malicious violence against a face that I happen to spend a considerable amount of time looking at. Besides, roses are far more beautiful in their second bloom.'

Her smile broadened although her husband could not see it. 'I'll bear that in mind, OK? Gotta run.' As she stripped the husks off roasted ears of corn, the grin stayed on her face: her family were far more concerned about her turning forty than she herself was. She had known that tossing out the idea of plastic surgery to Luke would get it straight back to Julian, and she was touched by his need to make sure she wasn't serious. Forty was nothing but a number, and thirty-five had been a much more telling figure in her own mind. She remembered how she had felt then, her anger when she realized that thirty-five, which logically should have placed her approximately in early June of her personal calendar, had actually tipped her into September, with all the associated melancholy brought by the end of summer, and only the prayer of an Indian summer ahead. That was when she had genuinely considered a face-lift, and rejected it. It was grossly unfair that the female high season ran from the teens to the mid-thirties, after which women faced a precipitous slide into a long, protracted autumn. Unfair that the more medical progress extended life expectancy, the shorter the period society allowed women to be attractive. Unfair, Constance snorted, that people acknowledged the sexuality of one forty-five-year-old actress or another with surprise, as if a forty-five-year-old woman, or a fifty-five-year-old couldn't – didn't – enjoy good sex. Grossly unfair, Constance, at thirty-nine, felt again, but it was a fact. Face-lifts were nothing but a belated attempt to tidy up a neglected garden in preparation for winter. Under Lewis's openly admiring gaze, she sliced the kernels of corn off the husks with surgical precision, chopped up the cobs and threw them into a pot with the chillies and stock. Lunch service would soon start, and there was no time to waste on wrinkles.

When Constance had opened the Lonely Falcon she had looked forward to the intimacy of cooking for friends and neighbours rather than the anonymity of a London clientele. She could now count on knowing fifty per cent of her clients by name at any sitting, and initially this had seemed attractive. It had soon palled. Diners who knew the chef by name, who had the chef to their own dinner parties, felt entitled to be more demanding than the nameless clientele to which she had been accustomed in London. She could guarantee that at least one guest, every sitting, would peruse the menu and ask for something completely different, saying to the waitress, 'Sorry to be such a nuisance, just tell Constance it's me, I'm sure she'll rustle up something.' And in the kitchen Constance would curse and spit like a drunken sailor before smoothing her white jacket and stepping out front to beam and soothe and propose a simply grilled steak with a mushroom garnish and, yes, perhaps just a soupçon of the béarnaise, if she had it going. Most of the time, she knew, her regulars only made these special requests in order to demonstrate the 'special relationship' they had with her. It did not occur to them that rejecting her menu was offensive. No one, except for Julian, seemed able to understand that cooking was not a pleasant pastime, nor was it an occupation. It was not a means to an end, as she did not particularly enjoy the process of eating, and preferred food in its raw state to its finished one. Cooking was Constance's life. The pretence that it was a casual hobby was profoundly exhausting. As Constance's scanty reserves of good manners and tolerance were rapidly used up on her clients, it was not surprising that her staff and family found them empty.

Lucy called after the lunch service to check if Constance objected to having some shelves put up in the bathroom and after five minutes' debate over precisely what sort of shelves Lucy intended to install precisely where, Constance agreed.

'Great. I'll do it next week. Good lunch?'

'Apart from David Moore asking me "to rustle up" a slice of apple pie at half past two, it was fine. Honestly, I don't know why they bother to come to a restaurant.'

Lucy was unsympathetic. 'They're paying you for services rendered. They should be able to eat what they want, pay what you charge, and come back the following week. Simple. I don't see how you can ask more than that, Con.'

'If that's their attitude they shouldn't bother. They can buy perfectly good food themselves and ruin it in their own homes.'

'That's like a prostitute telling her clients to stay home and screw their own wives. You're missing the point. People don't go to a restaurant to eat.'

No, Constance had thought. That *is* the point. Cooking is top-drawer prostitution, when it's done professionally; it has nothing in common with knocking up a meal at home. You give a complete stranger the very best part of yourself in exchange for nothing but money, and the urge to go on doing it, regardless of the frustration, was not for financial gain but for recognition, and recognition was thin on the ground. She had considerable sympathy for the notorious chefs who evicted unsophisticated or unappreciative clients from their restaurants; she had sympathy, but she did not have the kamikaze streak required to imitate them, with the result that she took most of the roast corn and chilli sauce home that afternoon.

The nature of friendship between women is quite a different thing from friendship between men. However close the bonds between women, few are capable of keeping their relationship entirely free of competition. This did not mean that Constance did not love Lucy, or that Lucy did not love Constance. There were many ways in which the two women not only loved each other, but genuinely admired each other, but these were in the zones where they had subconsciously established non-compete clauses. Lucy felt able to praise Constance's cooking unstintingly, and did, but then she had no desire to be regarded as a good cook herself. Constance appreciated Lucy's easy warmth, but she did not crave it herself. On the deepest level, they loved each other for having something that each feared they lacked entirely. Constance Purcell went about her life without ever being certain that she was real. For all her well-developed and readily exposed ego, her perfect house, from her meticulously maintained wardrobe to her colour-coordinated linen chest, she sometimes found herself wondering if she were really there, fully, roundedly, *there*, rather than being a two-dimensional character in somebody else's story. There were times when she was actively frightened of being left alone in a room, feeling that when the others walked out, especially Julian, she might vanish altogether into thin air. In contrast, nobody was ever quite as real to Lucy, for all her empathy, as she was to herself, and she had the sense to know that this was a truly terrible thing. She did her best to conceal it, frightened that others would reel away in horror from her if they saw it, much as they might if she appeared with a pustulating boil covering her cheek.

That afternoon Mark Epstein was also preoccupied by the ignorance and ingratitude of clients.

'It takes time to build up market share, you know that.' Lucy was half listening to her husband and half watching the video of *Oliver!* that Grace seemed to play on a continuous loop. 'I thought you were thrilled with all the free publicity you've been getting.'

'I am. I'm just worried about getting the right balance between private clients and corporate ones. I need more restaurants and retailers and fewer well-meaning gents picking up the odd case of burgundy. That's the problem with setting up outside London.'

'Adnams never found it that hard, according to Samantha.'

'Thanks, Luce, that's really reassuring.'

Catching the resentment in his voice, Lucy looked at him in surprise. 'I'm sorry, but you are being irrational. Two weeks ago you were cock-a-hoop, and now it's all doom and disaster. What's changed?'

'Crappy results from the mail-shot we did. Lots of thanks but no thanks.'

Lucy turned back to Fagin's den. 'Oh, well. You'll have to give it more time . . .'

'Yes, I know,' Mark retorted crisply. 'Thanks for your insight.'

Lucy licked her lips. It was unlike Mark to be edgy, and very unlike him to start talking about the business on a rainy Sunday afternoon in front of a video with the children in the room. Lucy moved further away along the sofa and placed a cushion between herself and her husband. An uneasy silence settled in the sitting room while Nancy and the Artful Dodger danced.

'I have to be in London for a meeting next Wednesday afternoon.' Lucy nodded in reply to Mark, watching the screen. 'You said it would be good if we could go to the flat together.'

'Mummy, where's the bad man? Is that the bad man?' Grace stood in front of the television pointing to Fagin, provoking shouts of 'Get out of the way!' from Charlie.

'No, darling, he's not really bad.' Lucy bent down to take the dog's rubber bone out of Abigail's mouth.

'Have you arranged with Amy whether you're going on Wednesday or Thursday?'

'He is too bad, Mum. He steals.'

'Yes, I know, Charlie, but when Grace talks about the bad man she means Bill Sykes.'

'Are you deliberately ignoring me, Lucy?'

'No, Mark, I'm not,' Lucy denied crossly. 'I'm trying to deal with Grace and Charlie, and look after the baby, if you hadn't noticed. I haven't even thought when to go to London. I have to get the shelves sorted out . . .'

'If you make it Wednesday, we could go together in the morning.'

'That sounds fine,' Lucy said coolly.

Mark rose heavily. 'I'm going to the garage.' He loomed above her. 'If that's all right by you.'

Lucy shrugged in reply, not taking her eyes off the television. By the time she heard the back door slam her eyes had welled up with tears of frustration, but whether she regretted being uncooperative with Mark, or whether she resented his being cool to her she could not decide. There was always a bloodiness about wet Sunday afternoons, a fitting time for trouble to start in paradise, and the thought of Constance working passionately away in her meticulous kitchen, earning her living and fulfilling her dreams, made Lucy feel worse.

'Darlings, shall we all put our boots on and go out and splash in the rain?' she suggested in a bright yet brittle voice, the sort of voice Lucy imagined Constance would use in a minor domestic crisis.

'Mu-*um*! We're watching *Oliver!*.' Charlie was the only one who still was.

'OK. I'm going to make some tea.'

Lucy walked through the relentless drizzle down the path to the garage with a cup of tea in a gesture of truce. Through the little window she could see Mark standing at the easel, his back presenting an insurmountable barrier. She stood silently for a moment in the rain. Lucy loved the back of his head; she loved the way his hair sprang into curls that always made her want to scrunch it up in her fingers. She was suddenly not certain that she would recognize him if he turned around to face her. She tapped on the window and he swung round, shielding his painting as if he had been caught in a crime. She put the tea down on the window-ledge and left.

Lucy did not admit that it was the gnawing sense of dissatisfaction with her own marriage that made her speculate so frequently about Constance's, and that it made her feel closer to Constance than she would have been able to feel had she believed Constance's marriage was unblemished. As she dragged the children out in the rain that darkening Sunday, pushing the pram roughly up the gentle incline from the house, she pushed her irritation with Mark out equally forcefully, and decided that she did not blame Connie for having an affair with Steven Armitage. Abigail beamed and cooed at her from the sheepskin-lined pram, and Grace's short legs pumped along trying to keep pace beside her. Charlie dawdled along the hedgerows, stopping to pick up small conkers, to examine a leaf or to coax a cow to the railing. Lucy swung round and as the words 'Hurry *up*, Charlie!' formed on her lips and she saw his pale, rain-washed face and innocent expression, she decided with a sudden, swooping certainty to dedicate her life to making her children all that they could be, and as happy, along with that, as they had every right to be.

Lucy believed, when she married and for a not inconsiderable time after, that marital happiness depended on doing things, generally together, but 'doing things' was the important part. Despite her niggling worry that she 'did' nothing, Lucy was a very busy woman: she oversaw a highly complex spider's web of relationships as intricate and interdependent as a six-team country dance in a rural meadow. She was just about able to take her eyes off one group for a moment or two, but if she entirely neglected any part of the field, the whole thing might collapse around her into chaos. Older practitioners of the subtle art of marriage, more seasoned hands, had learned the lesson that the doing is not nearly so important to the health of the marriage as the ability to undo what has been wrongly done, a rule that is equally applied by the most skilful of dancers, actors, chefs and seamstresses. Lucy Epstein was full of conviction and good intentions, but she was not yet very skilful.

Chapter Eleven

I don't know anyone who doesn't fancy a fishcake when the time is right.

Simon Hopkinson

From Waterloo station, Mark headed for his meeting and Lucy made her way by tube to Charlotte Street. She went straight into the deli and was disappointed to find that Enrico was not working, but bought gnocchi and a tub of roast red pepper and tomato sauce from his assistant. As she headed through the side door to her flat Stefano called out: 'Signora! I forget – Enrico left this for you.' He handed her an envelope and a bottle of wine, and shrugged when she asked what she had done to deserve the gift.

Lucy opened the envelope as she went up to the flat.

Dear Constance's flatmate, [read the compliments slip],
    Call me at the number above if you can make lunch either Tuesday, Wednesday or Thursday of this week. Call me if you can do it Tuesday, Thursday or Friday of next week. Call me if you want to do it next month. Call me if you don't ever want to have lunch with me.

Call me if you don't like the wine I sent. So long as you
call me.   Regards, Steven (Armitage)

Lucy propped the card on the mantelpiece, put Vivaldi on the CD
player, went into the bathroom and turned on the taps. She was
surprised and pleased that he had contacted her; it was impossible
not to feel flattered by his attention. Maybe she'd go, just for a lark
and a good free meal. She wondered if she should check with
Constance, but Constance had let her know she did not welcome
inquiries about her private life, and if Steven raised the subject it
would be pretty obvious what he was getting at. Curiosity and the
spirit of adventure persuaded her to accept: maybe she'd do it next
week. As the steam rose in the bathroom and fogged the mirror so
that she could barely see her own reflection, Lucy realized that the
note would read very oddly to Mark, particularly as she had
omitted to mention the encounter at all. Uncertain quite why she
had concealed the meeting from Mark, she hurriedly retrieved the
card and put it in her handbag.

After her bath she called the number on the card and was put
through to the paper's voicemail system. 'This is . . .' a clipped
female voice intoned '. . . Steven Armitage' his voice drawled, in a
lazy way, as if he couldn't be bothered to speak at all, but had
managed to trawl his memory bank and retrieve some vague trace
of social civility from deep within. 'I am afraid that . . .' the female
operator apologized '. . . Steven Armitage,' he interjected brightly,
'is unable to take your call,' she explained. 'However, if you would
like to leave a message for . . .' '. . . Steven Armitage,' he growled
threateningly, 'please speak after the tone, and . . .' she paused,
with the faintest intake of breath '. . . Steven bloody Armitage!' he
bellowed '. . . will return your call,' she promised, with empty
conviction.

'Hello. Um, this is Lucy Epstein. Thanks for your note, but you didn't need to leave any wine. Thanks anyway. Uh . . . OK. That's all . . .' Lucy hung up. The whole thing was ridiculous. If he had genuinely wanted to have lunch with her he would have asked Constance for her home number. He'd probably had a bloody good laugh with Constance about her kicking him out of the flat that night. Lucy stood indecisively, wishing she'd never called him in the first place, and imagining how he'd laugh when he heard the message she left. For Christ's sake, she told herself with disgust, I'm a professional woman, not a gauche teenager! She hit redial on the phone, listened patiently to the double act and then spoke again. 'I'm sorry about my last message; I was interrupted. It's Lucy again, the flatmate. I'm in London now, it's Wednesday afternoon, and I *could* do lunch tomorrow, if you really want to. It's probably too short notice, so don't worry about it . . .' She winced at her apologetic tone. 'I haven't fixed my schedule for next week. If you like you can reach me on . . .' About to give the number of the flat, she paused and left her mobile number. 'OK. That's all.'

If he called, and lunch was on, then he'd doubtless want to talk to her about Constance, and he'd probably ask a lot of questions about Julian, and Lucy didn't know how she'd respond to that. She did not want to be a go-between. But if he called, and lunch was on, it might as well be because he liked her, and it would be fun to go out with a restaurant critic, and a friend of Constance's, and it couldn't do any harm if he didn't talk about Constance, which he hadn't the first time they'd met, and if he did talk about her, Lucy could make it perfectly clear that she wasn't going to be party to anything that made her feel a sordid accomplice. But he wouldn't call.

He called about twenty minutes later, but Lucy was blow-drying her hair in the bedroom and didn't hear her mobile's faint trill. She went out to look at shelving and arrived home just before Mark in the late afternoon.

'Hello, darling.' Lucy kissed him and handed him a cup of tea. 'How did it go?'

'It was OK.' Mark pulled off his tie and rubbed the back of his neck. 'They were pretty impressive. I just don't buy the joint-venture idea. It seems to me you either run your own ship, with all the risks, or you're an employee with none of them. And none of the benefits.' Mark had told her on the train that morning about the approach from a private Scottish wine dealer with a good reputation in New World wines, who was looking for a regional partnership and felt the classical French wines in which Epstein & Rose specialized would be right up his street. 'I had the distinct impression they were not thinking of equal partnership, but I'm not feeling confident enough to blow them off entirely.'

'It might not be a bad idea. It would take some financial pressure off, if you could share overheads a bit more and still expand the catalogue.'

'I just feel we should only do it when our backs are right up against the wall. I don't want to surrender half my business – or more – and then find we're turning the corner. I've struggled too long for that. There's a lot we can give up before independence.'

'Well,' Lucy said doubtfully, 'if you're sure. Maybe you should wait until you see the numbers.' She wanted to support him, but there were times when she wished he still had the security of a salary from a major dealer. No one ever made their fortune from wine-broking, and although Lucy didn't crave wealth, she didn't like the sound of the 'lot' they could give up to preserve the independence of the business.

'I'll talk it through with Samantha,' Mark said casually, and Lucy bit her tongue. She was not, absolutely *not* going to let herself get provoked. 'Everything OK at home?'

'I'll just check my messages. Amy always calls on the mobile and I forgot to take it when I was shopping.' Lucy tapped in to her service to learn that she had two new messages.

'Hi, Lucy, this is Amy,' the nanny said breathlessly, 'just to stop you worrying and let you know that everything's great at home. Charlie got a merit for his reading, and Gracie was good as gold at nursery, and Abigail's eaten all her tea. I told them we'd play safari parks tonight, so if you call and I don't answer, we'll be tracking lions! 'Bye, then. Hope you're having fun.'

'Lucy, this is Steven. Let's meet at twelve forty-five tomorrow, at a Vietnamese place called Saigon. That's S, I, G, H, hyphen, G, O, N, E. It's on the corner of Dean and Wardour, not too far from you. I'm looking forward to it.' Lucy clicked off the phone nervously.

'So, is everything OK?' her husband asked.

'Yep. Amy left a message.'

'A long one.'

'Oh, she was just prattling on about the kids, and how they were playing some sort of a safari game. You know what she's like.'

'Where shall we have dinner tonight?'

'I bought some gnocchi. I thought we were trying to save our pennies.'

Mark sighed heavily. 'We are. I just thought you might like to go out . . .'

'Christ, Mark, you can't lecture me about money one minute, and suggest dinner out the next. We can eat in.'

'I know. But if we weren't paying the mortgage on this place, we could eat *out*.'

Lucy stiffened. She'd eat in every meal for the rest of her life rather than give up the flat. It always happened this way: because he earned and she didn't, his priorities took precedence over hers when it came to how to spend it; not that Mark ever admitted that.

'It's a bit late for that, isn't it?' she asked, in a milder tone than she felt.

'I suppose. I just couldn't help thinking that if we hadn't bought the flat, we could hire Amy for only twenty-four hours a week, and afford to stay at the Lansdowne and go out to dinner. You could even buy some new clothes.'

'What's wrong with my clothes?' Lucy asked, inwardly wondering what she would wear to lunch with Steven Armitage. She didn't have that big a choice, as she kept only a few outfits in the flat. Unless she went shopping first thing in the morning . . .

'Nothing, sweetheart. You'd look good in a sack.'

'A sack, or *the* sack?'

'Both.' He smiled with relief at her playful tone. 'What did you get up to today?'

'Oh, nothing much. Odds and sods.'

'Anything on tomorrow? Can we head home in the morning?'

'I've still got to find the bathroom shelves – I promised Connie I'd look for something chrome. Maybe I'll check around King's Road.'

'There's nothing wrong with MDF. If Connie wants smart shelving she can pay for it.'

Lucy's mouth tightened as she listened to him. How he had the nerve to bang on about money after he had gaily dismissed all her financial objections when the flat was first proposed. 'Anyway, I'm having lunch with Dash tomorrow. You don't have to wait for me, though.' Lucy stood in the archway to the little kitchen and watched her husband while he studied the Scottish catalogue. Several seconds passed before Mark looked up. 'Shall I start the gnocchi?'

'Sure. They've got some very good stuff here – good notes too, unpretentious.'

'Mark?' Lucy folded her arms across her chest.

'Mm-hmm?'

'Are you happy? I mean, apart from worrying about work and money, are you happy?'

'Of course I am.'

'Are you happy with me?'

'Darling, of course. Very happy. You and the children are the things that make me happiest of all. Why are you asking me?'

'I just wanted to be sure.' Lucy paused. She resented that he had lumped her in with the kids in that 'you-and-the-children' domestic unit. 'Because . . .' she paused again. Because it's important, she thought, more important than the business or the overdraft or anything else. Because I don't think Connie's happy with Julian. I think she's seeing a smoothie slick bugger who must do something for her that Julian doesn't. And I happen to be having lunch with him tomorrow. Because what is the point of all those marriage vows if all we do is talk about whether joint ventures are a good idea or not, whether Charlie should have extra tennis coaching, and whether the girls should go to the same school as Charlie, and what's on telly, and should we have the Martins to stay next month or not? And what is the point of anything if when I look at you I feel cross, and I don't know an earthly reason why, except you never look at me the way you used to look at me, you never properly *look* at me, and I don't like this odd feeling of neglect I'm getting from you, and I don't like myself for being so childish about it? In fact, I don't like me at all, so how can you possibly love me? Lucy did not say any of this. All she said was, 'You just don't seem very happy. I wondered if it was me?'

'Oh, God, Luce, no, it's not you.' He put his head in his hands briefly, rubbing his eyes. 'Have I been that bad? Sorry. It's nothing to do with you, it's the business: I want it to go well, and I know it doesn't happen overnight, but every time I talk to an old chum it's all going swimmingly for, well . . . It makes you think.'

'What?'

'It just makes me think, that's all. Whether I should ever have tried this. Whether I'm doing the right thing at all.'

'Of course you are,' Lucy said firmly, without the faintest idea whether he was or not, and with a niggling doubt whether it was relevant to her question anyway.

'I can't stand you thinking that I'm not happy with you.'

'Do you still fancy me?' she probed.

'You know I do,' Mark confirmed. He did not really hear her question, beyond a flash thought that it was typical of Lucy to shift the subject back to the personal when he had for the first time voiced a real concern about his professional life and his wavering self-esteem. Her questions seemed to have far more to do with her state of mind than his own. 'I love you. You're my wife.'

'That's not what I asked. Do you desire me?'

'I fancy the knickers off you.'

'No, you don't.'

'Yes, I do. I fancy you every single conscious moment. Shall I ravish you here on the floor?'

It would be interesting to speculate what might have happened if he'd just done it without asking permission, but he did not. They were like two trains on neighbouring tracks, passing each other by at high speed, close enough to touch, and for their rumblings to disturb each other, but too intent on reaching their own destinations to be distracted.

Lucy could not allow herself to buy a new shirt to wear to lunch with Steven because it would have made her despise herself. The best one she had in London, a pale pink silk shirt, had lost all colour in a little bleached patch above her left breast, probably where some baby sick had been scrubbed off. She arrived at the restaurant early and stopped round the corner for coffee in order to arrive ten minutes late but not later than that. Steven was reading the *Evening Standard* when she was shown to his table.

'I'm so sorry I'm late.'

'Why?' He stood to greet her with an equivocal smile.

'Why am I late?'

'No, why are you sorry?' He pulled out her chair for her. 'If you're honest, you aren't sorry at all. No one is, unless they're more than half an hour late, and even then they're not really sorry, they're simply embarrassed.'

'In that case I take it back. I'm absolutely not sorry.'

'Excellent. I'm glad we've established a rule of complete honesty. Now, how much do you know about Vietnamese food?' His eyes were on the menu and Lucy instantly regretted coming. He signalled to the waitress, who poured wine into their glasses and withdrew backwards. Lucy didn't feel like red wine, not that he asked.

'Nothing at all.'

'Excellent. More honesty. Then may I order for both of us?'

Lucy's stomach knotted. He was completely different from how he had been on their first meeting, on her turf. He acted as if he had only invited her in order to patronize her. 'Is that what you normally do?'

'It depends whom I'm with,' he answered smoothly.

'And with me, you feel you should take charge?'

Steven smiled slowly. 'That's an interesting – and tempting – suggestion.' He pointed to the menu that lay beside her. 'Help yourself, if you want to. Order for me too.'

Lucy shook her head and shoved the menu towards him. He beckoned the waitress, ordered immediately, obviously having decided what they would eat well before she arrived, and raised his glass. 'Here's to us. To new friendships.' Clink. 'So, Constance's flatmate, tell me everything you've been up to for the past week. How's your gorgeous daughter?'

Why does he make me feel so nervous, God damn it? Lucy

thought. Why does he make me feel so fantastically uncool, such a scared little rabbit? 'She's fine.'

'And the specialist?'

'I'm sorry?'

'The last time we met you were taking the baby – Abby, isn't it? – to a specialist.'

'Oh, that. It was nothing, just me being neurotic about her hearing. There's no problem.' Lucy sipped her wine. 'What have *you* been doing this week?'

'Eating. That's all I do every week. Some people eat to live, some people live to eat, and I eat for my living . . .' It was clearly a line he had used before; he probably used it every time he picked up some poor stray and bought them lunch on expenses, Lucy thought, wondering what on earth had possessed her to see the arrogant jerk again, and wishing she were safely on the train with her husband. He had turned sideways in his chair so that he faced her, no doubt waiting for an appreciative giggle to reward his witticism. Her lips tightened and he observed her closely, seeing her hand gripped around the stem of her glass. She looked like some beautiful, woodland creature ready to spring away if he moved a muscle, almost a-quiver with watchfulness. At once Steven wanted to soothe her, to assure her that he was not a threat. 'May I make a confession, Lucy?'

Here it was . . . The ulterior motive, the confession about Constance, and investigation of Constance's marriage; it had come far sooner than Lucy had expected. 'If you like.'

'I've found myself thinking about you a great deal since we met. I keep catching myself at odd times of the day wondering what you are doing, and whether you are playing with your baby, or standing in the supermarket. Imagining what you're saying, and how you're looking. If you've had a good night, or if the baby kept you awake . . . All sorts of peculiar thoughts.' Lucy stared at him in

172

confusion, but with a growing sense of horror that he was mocking her. 'I don't have any business prying into your life, I know that,' he continued, 'but, as I explained, I have no time for lying or hypocrisy. That's my one rule. There's no point at all in putting on an act, or pretending that my interest in you is casual. Ah, good!' The waitress placed a variety of small dishes on the table, naming them in turn. Steven passed Lucy a pair of chopsticks and paused as she sat frozen in her seat, one hand loosely holding the chopsticks, the other gripping the edge of the table. 'Have I already spoiled your appetite?' he asked, with concern.

'I think you are insane,' Lucy said very quietly, not looking at him. 'You are either quite, quite mad, or you are cruel.'

Steven Armitage looked baffled. 'Cruel?' he repeated slowly. 'How could I be cruel?'

'To invite me to lunch just to make fun of me like this.' Her face was blanched of colour, her voice so quiet that he could hardly hear her. 'Why would that possibly amuse you? Did Connie put you up to this? Did she say it would be an enormous laugh, to make me think you were interested in me, not her, and see how I reacted? Just so she can test me, and see –'

Steven's brows were pulled together in a frown, his face serious and intent. 'I haven't spoken to Constance since I met you.'

'So this was your own idea? Well, that's some comfort.' Lucy pushed her chair away from the table, and half moved to stand, as he simultaneously took her hand in his and held it down on the table.

'You don't understand – I meant what I said – please don't go – you have utterly the wrong idea of me –'

'I have no idea about you at all. I can't understand why you should take any pleasure at all in making fun of a complete stranger – what have I possibly done to you?' she whispered in outrage, acutely aware of the handful of other diners' curiosity.

'Sit down, please.' He held her upper arm, pulling her back into her seat. 'Let me finish, for God's sake.' She sat reluctantly, not looking at him, aware that he still held her hand tight in his on the white tablecloth. 'I never dreamed you'd even reply to my note. I wrote it on an impulse, I couldn't stop myself. I told myself that if you didn't call, that would be that, and I'd just fuck off and make no attempt to see you again. But that if you *did*, if you *did* agree to lunch, then I would have to tell you that my intentions were not – well, not innocent. Does that make me such a villain? In my book it makes me honest. Good God, why would I invite you to lunch if I wasn't interested in getting to know you?'

'Let me go now.'

'Not until you believe me. I think you are entrancing –'

'Oh, for God's sake, stop it.'

'Entrancing,' Steven repeated firmly, 'and I have spent a week telling myself that you're a married woman, with a baby, and I have no business even thinking about you at all, but I do, and that's a fact. When I say my intentions are not innocent, don't think I intend to ravish you. I simply want to spend some time with you. I like you enormously, Lucy. I'm very attracted to you. I was as soon as you walked into the flat that night. Isn't that why you came? You must have known that?'

'No. I don't know why I came. And you know nothing about me.'

'I'm sorry. I was wrong. I thought it was obvious that I was attracted to you, and I stupidly thought it was mutual. I apologize.'

'All you know about me is that I'm Connie's best friend, live in Dorset and am married, very *happily*,' she emphasized, 'with three children.'

'I didn't know you had three children.' Lucy remembered saying she had three children, because he'd said it was a pity she wasn't going to have any more. 'I didn't even know you lived in Dorset. I haven't a clue about your marriage or whether it's happy or not. All I know as fact is that you share that flat with Constance, your husband is a wine-dealer, and that I'm bloody jealous of him.'

'And Connie? What about Connie?'

Steven leaned back in his chair in genuine bewilderment, releasing her hand at last. 'What does Constance have to do with any of this?'

Either Constance hadn't yet let Steven know she was up for an affair with him, or Steven was a masterful actor. Lucy put her head in her hands. As Steven moved his arm towards her, the edge of his cuff caught the bottle and tipped it over the table, splashing wine over himself and over Lucy's pale pink silk shirt before he righted it.

'Oh, fuck it,' he swore furiously under his breath, as the waitress tried to mop the table, Lucy and himself all at the same time. 'Fuck it, fuck it, *fuck* it.'

'It's quite all right,' Lucy assured the waitress, 'honestly, it doesn't matter.'

'It was my fault, and it *does* matter,' Steven corrected crossly. 'Let's have another bottle, and I'll buy you a new shirt. Sorry,' he called to their fellow diners, 'bit of a cock-up on my part . . .'

As both Lucy and Steven refused further assistance the waitress changed the tablecloth, brought clean plates and finally backed away. For a moment they sat in silence, Steven shaking his head sheepishly, his coppery hair falling over his forehead. Then he laughed. 'OK. Can we start all over again?'

'Absolutely not. It was a very nice lunch, thank you, but I really must leave now,' she said gravely. 'I don't understand the game you're playing, but that doesn't matter. What matters is that I don't want to play it with you.' The waitress presented another bottle of wine.

'Lucy, please give me a chance to explain. And you haven't eaten anything. Ten minutes, all right?' He looked so boyish, his eyes so full of entreaty, that she relented.

'Ten minutes,' she said firmly, looking at her watch and accepting a spring roll. 'Then I have to go.'

'All right.' Steven put a steamed dumpling into his mouth, chewed thoughtfully and swallowed. 'It goes like this. I'm the sort of sad bloke who makes wonderful plans, and always manages somehow to put his foot in it. When I met you at your flat I thought you were delightful – so different from the women I normally meet. Then you suddenly put the freeze on, kicked me out, and I thought, well, why the hell not? Why shouldn't I want to see you again? There's nothing wrong with being friends with a married woman you admire.' He paused, studying her expression intently. 'Is there? Once you agreed to meet me, I thought, I can't pretend I'm not attracted to you, so I'll say it straight out, and if you laugh at me, fine, we'll just be friends, but *maybe* you won't. *Maybe* you don't love the wine-dealer. I have plenty of married friends who aren't all that happy. Most of them, in fact. Maybe familiarity *does* breed contempt.'

'Maybe it breeds content.'

'*Touché*. If that's true, it's a shame for me, but bloody lovely for you. Is there anything wrong with having an admirer, so long as I promise to be a good boy and keep a respectful distance?' Lucy did not reply. 'Tell me about him, this paragon of a husband. What makes you love him?' Lucy looked hesitant as he pushed a plate of crab towards her. Immediately he took the dish back and began to crack the shells himself and extract the spicy flesh for her.

'You can't analyse love like that,' she began cautiously. 'You just know when you love somebody. I've always loved Mark, and I always will.'

'So his name's Mark. Who does he work for?'

'Himself, if you must know. Are you always so nosy?'

'I like to get the basic facts straight before we get into the more interesting stuff. Set the framework, you know. Were you childhood sweethearts, you and Mark?'

'No. We met when I was twenty-four.'

'Tell me everything. What were you doing, at twenty-four? What were you like, then?'

'I was a junior management consultant.' Steven guffawed, and Lucy took offence. 'What is so funny about that? It's a perfectly serious job.'

'Certainly – very serious . . . It's just a surprise, that's all, not what I imagined. I assumed you were an English teacher, perhaps, or an artist. A designer. Something creative.'

'You shouldn't assume so much.' Lucy sipped her wine and looked thoughtful. 'Mark's the one who's artistic. I've always been on the business end of things.'

'You astound me. Tell me more about Mark. Does he write wonderfully poetic catalogue notes? Impudent bouquets, that sort of thing? The aroma of a freshly oiled cricket bat? What would he say about this,' he swirled the wine in his glass, 'a Côtes du Rhône with the cheeky effrontery of a curate trying on a bishop's mitre?'

She smiled at him, reluctantly acknowledging his effort. 'Not quite. Mark doesn't believe in describing wines like that. He thinks words are unreliable, that all young reds can be peppery, or spicy, or prickly in their own way, or to different palates. He prefers to talk about the real people involved, the growers. His last catalogue was very funny about one man: he said, "When will this besotted parent abandon hope that his latest monstrous offspring will mature into a sensible member of his highly respectable family?" Or something like that. He put it better than I can. But that's not what I meant by being artistic. I meant that he paints. In our garage.'

'In your garage?' Steven controlled a smile, conscious of the wary look that still lurked behind Lucy's blue eyes. 'And you handle the finances and the children?'

'I suppose.'

'While he paints?'

'He needs to paint,' Lucy said defensively. 'It's how he relaxes.'

'And how do *you* relax, Lucy?' Steven refilled her glass.

'Me? Oh, I don't really need to. I don't work any longer.'

'Tell me about your children.'

'I don't believe you're interested in children at all.'

'I am in yours. Your little girl is a beauty. First baby I've ever liked . . .'

'Maybe it's time you had one of your own. You always like your own.'

'If only the right woman would come along . . . Go on. Tell me everything.' He spoke with the easy intimacy and unapologetic curiosity generally found between close female friends. It made Lucy feel alive, if uncomfortable.

'We have a son, Charlie. He's eight, very bright, and lovely. Then there's Grace, she's nearly five. You met Abby. That's all there is to know, really, nothing unusual, just the ordinary stuff. We're an ordinary family with an ordinary routine. I'd rather talk about you.'

'Would you, indeed? I'd find that flattering, if I didn't realize you were just trying to change the subject.'

Lucy dropped her head, and her hair swung forward to hide her face. 'So the right woman's never come along?'

'She did, once. I was too young, and she was too married.' He feigned waggling a fat cigar in a poor W. C. Fields impersonation, 'End of story . . .'

'You can't stop there.' Lucy leaned closer.

'It's not a pretty tale. I need to top up my courage first.' Steven refilled their glasses. 'It was my first proper job in journalism. I was working for a financial magazine, called *Planned Investment* – as if you could ever invest spontaneously. That's why I laughed when you said you were a management consultant. I used to quake interviewing people like you.'

Lucy smiled easily for the first time. 'I doubt it. How ever did you end up as a restaurant critic?'

'Long, boring story. It was stranger that I started off with *Planned Investments*. Anyway, d'you want the quick CV or the doomed love life?'

'Both. Start with the doomed love life.'

'I was twenty-four, just to add another coincidence, and fancying myself no end as a bright young hack about town.' He waved one arm, describing an arc in the room. 'The world was my personal oyster. There I was, a future media tycoon, eagerly anticipating inch-high bylines, flattering photo, the works, in all the glossies and a couple of broadsheets too, editorials being flung at me right, left and centre . . . I set my sights high, though I was barely more than the coffee boy. Then, one day, a woman joined the staff. An extraordinary woman. She was my boss, about ten years older than me. And I fell for her in every way.'

'And?'

'Christ, it was so long ago. I can't remember when I last spoke about her.'

'You don't see her now?'

'No. She was married, had a child. In fact, she was married to the proprietor of the magazine – nepotism riding high, not that it bothered me. Her husband looked after her career, and she looked after mine. We had an affair. She always told me it was just a fling, and I always said that was fine, that I understood. But I didn't understand anything. In the end I left the magazine. I had to. I couldn't stand to be in the same room as her and not touch her.'

'How awful for both of you.'

'Yes, I suppose it was, but as far as I know it didn't scar her unduly. I didn't even leave a surface scratch. I set my sights on ambitious single girls and the odd pretty waitress, until a little while ago . . .' His voice trailed away.

'Don't say anything stupid,' Lucy warned, holding up a finger. 'I've only just forgiven you for making me feel like a fool. Remember, we're going to be just friends.' Then she guessed in one intuitive leap that he had been referring to Constance, and she blushed. 'It's not my business if you have affairs with married women – I'm not being judgemental. I think it's up to the individual.'

'And you, Lucy, have you ever had an affair?'

'I'm not the type.'

'What is the type?'

'Oh, Connie, perhaps, someone tougher. Or prettier.'

'Pretty girls are common,' Steven said quietly, 'you can find four or five in any classroom, on any street, on any bus or train you step on to. As for toughness, well, it's not an attribute I'd seek in a lover. Interesting women are rarer, much more challenging, and much more beautiful. Besides, pretty girls almost always age badly. And if they're really pretty, they don't have any souls.'

It was a walloping generalization, equally unfair to both youth and beauty, *but* . . . How often Lucy had wanted to hear a man say that and believe it was true, that the truly lovely had an emptiness inside that took away all their beauty once you got to know them. Constance was beautiful; Constance was successful, and in charge of her life; sexy, confident, tough; it was clear she had never experienced a moment's self-doubt. But maybe, just maybe, she didn't have quite the lovely, rounded soul that Lucy hoped she herself had . . . Lucy shook her head in denial. Constance had a soul, all right, a robust, mighty one; a soul strong enough to knock you backwards, if it wanted to. She swallowed, and said, 'That's nonsense. And you know it.'

'I wanted to pay you a compliment.'

'By saying I'm not pretty?'

'By saying you are beautiful.'

The bottle of wine was empty. It was nearly four o'clock. Steven had rolled his shirtsleeves up, and was now tipping his chair back, his hands behind his head. Lucy glanced quickly at the thick hairs on his forearms, and back to his head, dark copper-coloured locks that sprang stiffly off his forehead, too long, too rough, and clearly hadn't been washed for quite a while, but seemed enhanced by that. He had the look of an undergraduate in a 1930s photo album. Nothing about that lunch seemed real to Lucy, it was all mock movie scripts, all part of the external upholstery of flirtation she had tried to engineer in the Charlotte Street bar with her husband. If Mark had played along, it would have been just that, a silly game in which he indulged her whims, before they resumed the normal discussions of the state of the overdraft, whether or not they'd attend the school fund-raiser, and who was going to collect the children the following Friday afternoon. With Mark, game-playing was as safe as houses – even when it was about houses. Real life found it perfectly easy to barge in and reassert itself. But with Steven the game had no purpose and no rules – it could swing wildly out of control, like a roller-coaster running off its rails, and she didn't even know how she'd ended up playing it. The more she drank, the more attractive he looked, and the less she could summon up the energy to leave, the more she justified it by saying it meant nothing; it was a one-off.

Steven beckoned the patient waitress. 'Could we have some coffee – espresso – and a couple of cognacs?' He swung back to Lucy. 'You know, you could always let me *try* to seduce you, then rebuff me. There'd be nothing to lose on your part. I won't be offended. I'll probably think even more of you.'

'Then what's the point in trying?'

'What's the reason not to?

'How many times a week do you do this?' Lucy teased. 'Pick up some stray woman to take to lunch, so you can write a review and not bore yourself stupid. Whenever I read restaurant reviews, which I don't much as I never get the chance to eat at the places they talk about, they always say, "My companion tucked into her cassoulet with gusto." Is that what you'll write about me?'

'No. I'll say, "I hi-jacked a gorgeous mother of three to the Sigh-Gone with high hopes of post-prandial sex, but after tasting one Vietnamese spring roll and picking at the cracked peppered crab in a desultory fashion, she declined my offer. This may have been because I inadvertently tipped an entire bottle of Côtes du Rhône – house, and good value at sixteen ninety-nine – over her". I don't know that the sub would pass it. Drink up.' He nudged a large brandy glass towards her.

'I never normally drink at lunch. I'll have to go home and go straight to bed.'

'To Charlotte Street?'

'Mm-hmm.' She didn't know why she pretended she was going back to the flat.

'No husband?'

'He's in Dorset.'

'No children?'

'No . . .'

'But no room for me?'

'Absolutely not.'

'I don't suppose you'd like to have lunch with me again next week? I have to do a place in Charlotte Street, by coincidence. I promise I won't pour wine over you, or ruin your clothes, or do anything else improper, just talk.'

'I don't think that's a very good idea, do you?'

'You don't like talking to me? Since when was conversation between two consenting adults dangerous?'

Since it made her feel she was the most interesting person on earth, and each banality that fell from her lips a pearl, Lucy thought. Since each exchange went that little bit further in the give and take, until she didn't know who was giving and who was taking. Since she'd learned, at about the age of eighteen, that conversation was always the heart of sexual attraction for women. 'I suppose there's no harm in talking.'

'So you'll think about it?'

'I may . . .'

'You have my number. And I have yours.'

Five minutes later he saw her into a taxi, told the driver to take her to Charlotte Street and kissed her fraternally on the cheek, leaving Lucy as confused as Abigail was when Lucy tried to coax her to put the little red triangle in the triangular hole. She redirected the taxi to Waterloo station, spent three hours staring out of the window into the dusk without seeing anything, and caught another taxi home. When she arrived, she noticed that the curtains were drawn in the garage, but didn't stop to see if Mark was there or not. In the hall she studied her face in the large gilt mirror. Ugly? No, just nondescript; unimportant. She didn't really look any worse than she had that morning. She was watering the tubs at the side of the house when Mark's car pulled up. She watched him get out, glance towards the garage, then walk briskly to the front door. He caught sight of her and stopped, looking at her without speaking.

Lucy set down the watering can at her feet. 'What?' He didn't reply. 'Mark?' He continued, with a slight stiffness in his step, towards the house. She followed him. 'Why did you look at me like that?'

'Sorry, I was in another world for a minute.'

'You gave me a really dirty look.'

'No, I didn't, I barely saw you. I was thinking about work. I wasn't looking at you in any particular way.'

'Yes, you were. Why? Have I done something wrong?'

'Not that I know of,' he said mildly. 'Why? Have you?'

Chapter Twelve

All beings seek happiness; it is the purpose of life.

The Dalai Lama

It was a little after eight p.m. As Julian was up in London, and her children safe at school, which was the bare minimum you could expect in exchange for quite gargantuan school fees, Constance wandered aimlessly around her house, smoking, to escape the feeling that somehow she had vanished now that she was alone. She drew comfort from the security of her home.

Like many women, Constance had begun by unconsciously colonizing the rooms one by one, annexing first the drawing room, then the master bedroom, then the kitchen and finally the little sitting room, before she openly embraced totalitarianism and overran the halls and corridors. Her children staked mini-Stalinist claims to their bedrooms and their den. Like many men, Julian had retreated in time into the little nooks and corners she couldn't be bothered with, the cellars and attic, and the one decent room she had designated his office. Funnily enough, that was the room where Constance always ended up when he wasn't home. She missed Julian, found herself pining for his physical presence, and all the incidental things that he did and said that filled her house and heart. In exactly two months, just before Christmas, it would be her fortieth birthday, and there was still so much to achieve. She sat down at his desk to leaf through the perpetual pile of architectural drawings that covered it. The very sight of them made her reach for the phone and call the flat. It rang without answer.

Constance had one instinct sharper than her others: to run from boredom. Ironically, she was a woman who was more easily bored than many, and she was bored most of all by her own company. When she married, she had chosen the whole package, not just Julian himself but all that he represented. The mannerisms that others saw as pompous were quite the opposite to her: they formed part of his surrounding shell, an essential part of him that was quite inseparable from his innate modesty. Without him she felt rudderless, an unpleasant condition at any age, but highly unwelcome when one is rapidly approaching forty. Constance opened the desk drawer that held her husband's private CD collection, those that were restricted to his office, as the children were too shamed by their lack of credibility to allow them to be stored with, let alone played on, the main family system. Van Morrison, the Doors, even the complete works of Simon and Garfunkel skulked inside his mahogany bureau. Constance put on *Bridge Over Troubled Water*. While she sat smoking at his desk, it struck her suddenly that she was now roughly the age of the legendary Mrs Robinson. Transfixed, she began to work it out on a scrap of paper: Anne Bancroft had told Dustin Hoffman that she'd been at college when she got pregnant, say, maybe twenty, maximum twenty-one, and Elaine was then at college, say nineteen . . . Bingo. Mrs Robinson was only forty. Constance slumped back in Julian's chair, inhaling deeply, stroking her upper lip with her thumb. She was about to be the same age as Mrs Robinson, a woman who had embodied, in Constance's teenage years, the last shameless throes before the decline into old age. At least the subject of her amorous fantasies was a forty-five-year-old restaurant critic and not a recent university graduate. She stopped the CD and dialled the flat again. She just wanted to hear his voice, but there was no answer from Mr Robinson.

In the kitchen, she poured out some wine, turned the radio on loud and started to make risotto. She wasn't even hungry, and never cooked for herself, being quite content with a bowl of cereal or a hunk of cheese, but she needed to do something that required patience and concentration. And risotto always put her in the right mood, a weighty, sultry mood as the scented vapour warmed her face. The act of making risotto summoned the spirit of Silvana Mangano in *Bitter Rice*, with her skirt hitched up into her knickers, bare feet, strong muscular calves, gleaming thighs . . . Constance hummed throatily as the stock simmered. Good cooking and loving marriage were sisters; both required intuition, commitment and careful timing. Even for a perfectionist like her, cooking could go wrong, and it occasionally did. And her marriage had gone wrong, only once, shortly after Luke was born, when she had neglected her timing and commitment, and her much prized intuition had abandoned her. She'd never talked about it since, not even to Lucy. She did not see the point of post-mortems, certainly not ones that involved outsiders. All you could do was identify the problem for yourself, cut it out, bury it, then sterilize the surrounding area. She had never talked about it, but when she was alone, sometimes, she thought about it, how close she'd come to losing Julian. On impulse she grabbed the phone and hit the stored number for the Epsteins, still stirring the stock.

'Mark? It's Connie.'

'As if I wouldn't recognize your voice. What's up?'

'Nothing much. I just thought maybe you and Luce would like

to come over for a kitchen supper. I'm on my own, and the risotto will be done in the time it takes you to get here.'

'Risotto . . .'

'Pumpkin. I've been turning autumnal.'

'God, *pumpkin risotto*. And there I was, getting excited about the children's leftover chicken nuggets.'

'I've got some late raspberries, too,' she seduced him, 'as soft and downy as my mother-in-law's chin, and some organic cream from Bill Marshall . . .'

'Enough, *enough*!' Mark groaned. 'We haven't got a hope of a babysitter.'

'I don't suppose just one of you would like to come?'

'Are you OK, Connie? Is something wrong?' Mark asked, with concern.

'I'm just bored and lonely. Julian had to go to London, and stupidly I said I'd stay at home and work. Now I don't know what to do with myself.'

'Let me have a word with Luce. Hang on . . .' After a couple of minutes Mark came back on the line. 'Well, if the offer's genuine, and you really don't have a preference, then I got the long straw. Or you could say you got the short one. Luce wants an early night, and she says she loves cold baked beans. No taste, that girl. Don't know why I married her.'

'Drive fast, OK? The risotto won't wait.' She was glad it was Mark who was coming: Lucy had developed a worrying habit of pressing her about infidelity.

Two hours later, Mark was sitting with his legs flung over the side of an armchair in front of a spluttering fire in Constance's little sitting room. His hostess was lying on the carpet opening her second packet of Marlboro Lights that day.

'I've never been much cop at lighting fires,' he said glumly, leaning down to light her cigarette.

'Nor me. Julian always does it. He must have been a boy scout.' Connie rolled on her back, blowing smoke at the ceiling. 'Mark? Do you like being married?'

'Why is everyone so interested if I'm happy all of a sudden?' Mark countered, with mock irritation. 'Yes, I like being married.'

'Unreservedly?'

'Unreservedly.'

'God, it's so easy for men, isn't it?' Constance turned on to her stomach and propped herself up on her elbows. 'I think that marriage is a state you have to enter from a position of complete ignorance and naïveté. No one who actually knows anything about it would be prepared to face the consequences.'

Mark grinned at her. 'You're full of crap, Connie. You don't believe that for a moment, and I'm not jerk enough to fall for half the cynical stuff you spew.' Constance pouted as if to say, 'Well, it was worth a shot; you can't blame me for trying it on.' Mark continued reasonably, 'Let's face it, the only alternative to marriage is not being married. I didn't enjoy that nearly as much.'

'Nor me.'

'That's sorted then.'

'So you and Luce have never had any problems?' Constance pressed him. Lucy's last visit had been distinctly odd.

'Not big ones. She gets pissed off with me, with plenty of justification, and she's no saint herself, but we muck along. We love each other, even when we fight.' Mark wondered if Lucy had said anything to Constance about their most recent fight. 'Lucy is the most remarkable and lovely woman I have ever met. I know I wouldn't want to be with anyone else.'

'Do you think Julian feels that?'

Mark laughed. 'Julian? *C'mon*, Connie, my love. Julian Middle Name Uxorious Purcell? Pull the other one.' He took her cigarette-free hand and tugged her little finger. 'This is where Julian lives, and he loves it.'

'Not always, he hasn't,' Constance said darkly, and sat up, crossing her long legs and looking at Mark seriously. 'I haven't always been . . . well, that easy to live with.'

'Con, I don't believe you've *ever* been easy to live with. That's what makes Julian so extraordinary. You are his calling.'

'Piss off, chum,' she growled, and looked at him with the direct, confrontational gaze that scared the hell out of her staff. 'I know Luce has never considered having an affair, but have you?'

'Nope. I'm as pure as driven snow. Cross my heart.' And Mark did.

'What stopped you?'

'Nothing ever started me, Con.'

'Maybe you're still too young.'

'Me? I'm older than the hills, older than the earth's crust.'

'Rubbish. I bet you still believe Clearasil actually works.' Constance yawned. 'No, it's not age with you. You're different. Maybe you're just inherently faithful?'

'I don't know if that makes any sense,' Mark mused. He was not a fool: he suspected what Constance was trying to tell him, but he had not yet decided whether it was something he wanted to hear. 'I think . . .' he began cautiously, and paused.

'Yes, what do you think?'

'I think it's all a chemical reaction. I wouldn't describe it that way to Lucy: it would be like saying Father Christmas doesn't exist. But it is chemical, isn't it? You're a rational person, like me. We know it's all a chemical compound of endorphins and oxytocin.'

'Love?'

'Not love, no, not love the way we mean it. Love is something else. I meant the down-and-dirty stuff – lust, sex, the business of "falling in love". When people say it's all in the head, they are spot on. Falling in love is just a state of mind . . . Con, what are we talking about here? How did we get up this alley?'

'The booze,' Constance said sagely. 'Carry on about falling in love.'

'I haven't done it for a long time. I only ever did it once.'

'No, I don't mean the big romance, when you fall in love and get married and live happily ever after. I mean, what makes people stray? Why do they fall for someone else?'

'Why are you asking me?'

'Because you're here, and I'm pissed.'

'That's OK, then. I think people get some vague feeling of dissatisfaction — that there's something not properly aligned, something missing somewhere.'

'So you think infidelity starts inside the marriage?' Constance asked, thinking about her own.

'If you want to put it like that. You look around yourself, at the people around you: if you try hard enough, and look long enough, one of them is bound to float to the top.'

Constance smiled. 'Like scum?'

'Or like cream . . .' Mark grinned back at her.

Constance wagged her finger at him. 'And *there*'s the problem. It can be so hard to tell them apart.'

In over five years of friendship, Mark and Constance had never before talked so intimately. When they had been alone, they generally talked about the wonders of wine or the frustrations of work. They were both naturally wary of introspection, and not people who voiced their more intimate feelings even when they were prepared to recognize them. Mark found it faintly embarrassing to be talking in such a manner about things that he felt should be relegated to the territory of the under-thirties; he was surprised to find that he was enjoying himself.

191

Constance poured two slugs of whisky and waved one at Mark. 'I won't be able to drive,' he cautioned her.

'There are four empty bedrooms if you want to stay. You know, somebody once described a model for extramarital sex to me.'

'Tried and tested?'

'It went like this. You get a lover. You meet once a week at a hotel, a smart hotel – Claridges or something. You have great sex, order great room service in bed, have a Jacuzzi or something, then put your clothes back on and off you trot home, bright-eyed and bushy-tailed. No ties, no complications, just like you were booking a massage, or a facial or something. Just to step out of the domestic routine, once a week. What d'you think?'

'It has a certain appeal, I'll give you that . . .' Mark stared at a spot on the ceiling. 'But I could never afford Claridges. Maybe the Thistle Hotel in Bristol.'

'That's the whole point of the story. You start off at the Dorchester. As the novelty fades, you shift to a Hilton. A couple of months later, it's once a fortnight at the Holiday Inn. As the affair becomes routine, the location gets seedier and seedier, and the whole thing more and more guilt-ridden.'

'Until you end up at the Master Brewer on the A40?'

Constance howled. 'Any affair would end before that. Romeo and Juliet would have said, "*Sayonara*," before hitting the Master Brewer.'

'Well, in my present financial condition, an affair would have to *start* at the Master Brewer. What would your friend say about that?'

The 'friend' who had described the downhill course of adulterous love had been Julian, but Constance wasn't drunk enough to tell Mark that. 'Probably that you were the last of the great romantics . . .' Constance teased. 'Maybe that way round would be better – a real test of desire. By the way, Mark,' she added seriously, 'seeing you brought money up, if you ever have any financial worries, you know, about the mortgage, any worries at all, you only have to say the word. We could always pick up the payments for a bit.'

'Pick up the payments, my arse. If we have financial worries then I intend to rent the flat out at weekends to ladies of the night. Or American tourists.'

'They might be more hassle than the hookers – and they'd use my kitchen. Bloody hell, they'd even use my knives.'

'And you think the hookers wouldn't?'

'What a revolting thought. I can't believe men really go in for all that S&M stuff. What kind of pervert really wants that?'

'I have it on the best authority that it's mainly bank managers and CEOs. Now, you tell me something, Constance, something I've been puzzling over for a very long time. What is it *women* really want?'

'Credit cards.'

'I'm serious.'

'What do women *want*?'

'That's right.' Mark nodded. 'From men.'

'There are three acceptable husband models. Even if they get marginally updated every decade or so, there are only three basic types a woman can be expected to put up with long-term.' Constance rattled away, raising three fingers and counting them off. 'The bloody good fun, laugh-a-minute husband, the insatiably passionate husband, and the simply perfectly good, never-puts-a-foot-wrong husband. All the others are a complete waste of time for anything more than a test drive.'

Mark sucked in his breath, shaking his head. 'You're doing it again, you cow. Stop taking the piss. It was a perfectly serious question.'

'And I gave you a serious answer.'

'Not to my question. What do women really *want* from men? Their husbands, their lovers, whatever. What do they want in life?'

'I'm sure you know if you think hard about it.'

'I'm not at all sure I want to think hard about it.' Mark helped himself to the bottle.

'It's simple,' Constance said solemnly. 'Women want to be hopelessly, helplessly and endlessly adored. That's all.'

'That's *it*?' Mark queried in mock shock, as if she had said women wanted a nice cup of tea in the morning. An inveterate optimist, Mark had the typically English characteristic of laughing when he was most serious, and appearing to dismiss those things he cared most about.

'Yep. That's it. Helpless, hopeless adoration, as long as the blue of the night . . .'

'. . . meets the gold of the day. Don't tell me, I get the picture.'

'It's true, Mark. The key thing about women fantasizing about men other than their husbands is that they *don't*. It hardly ever happens. All of us just crave some man desiring us madly and for ever, whether it's ever consummated or not. In a way it's better – for the fantasy – if it *isn't* ever consummated, because then you know he's going to desire you for ever even though it's hopeless. Husbands can't do that.'

'I wonder if you're right. Can't husbands pretend?'

'They can try, but they have to practise very, very hard, and get very, very good at it.'

'Yeah, well . . .' Mark's eyelids were heavy, his voice slurred.

Constance stood up and stretched. 'Listen, on that authoritative and compelling note, I've got to hit the sack. Why not call Luce, so she's not worried, and stay the night?'

'Lucy, yes, I must call Luce. I miss her.'

'God, you're even dear when you're drunk as a skunk. You can sleep in Luke's room, then I don't have to remake a bed.'

Lucy was neither worried nor suspicious when Mark asked if it was all right if he stayed at Constance's, rather than getting a taxi home. She was perfectly sweet about it.

While Mark, in Luke's bedroom, fell at once into deep and dreamless sleep, his wife, seven miles across country, found it impossible to settle. She checked on her children one by one, first the girls and then Charlie, all sleeping soundly. Like most mothers, she loved her children most ferociously when they were asleep. These were the times when she made deals with a God she did not believe in, asking for his protection not of her but of her babies. She knew she could not shield them from every blow, not from all the moments of small unhappiness that lay ahead – the future lost football matches, grazed knees, disappointing exam results and the rejection of first love. Dear God, she'd plead, let all their trials be little ones. Anything but the big ones, anything but death, and illness and absolute heartbreak. *Protect them from evil.* She prayed for divine protection because she did not know how to arm them to face evil and defend themselves; she had no reliable weapons to give them.

Lucy lingered in Charlie's room, straightening his bedclothes and refolding his school uniform. For once, she hoped that her son would wake up. She had always felt able to talk to Charlie, even when he was very tiny, and had drawn comfort from his quiet, serene presence. Lucy tried to conceal that Charlie was her favourite, and caught herself drawing up lists of perfectly rational reasons, both in support and in denial of her feelings. Charlie was her first-born, and her only son, and that justified her feeling differently about him. He was that much older than his sisters, so naturally a better communicator; when the girls were older, she wouldn't feel that way at all. He had a gentler spirit than his sisters, so needed her protection more than they did. She had a special, female bond with the girls, from which Charlie was excluded. Above all, she told herself that whatever she felt she was clever enough not to display it, and that she loved each of her children more than some adults loved any of theirs. Lucy was misguided to draw comfort from this last fact, whether true or not, for her children had no notion whether they were loved more or less than other children, but were each exquisitely sensitive to favouritism shown to a sibling. After two or three minutes of his mother's cool hand on his brow, and the pressure of her lips on his cheek, Charlie sat up, rubbing his eyes.

'Hi, Mum.'

'Hello, darling . . . I didn't mean to wake you up. I just wanted to say goodnight.'

The boy yawned and draped an arm sleepily around her shoulders. 'Why are you sad, Mum? You look really sad.'

'Sad? Rubbish. I'm fine. A hundred per cent. Now you go straight back to sleep.'

Then Lucy felt lonelier than ever, and there was no one to stop her feeling so alone. She coaxed Mungo, their long-suffering Labrador, out of his basket and into the playroom to keep her company while she watched the late-night film, a made-for-TV western that should never have been made for anything. When she murmured, 'Life's just not fair, is it, old boy?' into his ear, and inhaled the faint warm odour of roast chicken that only Labradors' ears have, the dog decided enough was enough and sloped back to his bed.

Lucy took a heavily creased envelope out of her dressing-gown pocket and studied the address. 'Mrs Lucy Epstein, c/o Fratelli Camisa. Please forward.' The scrawled note inside read:

Here is a carefully considered list of the best things in life:

1) Constance's flatmate

2) Love

Tied 3) Lust, and other people's burgundy

5) Other people's children

6) Foie gras mi-cuit

Tied 7) Fixed contract journalism and an abundant supply of taxis

9) Rocket

10) London

2,157) A sad bastard called Steven Armitage, who is wondering whether Constance's flatmate will ever call and have lunch with him, and is increasingly forced to conclude that her two-week silence spells a large and reverberating 'No'.

Lucy refolded the letter and restored it to her pocket. More than anything else she wanted to phone Steven and arrange to have lunch with him, but she could not see a way of achieving this without wilfully doing something she knew to be at best playing with fire and at worst simply wrong. Lucy could not accept the deliberate commission of a crime, only the accidental trip-up; she could live with herself as a bungler but not as a villainess. If she had to say one thing about herself, it would be that she sought to avoid trouble, to lead a nice, clean, easy life with no real complications, plenty of fun, of course, but nothing messy or difficult. It was OK to be scatty, fine to make occasional mistakes and be entitled to forgiveness, but, Please, God, she said to herself, please, God, let me never put my foot in it so badly that I really screw things up . . . Let nothing *happen* . . . She shouldn't call him. She would not call him. She could not. Her mind raced as she sat on the sofa, staring at the television screen without knowing who the good guys were. If he called her, and she picked up the phone, she would simply decline to meet him.

And if he called and left a message, and Mark heard it, and asked who 'Steven' was, she would say he was a friend of Connie's, that she'd bumped into him once, and he'd mentioned something about the three of them getting together for lunch, and she'd laugh it off, blame Connie, somehow, for getting her involved, and Mark wouldn't care, it probably wouldn't even register in his mind, because he wasn't very interested in trivial, social details like that. On second thoughts, Mark probably wouldn't even bother to ask who he was, because he was barely paying any attention to her life at all. But what if he called, and Mark answered the phone? What then? What would Steven say? How would he explain himself, and how would she know what he'd said before Mark interrogated her? He'd say, he'd say – *Oh, God, he'd said he never believed in lies . . .* He'd say he'd met her at the flat, shared a bottle of wine, met Abigail, even, and then they'd had lunch . . . Lucy's stomach heaved, feeling delightfully fluttery and nauseous at the same time. She went shakily to bed, studying herself again in the mirror as she passed the hall. No, she didn't look ugly, not bad ugly, not yet, but the face that stared back looked horribly guilty, and she hadn't even done anything, and wasn't going to do anything ever. She curled up in bed, hugging her knees, and thought, *My God, what if he doesn't call at all?*

After she had given Mark clean towels and a toothbrush, and closed the door behind him Constance went downstairs to clear up. First she called the flat again. There was still no reply, and it was after eleven. She set the breakfast table and made batter for cornbread muffins, Luke's favourite, as if her son were home from school and tucked up in his bed, rather than Mark. By midnight she had run out of things to do, and called Julian again, determined to wake him up. She counted as the phone rang twenty times, then checked with the operator, who confirmed there was no fault on the line.

Julian lay in bed, wide awake, reading. He had returned to the flat in the late afternoon, and could easily have caught the train and been home in time for dinner, but he had his reasons for choosing to stay alone in Charlotte Street. After he had heard the phone ring the first time and guessed it to be Constance he had made himself an omelette and eaten it standing at the window, listening to the phone ring. He had spent the rest of the evening quietly and alone, oblivious to the music he put on the system, and unmoved by the comings and goings on the street below. He had been asked by English Heritage to submit a proposal for the design of a new visitor's centre at Stonehenge, so spent some time on the Internet, trying to find out a little more about the properties of certain stones. His search did not inspire any design ideas, although browsing the multiple geological sites fed his thoughts about Constance. When he had first met her, he had called her his little volcano, a rather obvious nickname given her frequent explosions, but Julian did not pride himself on novelty or subtlety. He responded far more to history, whether personal or general, than to the future. Over time, he had elaborated the metaphor, and used to describe their union as built upon two contrasting rocks: Constance being igneous, formed from hot lava, and himself as the less glamorous sedimentary personality. Lava suited his wife's temperament: not only was it the product of eruption – and Connie loved as fiercely as she hated – but it cooled very quickly. It was several years since he had played with the idea: Constance was not as volatile as she had been in her youth. Nowadays she was far more likely to engineer the internal explosion of apples than to erupt herself. 'That's where the fluffiness comes from,' he'd once heard her say to Lewis. 'They have to burst from *inside*, to swell, explode, then collapse.' As Julian browsed the various sites, he refined his description of her to obsidian, the dark, shiny, volcanic glass that had cooled instantaneously. He harshly reclassified himself from sedimentary rock to metamorphic, particularly to slate. The process of compaction, by which clay was converted first to shale and then to slate, seemed to sum him up perfectly: his own grains had moved closer together; he had certainly become more dense; his porosity was reduced; and he was undeniably of dark grey character. At that point he turned off his computer. He could make a strong case for slate flooring in the new visitors' centre, but no rational one for why magical obsidian should choose to partner itself with slate.

He did not answer the phone when it rang shortly after eleven, nor at midnight. He was certain it was Constance. Had it rung every five minutes, he would have answered, fearing a crisis at home, but Julian knew his wife very well, and all her patterns. It had taken him nearly forty years to learn the key lesson in life: that the sole important thing is the certainty that you are loved. It lay, for Julian, at the heart of all happiness, far outweighing career success, financial reward, or public esteem. Secure that Constance loved him, he wanted to be always in her company, but he knew that in order for her to continue loving him, he had to elect to be alone from time to time. As he needed to be certain of her, so she needed to doubt. He correctly deduced from the pattern of the telephone calls that she was checking up on him. He blessed her for that, punishing himself, and rewarding her, by leaving her guessing.

Chapter Thirteen

How delicious, how sumptuous, how wickedly seductive and how
– at the time – you don't give a fig how you are going to feel after
too much of it . . .

Simon Hopkinson

Steven sat at his desk, chewing the end of the pen he used as a surrogate cigarette on his rare visits to the office. He was aware that two typists across the room were looking at him and pretending not to be, and just as aware that they were discussing whether or not they fancied him. He was not interested which side they came down on. He didn't know their names, and had never spoken to them. Normally he would have stared back boldly at them with a half-smile, just to let them know that one day he might, if the spirit seized him, but today he did not.

'You look like an unmade bed,' the paper's junior film critic at the next-door desk commented, typing furiously.

'Is that a compliment?'

'Let me just finish this and I'll have a better look.' Steven waited. He liked Marcella; he'd even slept with her a few times. After a minute or two she swivelled her chair around and appraised him critically. 'Yeah, it's a compliment. You look sexy, in a schmoozyold-bugger kind of way, like you haven't had a shower all week, slept in your clothes and have got the mother of all hangovers. I'm guessing you've got a new girlfriend.'

'How astute you are, Marcie. You, on the other hand, look far too tidy. You look like a model in a mail-order catalogue for cashmere twin-sets. Crossed with a plate of cucumber sandwiches.'

'Crusts off?'

'Undoubtedly crusts off.'

'That's not what you used to say . . . but I take it that's an insult.' She swivelled back to face her screen, smiling.

'How could I ever insult you, our Siren of the Silver Screen?'

'Oh, fuck off, Armitage. So who is she, your new bit?'

'Let's not talk about me, flower, let's talk about you, far more interesting. Did you get your raise?'

'You're not getting off the hook that easily. Does she work on the paper?'

'She doesn't even work.'

'Wow. So she's still at school.'

'No need to be catty, Marcie. It doesn't become you.'

'What do you expect,' she grumbled, 'if you call me a plate of cucumber sandwiches? A girl's got to have some self-respect. So,' she pressed on, 'is she The One?'

'Hmm.' Steven picked up the phone. 'Dunno. I haven't even kissed her yet.'

'Not off first base? Definitely a schoolgirl, then.' Marcella smirked. 'What's so special about her? What's she got that I haven't?'

A husband, he might have answered, and three bloody children; these appendages were never far from Steven's mind when he thought about Lucy Epstein. He dropped the phone back on its cradle. 'If I could put my finger on that, the whole thing would be a lot more manageable. Or avoidable.'

'She's pretty, I assume?'

'Yes, she's very pretty,' he admitted, in an impatient tone. 'She's just very, very . . . nice.'

'Have you seen a doctor recently, Steven? Let me check your temperature . . .' She laid her hand on his forehead. 'Hey, you're not in love, are you?'

'Piss off, Marcie.'

Marcella let out a long, low whistle. 'My God. It's true. You've finally fallen in love.'

'Rubbish.' Steven shrugged into his jacket. 'You know you're the only woman who's ever had my heart, blossom. See you next week.'

'By the way, what's her name?'

Steven swung round in the doorway, his shoulders hunched and hands shoved deep into his pockets. 'Charlotte.'

'Charlotte. How terribly English and proper. Pity that. I took a message for you this morning from some woman called Lucy. I thought it might be your *inamorata*, but it's probably an eager restaurant PR.' Marcella shoved papers about on her desk, then waved a scrap at him. 'Here it is. She said something about lunch, a review, and left a number. Well?' she asked expectantly. 'D'you want it, or shall I bin it?'

'You haven't been to the flat for ages,' Constance said critically. She had dropped in on Lucy to show her some material samples she'd picked up for the living room, and Lucy was taking very little interest.

'No, I missed a couple of weeks. Charlie was sick, and then Grace got it. She's still off school.'

'I thought I detected her dulcet tones.'

'She's in the playroom. I don't feel that good myself.'

'You certainly look awful . . .' Constance studied her swatches. 'I'm tempted to go for the white, seeing it's a childfree zone.'

203

'Fine by me.' The phone rang. Three minutes later Grace burst into the kitchen, twirling around and singing at the top of her voice, 'It's my darling daddy! It's my darling daddy!' with no visible sign of poor health. Amy popped her head around the door. 'Gracie talked to him, but I put the call on hold, Lucy, if you want to take it in here.'

Lucy picked up the extension. 'Hi, darling. What's up?'

'Lucy?' Steven sounded amused. 'Not darling Daddy, I'm afraid, it's me. Was that your four-year-old?'

'Yes, yes, it was,' Lucy turned her back on Constance and cradled the phone. 'Um, how are you?'

'Great, since I got your message.' His voice softened. 'And how are *you*?'

'Me? Oh, I'm just fine.'

'Stop comparing medical notes and ask him about the curtains,' Constance instructed.

Lucy briefly put her hand over the speaker end. 'He doesn't care about the curtains . . . But if you insist . . . Connie's here. She brought round some curtain swatches for the living room. Of the flat.' Lucy felt a nervous giggle bubbling in her throat. 'She thinks we should go for white.'

'Charming, I'm sure. Are you asking my opinion?'

'I suppose so. Connie is, anyway.'

'And she thinks you're talking to Mark. Are you coming to have lunch with me?'

'Ask him if he's willing to put them up,' Constance asked. 'Julian's useless at DIY. Ask him if he'd rather pay a bloke, or do it himself.'

'Connie wants to know if you'd put the curtains up.'

'I'd be happy to, on condition you agree to have lunch with me. Or dinner. Or both.'

'Hmm.' Lucy froze, suddenly realizing that Constance would

204

naturally refer to the curtains, and the conversation, next time she saw Mark. 'We'll talk about that later.'

'Did he say he wouldn't do it? Is he being rude about me? Bloody cheek. Let me talk to him, Luce.' Constance held her hand out for the phone.

'Are you going to have lunch with me or not? If you don't say yes right now, I'll start yelling,' Steven threatened. 'I'll tell Constance we're having a mad, tempestuous affair, and don't have time to put up her bloody curtains.'

'He says he'll do it,' Lucy told Constance.

'You better believe I'll do it. Will. You. Have. Lunch. With. Me. Next. Week?' Steven's voice rose ominously.

'Thursday, one o'clock?' Lucy suggested hurriedly.

'Thursday, one o'clock. At L'Etoile on Charlotte Street.'

'Let me talk to him.' Constance held out her hand but Lucy hung up. 'Where is he, anyway?'

Lucy looked at her blankly. 'Who?'

'Lord, Luce, maybe you are coming down with something . . . *Mark*. Remember him? Your husband? The man you've just been talking to?'

'Oh. He's in Sherborne. I think.'

Constance stretched lazily. 'You don't mind asking him about the curtains, do you?'

'Of course not. Why should I?'

'No reason at all. You just looked nervous.' Lucy gazed back at her friend with the wide-open eyes of a child. She had no reason to feel guilty. She hadn't initiated it, circumstances had simply intervened. She had left her home number with the intention of telling Steven she couldn't do lunch at all, ever. And she could always call him back and tell him exactly that.

The following Thursday Lucy caught the early commuter train to

Waterloo and went straight to the hairdresser's she had used when she lived in London, and still patronized on rare occasions. It was an indulgence she could not afford in more ways than one, but she pushed this thought aside. She asked the stylist to put up her hair elegantly but casually, as if she'd done it herself.

'Going somewhere nice, then?'

'Just a work do tonight – my husband's cronies.'

'Corporate-wife lark?'

'Something like that.'

'Want your nails done too?'

'Why not?'

She arrived at Elena's L'Etoile a little after one to be greeted by a sweet yet imperious old lady. Lucy knew her to be Elena, although she never assumed the familiarity to address her by name. Steven was waiting at a corner table at the very back of the room, and rose as they approached.

'See, Elena? I told you I wouldn't be stood up.'

'You should be stood up more often, Mr Armitage, all those rude things you write about nice people.'

'You told me you never read my stuff.'

'Sometimes I look. I only look.' She brought them each a glass of champagne and returned to her post at the front desk, from where she could keep an eagle eye on the front door as well as every corner of the dining room.

'My, how smart you look.' Steven looked at Lucy appraisingly, registering a faint slap of disappointment. He liked her better when she was less elegantly coiffed, when she looked more like a harassed mother of three in urgent need of rescuing.

Lucy's hand flew to her hair. 'I have to go to a wine do with Mark tonight, that's all.'

'And I thought it was for my benefit. I promise not to empty any bottles over you this time.'

'I'm wearing black. In case.'

'I didn't think you'd come.'

'I almost didn't,' she lied, 'but it seemed so rude.'

'I bet you're never rude.' Steven considered himself an authority on rudeness; after all, he made a very decent living from it.

'Oh, but I am. I can be dreadfully rude without even trying.' She picked up the menu, then hurriedly put it down again. 'I'm sorry, I forgot. Are you going to order for me again?'

Steven let out a shout of laughter. 'Is that what you mean by not even trying? I consider my hands well and truly slapped. I wouldn't dream of ever ordering for you again.'

It took all Lucy's concentration just to sit still. She would have welcomed his choosing what she should eat, but she looked over the menu and chose pâté and grilled Dover sole off the bone, on the grounds that they were easy to eat and would not make her vulnerable to nervous dribbling. Steven had no such fears and ordered escargots followed by partridge.

'So, how have you been?'

'Fine, doing all the normal stuff. Doctors' appointments, parent–teacher meetings, supermarkets, trying to find Charlie's football kit or Gracie's leotard when we're already ten minutes late for school. You can't imagine what an exotic life I lead. The last two weeks one or other of the children has been puking day and night.'

'The very first time I met you,' Steven said, as if he'd known her most of his life, 'I thought you were the type of woman who was born to motherhood.'

'That mythical beast, you mean.'

'You seem to thrive on it. I would have put you up for every babyfood ad in the business, were I an advertising man.'

'How very flattering.'

'It *is*,' Steven countered her sarcasm. 'There's nothing in the world more alluring to a predatory male than a beautiful and contented mother.'

'What rubbish. If it's true, then it's because there's only a handful of mothers who are either beautiful or contented. Probably not one who's both. Most mothers are too stressed to feel either.'

'What makes you happiest, Lucy?'

'My children,' Lucy said firmly, and smiled warmly. 'But they also make me a little bit mad. I adore them, absolutely, but sometimes, every so often, I just wish I could read a book in peace or have a bath without someone coming in and saying, "Grace just pinched me," or "Mum, where are my wellies?" Honestly, I can't even remember what it's like to have nothing to do, nothing pressing I've left undone, and no persistent worry, like could Charlie be mildly asthmatic, or should I be trying homeopathy for Grace's eczema, or is Abby going to be incapable of establishing full, warm and trusting relationships because I didn't breastfeed her as long as I did the others?' Lucy blushed, then shook her head and tried to look offended as Steven grinned at her. 'Stop it. You have no idea how guilty that makes me feel.'

'Breast-feeding is not something I've given much thought to,' Steven admitted, delighted that the Lucy he felt he knew was so rapidly reasserting herself over the suave woman who had first entered the restaurant.

'Someone like you can't possibly imagine what it does to your brain to spend your whole day looking for things other people have lost, or sorting out other people's battles. Honestly, there ought to be an exam you have to pass before motherhood. They should make women sit through Chinese water torture, be denied sleep for ten nights in a row, cook dinner with *at least* two green vegetables and one arm tied behind their backs, do seventeen loads of laundry, then referee a fight between Mike Tyson and the guy who had his ear bitten off, and *then* listen to a five-year-old trying to read, "John sees the ball. John runs after the ball. The ball runs down the hill. John runs down the hill." Twenty-seven times. With enthusiasm and constant encouragement. And have to be patient when the child reads, "John," perfectly easily the first twenty-six times, and on the twenty-seventh stares at it and says, "Mary."'

As she talked, Lucy's chignon began to slip, strands of fair hair escaping the clutches of the hairgrips to float around her neck. The more she talked, the more expansive her gestures became; she was painting a picture for him, sketching a scene of domestic chaos. She was deliberately caricaturing herself into a neat little bundle of disgruntled housewife, and not letting Steven say a word that might distract her. As she heard herself rattling away she recalled something she'd read, a terrible laboratory study that refuted the long-accepted notion of maternal self-sacrifice. The bastard scientists, instead of trying to find a cure for cancer, had taken a mother animal – Lucy couldn't remember which, but fervently hoped it was something unmaternal, a rat, or a reptile, not a monkey or a dog or something she could identify with – and put it in a special cage with its baby. There was no way out of the cage, no means of escape, no platform within it, and the scientists coldly observed the mother's behaviour while they gradually heated the floor to an intolerable degree. Mother and baby had become increasingly distressed. How Lucy had prayed, reading the article, that the mother would lay herself down on the ground to spare her child pain, but no: the mother had finally stood on her own baby to protect herself. Lucy did not describe this to Steven, she thought she might weep if she did. 'Anyway, I can't tell you how nice it is to sit at a table without a plastic cloth on it.'

'On second thoughts we'd better scrap the babyfood ads.'

'I'm sorry, I know I'm being boring. There's just such a big conspiracy, you see. Mothers have to know each other incredibly well before they dare whisper the dreaded secret.'

'Which is?'

'Which is,' as Lucy dropped her voice, Steven bent his ear to her lips, '*sometimes I wish I didn't have them*. There. Look at you. You see? You're shocked and appalled. And I thought it was safe confessing to you because you're not a woman. You're not even a parent.'

'Thanks. I now feel like some lower life form, a sub-amoeba.'

Lucy laughed. 'You know what I mean. It's safe to tell you. You won't think I should have my children taken into care and be locked up for twenty years. Women aren't honest about all that stuff.' She waved one hand airily. 'Women aren't honest about anything at all.'

'Let me into the secret world of women. It's mystified me for years.'

'All right. Women lie all the time. They lie about the fact that they have half a bottle of wine alone, maybe a whole bottle. They lie about being blissfully in love with their husbands. They never admit that sometimes they let their children play Nintendo till ten p.m. without even checking whether they've done their home-work. Women,' Lucy stated authoritatively, 'or rather mothers, lie to other mothers about everything, because they are obsessively worried that every other mother on earth is perfect. Men don't do that, they don't lie to each other.'

'Oh, rubbish. Men lie about their careers all the time. About how far up the ladder they are, and their bonuses. Constant bragging.'

'That's not the same. That's lying about how much money they make, not lying about ordinary everyday stuff. Is it that men have naturally lower expectations themselves, or is it that less is expected of you lot?'

'I don't know, but I get the feeling that either way we're pretty much sunk in your book.'

'No, you guys are instinctively more secure, you're just not frightened about not being perfect.' Lucy shrugged. She could barely believe she was talking like this to Steven of all people, but it was so long since she'd had that sort of conversation with Mark.

Having already gone too far to recover herself, Lucy saw no reason to stop. 'This morning, just this morning, Gracie threw a fit because she thought Charlie's slice of bread and chocolate spread was bigger than hers. I spent five minutes discussing who had the bigger slice of bread, saying. "Well, Charlie's is larger, but yours is thicker . . ."' she laughed at herself. 'Can you imagine that?'

'Isn't that perfectly healthy sibling rivalry?'

'Perfectly healthy for whom? Not for me.' Lucy shook her head vehemently, liberating more hair. 'It nearly gave me a migraine.'

Steven held out his hand, palm up. 'Let's make a pact. Whenever we meet, which I hope will be frequently, let's agree never to talk about children, yours or anyone else's, never to talk about families. Let's pretend you are a child-free, independent and exotic world traveller and committed career woman.'

Lucy closed her eyes and shivered. 'I can't imagine anything more horrific.'

'Why?'

She answered simply. 'Because my children are my whole life. The whole of it. I adore my children, and I'd be lost for ever without them. But coming to London, being free of them for a few hours, a day or so, keeps me sane. At home I orbit around them, all the time, in a crazy, somehow regular pattern. OK, sometimes it's monotonous, but without them I'd just be adrift.' Her eyes were shining with conviction, and Steven was mesmerized. 'When I'm here, at the flat, I look out of the window and see all these people going on with their own lives . . . Sometimes I feel sorry for them, and I ache at not having my children in front of me, not holding them that minute, and being able to squeeze them. And then other times . . .' She shrugged. 'Sometimes it's hard not to envy people who don't have anything or anyone to – well, orbit around. People who can just do whatever the hell comes into their heads. See? I warned you, I'm a total nutcase.'

'I don't think so. I think you are remarkably sane. Grounded.'

'Grounded? Me? I'm just hanging on by my fingernails.'

'Your beautiful fingernails.'

Lucy had forgotten about the impulsive manicure. 'Oh, that's just corporate-wife stuff. I told you, I have to meet Mark later.' Second time around, the lie came perfectly easily. 'Take you, for example, you're free. You don't orbit around anyone.'

'The danger with poor sods like me, we sub-amoebas,' he smiled self-effacingly, 'is that we orbit around ourselves. That's a far more dangerous predicament.'

'You don't strike me as self-centred. You've been very patient listening to me ranting like this,' Lucy said, blushed, and reverted to the safer theme of maternal resentment, feeling quite mistakenly that Steven needed to be reminded of her parental and marital status. 'Please don't think I don't love my children, I do. I just want to have them, say, five and a half days a week.'

'Hence the bolt-hole in Charlotte Street?'

Lucy nodded. 'Exactly.'

'So you want to have your cake and eat it.'

'Of course I want to have it and eat it. I just don't want to have to *bake* it.'

'Talking of food, how's your pâté?'

'Absolutely delicious.'

'Good. Have some more wine.'

'I have to warn you, I'm now in the mood to get completely smashed.'

'Excellent,' Steven said. 'That makes two of us.'

All the time she talked, he bent his head close to hers, although the restaurant was not full, and the acoustics excellent by the standards of most London restaurants. He gave, both to Lucy and their fellow diners, the impression of complete absorption, as if her every observation struck him profoundly. Lucy found this a new experience, or at least a long-forgotten one, and the wine, and the otherworldliness of her situation eased her slowly back towards an ability that many women lose when they have children: the elusive ability to surrender to the mood of the moment.

Two hours later they were alone at the back of the restaurant, although towards the front two men still lingered over coffee. Elena had tutted over Lucy's half-eaten chocolate tart and refused to take it away, instructing Lucy to nibble at it. She said they were welcome to stay until six when they'd need to clear the table, providing Steven gave her a glowing review. It was raining outside, cold and gloomy, but they did not notice.

'Don't you have to file your copy?' Lucy asked.

'Not today. I have all the time in the world.' Steven looked at her, her expression so gentle and so hesitant, and felt responsible for the first time in many years. 'I'm quite happy just to sit here and talk, for as long as you can spare me the time.'

'How sweet.' Lucy dipped her head. 'It's very easy to talk to you.'

'You didn't feel that last time we had lunch.'

'That's true,' she admitted, 'but I feel . . . It's different now. You're different. You're . . .'

'What? What am I?' He covered her hand loosely with his.

Seductive, she wanted to say. Oh, God, you're so terribly seductive, and I don't know if you truly, genuinely want me, or you're just playing games, and I don't know if I have the strength to stop myself, or if I even want to, or what it is that has brought me here, if I'm not a bad person, and if I am . . . 'Foreign,' she said simply. 'You seem very foreign to me.'

'First an amoeba, now an alien . . . Maybe that's a promotion, but it's still going to take a long time to recover my self-esteem after this lunch. I'm quite human, you know: I worry about all the normal things, growing old, being alone, things passing me by.' He squeezed her hand, and looked serious. 'I'd like to tell you about something. I'd like you to help me make a decision.'

'Of course. If I'm any use.'

'I don't know anyone whose judgement I'd value more.' Steven put both hands to his forehead and rubbed out the wrinkles, then ran his fingers through his thick auburn hair. He clasped his hands behind his head and leaned back against the high maroon velvet bench. 'This will sound very silly, I warn you, but I'll tell you anyway. When I left university, five friends and I made a pact. We called it the Parachute Plan. We were twenty-one, with the world at our feet, or so we thought. We decided to meet up in 2000, when we'd all be roughly forty-five, near as damn it. We arranged to meet in the international arrivals hall at Mexico City airport at noon on the fourteenth of February. It's only a few months away.'

'How wonderfully exotic. I'd go like a shot.'

'You don't know why we agreed to meet. The idea was to throw our lives over altogether. To jettison them, and all our responsibilities.'

'What do you mean?' Lucy asked curiously.

'It was painfully serious at the time. We were close, a real clique. And so confident. At twenty-one, we decided that by the age of forty-five we'd probably have dull marriages, dull children, dull jobs, and our lives would be over.'

'I don't know if that's pessimism or foresight,' Lucy said slowly, looking straight into his green eyes, and then down into her glass.

'It was just student wank, as far as I'm concerned. Forty-five sounded a long way off, and very grim. So we agreed to throw it all up. Reconvene on neutral territory, have a splash-out lunch and review each other's lives. If there was a majority vote against any person's state, then they'd chuck it in and start afresh. I suppose it was about trying to be young for ever, for the next seventy years, not just seven.'

'Why Valentine's Day?'

'It happened to be Valentine's Day when we made the plan. We considered ourselves very, very cool back then,' he said, self-mockingly. 'We were above anything as conventional as dividing into cosy little romantic *têtes-à-têtes*, so we spent the evening together.'

'It was three men and three girls? Were you going out with one of them?' As the question left her lips, Lucy felt suddenly and absurdly jealous.

'One of the men, or one of the girls? Funnily enough it was *four* men and two girls – and I was slightly involved with both of them,' he winked, 'but only slightly. That's one reason why I suggested the six of us should go out together. It made Valentine's Day less complicated for me. The strange thing is that I can't remember who one of the men was – the Fourth Man, I call him to myself. It will be interesting to discover who he is, if he turns up.'

'You're going to go?'

'That's what I'm asking you. Should I?'

Lucy looked away. It sounded very tempting to her: she had no emergency escape route, no cronies with whom to meet and review her life. 'You have nothing to lose.'

'Absolutely nothing.' He turned his hands palms up. 'No wife, no children, no ties. Nothing to throw over. Nothing but the job. That's half the problem. The other half is, what if nobody else shows?'

'If they don't, no one will know that you did,' Lucy commented practically. 'Do you still see them?'

'Only one. Then there's the Fourth Man, whose face I can't even remember, let alone his name. The other three I haven't spoken to in over ten years.'

'Is the one you still see planning to go?'

'She's worried what her husband will think. She says she'll go if I go.'

Lucy pretended to be thinking hard. All she was capable of thinking was, He has a life, a full, separate life, friends, women. He'll go to Mexico City, hitch up with this old girlfriend, travel the world, and she'll be free, with him, and I am nothing but a sad housewife he's befriended, nothing at all . . . 'Of course you should go,' Lucy said, in the jolly-them-along voice she used when Charlie didn't want to go to school. 'If it's just you, then that's fine. If your girlfriend goes too, the two of you can have a holiday, and stuff her husband. And if everyone turns up, well, how interesting that will be . . .'

'I didn't say she was my girlfriend. I said we had been slightly involved a long time ago.'

Meaning, Lucy deduced, that they'd had sex, but it hadn't counted. Maybe he was the sort of man for whom it never counted. She shrugged. 'You know what I mean.'

'There's still the hitch that we made the plan to escape all our responsibilities, and here I am, forty-five, without any responsibility other than writing weekly crap that ends up in cat litter trays by Sunday. God, what a thought. I'm going to get another bottle of wine. Don't feel you have to drink it, if you don't want to. I can manage it all by myself. I know you have to meet your husband soon.' Steven attracted the waiter by waving the bottle, then swung back to face Lucy and asked abruptly, 'Would you come with me?' She met his eyes, and felt her diaphragm clench so hard that she couldn't breathe. 'To Mexico City?'

'No. Certainly not.'

'Because of Mark?'

'Oh, Steven. How would it look to say to your husband, "Hey, you don't mind if I piss off to Mexico City to spend Valentine's Day with a bloke you don't even know exists, do you?"'

'Doesn't Mark know I exist? Haven't you mentioned meeting me?'

'No, I haven't,' Lucy murmured, realizing, as surely as Steven did, what that meant. 'Is that a mortal blow to your pride?'

'No, not at all, it's perfectly understandable.' Steven felt triumphant.

'But it's not just because of Mark that I can't come.'

'It's because of me, then?'

'It's because it would just be a stupid mistake – the kind of mistake I always make.'

'Is it the sort of thing you've done before?' Steven asked quietly, dreading her answer in case she revealed herself as a different woman altogether, or went back to the cold, controlled female Elena had shown to his table.

'No, it's just the sort of mistake I'm likely to make, to do something without thinking at all, or just because it sounds like fun, and then find myself up shit creek. I'm a banana-skin person, quite literally.'

'What does that mean?'

'I don't know if I can explain it. OK. I'll just tell you the facts. Well.' Lucy closed her eyes for a moment, then stared at the table so she couldn't see his face. 'When I was a little girl, I left a banana skin on my parents' bedroom floor one Christmas Eve. We were only allowed to eat food in the kitchen or the garden, but I dropped it and didn't bother to pick it up. When my father asked if I'd done it I lied. I was a very bad liar. I still am. Anyway, he knew all the time it was me. He said he was cancelling Christmas and sent me and my little sister to bed. Everything was fine the next morning, but ever since, I've worried that if I don't think through all the consequences, Christmas will be cancelled. It's my fault: I slip up. I leave the evidence all over the place. I can't go to Mexico with you. I can barely have lunch with you.'

She raised her eyes slowly and Steven kissed her at once. Lucy saw it coming, and she did not move away. She let him kiss her mouth, and inside she felt the panicky, liverish feeling in her stomach that it was all going wrong slowly dissolve into a warm, fizzy feeling that it was all going *right*.

'Do you love Mark?' Steven asked quietly, his lips against her cheekbone.

'Yes, I do. It isn't about Mark at all.'

'You said women always lied about being in love with husbands.'

'Not me. I haven't lied about anything, not to you,' Lucy said earnestly, 'and if there's anything wrong with our marriage, it's not Mark's fault.'

'What's wrong with your marriage?'

'Nothing,' Lucy asserted, holding her fingertips against her mouth as she spoke. 'It's just that when you've been married for a while, it's so different from when you first fell in love. The *romance* of love goes, it has to. Sometimes you can hear it go *phut*, like a tiny little gasp. Anyway, you drift into something else, something solid and wonderful, but it's not the same, not awfully exciting. That's OK. And if you do hit a bit of a bad patch, you simply have to say to yourself, I'm going to look back on this next year and think, yes, that may have been a rough patch, but look how we pulled through.'

'And that's why you're here with me now? I just happened to appear in the middle of a sticky patch with Mark?'

Was he right? Was it just that the timing was right, and anyone would have done for her, had the same neurological effect on her that even now she could barely speak, and hardly breathe? She had not been conscious of anything being wrong with Mark until she had met Steven; even now Mark's only failing was that she was not his sole focus in life. *Now is the time*, Lucy instructed herself, for the light remark, the casual flippancy that would have brought them both soundly back to earth, stopped them peering over the precipice like daredevil teenagers. Love was in the balance, and could be tipped either way by the slightest thing. All the warning lights were flashing, the 'destruct' button glowed red, and she knew that if she pressed it there could be no going back, no abort system that could be applied later, in a reflective, more sober mood. She ran the tip of her tongue over her dry lips. The safe remark, the light remark, did not come; it did not come in time. Steven simply saw her looking uncomfortable.

'I'm sorry. It was idiotic to ask you to come to Mexico.' Steven inwardly cursed himself for his new-found and unsought moral sense. 'I had no right to do that, and even less to ask about your marriage. I'm sure you have a wonderful marriage. Mark's a lucky man.' He pushed away both their glasses simultaneously. 'What time are you meeting him? The least I can do is put you in a taxi and send you safely on your way. As soon as you've finished your chocolate tart.' He scooped up a forkful of the sinful stuff and Lucy opened her mouth obediently.

Everyone knows, or can at least imagine, the first stages of an affair when, however threatened one feels, one wriggles with the delightfulness of being desired. The first semi-innocent flirtation, the growing awareness that someone finds you interesting, intelligent, provocative, entrancing: that is irresistible, regardless of the admirer. The best moment is teetering right on the brink, when you can still choose to step backwards or forwards. Lucy found herself wobbling with a sudden sense of vertigo, and the more rationally she warned herself, and the more she saw how dangerous it all was, however delicious, and that if she went too far, had too much, it would cease to be delicious but would make her sick, once she'd tasted it she couldn't stop, because having a little bit, just a tiny bit more, was better than having nothing at all.

She pulled her head up and thrust her chin out. 'Mark's in Dorset. I'm here on my own.'

'In that case,' Steven said slowly, 'why don't you let your hair down?' He reached forward and felt through her hair with gentle fingers. As he withdrew two grips her chignon collapsed in a drift of blonde as soft as cobwebs.

Chapter Fourteen

The precursor of the mirror is the mother's face.

D.W. Winnicott

Lucy caught the last train that night and arrived home in the small, dangerous hours of the morning. The house was dark and mercifully silent; she had not phoned to say that she was returning, as she had not been certain, until the train pulled out, that she would be able to catch it, let alone stay on it. She dreaded finding Mark still up. As she walked upstairs on shaky legs she heard his muffled voice, and froze. The door to Grace's room was ajar. Lucy held her breath and pushed it softly open.

Mark was lying on the very edge of his daughter's bed on top of the Forever Friends duvet, barely clinging on. One arm was propped up on its elbow, and his hand clutched a pocket tape-recorder inches above Grace's head. The tinny sound that had halted Lucy in her tracks was a personal recording of *The Railway Children*. Six months earlier Mark had taped himself reading the story so that the children would be able to hear his voice when he was away on business trips. He had annotated and simplified the text for Grace's benefit, and interjected funny comments, such as, 'Now, Gracie, are you quite sure you brushed your teeth? Top *and* bottom?' 'Charlie? Was that a fart I just heard?' and 'Grace! Get back into bed this instant!' Mark's interruptions entertained his daughter far more than the story itself, and she knew exactly where they fell in the narrative, making rude noises before the fart reference and scrambling out of bed seconds before the instruction to get back into it. She adored the tape and insisted on hearing it most nights at bedtime, but the scheme had backfired: far from listening to it when Mark was away, she demanded his physical presence. Grace now gripped the two edges of her father's dressing-gown with tightly clenched fists. They were both fast asleep, Grace's dark lashes almost brushing her cheeks, Mark's flickering when his own voice became particularly emphatic.

Lucy did not rouse him. At some point he would awaken, chilled and stiff, and stumble back to their own bed, and be surprised to find her fast asleep in it. They were all accustomed to going to sleep with one family member, and waking up with another, or in a different bed altogether. Lucy prayed she would be asleep before Mark returned to their bed. She had the sort of face that revealed everything behind it, all the minute variations between joy and sadness, fear and guilt; a complete stranger, let alone Mark, could take one look at her and know everything. Even if she were asleep, her face might betray her. She could not let Mark look at her, not for a while, not until she had transformed herself into somebody quite, quite different. She took two sleeping pills. Across the vale, the Purcells slept deeply, hand in hand.

The children were surprised to see Lucy sit down groggily at the breakfast table the next morning.

'Mum – you said you had to stay in London!' Charlie helped himself to a second bowl of Corn Pops.

'I missed you all too much. I got home very late.'

'Tea?' Mark held up the pot and she nodded, hoping it wouldn't make her vomit.

'I tried to wake you up last night,' she told him, heaping sugar into her cup although she hated sweet tea, 'when I found you in Grace's room. You were dead to the world.'

'So were you. I came in at four, but a sledgehammer wouldn't have made any impact.'

'I took temazepam. Felt dreadful. Still do. Gracie,' Lucy scolded, 'what was Daddy doing in your bed?'

Grace looked innocently from one parent to the other, and lowered her eyes. 'I slept in my *own* bed,' she asserted. 'Maybe Daddy had a bad dream.'

'*God*, I feel terrible,' Lucy said, to no one in particular, shielding her eyes.

'Probably your normal pre-Christmas virus, darling. Remember, "'Tis the season to be jolly, fa-la-la-la-la . . ."'

Lucy held her head. 'Don't say that. It can't possibly be Christmas-time yet. It feels like it should still be September.'

'Christmas isn't far off.' Mark picked up the newspaper. 'My mother called yesterday to ask if we'd made any plans.'

'It's exactly thirty-six days to Christmas,' Charlie said authoritatively as Grace, unobserved by anyone except Abigail from her high-chair, carefully filled her bowl with milk and carried on pouring a drop at a time, watching it trickle over the sides and on to the table.

'Does she want to come here?'

'I had the feeling she wants you to invite her. What did you get up to last night?'

Lucy picked up the sports section and turned pages. 'Oh, nothing. I said, I felt awful.'

'You didn't see Dash?'

'Gracie! What on earth are you doing? What a mess!' There were

223

times when Lucy inwardly blessed the constant interruptions by her children; she conveniently forgot that just a few months, even a few weeks ago, she had been bemoaning the fact that she and Mark never had the chance of a private conversation. Now she busied herself with a sponge.

'How is she?'

'Who? Dash? The same as she always is, just fine – getting big.'

'No problems?'

'No. She takes to pregnancy very easily.'

'It must run in the family. Come on, Charlie!' Mark held out a toothbrush. 'Let's get this show on the road. Gracie, are you going to eat any of that, or just play with it?'

'I'm making a *painting*,' Grace explained scornfully, as if it were perfectly obvious.

Her father smiled indulgently.

Lucy rose. 'I'd better get some clothes on and take them to school.'

'I'll take them – you finish breakfast. Are we meant to be collecting Hannah Lewis?'

'That shows how often you do the school run. We never take her on a Friday.' As soon as she'd said this, and seen Mark's face harden, Lucy felt nervous. 'Sorry, Mark, I didn't mean that. We changed the routine a month ago or so.'

'If you're not happy with the distribution of labour in this family I suggest you think about going back to work.'

'For God's sake,' Lucy snapped, 'what's the big deal about taking the kids to school once in a blue moon?'

'I suppose you want me to take Abby too, so you can go back to bed?'

Lucy picked up the baby and stormed out of the kitchen.

In the time it took to stuff the two older children into their coats and buckle Grace into her car seat Mark had regained his equilibrium. He excused Lucy's short temper and apportioned it equally between the perennial marital dispute of who did what domestically – or, rather, who did *more* – and the fact that Christmas was coming. Lucy suffered from her own seasonal affective disorder: it had nothing specifically to do with lack of sunlight, rather the proximity of Christmas. She claimed to adore the festive season, and it was certainly the period when she shifted her maternal duties into a higher gear, believing that if normality was allowed to surface through the magic for one brief moment during the holiday she would have failed utterly. Mark did not see that it made any difference whatsoever to the children if they ate home-baked muffins on Christmas morning or shop-bought ones, and adopted the rational attitude that if it mattered so much to Lucy then she should be solely responsible for the production of the magical ingredients. This resulted annually in Lucy spending six weeks in a state of rising hysteria, followed by three days of frenzy, followed, on Boxing Day afternoon, by the realization that she had left all the home-baked muffins in the freezer, and insisted on everybody eating them then and there whether they liked them or not. After which she spent two days in bed with complete nervous exhaustion. No, all in all Mark was not a devotee of Christmas. As he grilled Charlie on his times tables, he did wonder how Lucy had seen her sister the day before: Dash had left a message on the machine in the late afternoon begging off dinner due to swollen ankles. Maybe she had rallied; maybe Lucy had gone round to her sister's house and seen her there. Seeing her sibling often put Lucy in a bad mood. Mark did not give the matter further thought. He was more concerned that two of his major clients had hinted they might have to transfer part of their business to a London dealer.

'Dad?'

'Yes, Charlie?'

'I've forgotten my homework.'

'It's too late to turn back now.'

'I'll get into trouble.'

'No, you won't. Homework's not that important when you're eight, believe me.'

'*Dad* . . . It *is*.'

'Nah. Nothing's important when you're eight, except listening to your mum and having a good time.'

'But, Dad . . .'

'It couldn't matter less, Charlie. Just blame it on me. Or say the dog ate it.'

There were distinct advantages in illness, Lucy decided, as she phoned Amy and asked if she could possibly look after Abigail, explaining that she felt like death. Amy could only offer two hours, as she worked for someone else on Friday afternoons, but Lucy leaped at it. When Amy bounced into the kitchen and swooped up the cooing, Readybrek-splattered Abigail, Lucy went back to bed and put a pillow over her head.

Mark met Samantha in the drive when he returned home to work, and although he had intended to check on Lucy, and apologize for being gratuitously shitty about the school run, Samantha was eager to draft a proposal to the two vacillating clients; a priority, he agreed, that could not wait. He settled down at his desk in the barn and resolved to take Lucy away for a long weekend after Christmas, finances permitting. Lucy loved romantic gestures, and he had been too preoccupied to make any recently. A weekend in Edinburgh might not break the bank.

While Mark struggled to preserve his clients and Lucy slept dreamlessly, Steven Armitage was also in bed but wide awake and smoking, thinking about Lucy. He lived in a top-floor flat in Bayswater, a place where people on their way up and people on their way down live cheek by jowl for a little while, among those who could go either way. The flat was surprisingly Spartan for a man who was so very much of the world. He took his pleasures outside the home, not in it, and found that the sharp contrast between one and the other enhanced his enjoyment. For all his apparent advocacy of the *bon viveur* creed, Steven was a solitary animal, and he needed somewhere private and plain to which he could retreat. Now Lucy had invaded this space. When he had first met her, he had popped her into the pigeonhole of endearingly scatty happily married woman. She had seemed both beautifully neglectful and beautifully neglected, and he had inwardly blessed her poor mug of a husband. Lucy made an appealing contrast to most of his female companions, who required ceaseless recognition of their attractiveness and forelock-tugging acknowledgement of their independence to boot. At the Vietnamese restaurant he had found Lucy perplexing – wary and suspicious where he had predicted childlike enjoyment of his blatant flattery, and fluttery flirtation. At Elena's he had realized that he was falling in love with her and there was nothing he could do about it. When he had unpinned her hair, and after, as they left the restaurant, she seemed to Steven to be a woman for whom everything could be sacrificed, if only he had anything worthy of sacrifice. She had quite inadvertently triggered a catch that opened up a secret room in himself. He found himself paralysed by her incertitude, feeling possessive and protective, and Steven had not known how to respond to those feelings, or how to escape them. When, after several long, slow hours of kissing her, Lucy had leaped to her feet, buttoned her shirt, and told him to leave *now*, *right away*, he had accepted it, when it would have been effortless to draw her back into his arms. 'I didn't mean it to be like this, for this to happen,' she had whispered at the door, her eyes wide as a doe's, 'I couldn't have meant this to happen.'

He had always divided the world into people with virtue and people without it, and was firmly of the opinion that virtue was not only grossly overrated but could be an enormous handicap. There were circumstances when it was the very last thing you wanted to discover in a companion. Steven Armitage was intimately acquainted with both virtue and the lack of it, but he had never before found himself positioned so firmly on the wrong side of the barrier.

There are many stages in the long slide into parental selfishness, and parents draw comfort from the conviction that their own crimes are insignificant relative to the neglect that others perpetrate on their offspring. The most common manifestation of neglect is trying to buy a little extra time of peace and quiet, something Mark labelled the Sunday-morning-reading-the-papers scenario, and Lucy thought of as the in-a-minute tactic. Lucy, at home most of the time with her children, employed it frequently. Charlie was too old to fall for it: he had a second hand on his watch and would stand waiting for it to complete a full circle, then say, 'OK, Mum. Time's up.' Grace still made no real distinction between ten minutes and next week. That afternoon, after she had fed Abigail and collected Grace from nursery, Lucy tried to write a letter while Grace played and Abigail had her afternoon nap.

'Mummy? Shall we make a safari park out of the cushions? Shall we? Yeah?'

'Umm, in a minute, darling, when I've finished this.'

'Let's make it now. I want to do it now.'

'In a minute, Grace, OK?' Grace began to whimper, and Lucy's face grew more stern. 'No, darling, I said *in a minute*. You must be patient. This is an important letter. Besides, if we make any noise it might wake Abby up.'

'We'll go in the garden, Mummy? That won't wake Abby.' Pause, as Lucy continued to write. Grace tucked her elbows to her sides and held her palms turned up, her head slightly cocked to one side, unconsciously imitating a pose that said, I am being so reasonable, don't you agree? 'Shall we? Shall we play in the garden?'

'In a minute, darling . . . You can go and play in the sandpit if you like, so long as you put your boots on. And don't turn the hose on.'

'And you'll come out and play later? OK? OK? In a minute?'

'Yes. In a minute,' she called after her daughter's disappearing back.

Twenty minutes later a wet nappy woke Abigail from her slumber on the sofa. Lucy screwed up her fourth attempt to explain to Steven why she could never see him again, and took the baby upstairs to change her. As she was securing the tabs she heard Grace screaming hysterically and raced down, her heart in her mouth, to find her daughter battering at the garden door. She was soaking wet and sobbing. The relief that she was only wet released an explosion of anger in Lucy. Grace had deliberately turned on the hose and drenched herself, despite being expressly forbidden. She was still wearing her sequined fairy slippers, now almost certainly ruined. Lucy tucked Abigail tightly under one arm, grabbed Grace's upper arm roughly with her free hand, almost dragged her into the hall and screamed, 'Grace, how *could* you be so silly!' Grace stood shivering and shocked: she looked warily at Lucy, turning her head away, as if her gentle mother had turned into a stranger before her eyes. It took only that newborn guarded expression in her four-year-old's eyes for Lucy's anger to turn on herself. That mistrustful look made even Lucy's teeth ache: she could feel each one as if they were inches apart; it didn't even feel like her own mouth any more. It was her fault that Grace had been alone and frightened, and instead of comforting her, when her daughter looked for safety, she had terrified her further. Lucy dropped to her knees, embracing both her daughters as the tears fell down her cheeks. Grace stood stiffly in the circle of her mother's arms. Each time her mother squeezed, she pulled back a little.

'Oh, God, I'm sorry, Gracie, Mummy's so, so sorry . . . I'm the most horrible mother that ever lived, and I don't deserve you. I'm sorry for everything . . .'

Grace put her arms stiffly around her mother's neck, and laid her cheek against Lucy's. 'Don't cry, Mummy. Here, you can cuddle my baby if you like,' she said soothingly, as Lucy's tears fell harder and faster.

'God, what on earth is wrong with me?' Lucy wailed to no one at all.

Her daughter's love was as easily reclaimed as it had been casually tossed aside, but Lucy was not certain if her trust could be so restored. Mother and daughters spent the remainder of the afternoon telling stories about princesses to each other, though Lucy's imagination was stretched thin. While she talked about Sleeping Beauty and raced to make brownies ready for Charlie's return home, she was also mentally drawing up a list of Christmas activities. She was determined to compensate for every harsh word and oversight she had ever committed. She yearned for rigorous penance. She resolved that there would be homemade advent calendars rather than the shop ones, which she always ended up opening herself after the fourth or fifth day, when the children had lost interest and she had to feign delight at the unveiling of yet another little lamb or star. She could fill each pocket with a sweet or a tiny toy. The children could make truffles together, and Lucy would sew new stockings – each child could choose their own material, and she could stitch on bells and ribbons and make stockings they would keep even when they were grown-up and had children of their own. This year, she swore, she'd remember to stock up on hundreds of batteries, and she'd remember to use a different wrapping paper for the presents from parents and those from Father Christmas. Charlie's belief was too frail to risk any logical deductions.

'Sometimes I'm a princess, you know,' Grace confided, licking out the chocolaty bowl, and putting her fingers into Abigail's mouth once for every third time they went into her own.

'I know you are, darling. What do you like doing, when you're a princess?'

'I have lots of pretty dresses, with frills and ribbons and everything, and lots of jewellery, and a *beau*-ti-ful palace, and lots and lots of princes.'

'What do the princes do?'

'They kiss me and buy me presents,' Grace replied airily. A sensible mother, a mother like Constance, would probably tell her daughter that was a load of nonsense, so that she wouldn't grow up to hit forty and face the fact that none of that was going to happen. A sensible mother had it in her power to spare her daughter romantic notions that would result in disappointment. Lucy caught herself wondering where her own many princes had gone, or if they still waited, just around the corner. She could not imagine Mark contemplating his dreams lying in dust about his feet, and trying to fall back on myths and magic and make-believe. Mark was far too mature, she thought nervously, happily occupied sorting out his catalogue and playing with his paints.

'OK, Grace – into the oven!'

'Me?' Grace giggled.

'Not you, you goose, the brownies.'

When the phone rang, Lucy held it in the crook of her neck as her hands were covered with flour and melted chocolate.

'Hello?'

'It's Steven.'

'You can't call here,' she said, in a low voice. 'You must never call here again.'

'Listen for a minute, and I promise I won't call you at home again.' Lucy didn't reply. 'Are you still there?'

'What do you want?'

'I need to see you –'

'No. I'm afraid that won't be possible.' Lucy spoke firmly, as if she were talking to a deliveryman, while her mouth filled with so much saliva that she had to keep swallowing and thought she'd be sick if her stomach weren't so hollow, and her head began to pulse with a nervous, sinusy pain.

'I must. Is Mark there with you?'

'No. That doesn't make any difference anyway. I just can't do it. I'm sorry, but there it is.'

His voice dropped, and she ached. 'Lucy, please think. We have to meet, if only to end it.'

'There's absolutely nothing to end,' she insisted, knowing then, all at once, that she'd fallen in love with him.

'Yes, there is. It will never be finished properly, not for you and not for me, if we don't meet. See me for your family's sake, if not for mine.'

'You shouldn't have called.'

'What should I have done? Haunted Charlotte Street? We have to meet. Tomorrow.'

'I can't. Tomorrow's Saturday.'

'If not tomorrow, then next week.'

'I can't know I'm going to see you and then wait a week,' Lucy whispered, with longing. If she had to do it, if there was nowhere to run away to, then it had to be done swiftly and savagely, like putting an injured animal out of its misery. 'I can't think about you for a whole week . . .'

'Oh, Lucy . . . Tomorrow it is, then. Tell Mark the truth, or make an excuse, I don't give a damn. Yes, yes, I do. I'd rather you told him the truth.'

'I can't. You don't understand.'

'I understand you perfectly. Meet me for lunch tomorrow. One o'clock?'

'No . . . I can't have lunch with you.'

'Fuck, Lucy, I don't care what we have. I'll be outside the flat at one o'clock.'

After collecting Charlie from school Lucy set about preparing roast chicken and gravy, a firm favourite with all the children, and making bread sauce. After dinner she insisted she would put all the children to bed single-handedly.

'Really, Mark, I want to. I was vile to Grace this afternoon. I lost my temper with her for no reason at all, and scared her half to death.'

'What happened?'

'Nothing, I don't want to talk about it. I was just a selfish pig.'

Grace wrapped herself around her mother's leg. 'You're not a pig, Mummy. You're not. You're my mummy.'

'If Mum's a pig,' Charlie started laughing, 'that makes you a piglet, Grace.'

'I am not a piglet! You're a piglet!' Grace stamped her foot and Lucy picked her up.

'Are you sure you don't want me to help?' Mark asked doubtfully.

'Absolutely. Honestly. I'd enjoy doing it.'

Mark stood at the sink, washing his hands. 'In that case, do you mind if I muck around in the garage for a bit?' He made it sound as if he were some old bore who spent his free time fiddling about with a car engine.

'Why should I mind?' She put down Grace to fill the dishwasher with soap. 'Oh, by the way . . . do *you* mind if I go back to London tomorrow? Just for the afternoon?'

'Oh, Mum . . .' Charlie complained. 'It's the weekend.'

Mark raised his eyebrows. 'To see Dash?'

'How did you know that?'

'I know you didn't see her yesterday.' He stood looking at her quizzically, until Lucy shrugged and turned back to the sink.

'You're right, I didn't see her. I lied about it. I didn't feel up to seeing her last night and I've been feeling guilty about it all day today, so I thought maybe I'd go tomorrow.'

'Of course you should.' He wiped his hands on his sweater. 'Remember we're having dinner at the Purcells' tomorrow night – we've got Amy booked.'

'We are?'

'It's Luke's birthday.'

'Oh, yes, I'll make sure I'm back in time. Or I'll take the car and meet you there.'

'Fine. You know where I am if you need a hand.'

'Mark?'

'Yes?'

'What happened to that client – the one who might leave?'

'Which one? There were two of them.'

'Either. Both.'

'I think we've probably lost Henchard's. We might just be able to hang on to Blandford Wines. If not, we're really going to have to tighten our belts.'

She watched him walking slowly across the cobbled yard to the garage with his torch. She hadn't set foot in it for nearly three months, or laid eyes on the painting he was working on. She wanted him to invite her into his den and request her opinion, but if he didn't choose to she would not force herself upon him. He hadn't once asked her to look at a painting since they'd bought the flat.

'Come on, darlings, upstairs, and we'll read as many stories as you like.'

'*The Wind and the Widows*!' Grace shrieked delightedly.

'Oh, God, I wish I didn't have to live with all these babies . . .' Charlie trudged up the stairs behind his mother.

Chapter Fifteen

Experience is a good school but the fees are high

Heinrich Heine

'Chef?'

'Lewis. You have a brain like a sieve. How many times do I have to tell you?' Constance growled, taking out her frustration on the Hollandaise. 'If we were a proper establishment, with a proper brigade, then you could be *sous chef*, and we'd have a *chef de partie*, and a *commis chef* and various other sub-chefs and underlings. As it is, it's you, me and that strange thing in the corner,' she jerked her head at the work-experience boy who was washing up while dreaming of Michael Owen, quite oblivious to her insults, 'so *don't* call me Chef.'

'Right. Constance? Why are single men always thinner than married men?'

'Is this a joke? You know I have no sense of humour at work. Not much of one at home, either.'

'Answer.'

'Because men can't cook? Lewis, what the hell are you doing with those lamb shanks? Waiting for them to grow wool?'

Constance sighed long-sufferingly. 'OK. I give up: why *are* single men always thinner than married men?'

Lewis smiled. 'Because when a single man gets home, he looks in the fridge, and then goes to bed. And when a married man gets home –'

'He looks in the bed, then goes to the fridge. Very, very funny, arsehole. It's a known fact, Lewis, that married men have sex, on average, three times as often as single men.'

'Do they?' Lewis stopped in surprise, whisk upheld. He stood gazing at her, thinking that if he was her husband he wouldn't ever get out of bed.

'Of course not, you berk! Married people never have sex at all, not with each other anyway. And you won't be capable of ever having it again if you don't bloody do something with those lamb shanks!'

'Yes, thank you, Lewis, you're a joy to work with. No, no, I insist.' Lewis swung round to the oven, having adopted a light, feminine voice in a poor imitation of his boss, 'and it's *soo* sweet of you to take over tonight so I can have a Saturday night off with my hubby . . . Pay rise? But of course you can have a pay rise, just name your figure.'

The dishwasher smiled dreamily into the sink, and Constance grinned at Lewis. 'You say one single word that even resembles "pay" or "rise" and you'll be cooking scampi in the basket at the Dog and Fiddle,' she warned, and slapped his backside with the flat of a Bunmei knife. 'I told you, I want tonight off because we're celebrating Luke's birthday.'

'Blame it on the children. That's what women always do when their blokes think they're going to get lucky.'

'Are you sure you're going to be OK?' Constance asked three hours later. 'I've asked May to come in two hours early, Sally will be in as usual and you've got Bozo the clown over there all night.

You've checked the bookings?'

'Of course. What are you cooking tonight?'

'Fish to start, then beef Wellington, nothing fancy. Luke loves beef. Lewis, did you remember to take the duck off the menu? You can't possibly do the duck on your own.'

'Constance, we've only got fourteen bookings tonight. Spread over three hours. I can manage fourteen covers. It's not as if it's the first time you've left me in charge.' Lewis sniffed, and summoned his courage. 'Go and have fun. Or go and have sex – have one for me.'

'You're such a smart-arse!' She patted his cheek and stepped outside, carrying her coat over her arm. It was freezing cold and raining; her car windscreen had misted up, and a heavy fog drifted and coiled blowsily around the Lonely Falcon. She loved winter weather and was invigorated by it. Stamping her feet, Constance lit a cigarette, paused at her car door, then walked back and rapped on the kitchen window. 'Lewis? Don't worry about the cold starters – you won't get orders for any tonight.'

'A tenner says you're wrong.'

'Fifty quid says I'm right.' She winked slowly. 'Always put your money where your mouth is, child, or you'll never get anywhere in this business. And remember, a good chef isn't the one who never makes mistakes – a good chef is one who learns from them.'

Lucy decided to drive to London so that she would not be able to drink. She hated admitting that she was being so calculating; she had lain awake half the night trying to resolve much more than the matter of transportation. In the morning she stared at herself in the mirror and knew she looked horrible. As she was leaving she saw Mark with all three children at the door of the garage and tooted the horn. Charlie came to the car window. 'Give Auntie Dash my love.'

Mark, holding Abigail in one arm and with Grace tugging the sleeve of his sweater, approached more slowly. 'We're all going to do some painting.'

'I'm amazed you're letting them into the holy of holies . . .' Lucy wished she hadn't said that: it had sounded more caustic than she'd intended, like everything she had said to Mark the past few weeks, and most things he had said to her. She had no time to repair the damage. 'Have fun. I'll see you all later.'

'At the Purcells', remember?' Mark called after her.

Steven wasn't even wearing a coat. As she drove slowly down Charlotte Street looking in vain for a parking place, she saw him waiting outside the door of number 53, blowing on his fingers and holding a bunch of flowers. Fifteen minutes later he was still there, stamping his feet.

'These are for you.'

'How lovely.' Lucy held them stiffly. 'But what am I going to do with them? I can't take them home. I'll have to take them up to the flat.'

They were both ill at ease. Steven waited at the foot of the steps, but when she glanced back from half-way up he changed his mind and followed her. He closed the door behind him in the little hall, and leaned against it, waiting while she found a vase and filled it with water. 'I'm sorry, Lucy. I've put you in a tricky position.'

'Oh, don't say that! You can't claim all the credit.' Lucy stood on the far side of the room and found the flat cramped for the first time. All that wide-open space, all the secrets of former occupants, the little duets of joy and distress that had passed within those walls crowded in on her.

'I've fallen in love with you, Lucy.'

'That's a bit premature, isn't it?' Lucy tried to speak lightly, but her voice rang false and brittle in her own ears.

240

'I don't know if it's premature or not. I only know it's true.'

'I thought we were meeting to say goodbye.'

'That's what I'm trying to do.'

'Well, I don't know what I feel about you,' Lucy said quickly, 'but I can't see you any more.'

'If you don't care about me, why bother to stop seeing me?'

'Because I think about you too much.' Lucy paced the galley kitchen, banging the brushed steel cupboard doors randomly. 'And thinking about you is stopping me from thinking about Mark. Maybe it's even getting in the way of my loving Mark. I can't think about both of you at once, I just can't. So I have to stop thinking about you.' He began to walk slowly towards her, and she pressed herself against Constance's slim-line kitchen units, the greatest distance she could put between them. 'I'm going to stop thinking about you, today, right now. Before anything starts.'

'I thought something had started.'

'No, it hasn't. That was a mistake.'

'Look – I won't hurt you. I couldn't.'

'You already have. If you hadn't been here that night, when I came with Abby –'

'If you hadn't come – if you hadn't been trying to score a point over Mark that night –'

'Just leave Mark out of this!'

'I'd love to, but you told me about walking out in a strop, remember? You told me when we were kissing on that sofa.' He pointed to it as if her memory needed jogging.

'Just don't come any closer, not an inch.' Lucy held up one solitary index finger, and Steven paid it even less heed than her children did.

'Lucy, darling, you have to let go sometimes, you just have to let go for once, or it will never stop mattering . . .'

'Please don't,' she said, as he kissed her neck, 'oh, please don't,' as he kissed her mouth, 'Oh, God, no, don't,' as he picked her up in his arms and carried her to her bedroom, kicking the door open, 'My God! Steven, if you care for me at all, please don't . . .'

'Why is it that the people who believe least in God and most in fate are the first to yell for God when they want help?' Steven sat on the edge of the bed looking down at Lucy who lay in a position of complete abandonment. 'Do you really want me to leave?'

'Yes. I want you to have never come. I was happy before I met you.' I want to let go, she thought, I want to let go and be shameless, so long as I don't fall apart altogether.

'You weren't happy. If it wasn't me, it would have been somebody else, sooner or later.'

'No – that's not true! I'm not a bored housewife, I'm not – It's you . . .' Lucy twined her arms around his neck and felt the tendons tighten. 'Have you been involved with other married women?'

'A few,' he replied curtly. 'But I've never felt what I feel about you. I haven't cared that they've been married – I've even been glad about it. I love you, Lucy. I don't know what to do about it, but I love you.'

'You don't know me; you don't know how mean and selfish I am.'

You may well be, but that doesn't make any difference. I love you.' He buried his face in her hair.

'Doesn't it matter what I feel?'

'Even if you loved me, you'd have to deny it, so no, it doesn't bother me. I can let myself believe whatever I like.'

'Steven . . .' She pulled him closer.

'Go on, Lucy. Tell me you don't love me. Tell me you don't even like me, and that you don't want me to make love to you. Go on, say it.' She shook her head mutely then let it drop back, exposing her white throat. Steven let her fall gently against the pillows.

If Lucy had thought, however briefly, of the possible consequences of her abandoned gesture, she would have reeled away from herself, and him, in horror. She did not think: it was of crucial importance that she hang on to the idea that she had no choice. Steven was right that the deal had to be finished: she could not live in guilt for the rest of her life with no concrete reason for it other than kissing; clinging on to virtue by the skin of her teeth was less rewarding than she imagined it would be. She had come to London in all innocence – *oh God, if only, if only it could have been like that* – and if he hadn't brought her flowers they would never have gone to the flat at all. That these things happen because of a series of random and supposedly unconnected events is one of the comforts of the guilty. How many short-lived butterflies – as if their brutally reduced life span wasn't enough to put up with – have been blamed for earthquakes and tidal waves, as well as the relatively minor seismic tremors of adultery? But time and again, myths stand in to take responsibility, and lead people back to the dares and games of childhood: if I say my eight times table backwards, the teacher won't know I cheated on my exam paper; if I don't step on the pavement cracks, Mummy will be in a good mood; if he loves me, he won't ever betray me; if I never admit it happened, even to myself, it will be *just as if it never happened*.

If she could have him, absolutely, once, be a girl again, a bad girl, even, as she had never been, and hang the consequences, that was not so mighty a crime. It was a crime one could be forgiven. This was her last chance to meet a prince, to leap on a boat, destination unknown, with nothing but a change of knickers in her handbag, to give it all up, yet have the certainty that two hours later she could claim it all back again as if she'd deposited her marriage in a left-luggage locker. Steven was lovely and loving, and wildly different from Mark – the way he touched her, the feel of his hands, so smooth, so silken, the smell and the touch and the feel of him, the way his voice caught in his throat, the way he pulled back to stare at her face, the way he *loved* her . . . Lucy stopped thinking at all. She had thrown caution to the winds, and when you do that, you invariably overlook what the winds might throw back in exchange. Then she heard the flat door open.

'Don't move,' Lucy hissed.

'Oh, Christ,' Steven groaned, trying not to move, holding himself up above her and feeling that he had suddenly slid from the pages of *Anna Karenina* into a farcical whodunnit.

'Mark?' Julian's voice boomed. 'Luce? I know you're in there . . . You don't have to sneak off to have sex when you're married, don't you know that?' His approaching footsteps rang sharply on the bare wooden boards. Lucy pushed Steven off her and fought her way out of the gauze-draped bed. She stumbled over their discarded clothes and grabbed a towel.

'Julian!' She pulled the door closed and instinctively held on to the door knob behind her back. 'What on *earth* are you doing here?' she said, in a overly bright and busy voice.

Julian glanced over her head at the closed door. 'Do you want me to wait outside, Lucy?' He gazed steadily at her with the gravest expression.

'Mark's not here,' she said in a rush. 'I was just having a shower. If we share a flat, you're going to have to get used to seeing me in a towel without getting shy . . .' Her eyes pleaded with him not to say another word, to take what he wanted and get out, to pretend he'd never been there. Julian looked at her unblinking. 'Get dressed. Tell whoever's in there to get out. I certainly don't want to know who he is. I'll wait for you downstairs, and we'll discuss this on the train home.'

'You can't speak to me like that!'

'It would be very easy for me to go into your bedroom and

confirm my suspicions. Would you like me to do that?' Lucy looked away, clutching the towel over her breasts. 'No, I thought not. And, frankly, that's a relief. Right.' He checked his watch. 'You – and I – are expected at my son's birthday dinner in less than four hours' time. I'll give you ten minutes to get dressed. At three thirty I'm taking a taxi to the station. If you are not on the train with me, I'll make your apologies, and explain how you were otherwise engaged.'

'Julian, don't be bloody outrageous . . .'

'Ten minutes, Lucy,' Julian said coldly. 'Then I'm leaving.'

'My car's here . . .' Her voice finally faltered.

'Fine. I'll drive. I'll be outside when you're ready.'

'Julian's waiting for me.' Lucy's face was white.

'Tell him to fuck off, whoever he is.' Steven put his arms around her.

'He's Connie's husband. He knows about you – he knows someone's here – everything. I have to go.'

'Lucy, don't cry . . .'

She turned on him in a rage. 'How dare you? This is my life, right? My husband, my marriage, my children. My *flat*. How dare you tell me not to cry when I ought to be screaming?' She began to pull on her clothes, the M&S knickers, the worn bra, the black tights, the short skirt and long cardigan that she had chosen with such deliberate carelessness that morning. 'It's all so easy for you, isn't it?'

'Lucy, Lucy, don't panic, sweetheart –'

'Just go, please? Wait ten minutes after I've left – no, no, you go first. Right now. Julian doesn't know you, does he? Just go!' She began to weep noisily, wiping her face with the sheet.

'I'll talk to him, I'll fix things.'

'Don't even look at him! Walk straight across the street, for God's sake.'

Steven put on his clothes as Lucy sobbed, then cradled her wet cheek. 'I will be waiting for you next week, just as we arranged. Lucy, I love you, that's all that matters. I'll always be there when you want me.' When he closed the street door behind him he saw a tall, bulky man pacing restlessly outside the deli. Their eyes met for an instant, then Steven strolled across the street, fingering the coins in his pocket, and entered the café across the road.

Julian took Lucy's keys when they reached her car and held open the passenger door for her. Neither of them spoke until they were on the M3.

'I'm very . . .' Julian's eyes were fixed on the road. *Oh, please, God, no, don't let him say that*, Lucy thought, *not that!* as he uttered the words 'disappointed in you'. She made no reply. 'It's possible, however, that we can keep this between ourselves,' he continued, 'so long as you can give me certain assurances . . .'

Lucy hunched into the far corner of the passenger seat. 'Who the fuck do you think you are, Julian? Bloody NATO? Or are you practising your speech for when Chessie gets kicked out of school? Save it, OK? You can talk to your own wife like that, but not to me.'

'My own wife hasn't given me any cause.'

'That's what you think.'

Without comment Julian stared ahead into the freezing fog and stream of cat's eyes rushing past them. He did not enjoy the role of stern parent: it was one he had always gratefully allowed Constance to assume. Now he searched his conscience. 'I'm sorry, Lucy. I'm sorry that I came in, that I had to be the one –'

'You jumped to conclusions.'

'Did I?' Julian glanced quickly at her, hoping that she was right. 'Tell me I'm wrong, that there wasn't anyone there with you. That you are not having an affair.'

246

'I am not "having" an affair,' Lucy said sulkily, then covered her face and began to cry again. 'It was the first time, just today, just now. Oh, Christ, I hate you, I hate myself, I hate everyone . . .'

'Then it's not the end of the world,' he said uncomfortably. 'I'm sure there's a way out of all this.'

'Yes, there is. You can say nothing about it and let me get on with my own life.' Lucy sniffed noisily, pulling herself upright.

'Do you regret it?'

'I don't know what I think. What does regret matter, anyway? You're so bloody Catholic about it all, like you can have a fling on Saturday, be bloody sorry on Sunday and go back to it on Monday. Does it change anything at all if I regret it?'

'It changes everything.'

They listened to the rhythmic *thwup thwup* of the wipers as the rain started again.

'I don't have a present for Luke.'

'I don't think that matters in the scheme of things.'

'I can't go to dinner, I can't. I can't sit there feeling you condemning me. You'll have to leave me at home.'

'You have to go, or you won't be able to look at any of us again. And I don't condemn you. Who is he, Lucy? An old friend?'

'I thought you didn't want to know anything about it.'

'I want to know what led you to start an affair.'

Your wife, Lucy thought. She put it in my mind, and she was responsible, which probably means that you are indirectly responsible, you superior bastard . . . Except that it was me who did it, and me who got caught, and it's all bloody banana skins all over the place . . .

'Lucy? Do you know why?'

'It just happened.'

'That's not good enough.' Julian winced as the words tripped off his tongue. 'Listen, Lucy, I do understand, and I'm not prying. I'm

247

trying to give you some good advice. Work out now what it was that led you into this, and you can find your way out.'

'I can?' she whispered.

'If you want to.' He leaned closer to the windscreen, struggling to see the way ahead. He wished very much that it was Constance who had walked into the flat unexpectedly, and that she was here to sort things out: she would have known absolutely the right thing to say. He tried, not for the first time in his life, to put himself in his wife's mind. 'Do you love him?' he asked quietly.

'I don't know. I just don't know. I've never doubted loving Mark, but somehow –'

'Constance says,' he began, 'Constance believes that a man can love two women at the same time, but that a woman can only love one person at a time.'

'That's nonsense.' Lucy said bitterly. 'Women are the ones who are expected to hold everything together, love hundreds of people at once – families, children, friends.'

'I meant romantically, sexually even.'

'I don't think Connie's right. I did love Mark. I do love Mark. But . . .'

'It wasn't enough?'

'How can you love someone "enough"?' Lucy exploded. 'What does "enough" mean, for God's sake? I mean, we have just "enough" money to live nicely on, way more than most people, but does that stop us wanting more? Isn't one child "enough" – or two – or three? Why do some people go on? Enough doesn't mean anything. *Everybody* wants more than "enough".' She sneaked a look at him. 'Everybody except you, apparently. I thought I had enough. I thought I had everything. I didn't want a sodding flat in London, or a lover, or anything else. I was perfectly happy.'

'Except that you weren't. What was missing?'

'The magic. The thing that makes it all suddenly special.'

'Which is?'

'You'd never understand.'

Julian did not to try to convince her that he might be able to, and had some experience in the subject. 'Lucy, you have put me – inadvertently, I know – in a very difficult position. If this affair continues, I don't think I can hide it from Connie. Or Mark.'

'I'm not asking you to hide anything, just not to mention it.'

'That's the same thing.'

'I guess you'd tell Mark for some sort of male-solidarity thing, but why would you have to tell Connie?'

Because she is the person who puts me straight, and I need her judgement to shore up my own . . . 'Because she is my wife, and I have no secrets from her. If I believed that the affair was over, genuinely over, I could sleep easily without mentioning it.'

'You're threatening me.' Lucy had turned sideways in her seat. Julian could feel her wide, shocked eyes staring at him, but he did not look at her. He cleared his throat to deny her accusation and found she had been quite justified in making it.

'That's correct. End it, as soon as you can. Tonight I will tell them both what happened, unless you give me your word that you won't see him again.'

'You have no right to do that.'

'Do you honestly believe I enjoy it?' he replied angrily. 'Do you think I have nothing better to do with my time than involve myself with your private affairs?'

'That's the impression I'm getting, yes. Is this because we share the flat, is that what's upset you, that some golden rule has been broken?'

'No. If it helps you to believe that, you may.' Julian had never been able to understand why so many people saw him as a slavish follower of rules. Since he was a boy, he had been teased for respecting authority, for paying too much heed to the laws of good conduct. In his own heart he had never consciously observed them.

'If I give you my word, that's enough?' He nodded curtly in reply. 'You still think my word's worth having?'

'Yes, I do, Lucy. You have never given me any cause to doubt it.'

Lucy felt childishly grateful for his confidence, but she was still resentful. 'You can't treat me like a child.'

'Do whatever you have to do, and I will follow suit.'

Lucy couldn't breathe; she was gasping for air in the close confines of the car, wishing herself elsewhere, yet in some strange way relieved that she had been exposed. She would do as little as she could to support life; she would shut down all operating systems; she would not show her heart, not by a word, not by a glance; she would be stone.

'All right, Julian. I give you my word. It's over. Truly, it had barely started.'

He stopped at her house so she could change. Lucy hugged her children, wishing she could crawl into bed with them and hide in one of their let's-pretend worlds. Mark had already left. She felt she ought to wear red to complete the branding that Julian had started, but she settled for a black dress, and they drove on to the celebration.

Chapter Sixteen

Love ceases to be a pleasure when it ceases to be a secret.

Aphra Behn

'At last! We'd nearly given up on you!' Constance came out into the driveway with Mark at her side. 'What happened to your car, Julian?'

'I left it at the station. I bumped into Lucy by chance at the flat, and we decided to travel together. Where's my boy?'

'He's waiting for you in the drawing room, all the young ones are there, looking terribly grown-up and nervous. Don't forget to tell Chessie how marvellous she looks. Lucy, you look lovely – come and have a drink. Mark and I started without you.'

Mark kissed his wife's cheek and slipped his arm through hers, bending close to whisper urgently in her ear, 'Did you bring a present for Luke?'

'No. You said you would.'

'Did I? Blast. Do you think we can give him cash?'

Lucy did not reply. She followed her host and hostess inside and began to count the minutes until she could leave. In the drawing room she barely noticed the effort the four youngsters had made to blend with the adults. Francesca had invited a girlfriend from school, both of them contriving to appear bored and sophisticated but instead looking delightfully fresh and pretty. Luke and his best friend, Spig, balanced tentatively between impulsive boyhood and wary adolescence, looked stiff and buttoned up. Julian held out his hand to his son, then just as Lucy's lip curled, pulled him into an embrace and tousled his hair.

'Right!' Julian said boisterously. 'Who's for champagne? Luke? Miranda? You'll all have a glass, won't you? Spig, be a good chap and fetch another bottle from the fridge. Mark will teach you the proper way to open it.'

Lucy took Luke's arm and led him away. 'Luke, I've been a twit and left your present at home. Can I bring it over next week?'

'Of course you can, Lucy,' Luke blushed becomingly, 'but you don't have to buy me birthday presents. I know you did when I was a kid, but you don't have to now. How's Charlie?'

'He's fine, really well. He looks up to you so much, you know.'

'He's a good bloke,' Luke acknowledged, as if they were talking about a teacher at school, and not an eight-year-old. 'His head's screwed on right.'

'I'm so glad you think so.' All the time, Lucy felt Julian's eyes watching her, waiting for her to put a foot wrong. Even as the thought crossed her mind, he took her elbow and led her back into the centre of the room.

'Lucy, have you met Chessie's friend Miranda?'

Constance kept dashing off to the kitchen. Lucy trailed after her to get away from the two men and intending to confess, and found Connie trickling a pale yellow, sticky substance over an empty magnum bottle.

'What on earth is that?'

Constance smiled. 'Parmesan.'

'It doesn't look like Parmesan.'

252

'Wait and see.'

The cheese cooled into a delicate curved tracery of cobweb, which Constance expertly slid off the bottle. 'It's a tuile roof for the sea bass,' she explained, 'something like a cheese brandy snap. I have to leave them to crisp up.'

'Incredibly grand food for a fifteen-year-old's party, Con.'

'This isn't really Luke's party. He's having a disco in the holidays, renting a hall. Which, of course, has made Chessie furious, so she now wants to have a New Year party here. Over my dead body.' Constance winked. 'No, this dinner isn't for Luke, it's for me, *my* celebration. Do you think I'm selfish?'

'Of course you are, but you're entitled to be, I guess.'

'What were you doing in the flat today?'

Lucy swallowed. 'Odds and sods. Is there any champagne in here?' Constance nodded towards an open bottle, her hands busy with the next tuile. Lucy struggled to keep her composure and not break down. *I will be stone*, she reminded herself, *for ever*.

'What's up, Luce? You look like you've seen a ghost.'

'Oh, I'm OK. Your children are so grown-up, I can't believe it.'

'I know. Would you take those canapés out for me? Warn the kids they're anchovy. The girls may eat them, but I bet the boys won't.'

Lucy wanted to beg Constance to help her; she wanted to hide away in the kitchen and collapse in the arms of a veteran who would instantly make it all better, calmly and smoothly, but instead she passed canapés.

The sea bass first course was the type of dish that stopped conversation for a good three minutes. Spig was the first to speak.

'This is just . . . It's bloody – Sorry, it's amazing, Mrs Purcell, really wicked. My mum never makes proper restaurant stuff like this. I won't even eat the fish she makes at home.'

Constance threw a warning glance at the two girls, who were giggling and making faces. 'Thank you, Spig, it's very sweet of you to say so.'

'Spig's always got a really good line for the grown-ups,' Luke teased his friend. 'He spent all afternoon thinking that one up.'

'It's a *tour de force*, Con,' Mark seconded.

Lucy smiled wanly and wondered how she could swallow a second mouthful.

Julian, at the far end, beamed down the length of the table at his wife. 'I'd like to propose a toast to my son. Would you all raise your glasses to Luke, on the occasion of his fifteenth birthday? Luke, we are enormously proud of you,' the boy blushed as Spig elbowed him in the ribs, 'and we always will be.'

'Dad, please, that's enough,' Luke growled, his voice crackling with self-consciousness. Constance stroked his arm.

'Not quite,' Julian persisted. 'I know how mortifying it is to have parents, let alone have them stand up and make humiliating speeches in front of your friends, but there is a time when these things have to be said. Your mother and I are certain that you will lead a good and valuable life. Our only wish is that it is happy, and that you make others as happy as you have made us. To Luke.'

'To Luke,' they echoed, standing up. Miranda was torn between the wish that Luke were two or three years older, and the wish that her own parents were more like the Purcells. She looked wistful until Francesca pulled a face at her.

'Now,' Julian continued, 'why doesn't everyone say what they remember most about being fifteen. Mark?'

'Oh, come on, Julian,' Lucy remonstrated. 'That's worse than the worst kind of party game, and it's an agony for Luke.' The birthday boy smiled his gratitude at her.

'Mark?' Julian repeated.

'Christ. I don't know if I have any words of wisdom . . . OK,

Luke, when I was fifteen, all I wanted was to play football, for my school, my town, for England. Only problem was I was complete crap at it.' They laughed in relief. 'A couple of years later, I'd forgotten all about football. All I'm saying is that when you love something, just go for it. Don't be rational, don't doubt yourself, just do it. And never waste time worrying. If something's not meant to be, it won't happen, and something better will take its place.'

'Like wine?' Constance suggested with a smile.

Francesca tossed her hair back. 'When I was fifteen, I only wished I didn't have to put up with such a complete prat for a little brother. But Mark's right, things change. Now I think you're OK. Go on, Manda, it's your turn.'

Miranda blushed. 'I haven't got anything to say . . . When I was fifteen I wasn't any good at anything. I was useless at school, and I didn't have any friends. I hated it. But I'm much happier now . . .'

'And you're incredibly smart, and you don't even have to try at school, which makes the rest of us really sick.' Francesca finished supportively.

'Luce?'

Lucy pushed the fish around on her plate, her heart beating far too fast. 'I really hate this sort of thing. Can any of us even remember what being fifteen really felt like? I don't think I can. I don't know if I can remember being twenty. Even if I could, I don't see why Luke should take advice from any of us.' She was trying not to look at any of them but she could not continue to stare at her plate and allowed her eyes rise to meet Luke's. She seriously doubted that she could control her voice much longer. I don't know if I was happy or sad at fifteen, she thought; I don't know if it even matters. I don't know if I was happy last year, or happy in bed with Steven a few hours ago, or ever happy. I wonder, Luke, if you will find yourself in my position when you're thirty, or forty, or fifty, just not knowing anything at all? I wonder what your dad will say to you then? 'The only thing I can say is I hope my Charlie's as nice as you when he's your age.'

'Very well put,' Julian said smoothly. 'Constance?'

'I remember being fifteen very well. I felt I was too young to do anything, and frustrated. I was in such a hurry to get on with life. I haven't learned my lesson –'

'Except now you're too old to do anything, Mum!'

'Thank you *very* much for reminding me, Chess. Sometimes you just need to slow down and take time to look around, to appreciate exactly what it is that you have, right then and there, at that moment.' She held Luke's hand. 'At *this* moment.

'Oh, no, Mum's going all weepy and sentimental!' Francesca joked. 'Somebody fetch the mop!'

Their laughter broke the moment.

'Now that's over, let's get on to the serious stuff. Run us through your presents, Luke.' Mark leaned forward with his elbows on the table.

The children talked about school, teased the grown-ups with increasing daring, and dominated the conversation easily. The beef was praised, most highly by Spig, who ate as if he had never had a square meal in his life and had rather too much wine. Lucy alone did not enter into the spirit of things, despite Julian's persistent efforts to involve her. She could not play happy families, when her family's future was in the balance and knowing that it lay in Julian's power to tell Mark how he'd found her that afternoon. She mentally ran through twenty possible reactions Mark might have, from kicking her out of the house and throwing her clothes after her, to laughing and refusing to believe it. Somehow she didn't think he'd laugh.

'Luce, can you help me carry something?' Constance finally pushed back her chair and beckoned Lucy to the kitchen. 'What's the matter with you, Lucy? You look like someone's dying.'

'I . . . It's a long story, Connie. This isn't the place.'

Constance put a hand on Lucy's arm. 'If something's wrong, you can always tell me. Is there something I can do? You've been looking wretched all night, all hollow. It's not your sister, is it? Mark said you'd gone to see her today.'

'No, it's not that. Don't worry, Con, I don't want to spoil the evening. I'm fine.'

'Let's have a real heart-to-heart soon, OK? Now look. This is as close as we get to real magic.' Constance removed a crystal dish from the freezer, a pink mountain of ice. 'Actually, you've missed the magical moment itself, that's when you make the thing. It never fails to thrill me.'

Never fails to thrill me . . . What a thought. Lucy felt that she would never be thrilled by anything again. 'What is it?'

Constance spooned a tiny amount off the top and offered it. 'A granita. You tell me what flavour.'

Lucy tasted it on the tip of her tongue. 'It's . . . extraordinary.' Constance's eyes danced. 'I know what it is, I just can't quite . . . It's so familiar. Not pomegranate?'

'No. Try again. Close your eyes. You'll taste it better.'

'I can't. It's not fruit, and it's not a herb. Tell me.'

'Isn't that just how love should taste? That perfect, indescribable flavour, when you can't say what it is and you know everything it's not, and you can breathe it, you can inhale it, and you can't put your finger on it?'

Lucy looked at her blankly. 'I've never considered what love tastes like.'

'Philistine. Come on, Lucy! Food is about all your senses, not just taste – you have to listen to it, and smell it, and feel it.'

'I get the picture,' Lucy snapped. 'Look, some of us aren't quite so obsessed.'

'You haven't the foggiest, have you?' Constance stood with her arms akimbo. 'I just gave you about twenty clues. With this,' she nodded at the pink ice, 'you just have to *inhale* . . . What does summer smell like?'

'Oh, God!' Lucy groaned. 'Do you want me to take this out now?'

Constance gave her a piercing look. 'What *is* wrong with you?' She shrugged. 'Go ahead. I'll bring the cake.'

Julian was sworn not to identify the secret ingredient. No one else could either. The children did not take to the sorbet but had huge helpings of cake, with a little granita on the side, just for the contrast of the icy fuchsia against the chocolate.

Miranda suddenly sat up straight and turned to Connie. 'I've just twigged what it is. You don't taste it, you smell it in your mouth.'

'That's right.' Connie's smile was as rewarding as if Miranda had just solved one of the mysteries of thermodynamics.

'Roses.'

'Spot on. Full-blown, English country-garden roses.' Constance looked no more than sixteen herself. 'After you steep the petals, and strain off the syrup, your heart stops. It looks like pale green tea, and you don't believe anything can happen. Then the magic: a few drops of glycerine and lemon juice – bang. Suddenly it's a Lacroix party dress.'

'Bit poofy for a boy's birthday, Connie.' Mark laughed. 'Do you like it, Luce?'

'The colour's pretty. I don't like the taste much.'

'The problem with you is that you divide everything. You don't let your senses work together,' Constance grumbled. 'Food, like painting,' she enrolled Mark to her support, 'is about the marriage of the senses.'

Lucy jerked her head up and stared at her husband. 'Do

paintings talk, Mark? I may be a complete Philistine, but I've never heard them so much as whisper a word. Not a squeak.' Mark's gentle eyes rebuked her with a look that said, 'Stop it, Lucy. You're being rude, and it's unnecessary.' Lucy heard him loud and clear, and ignored it. 'Well, do they?' she persisted. 'Talk?'

Constance was dumbfounded by the sharp aggression in Lucy's voice. 'Children, why don't you all go upstairs? You don't have to hang around if you are bored.' The boys leaped to their feet and fled, after a kiss from Luke to Constance and profuse gratitude from Spig. Francesca, elbows on the table, was listening to Lucy intently. Her mother was eager for the children to leave because she wanted to shelter them from the unpleasant mood that was settling like a crow over her dinner table, and because she was dying to smoke. She jerked her thumb, gesturing upstairs. 'Go on, girls, git. Go paint your nails or tattoo each other or something.'

When the youngsters had left, Mark replied slowly, 'Yes, they do talk. To me at least. Not very intelligently, when they're my own paintings, but they do.'

'I'll have to visit the garage more often in that case. Maybe I'd learn something.'

'Maybe you would.'

Their tones were too edgy to be flippant.

Constance broke the following silence. 'Is there anything to raise on the flat?'

'Ah, yes, our management meetings . . .' Lucy glared at Julian. 'Why don't you start, Julian? I bet you've got some objections.'

'None at all. You, Lucy?'

'Not a thing. Mark?' Lucy knew that he wouldn't raise any of the objections in front of the Purcells that he constantly cited to her. 'I guess not. See, Connie? We're all as happy as bugs in a rug. Now I'm sorry to break up the party, but I feel absolutely deathly and

I'm longing to crawl into bed. Do stay, Mark, you've got your own car. I don't want to tear you away.'

Lucy left as quickly as she could, not knowing how to reverse her bad behaviour and fearing it would only deteriorate. There was no safety except being on her own. She kissed Constance goodbye twice and apologized three times, but her lips did not so much as graze Julian's cheek.

'Who the hell was that? It certainly wasn't Lucy.' Constance stared after Lucy's car as the three of them stood on the porch. 'Mark? What the hell happened to her? She walked in as white as a sheet, barely said a word, then bit our heads off.'

'It's probably just a physical thing,' Mark explained, causing Julian to look away. 'A virus. She's been saying she felt ill for the past few days. Maybe she picked it up from the kids.'

'She mentioned something like that in the car,' Julian concurred.

'Look, I'm sorry, I know she'll feel terrible about it. Lucy really doesn't have a mean bone in her body, poor lamb. I'd better go home and make sure she's all right. Thank you, Constance, it was a delightful evening, as always . . .'

Constance took a long drag to finish her cigarette. 'Well?' she demanded of her husband when both cars were out of earshot. 'What happened when you and Lucy were in the car? I'm waiting.'

Julian studied his wife's grave expression thoughtfully. He had pledged Lucy his silence, and felt obligated to resist at least a little before surrender. 'I don't think she's very happy, that's all.'

'She told you about it?'

'No.'

'She said something odd in the kitchen.' Constance chewed her lips pensively. 'She's having an affair, isn't she? Julian, just get on with it and tell me everything. You know you're going to, so hurry

260

up.' Arms folded, toe tapping, Constance confronted him and Julian yielded swiftly. It was less than eight hours since he had promised Lucy not to mention it, but Constance guessing wasn't strictly the same as his spilling the beans.

'Yes, she's having an affair.'

'With?'

'I don't know.'

'But you met him?'

'No. I walked in on them in the flat. Lucy came out of her bedroom, and I knew from her face what was going on. I've never seen anyone look so frightened.'

'Oh, poor Lucy!' Constance's face crumpled in sympathy. 'What did you say to her?'

'I told her to get rid of him and come home with me. And then I told her that if she ever saw him again, I'd tell Mark. And you.'

'And?'

'She gave me her word.'

'Poor, poor Lucy' Constance said again, and slumped into an armchair. 'Why didn't you tell me at once? What a hellish evening she must have had.'

'On her own head be it.' Julian looked at his wife sadly. 'We all have to learn to take responsibility. You've said that a hundred times.'

'It's different for me, but for Lucy . . . I don't know if she can handle it. I think you've gone about this all the wrong way.'

'Me? I haven't gone about it any way. I don't see how I can be blamed.'

'Yes, you,' Constance said crossly. 'You never think before you start talking.'

'I assure you, I thought very hard indeed about it. After all, it isn't as if I have no experience in the matter.'

Constance waved her hand dismissively. 'Your experience is

utterly different from hers, or Mark's, or anyone else's.' She chewed her thumbnail, gazed at it with obvious irritation and lit another cigarette. 'What are we going to do now?'

'It's not up to us to do anything. It's up to Lucy.' He observed his wife carefully as she sat curled up in the large chair, her skin so startlingly white, her nose uptilted, her chin sticking out defiantly, scalpel sharp. He could hear her mind whirring away and he momentarily regretted telling her. She would not rest until the matter was resolved. He repeated softly, 'It isn't anything to do with us, Con. I like Mark, that's all. He's our friend.'

Her aquamarine eyes met his. 'I like him too, and I like Lucy. They are *both* our friends. It shouldn't be our business, but now you've involved us in it. You should have walked straight out again. Don't you see? Don't you understand? It's too late. Now it's all changed. Now you know, and I know, and probably Mark knows by this time. Lucy can't possibly not tell him, not after tonight, and nothing will ever be the same again.'

'Nonsense. All that matters is how Mark reacts.'

'You would say that. What *matters*, what makes the difference, is if Lucy knows what the stakes are. If she does, then that's fine, but if she doesn't then somebody has to tell her before it's too late.'

'Meaning you?'

Constance shrugged. 'I have some relevant experience, that's all.'

'Wouldn't it be better if she talked to someone impartial? Like a counsellor? Shouldn't you be a little cautious?'

'God, yes,' she agreed at once. 'Caution is the key. It's the only thing that saves any of us, caution and a bit of luck.'

Charlie lay awake reading and waiting for the scrunch of his mother's car on the gravel. He switched off his torch when the front door slammed, kicked it down the bed and listened until he heard Amy's car leaving. He smiled as he edged under the duvet, feeling the torch with his toes, anticipating the familiar tread of his mother's footsteps coming quickly up the stairs, then down the corridor to his room, and then the feel of her breath against his cheek. Every night, when she did that, Charlie knew for a certainty that she loved him better than anything on earth, better than anyone. Most of the time he was asleep, sometimes he only pretended, but he knew that she always came, it was their routine, and it made him feel safe. He waited, tired but eager, to hear her approach. She was walking around downstairs, her high heels clicking back and forth along the passageway between the hall and the kitchen, passing the staircase twice. Now she's putting her coat away, he thought, hugging himself. Now she's getting a glass of water. Now she's letting Mungo out. Any minute now he'd hear her clearly on the stairs, more muffled along the carpet of the corridor, and then she'd be there, hunkering down next to his bed, in a warm cloud of perfume, kissing him goodnight . . . He closed his eyes and wriggled his bony shoulders deep into the pillow. The front door slammed again, and he heard his father calling, 'Lucy? Lucy, where are you?' and then he heard their voices rising clearly from the kitchen. They sounded angry, and Charlie screwed his eyes shut tight, and clamped his hands over his ears.

Mark threw open the kitchen door and found Lucy making a cup of tea. 'What was all that about?'

'All what?'

'Lucy! For God's sake!' Lucy began to tremble uncontrollably. 'You were sullen, and awful, and rude – bloody rude to Julian. And to me. What is the matter with you?'

'If I told you, you wouldn't understand. You wouldn't even care.'

'Try me.'

'I can't. You'll just hate me.'

'It's bloody hard to like you when I don't know what the hell is going on. You've been nothing but petulant and hypersensitive for weeks now. What? What are you so angry about?'

'I'm not angry about anything.'

'Then what is the matter? What have I done?'

She wanted to say that he hadn't paid her enough attention, hadn't even noticed she was falling apart until it had hit him on the head, and in public. If she found the courage to tell him about Steven, she wanted to be certain that he would listen and forgive, and she had no indication of that. He looked furious. 'You haven't done anything, Mark. I'm bone tired, and I don't think I can face talking about it. I'm sorry.'

'Fine. I'm going to bed.'

Never go to sleep on a row, Lucy's mother had advised her on her wedding day. Always clear up everything before, and keep the bed free of bad feeling. It wasn't the first time she had found herself unable to follow her mother's advice.

Chapter Seventeen

Those who know when to stop do not find themselves in trouble.
Tao Te Ching

Mark was a naturally cautious man, particularly where his own feelings and temper were concerned. Lack of control distressed him, and it was always his inclination to leave the room, to close the door gently rather than risk encountering unpleasantness face to face. He handled conflict as one might encounter a rat sitting in one's kitchen: it was wisest to retreat in the hope that in an hour or two the rat would think better of things and take itself away. As his wife became increasingly remote, and indifferent to her home, the only visible sign of his resentment was the way he followed in her path around the house, silently clearing up after her, turning off lights and straightening paintings. These minor rebukes were enough to tell her that in his opinion she had dropped the reins and was neglecting her responsibilities. It was a soft, silent condemnation that she could not tolerate. Lucy scented the first sulphurous whiff of martyrdom in the marital air, and a state of hostility was officially declared.

A few days after Luke's birthday dinner, Mark found Lucy at the kitchen table, writing a list of Christmas presents to be bought.

She had divided the page into two columns, with Mark's name heading one and hers the other.

'I've put some of your family on your list this year.'

'I'd rather declare a moratorium on presents.'

Lucy ignored his comment. 'I'll do your godchildren, but I don't have time to do your whole family.'

'We have to talk seriously about money, Lucy. We can't keep extending the overdraft month after month. The bank manager's fed up, and so am I.'

Lucy looked at him blankly. 'I'm certainly not spending any more than normal – if anything, less.'

'What about London?'

She was at once indignant. 'I haven't bought a thing, not a thing. Apart from clothes for the kids that once, when you told me to charge them, remember? Otherwise I haven't spent anything in London. I never even bought the bathroom shelves, and I told Connie we didn't care about curtains.'

That was quite true. She didn't appear to spend anything at all on her excursions to London: she never came back laden with bags as she had on odd day trips before they'd bought the flat. Sometimes Mark wondered quite what she did there; it certainly wasn't costing him anything. 'I didn't mean shopping, I meant the costs of the flat itself. It's a huge increase in our outgoings.'

'You were the one who was so keen to buy it in the first place. Correct me if I'm wrong, but didn't you say we'd pay for it all "through the company"?'

'I did say that,' Mark acknowledged coldly, 'but at the time I was more optimistic about the business. I was wrong.'

'It's too late now. We're committed.' Lucy's tongue peeped from between her lips as she concentrated on her shopping list; she drew another column and headed it 'food'.

Mark bent over the table, wondering if he would have to place his head between Lucy and her list before he had her attention. 'Look, Luce, aren't you even concerned about the business? It affects you too, you know, we're both involved in this. We're meant to be partners. You used to care.'

'Of course I care, but the business isn't the only thing in our life, or the most interesting.'

'I see. I'm sorry it bores you. I realize it isn't as urgent as your Christmas shopping, but could we talk about it for a minute or two? Good God, you're a bloody management consultant!'

'No, I'm not,' she said stonily, continuing to write. 'I'm a housewife. That's what we agreed when we moved here, wasn't it? That I'd be a full-time housewife, and you'd earn the money? That was the deal we made.'

'And you resent it?'

'I'm not the one who's resenting anything. It's you who's complaining.'

Mark sighed heavily. 'OK. Let's start again. Would you look over my forecast and tell me where you think we're going wrong?'

'Sure, but it will have to wait until after Christmas,' she began, grudgingly, and then the devil tweaked her tongue. 'But I don't have to do a formal study to know one thing. You seemed perfectly happy with the business until you hired Samantha. All you have to do is look at where your costs have increased. That's not too taxing, is it? If you want to talk about tightening belts, I suggest you start there.'

'Meaning?'

'Sack her. You didn't seem to need an assistant before. All she's done in exchange for her salary is make you worry about your strategy. That's hardly an efficient use of cash flow, is it?'

'You can be such a bitch, Lucy.'

'I call it like I see it.'

'And so do I.' Lucy would have winced at his wounded

expression if she had looked up from her list, but she did not. Her jaw set even more firmly before he continued, 'In the long run we may have to sell the flat. You and I need to talk it through first. Then, if we have to, we'll discuss it with Julian and Connie.'

Now she looked at him. 'I don't want to sell the flat.'

'You think I do? Do you think it's easy to admit we can't finance it, after all?'

'We've owned it for less than six months. After buying and selling costs, we'd be bound to lose money on it. It's just stupid.'

'The loss would be smaller than the carrying cost of running it for another six months. We have to do something, Lucy.'

'Not the flat,' she said adamantly. 'If it's that bad, there must be other things we can do, stuff we can sell. Other ways to cut back.'

'Like what?'

'We don't need a cleaner.'

'Lucy, that's twenty quid a week, max. It won't make a difference.'

'What about Amy? We could manage without Amy.'

'If we didn't have Amy, how would you ever go to the flat anyway?'

'Well, there must be something. We could sell that field.'

'We've let the field, Lucy, for the next five years. We couldn't sell it even if it was worth something.' At last he had her undivided attention. 'We've only got the flat. I know you love it, but it's the only thing that will make a difference to our budget. I worked out we'd save over eight hundred pounds a month.'

'What about selling the barn?'

'It's the company office, in case you'd forgotten.'

'Well, there must be something else we can do. The garage?' Mark looked at her with something very close to dislike. 'I guess we'd hardly get anything for it.' Lucy knew she was being wilfully cruel and that she had to pull herself together, if she could only get out of the rut. She laid her hands flat on the table with finality. 'It looks like you've already made your mind up, so that's that. It would have been nice if you'd bothered to discuss it with me first.'

'I give up. I tried, Lucy, I've tried a hundred times to talk to you. It's all I've talked about but you just won't listen. You don't care, you won't help, you won't take responsibility for anything. Why do you leave me all alone like this?'

When Mark left the room, Lucy sat tensely for a few minutes. She knew she had been vile and that Mark had done nothing to deserve it, nothing except that he would make no attempt to fight for her; it was the very fact that he did nothing that made her so enraged. He did not even realize that she herself, along with their marriage, were the trophies at stake and the recognition that he was, strictly, blameless didn't help at all. If only he gave some sign of caring whether she was there or not, beyond who did the dishes or who did the school run, it would be so much easier to remember what she was risking. As their relationship deteriorated like a patient suffering from a degenerative disease Lucy knew that she could not be with Steven because of the harm it would do to Mark and the children, but if she could snatch moments of happiness here and there, it had to be better than nothing at all. If Mark had simply asked her what it was that she did all day and night in the flat, why it was that she spent no money there, it would have indicated some level of interest in her life, and she could then have met him half-way. Having told herself ten times a day that she must see Steven if only to explain why she could never see him again, and twenty times a day that she would not go to Charlotte Street and meet him as they had arranged before Julian walked in, Lucy decided to go the very next day and that would be an end to it.

She called Constance in London to check when she was leaving. When Constance suggested they had lunch together Lucy refused without explanation. She had already turned down Dash just as perfunctorily.

'Are you feeling OK now, Luce?' Constance had asked gently.

'Why shouldn't I be?'

'You said on Saturday night you'd been feeling sick. I just wondered . . .'

'I'm OK. I'm sorry I didn't call to thank you for dinner – it was great. And I'm sorry I was rude. It turned out to be nothing in the end. I must send Luke his present,' Lucy added, thinking she'd have to buy it first.

'Hey, Luce, it's me you're talking to, your buddy, remember?' Constance said gently. 'You don't have to keep saying sorry. Can't we just have *coffee* tomorrow? I haven't seen you alone, not properly, for ages.'

'I can't, Connie, honestly. I've got thirty things to do. You of all people know what Christmas is like.'

'Oh, stuff Christmas! I'll give you a couple of Christmas puds and all the mince pies you want.'

'I have to go. I have to pick up Grace in twenty minutes.'

'Lucy, you and Mark are coming on New Year's Eve, aren't you? To the restaurant? Please say you'll come. I wish I hadn't decided to open, but Julian thought it was such a great idea . . .'

'We haven't had a chance to talk about it.'

'Say yes.'

And Lucy, no longer capable of saying no to anyone, accepted.

'I didn't think you'd come,' Steven confessed in Chez Gerard the next day. 'I hoped, I prayed, but I didn't think you would.'

'I can't do it any more, Steven. I'll go mad. At home I can't think about anything except you. When I'm with you, I can't think about anything except what I'm doing to the children.' She hadn't mentioned Mark, Steven thought, with triumphant relief. He'd beaten Mark. 'Anyway, Mark wants to sell the flat,' she continued.

'He knows about us?'

'Oh, *God*, no.' Lucy said vehemently. 'It wouldn't cross his mind that I'd have an affair.'

'Is that what we're having?'

'What would you call it if not an affair?'

'I'd say I'd chanced upon the woman of my dreams.'

Lucy shook her head sadly. 'There's no point talking like that, Steven. It isn't true, and it wouldn't make any difference if it were. No, Mark's just worried about money.'

'I bet it's not that. I'll bet he suspects something, wants to keep you all to himself, safely tucked up at home.'

'That's nonsense. Sometimes I think Mark might dance up and down with joy if I said I was leaving him.'

'So say it,' Steven said urgently. 'Say it, say it.'

Lucy shivered. 'Of course I can't. I can't leave Mark. I can't leave the children.'

'You don't have to leave the children. Let Mark leave.'

She looked at him in bewilderment. 'You don't understand, do you? My children belong to Mark, they're part of him, they always will be. I can't take my children away from him, or take him away from them. If I felt I couldn't live without you, I'm the one who would have to go. I will never do that.'

'What if he were violent? What if he cheated on you persistently? Don't tell me there's no way you'd be willing to end the marriage.'

'Mark isn't violent and he isn't unfaithful. Mark is loyal and gentle and kind. It's me, Steven, who should be kicked out. Mark hasn't done anything wrong.'

'Do you love him?'

'Yes, yes, I love him.' Lucy looked away. She didn't know at all. She told herself that if she were in love with Steven she could not simultaneously love Mark and she would be prepared to hurt him, which she was not. Yet if she did not love Steven, then what had she done, and for what? She could not contemplate that she had been so bad for nothing. The more Lucy questioned her love for her husband, the more she asserted it; fervent orthodoxy takes root in doubt far more frequently than in faith.

'How can I make you love me more?' Steven asked her softly.

'I don't know that you can.' The ambiguity of her reply was potent. 'Julian said he would tell Mark at once if he found out that I'd ever seen you again.'

'He sounds like a complete prick. People like that should be strung up. What the hell does he know? What business is it of his? God, I hate moralizing shits . . . There are too many of them.' Steven undid his top button, and ran his hand around his neck as if he felt strangled. A waiter approached for the third time to take their order.

'Lucy?'

'I've completely lost my appetite. You go ahead and eat.'

Steven thrust both menus into the waiter's hands and shoved his chair back. 'We've changed our minds. Sorry about that. We'll come another time.'

On the pavement outside the restaurant Lucy shivered and Steven pulled her against him. 'Where do you want to go?' he asked gently. 'We could see a movie. We could sit in the back row, through some weepie, weeping.'

'Let's just go to bed,' she whispered.

Enrico, standing behind the deli counter, watched the couple as the big man took Lucy's house keys and kicked the bottom of the door while tugging and twisting the key like an old hand. Enrico shook his head sadly, but they did not even look up: they were too absorbed in each other. Enrico listened to their footsteps above him, then resumed sorting the cheese delivery. Charlotte Street had that quality, a magical mixture of intimacy and anonymity. It was full of neighbourhood restaurants and shops where you could be recognized and greeted by name, and brought your regular order without being asked what you wanted, where people would keep your keys for you, serve you after hours, note your comings and goings without comment, and forget you the moment you left.

'Are you hungry?' Steven asked her, some time between the late afternoon and early evening.

'No.' Lucy rested her chin on his chest with her eyes shut.

'Thirsty?'

'No.'

'Cold?'

'I'm fine.' Lucy flung back the duvet.

'Too hot, then?'

She opened her eyes and studied him with a smile. 'Why are you so worried about my bodily needs?'

'I think constantly of your bodily needs. I think of nothing but. I just want to do you some small service, dedicate myself to your comfort and happiness.'

Lucy rolled on to her back, pulling the duvet back up to cover herself. 'You could put some music on.'

'What do you feel like?'

'You choose.'

In the living room Steven squatted by the pile of CDs. 'You've got some good stuff here,' he shouted.

'It's probably all Connie's. I haven't brought anything here.'

Steven frowned as he looked through them. He didn't know anything about Lucy Epstein: he didn't know what music she liked, he didn't know what she liked eating, he knew none of the incidentals of her life. He put on the Chieftains and lit a cigarette, looking down on the street below, wondering if he had anything at all he could seriously offer Lucy. After a minute or two the smiles on the upturned faces of those below reminded him that he was naked. He partially closed the shutters.

Lucy was lying propped up on her elbows. 'That sounds like one of Julian's,' she smiled, 'the moralizing bastard.'

Steven squatted down next to the bed, stroking her hair and letting one finger trail slowly along the line of her shoulder-blade. 'It's the Chieftains. He must be as old as me.'

'Older.'

'What belongs to you in this flat, Lucy?'

'Nothing. Only this bed and a lamp . . . Connie chose nearly everything else.'

'Does that bother you?'

'No. It's still my flat. It's always been mine. I don't care what she puts in it. I don't care about the physical stuff.' They were inches apart and their eyes moved quickly over each other's face, committing the details to memory. Lucy frowned heavily. 'You shouldn't smoke in here. What if Mark smells smoke next time he comes?'

Steven opened the window and got back into bed, putting the ashtray on his chest.

'Now I'm cold,' she said, hugging her breasts.

'Then let me warm you up.'

Lucy took the cigarette from him and had a tentative puff. She grimaced in distaste and stubbed it out. 'Go on, light another one for me. Right now.'

'I thought you hated smoking.'

'I do, but I've got no choice if I want to be with you. I'm going to have to take it up. Mark will find out I'm a closet smoker in London. Then he'll definitely sell the flat. And that would be really ironic, because I'd lose my lover and my flat as a direct result of smoking, which happens to be my least favourite habit in the world.'

'Stop waffling, woman.' Steven put the ashtray on the floor and rolled on top of her. 'What are we going to do, my lovely Lucy?'

'Smoke and be damned.'

Mark picked up the call in the garage when Amy buzzed him on the intercom.

'Yep?'

'Mark? It's Greg here.'

'Hey, Greg. What's up?'

'We've had the baby.' Greg's voice was exuberant.

'Congratulations! Isn't it a bit early?'

'Thirty-seven weeks.' Greg laughed. 'They had to page me during press night, right in the first act. One poor midwife got confused and thought I was a surgeon because Dash kept yelling, "Get him out of the theatre – call him out of the bloody theatre!"'

'Is everything all right?'

'Yes, yes, we're all great. A little shell-shocked. It is rather . . . *shocking*, isn't it?'

'Bloody shocking, yes. And it gets even more shocking, believe me. Has anyone told you about the green stuff?'

'The what? Look, Dash is here, longing to talk to Lucy . . .'

'Lucy's in London tonight – I'll try to track her down right away. Let me have a word with the proud mum.' Mark waited for a moment until Dash came on the line, sounding exhausted and elated and drugged. 'Sweetheart! Congratulations – the proud father didn't tell me whether you've got a son or a daughter.'

'It's a girl. We're going to call her Hermione.'

'That's splendid, just splendid. Lucy will be out of her skin with excitement. I'll let her know right away, shall I? Are you up to visitors? Blood relations only, or can I come?'

'Of course you can come, Mark. You're her only uncle, after all,'

Dash said sleepily. 'Only I'm so tired I want to weep all the time . . .'

'Maybe tomorrow would be better, then. Or I'll come and take Greg out for a jar, and leave you girls to worship. I'll get hold of Luce right away, I promise. We're so happy for you, Dash.'

When Mark called the flat, the line was engaged. He tried five times over twenty minutes, alternating with her mobile number, but he could not get through.

'If we sell the flat, I won't ever see you again.'

'Isn't my flat good enough for you? It's perfectly civilized, I promise.'

'I couldn't. How could I stay the night in London if we didn't own a flat?'

'You wouldn't have to stay the night. We could spend after-noons there.'

'It's so *sordid*, meeting for a couple of hours. It makes me feel incredibly dirty.'

'And you don't like that?' Steven said, into her belly.

'No. Does that surprise you?'

'Nothing and everything about you surprises me. You are an unknown quantity.'

'That's the only reason you're interested in me,' Lucy drawled, and then thought, with a jolt, that it was probably true. Most people were interested in most other people when they first met, or until they had had time to bore each other. She tugged his hair. 'Why *are* you interested in me, anyway?'

'It beats me. You never want to eat, you have more bloody ties than Turnbull and Asser put together, and you're so neurotic I have to spend what little time we have together listing the reasons why I'm besotted by you. I can only see you once a week, if that, you won't come to Mexico with me, you won't deign to visit my flat –'

276

'I didn't say I wouldn't come, I only said I couldn't stay there –'
'We've never spent the night together as it is.'
'We could.'
'Tonight?'
'Perhaps. If you answer my question.'
'What question?'
'Why are you interested in me?'

He breathed in deeply, with his eyes closed. 'Because you smell of apples, Cox's Orange Pippins.' She cuffed him and Steven rubbed his head. 'You want an honest answer?'

'Yes.'

'When I first saw you, I thought you were very sexy and didn't even know it. You were scattering bits and pieces all over the place, and your hair was a mess, and you had the baby glued to you and you scrunched up at the end of the sofa as if I was going to bite you. I thought you were sweet, and incredibly charming.' His voice turned husky. 'And then you relaxed and you opened up like a flower, and I thought, My God, I can do that to her: I can make this woman forget all about her home and her family and all that stuff, and blossom before my eyes without even touching her. And I wondered what you'd do if you trusted me more . . . You're not like other women I've known, Lucy, not at all. They're all so keen on keeping control and having the upper hand. You're honest. That's one thing that interests me. I wonder how you've managed to get away with being so honest all your life?'

'I'm not, not at all. Not with Mark, for example.' *Except that she always had been, until she met Steven.*

'You are with me. Aren't you?'

'I suppose I am.'

'There you go. And I watched the way you put your baby to bed, and how proud you were when I said she was beautiful. Most women I know would only want to hear that they were beautiful.'

'Not if they were mothers.'

'So I don't know many mothers. Then in the Vietnamese place you were so innocent. And righteous,' he smiled. 'You honestly didn't believe I was coming on to you.'

'No, I didn't. Why was that attractive?'

Steven rolled his eyes. 'You don't understand men at all, do you?'

'I do.'

'No, you don't, you're convinced that men find women like Constance attractive. Constance *is* attractive – at least, I thought she was the few times I've met her, because she lets you know straight up she has no expectations whatsoever. That's very appealing, because you can't go wrong. There's nothing at risk with a woman like that. But you . . . are so much more trouble.'

'If you could see the way I treat Mark you wouldn't find me at all appealing. You think I'm soft and gentle like a little fluffy bunny rabbit, you haven't seen me being a prize bitch.'

'Maybe you never would be with me. Maybe you're married to the wrong man. Maybe . . .'

'He doesn't understand me?' Lucy smiled ironically. 'There's a nice twist to an old story.'

'So, madam, have I answered your question adequately? Thumbs up or thumbs down? Do I get to stay the night?'

'Possibly . . . I haven't decided yet.'

'Whether you trust me enough?'

'Whether you deserve someone as wonderful as you've just convinced me I am.'

'I've changed my mind. You're an arrogant bitch.'

'In *that* case . . .' Lucy yawned affectedly '. . . you can stay.'

'In *that* case, I'm going to have to eat. I can't remember when I last skipped lunch. I'm not as young as you are, I can't carry on without sustenance. Come on, flower, put your kit on. I'm taking you out to dinner.'

'Can't we just stay here and snack on something?'

'Let me look in the fridge.' Seconds later Steven stomped heavily back. 'No, we bloody can't. Your fridge is even worse than mine. There's nothing but two eggs, a bottle of San Pellegrino, some Greek yoghurt and coffee beans in the freezer.'

'Let's eat the yoghurt. It's too cold to get up . . .'

Steven pulled her arm until she tumbled off the bed. 'Do I have to dress you myself? Dinner. Now. Oysters, I think. We'll go to Sheelans and order bloody great platters of oysters and drink buckets of Guinness and champagne. If we're going to have an affair, we might as well do it properly.'

Mark called the flat again, as well as Lucy's mobile, from the service station at Fleet, but the flat number was still engaged, and the mobile was switched off. The best plan was for Lucy to call Dash tonight, once he'd finally managed to pin her down physically, and they could visit together in the morning as early as the hospital allowed. Lucy could never resist a baby, and holding their newborn niece together might just pull them out of a rut that Mark was finding increasingly hard to handle, and impossible to ignore. He drove on towards London.

Chapter Eighteen

Mayonnaise should taste of nothing but itself; you should not be able to taste any one ingredient, be it the eggs, the mustard, the seasoning, the vinegar or lemon juice, or above all, the oil.

Rowley Leigh

'Darling, what would you say if I said I was thinking of packing in the restaurant?' Constance sat at her dressing-table mirror and addressed the reflection of the *Telegraph*.

'I'd say you'd gone off your rocker.'

'Seriously.'

'Seriously.' Julian folded the paper neatly and laid it on the bedside table. 'Off your rocker. You're making a decent profit, Lewis is getting on well, and your front-of-house staff are finally settled. Why throw it up now?'

'Oh, I don't know.' Constance sighed heavily. 'I've been so determined to make a go of it, and now it's all tickety-boo, I'm rather antsy. I feel like an adventure.'

'You could always extend hours. Open every lunch-time.'

'We'd never get the trade to justify it. Anyway, I was thinking of something completely different. A shop, maybe.'

'Oh, God. You've been talking to Enrico.'

She swung round on the stool and beamed at him. 'Well, yes, I have, as a matter of fact. We had a chat this morning and talked about a joint venture, that I might prepare some ready-made dishes every week for him to sell in London, and he would set me up with his suppliers to open here.'

'Sorella Camisa, perhaps? From the Falcon?'

'No, I thought Blandford.'

'I don't know, Constance. You're passionate about cooking, why get into retailing?'

'Just a whim.'

'You and your whims. It would probably mean selling the restaurant. I doubt we could finance both, and the start-up costs on a shop could be enormous. You'd need very good advice . . .'

Constance knew that: that was precisely why she had started the conversation by saying she'd close the restaurant. Once Julian was hooked on the idea of the shop, she'd find a way of keeping the restaurant too. 'I wanted to sound Lucy out but she wouldn't see me, not even for coffee.'

'I doubt Lucy is in a suitable frame of mind to discuss retail strategies.'

Constance ignored his allusion to Lucy's more pressing pre-occupations, although that had been the primary motive to meet. 'We could sell wine, too.'

'I thought it was time we were slowing down, not taking on new ventures.'

'I have no intention of slowing down at all, and I won't allow you to either. You sound like we're about to take up golf and I'm not even forty!'

'Near as damn it –' Julian dodged the pillow thrown viciously at his head. 'Darling, come to bed. I can't think this late at night, and I'm lonely without you.'

Constance lay down next to him, her fingers entwined with his, but she could not sleep. Her mind raced through the several considerations that lay before her. She would only be able to offer Enrico a narrow range of ready-made foods, but partnership with him would allow her to concentrate on the sourcing of ingredients that lay at the heart of her cooking. It would mean a major increase in her working hours, and less time for the restaurant, but she could let Lewis take over the kitchen under her supervision. Cooking one night during the week would satisfy her need to roll her sleeves up, but leave her far more time for the children at weekends. Julian's concerns about capital investment could be solved by bringing an outside investor into the restaurant, if she could find the right person, and she already had an idea about that. Mark's business would benefit enormously from having a secure retail outlet. Constance had already planned to invite Lucy in as a working partner, if she could persuade her to take an interest. She lay motionless, staring at the ceiling.

'Darling? What did Lucy's man look like?' she asked suddenly in the darkness.

'I barely saw him. I'm not even certain that the man I *did* see was him. I didn't ask for ID.'

'Thin or fat? Tall or short? Young? Old? Fair? Dark? You must have registered something.'

'I thought he was rather unprepossessing. Quite large, rather shabbily dressed. Roughly in his forties. Neither fair nor dark, just brownish, I suppose.'

'I hope you haven't made a terrible mistake.'

'*Me?*' Julian frowned heavily. 'Constance, certain noises coming from behind a closed bedroom door cannot be misinterpreted.'

'I guess not. I'm sure you're right. I just wish you were wrong.'

Even before he'd pulled up on the yellow line, Mark could see through the chink in the shutters that the flat was ablaze with light. He was relieved that Lucy was at home, and assumed she'd accidentally left the phone off the hook, or had been talking to Dash all night. Either would be typical of Lucy. He smiled as he recalled the various 'accidents' of their domestic life, and Lucy's explanation of them: the time she'd filled the car with diesel, and said she hadn't bothered to look at the pump because the last time she'd been there it was *definitely* four star. The day she had bought seven cold-water fish and tipped them casually into Charlie's tropical fish tank, causing sudden mass extinction. Her determination to change a plug herself had fused all the lights in the house, and there had been certain culinary disasters of such stature and scale that they were almost triumphant . . . That such a scatterbrain lay beneath the smart, efficient management consultant he had first met amused him, and confirmed his philosophy that things were never as they first appeared. He would not object to the lights being left on for the next three decades so long as Lucy did not look at him as if he were a fish she'd accidentally left in the bread bin for ten days.

Mark let himself into the flat calling her name, but there was no reply. The stereo was on, as well as the lights; the fridge door had been left ajar and was bleeping frantically. Lucy's mobile was lying on the sofa, half covered by an open copy of some food magazine that Mark took to be Constance's. Mark began to tidy up, washed the dirty coffee cups and glasses, restored a degree of order. When Lucy hadn't returned after half an hour he decided to go to bed. The bedroom was freezing cold, and the bed unmade, but this did not at once strike Mark as peculiar: their bed at home was frequently made only moments before they climbed into it. Mark bolted the window shut and made a mental note to tell Lucy that security was far more of an issue here than at home. As Mark straightened the sheets an ashtray tipped off the duvet and scattered butt ends over the bed and a half-empty packet of

Marlboro Lights on to the floor. His first reaction was one of disbelief that Lucy had taken up smoking without mentioning it to him, but when he registered the cigarette brand he wondered whether she had been in the flat at all that day: either Constance must have been using their room, or a friend of hers had, and hadn't bothered to clean up the mess. Lucy had said something about calling Constance to check that the flat was free, and he hadn't pursued it. In either case Mark felt entitled to use the Purcells' bedroom.

As he settled into their bed, Mark heard the street door open and Lucy's laughter on the stairs. He had hoped to lie in wait until she went to bed, and then, hearing her annoyance when she saw the state of their own bedroom, pounce and give her the shock of her life. Realizing that Lucy was accompanied, he considered the option of remaining hidden until she'd got rid of her guest, but the prospect of lying in wait for hours while she gossiped with one of her old girlfriends was unappealing. He grabbed Julian's dressing-gown and was belting it as Lucy's key turned in the lock. He heard her say, 'I thought we left the lights on?' over her shoulder as she opened the door, and in a split second glimpsed a large figure holding her arm loosely in the gloom of the shabby hall. As she screamed, Mark stepped forward, Lucy stepped back with a gasp, and the man shrank back into the darkness of the landing.

'It's all right, Luce, it's only me!' Mark snapped on the lights.

'Christ, oh, Christ, Mark! *Mark*. What the *hell* are you doing here? You scared me to death. Jesus Christ. *Jesus*.'

Mark chuckled and pulled her into the living room. 'Shh, I'm sorry, I just got here.' He held the door wide and beckoned the stranger inside. 'Hello there, do come in, sorry about all that – I'm Mark. Come on, come in, it's quite all right, I didn't mean to frighten you both witless . . .'

Still shaking, Lucy stuttered, 'Mark, this is Steven Armitage. We've just had dinner.'

'Have we met?' He glanced from Steven to Lucy. 'I'm sure we have. You're a consultant, right?'

'What's happened, Mark?' Lucy's knuckles were white – there had been an accident – her babies, something had happened to her babies, except that Mark seemed calm, and was being unusually jolly. Determinedly cheerful. That was it: Julian had told him, and he'd driven down here to kick her out; he was going to punish her. In a minute he was going to announce that she could never see the children again.

'Everyone at home is fine, Luce. It's good to meet you, Steven.'

The two men shook hands. 'It's a pleasure, Mark. I've heard a great deal about you.'

'Come on in, you can't stand out in the hall all night.'

'Mark, what are you doing here? Is it the children?'

'Calm down, Luce! I said, everything's fine, it's good news. Dash has had her baby, that's all – a little girl. What was her name? Damn. Something Shakespearean – Portia? Anyway, she was born late this afternoon. I tried to reach you, couldn't get through so I decided to bring the news in person.' He glanced at his watch and strode across the room, Julian's dressing-gown flapping around his legs. 'Here's the number at the hospital. She's waiting for you to call. Steven, what can I get you to drink?' Mark opened his arms in a gesture of hospitality.

Steven stood in the centre of the room with his hands plunged deep in his pockets and looked first at Lucy and then towards the windows. Why the hell had he closed the shutters? He didn't give a fuck about being seen naked; if he'd left the shutters wide open they might have noticed that the lights were off, the flat dark, and had some inkling of disaster. Lucy was sitting on the sofa, her hand frozen on the telephone as if she were in a trance. Steven didn't know who Dash was, and resented not knowing: she hadn't mentioned any friends, any imminent babies, nothing. He could feel Lucy's eyes fixed on his back. He was profoundly shocked, not to have been discovered but by having to come to terms with Lucy in this new setting. He had barely been more than two inches removed from her over the past twelve hours, yet here she was miles away in the company of the man who was so very much her partner. It made him angry with her, not her husband. It had never once crossed his mind that he would meet the man who had shared ten years of Lucy's life, impregnated her, saw her virtually every night of every year, and least of all had he expected to see him in a full-length Paisley silk dressing-gown and bare feet, striding around his flat and offering drinks.

'Steven? How about that drink?'

Steven swung round to face Mark. 'I'm clearly in the way here – you and Lucy have things to talk about.'

'Nonsense, she'll be on the phone to her sister for hours, picking over placentas and things. Have a whisky.'

'All right. I will.'

Lucy shook her head frantically as Mark went into the kitchen. He called over his shoulder, 'Luce, call her now – you know what midwives are like, bloody despots.' She closed her eyes briefly and dialled the number.

'Here. That's a single malt that will put hairs on your chest.' The dressing-gown permitted Steven a fine view of Mark's. 'Hope it makes up for the shock.'

'Hello? Could I possibly speak to Dash – I mean Jemima English, please? Don't wake her up – Oh. Right. OK, I'll hold, then.'

English, Steven thought. *Her real name is Lucy English.* He'd never even asked, never cared until just then.

Mark swilled the whisky in his mouth contemplatively and swallowed. 'So, Steven, are you an old colleague of Lucy's, then?'

'Dash? It's Lucy . . .' Lucy's voice dropped several notes into the purring whisper that women always adopt when calling maternity wards. 'I'm so thrilled . . .' Her eyes swivelled to watch the two men as she talked to her sister. 'Hmm? Really? Wow.'

'No, I'm not a consultant, more in the food trade.'

'Oh, really? How interesting. I'm in the wine business myself. We have a very good friend – she happens to co-own this flat, in fact – who's a restaurateur.'

'Look, Dash, you must be shattered, you can tell me all about it in the morning . . .'

'Constance, you mean.'

'Oh . . . That's amazing, how lovely . . . Yes, of course I want to hear . . . Everything, yes . . . Of course I do . . .'

'Yes. Do you know her?'

Lucy held her hand up in front of Mark's face. 'Dash, hang on for a fraction of a second, OK?' She covered the telephone receiver. 'Mark, could you get me a drink too, please? With lots of ice?' Behind his back she mimed to Steven, first putting a finger to her lips and then stabbing in the direction of the door. He shook his head slowly in reply. 'No, I'm still here, Dash . . . Did he? That's just like when I had Gracie . . .'

'You were saying, Steven, that you knew Constance.'

'I've met her,' Steven confirmed. 'In a roundabout way that was how I met your wife.'

'Dash, you sound terrible,' Lucy said loudly. 'You *must* get some sleep. Every moment the baby's asleep you have to be too. Believe me, I know. I'll be there in the morning.'

'Constance is a tremendous woman, a powerhouse, don't you think? Have you been to the Lonely Falcon?'

'Her restaurant? Not yet, no . . .'

'Yes, Mark will be there too. OK, I promise. Kiss Hermione for me. And Greg.'

'You have a treat in store. Well, Luce? All shipshape?'

'She's fine. I said we'd be there first thing.'

'Greg did his stuff?'

'Oh, yes . . . Look, it's awfully late.'

'You haven't touched your whisky. And Steven hasn't finished his.'

Steven rose and buttoned his jacket. 'That's quite all right, I have to be pushing off myself. Sorry to intrude on this family moment.'

'Not at all. I was the intruder, so to speak, on your dinner. I haven't seen Lucy jump like that since I proposed to her. See? She's still in shock.' Mark nudged his wife; she stood beside him with an expression of dread on her face.

Steven smiled thinly. 'I'll say goodnight, then.'

'Hope we'll see you at the Lonely Falcon. Come and stay the weekend, if you like. We're very close.'

Lucy followed Steven on to the first-floor landing. 'Good-bye,' she said numbly.

'Come downstairs and say goodbye to me.'

'I can't.' As Steven took her hand and tugged it gently, Lucy called back into the flat, 'Mark? Enrico said he'd leave something on the table for Connie. Did you see it?'

'Didn't even stop to look.'

'I'm just going down to check, OK?

Outside, Lucy stared down the street, refusing to look at Steven. 'How could you do that? How *could* you?'

'Do what?'

'How could you have come in?'

'He didn't give me much option.'

'You could have just melted away.'

Steven grabbed her upper arms and twisted her round to face him. 'I'm not disposable, Lucy. I don't just fucking melt away, all right? And wouldn't it have looked more suspicious if I had? I love

289

you, you stupid girl. Frankly, I'm all for going straight back up there and telling him I love you. And that you love me. That's the simplest thing to do, and the most honest. Don't you think he guessed?'

'No.'

'Then he's an idiot.'

'I can't see you again. I can't speak to you, I can't hear from you, I can't meet you. You have to go away.'

'Grow up, Lucy. I'm tired of that old tune. You can't have it both ways. You can't pretend you didn't want me, and now you've got me you can't pretend to throw me away. It's not on, all right? I don't want any more clandestine crap. This was meant to happen.'

'*Nothing* was meant to happen. Nothing *has* happened. Good-bye, Steven.'

'You're crying. How are you going to explain that, hmm, seeing nothing's happened? Just come upstairs and tell him, now, with me, or run away, now, with me.'

'I'm crying for Dash, you fool,' Lucy said bitterly. 'I'm crying for *Dash*.' She slammed the front door and ran up the stairs to the flat.

'Was it there?' Mark asked casually, when she came back.

'No. He must have posted it.'

'Steven seems like a nice bloke.'

'Yes, he is.' Lucy picked up the three tumblers, frightened she would not be able to keep her grip on them for the ten paces it took to reach the kitchen. 'I barely know him at all. We met a few weeks ago.'

'How did you meet him?' Lucy turned the taps on full and stood gripping the rim of the sink. 'Luce?'

'What? Sorry, I can't hear . . .'

Mark came up behind her and slipped his arms around her waist. 'He said you'd met through Connie, in a roundabout way.'

'Yes. He came to see Connie, came into the deli, I mean, and Enrico thought he was looking for me, I suppose, and introduced him. I must have mentioned it. He does food stuff; reviews, that sort of thing.'

'And he asked you to dinner.'

'No, not at all, it wasn't like that.' Lucy cleaned each glass meticulously, twisted out of Mark's arms to get a cloth and dried them just as carefully. 'We bumped into each other on the street, and neither of us was doing anything for dinner, so . . .'

'So?'

'Mark,' she faced him, frowning. 'what's the big problem? I'm allowed to have dinner with someone, aren't I? Is there anything wrong with that?'

'No, I'm just curious. I liked him.'

'He's OK, I guess.' Lucy edged past him. 'I want to go to bed. Something about babies always exhausts me.'

'Talking of bed . . .'

'What?'

'Did Connie say anything about using our room?'

'No. Why?'

'When I got here it was just a hell of a mess, that's all. I wondered.'

'I had a nap this afternoon, but nobody's been here except for me. You're not going to make a fuss about my not making the bed, are you?'

Mark stared at her for a few seconds. 'You had a nap?'

'Yes, I had a nap. Is that so terrible? Or is it the mess? God, Mark, you're like an old woman. I can't stand this compulsive tidiness! I never wanted the flat to be "smart". I can't stand the way it's always so *neat*. I liked it better the first time I saw it, before all this,' she waved an arm to encompass the wall lights, the furniture, the elegant fixtures and fittings, 'all *this* happened!' She stomped into the bathroom to brush her teeth, stripped off and put on a dressing-gown, and saw that Mark had returned to the sofa and put his feet up. Lucy went into their bedroom. Her heart thumped erratically at the sight of the upset ashtray and powdered ash sprinkled over the sheet. For ten seconds she stood gripping her elbows till her knuckles turned white and her nails marked her arms, trying to think. She put the cigarettes in her pocket and stepped back out, leaning her shoulders against the arch.

'It's the cigarettes, isn't it? That's what this is all about.'

Mark shrugged. 'You tell me.'

Lucy's eyes fluttered and she licked her lips. 'I didn't want to tell you. I didn't want you to know. It only started a little while ago, and I've only ever smoked in London. Damn.' She ran her hand repeatedly through her hair. 'I'm going to stop, I promise. It isn't a habit or anything, I hardly ever do it.'

'I thought you hated smoking.'

'I did. Till I tried it.'

'It's a little disgusting, finding fag ash in the bed.'

'I'm sorry. I just had a couple this afternoon.'

'Did you have to smoke in bed?'

'I'm sorry,' Lucy said again.

'If that's your only vice, I can live with it. Only never smoke in bed, OK?'

'I won't, I promise.'

'You're longing for one now, aren't you?' Lucy nodded miserably. 'Go ahead. I'd rather you smoked in front of me.' Mark picked up a book of matches from the low table and struck one for her.

Lucy lit a cigarette and forced herself to take three drags before she stubbed it out. 'It doesn't feel right, not with you watching me. Not now you know.'

'Good. Then my turning up out of the blue had some purpose.'

He stroked her hair, then sniffed it and pulled a face that made him look like Charlie.

'I'll have a shower right after I've changed the bed.'

'Forget the bed. Let's sleep in Connie's. It's a good thing it was so late when I got here or I would have called her and bawled her out for using our room.' Mark watched his wife framed by the archway, hoping she would smile easily, just once: her expression confirmed far more than he wanted to know. She hunched her shoulders and ducked her head as if she were simply waiting for a blow to fall. 'Luce?' he asked softly. 'What is it? Tell me.'

'Oh, you know me. It's just Christmas, I guess. I wish we could cancel it.' She turned on her heel and shut the bathroom door behind her.

In the shower Lucy put the water on full force until her skin stung with the pressure; she wanted to cry until her tears washed her away into transparency. If only Mark would say straight out that he knew. She did want to run away, but not with Steven; she wanted to be swept down the plughole in an eddy of shame and misery. She would not see Steven again, she swore vehemently, never again. It was too late to come clean to Mark, and too late to ask him to love her, and too late for anything but some kind of awful stoicism. Leaning her aching forehead against the glass, Lucy doubted that someone who had demonstrated such one hundred per cent carelessness, almost as if she had wanted to be discovered, who had not so much pressed the auto-destruct button as slipped and sat on it, could ever clamber up the slippery pole to reach stoicism. She certainly couldn't do it without help, and there was no one to help her, not Mark, not Steven, no one.

Wrapped unhappily in Constance's pure linen sheets Lucy listened to Mark's steady breathing and resented him for being able to sleep. She wondered if sleep came easily because he was ignorant of the storm that was circling over them, or because he did not care about it. Could he love her so little that he no longer felt even the faintest spasm of jealousy, despite the greatest provocation? *God help me*, she thought. Snatching a little easy happiness had made her more unhappy than she had ever imagined possible.

Chapter Nineteen

Csipetke, or little pinched dumplings: cut the dough into six pieces and roll each to finger thickness. Bring four quarts of water with one tablespoon of salt to a boil. Sprinkle a little flour on the dough and pinch off little pieces, using the thumb and index finger, and drop them into the boiling water . . . Real experts can tell not only if the cook was left-handed, but can even identify, by the shape of the dumpling, the person who pinched off the csipetke.

George Lang

By the end of the second week of December the Christmas decorations that adorned the shops of Blandford Forum were beginning to look a little weary and jaded, if not as weary and jaded as the faces of the shoppers. Constance had clung to her autumn menu and resolutely refused to introduce a Christmas theme at the Lonely Falcon. The restaurant would be closed for ten days, only opening for a special dinner on New Year's Eve. Constance had offered her staff eight times the standard New Year rate to persuade them to midwife the new millennium. She had been assured that London rates – for staff and restaurants – would be hiked at least tenfold, but eight times plus the promise of hefty tips had secured her regular crew. She had not advertised the special opening until after she had filled the restaurant with her friends and favoured clientele; she had no desire to celebrate the arrival of 2000 with General Sir William Dawlish and his wife, nor with the local vet, a habitué of the Falcon who took every opportunity to persuade her that a dog would greatly enhance her life, when Constance knew that a dog would do nothing but foul it up. She had spent weeks devising the meal, a six-course *menu dégustation*, which would commence, after Lewis's sage and anchovy canapés, with a truffle custard served in eggshells, and end with a compôte of macerated winter fruits accompanied by Brandy Alexander ice cream. Neither expense nor effort would be spared.

'I don't see why Luke and I have to be there.' Francesca draped herself languidly over the kitchen counter and looked at her mother soulfully. 'God, Mum, it will be *so* boring . . .'

'It will be fun, I promise, Chess, and it's really for Daddy's sake. I'll be in the kitchen all night, so who will keep him company if you two don't come?'

'Mark and Lucy are going, aren't they? And those work friends of his, the Whatsits.'

'Daddy far prefers your company to the Whatsits'. Just be generous, sweetheart. You have at least fifty riotous New Year's Eves ahead of you.'

'All right Mum, but I'm *not* doing babysitting duty on the kiddies' table, and I'm not doing the hokey-cokey with ancient crones, and I'm *not* going to pretend I'm enjoying myself.'

When Francesca had slouched back to her bedroom Constance retrieved her reading glasses from the top of her head and settled back down to her menu; she was determined to squeeze some offal in somewhere, even if it gave Julian an irresistible opportunity to air his dreadful joke about what an offal cook she was. She glared at the telephone when it rang: she found that most things shut up when she glared at them.

'Constance? It's Steven Armitage here.'

'Steven Armitage, my, my, my . . .' Constance stretched out in her chair, crossing her legs seductively. 'What a bolt from the blue.'

'It's been a while, I know.'

'You promised to call. You swore on your mother's grave.'

'I've been to confession about that . . . How are you?'

'Not bad. You?'

'Very good, actually.'

'You've called at a *very* appropriate moment. Tell me, how do you feel about *crêtes de coq*?'

'Ignorant. How should I feel about them, assuming I knew what they were?'

'Possibly pretty ambivalent. They're coxcombs.'

'Jesus. You eat them?'

'I do. I'm just wondering if my customers will. I'm playing around with a *ragoût de crêtes de coq et sot l'y-laisse aux truffes*.'

'Can two play around with them? It doesn't involve testicles, does it?'

'You have a filthy mind.' Constance laughed appreciatively. 'They're chicken oysters, darling, the bit by the bum. Or as the French put it more poetically, the bit a fool leaves behind. I'm going to stick with the French – I don't think I'd get away with a stew of coxcombs and chicken's arses for New Year's Eve, would I?'

'Frankly, I'd let you get away with anything if it tasted good. That's actually why I'm calling. I want to review the restaurant.'

'I thought critics were always meant to be incognito and unannounced?'

'So I'm giving you a break. You only do weekends, don't you? How about next Saturday night?'

'Let me just check the book back, hold on . . .' Constance

297

unearthed her reservation book and flipped it open. She certainly didn't want to turn him down and could book him in the last Saturday before she closed, but . . . She hadn't seen him since that dinner in town, and wanted to know what Julian and the Epsteins made of him. 'Steven, feel free to say no, but I'm doing a special dinner on New Year's Eve, mainly friends, some regulars.'

'A millennium dinner? Thousand-year-old eggs, perhaps?'

'I'm sick and tired of all the millennium shit. It's just a New Year's Eve party. I suppose you've been booked up for a decade at least.'

'I don't know. I've had various invites, even accepted three or four, but nothing appeals much. It might make excellent copy.'

'How sad, that you've got nothing better to do than work!' Constance teased lightly. 'But it's my gain and we'd love to have you. You're welcome to stay the night with us.'

'I couldn't really write a critical review, then, could I?'

'I bloody well hope you won't need to. Tell you what, I'll book you into a hotel so you can keep your distance, literally and metaphorically.'

'Who else is coming?'

'About thirty people. No one you'd know. Our closest friends down here, Lucy and Mark, I told you about them, we share the Charlotte Street flat, and some colleagues of Julian's, and a few food people, the first chef I ever worked for and his wife. He's a honey – they'll be staying the night too. You've probably heard of him – Malcolm Hay, used to own the Bunestan Arms on Mull?' Constance waited for Steven's response, but he was silent. 'Steven? You must have heard of Malcolm Hay?'

Steven, momentarily lost in thought, was jerked back to reply. 'Of course, he was a legend. I thought he was dead. Is that where you started, Constance? As a wee Scottish lassie on Mull?'

'Mm-hmm; Bunestan then Leith's.'

'You have quite a pedigree.'

'You can award me the Best In Breed award.'

'That's got to be better than the Best Bitch award,' Steven said playfully. 'Right. You're on. I'd love to come.'

'Bring a guest, OK? We're just going to have long tables, so everyone mixes in.'

'It sounds . . .' Steven exhaled slowly '. . . *delightful.*'

'Great. Then just let me know whether you want one bed or two – and, Steven?'

'Yes?'

'I don't care who you bring, so long as she isn't a vegetarian, OK? I can't be doing with vegetarians.'

Lucy stood shivering in the playground, waiting for Charlie to be released from class for the holidays. Since returning from London she had committed herself to forgetting all about Steven. Like a forty-a-day smoker facing total abstinence, she could think of nothing else. She was consumed by the thought that she would never see him again, and when she felt too weak to face that, she let herself believe that once she had hurdled the first few months she might allow herself to see him once, once or twice a year, perhaps, quite casually, in company. When she was over it, and hadn't thought about him for ages, perhaps they would be able to meet as friends. But all the time she knew in her heart that it had to be all or nothing, that the 'once' would immediately trigger the craving for a second meeting, and then a third, and then there would be no hope for her. *He is not part of my life*, she told herself.

Lucy could accept that there were women who were sure and certain in their fidelity, and women who were sure and certain in their infidelity, but she knew no one else, no one over thirty, who was so pathetically uncertain as she in both. She had wanted to take the high road of fidelity not simply because she was naturally a good little girl, but because she believed in the relationship she had tended for ten years. Yet she had, she knew, dynamited the first path right before her feet, the route she had been following for ten years, as brutally as if she had hacked down a lovingly nurtured ten-year-old shrub, and that way was now barred for ever. She would always know that she had betrayed Mark, whether he knew it or not. She could not follow the second path and say to herself, *The hell with it*: I'll have them both, my happy marriage and my lovely lover. Lucy couldn't say it, because Lucy knew she was intended, fated, to be a faithful wife. As a result, she felt, kicking the climbing frame, she had nothing: no self-respect, no happy husband, and no lover.

Charlie raced out of the school block, laden with plastic carrier-bags stuffed with art work, muddy football boots, science projects and God only knew what else.

'Hello, my darling!' Charlie ducked his head to avoid her kiss, his eyes on his schoolmates. 'Ready for Christmas?'

He looked at her with his steady, serious gaze. 'I've got your present, but I have to make Dad's at home. It's going to take the whole of the holidays to make it, but Mr Belbin told me what to do.' Mr Belbin, the art master, was Charlie's favourite teacher.

'Will you tell me what it is? Can I help?' Lucy asked conspiratorially.

'I dunno. Will you tell?'

'Never.'

'I'm going to make him a box for his paintbrushes, and I'm going to carve his name on the top.'

'Charlie . . . That's the best present you could ever give him.'

'I know,' Charlie said confidently.

'We can decorate your room when we get home,' Lucy prattled, wondering what she could possibly buy Mark. 'Grace has finished hers – you should see it, wall to wall tinsel. She draped Abby's crib in it too.'

'I bet she used it all up.'

'No, I saved some especially for you.'

They went shopping to buy Charlie's presents for his grandparents and little sisters, or 'little blisters', as Charlie now called them, and Lucy was easily bullied into stopping for takeaway fish and chips. It was after seven when they reached Manor Farm, and very cold. Lucy bustled Charlie out of the car and down the drive, passing the garage. The curtains were for once undrawn, and the windows glowed pale orange from the light of Mark's oil burner; she saw him, in a flash, painting, wearing fingerless gloves and with an expression of complete absorption. He doesn't think of us at all when he's painting, she thought wretchedly, as she passed the garage. *He does not think of me.*

Samantha was in the kitchen with the girls. 'Hi, Lucy. Amy had to rush off and Mark was desperate to get on with his painting, so I stayed.'

'That's very good of you, but Mark shouldn't ask you to do that. I'm sure you've got a boyfriend who wants you home. And your parents.' Lucy slowly unpacked Charlie's various bags.

'I like being here. My Mum's dying, you know,' Samantha said simply, as if they'd talked about it a hundred times. Lucy looked up, startled. 'Sometimes it's nice being in a normal family.'

'Sam, I didn't know. I'm sorry.'

'Oh, she's been dying for years. It's OK, I'm used to it now. I've used up all my tears, if you know what I mean.' She began to help Lucy, washing the mud off Charlie's football boots. 'I left my boyfriend back in Suffolk when I moved here. I thought it would last, but you know . . .' she hunched her shoulders slightly '. . . it didn't.'

'Do you want to stay for supper, Sam?' Lucy said impulsively.

'Not to look after the kids or anything, just to have supper with me and Mark. We'd love you to.'

Samantha wrapped a great coil of dark brown hair around her hand and knotted it at the nape of her neck as easily as a thick rope. 'That would be great, if I'm not intruding.'

'Not at all.'

'Have you seen what Mark's painting?' she asked hesitantly.

'God, no – the garage is private property. If he wants my opinion he'll ask for it. These days that place is like Fort Knox – door locked, curtains drawn. I used to read there, sometimes, while he worked, but since Abby was born I haven't had a spare minute.'

'Well. I know he'll show you when it's finished. It's . . . extraordinary. Brilliant.'

Lucy bit her bottom lip as she flipped through Charlie's work books. She was stunned that Mark had invited Samantha into the garage and shown her his work. She couldn't remember when he had last talked to her about his painting; he seemed to talk only about the company and finances to her, as if she were his assistant, and Samantha his partner. For the first time Lucy faced the thought that not only was she going to have to give up Steven but that she might lose Mark anyway. It horrified her.

Lucy left Samantha peeling potatoes while she put the children to bed. As Charlie dawdled in the bath, and Abigail staggered around the room, reeling, like a drunken sailor, from handhold to handhold, she read Grace a bedtime story.

'Shall we have a Christmas story?'

'Not about Father Christmas. I don't like him, I don't want him in my house, and I don't want him to come down my chimney.'

'But, dearest, he's lovely . . . And who will bring all your presents?'

'Daddy will. I want Daddy to do it.'

'We'll see . . . So which story shall we read?'

'Tell me a story about when you were a little girl, when you were a naughty little girl . . .'

'OK.' Lucy lay down next to Grace and pulled her into the crook of her arm, keeping an eye on Abigail who had careened over to the bookcase, toppled over on to her well-padded bottom, and proceeded to pull all Grace's stories off the shelves, giving a chosen few a ruminative chew. 'When I was about your age, and your Auntie Dash was about Abby's age, I was incredibly naughty one day when Dash had to go to hospital. She fell over and she cut her head,' Lucy drew a line with her finger across Grace's forehead, 'right across, like that, and there was blood everywhere.'

'Was it a horrible mess?'

'Yes, quite dreadful. But what I remember is that my mummy, your granny, took Dash off to hospital while I stayed home with Grampus. When they came home, Dash had a new toy, a huge, gorgeous, cuddly dog, and for the next five days or so, everyone who came to the house brought Dash a present, and no one brought me a present.'

'That's not fair.'

'That's what I thought.' Lucy eyed Abigail, who was lying on her back with her legs in the air in a soft pink Babygro, dribbling over Tom Kitten. 'One day I climbed up on my mummy's dressing-table, and I took her lipstick, which was *really* naughty –'

'Really naughty,' Grace echoed, with delight.

'And I smeared it all over my face, everywhere –'

'Was it Christmas-time?' Grace interrupted anxiously.

'Ah, I don't know. I can't remember. Maybe it was. Anyway –'

'Because if it was Christmas-time, and you were naughty, then Father Christmas wouldn't bring you any presents. At *all*.'

'He won't bring *you* any presents,' Charlie stood in the doorway

303

of Grace's room, 'because you are always naughty, and you're a horrible little blister.'

'Charlie, get into bed and I'll be there in a minute. Now. Go.' Lucy soothed Grace's pouts. 'So, I smeared the stuff *all* over my face, and then I started screaming, "Mummy, Mummy! Help!"' Lucy yelped ever more histrionically as Grace giggled. 'Hee-lll-ppp! And my mummy came rushing in, and thought for a minute that I'd broken a glass and cut myself, and she was so upset . . .'

'Then what happened?'

'*Then*,' Lucy whispered, 'she saw her lipstick. And *then* she paddled my backside. And I didn't get any presents at all. Do you know the story about the boy who cried wolf?'

'No, tell it me.' Grace yawned.

'Tomorrow night. You have to get to sleep, or else Father Christmas . . .' Lucy wagged her finger.

'You were *very* naughty, Mummy,' Grace said, with immense admiration and sleepy delight.

'Yes. But I learned to be good. Sleep tight, my angel.'

'It's OK Father Christmas comes so long as he doesn't come upstairs. He can't come into my bedroom.'

'OK. We'll tell him.' Lucy kissed Grace, scooped Abigail up and carried her into Charlie's room.

'That wasn't a true story, was it, Mum?'

'Not exactly. I *did* do horrible things to Dash, and I was naughty, sometimes, but I would never have dared to touch my mother's lipstick. I was too much of a scaredy-cat. Goodnight, blossom. Sleep tight. I'm going to light your advent candle, and you can have the lights on and read until it burns down to seventeen, OK? Then blow it out and lights off. No cheating, Charlie, I'm trusting you. Now kiss your littlest blister goodnight, *nicely*.'

Charlie leaned out of bed and kissed the baby with a long-suffering expression. His mother carried Abigail to her cot feeling she had forsaken the right to trust anyone by being so un-trustworthy herself. She tucked the baby into bed, kissed her softly, and whispered close to her ear, 'Everything's going to be all right, my lamb, I promise, everything's going to be just fine.'

Abigail put her foot into her mouth and gazed at her mother with wide, trustful blue eyes.

'I swear to God, Mark, he hated it – he only ever drank beer.' When Lucy came back to the kitchen Mark had three bottles of wine lined up on the table and was in the process of opening a fourth. In front of the bottles were three glasses. Samantha was laughing, shaking her head at Mark, 'Mark won't believe that my boyfriend – my ex – didn't like wine. He thinks everyone on earth worships it.' Lucy smiled at them both.

'I accept there are some poor benighted souls who don't, I just can't believe you dated one of them, Sam.'

'Well, I did. I got used to ordering by the glass when we were out, and drinking the whole bottle at home.'

Lucy checked the casserole she'd spent half the day making. 'We're ready, except for the veg.' Samantha had left the vegetables chopped in individual pots on the range. 'Fifteen minutes?'

'Great. Time for a tasting.'

'Mark, I am not doing any of that frozen raspberries, wet dog, Bronx-baseball-stadium-with-the-lingering-odour-of-hotdog-and-the-faintest-hint-of-household-bleach stuff,' Lucy warned, hands on hips.

'But, Lucy, you're a natural!' Samantha raised her arms over her head in salute. 'I've actually drunk wine that reminded me of baseball stadiums and household bleach.'

'It was probably retsina, domestic strength, vintage ninety-eight,' Mark commented. 'Don't worry, girls, we're only experi-menting for Connie's New Year's Eve party. I've got her menu here somewhere. The truffle custard may be a bit of a thumb-sucker to partner. The beef will need something truly elegant, but firm – a Pommard, perhaps.'

Samantha flinched exaggeratedly. 'The three dreaded words: New Year's Eve. The end of the decade, end of the century, end of the bloody millennium. I can't stand it.'

'Where are you going, Sam? A rave?'

'Six months ago I expected to be with my bloke at the Crown in Aldeburgh. We planned a huge piss-up with all the gang, then swimming.'

Mark was aghast. 'Swimming? In the sea? You've got to be kidding.'

'Some of them do it every year. Last time we spoke on the phone, he went quiet and said he was "checking things out". I knew what he meant – *chucking me* out. So I'm staying put. I'll stay in with Mum and Dad. There are worse ways to celebrate than spending the night with your parents. It's cool. I don't know many people down here, anyway, apart from you two and my folks.'

Lucy was struck by the easy way Samantha linked her and Mark – 'you two': it made them sound inseparable. 'Maybe,' she suggested, glancing at Mark, 'Sam could come with us to the Falcon. I'm sure Connie wouldn't mind.'

'No, honestly, I wasn't begging for an invitation. Like I said, it's cool. I like the idea of being the only single woman on earth without a date for the thirty-first of December 1999. It makes me unique.'

'It makes you pathetic. You'll come with us,' Mark said firmly. 'You two start on the wine and I'll call Con.'

Constance agreed to include Samantha at once when Mark suggested she added the fifty-pound-per-head bill for her to his account.

'It's a deal. Sam, you're expected. Hey, Luce, guess who else is coming to dinner?'

'Who?'

'Connie's persuaded a critic to review the restaurant.'

'That's nice.'

'And it's your friend Steven.'

'Steven Armitage?' Lucy opened the oven door and put her hand straight in without thinking. 'Shit!'

'Are you OK? Put it under cold water.' Mark looked at her curiously, turned on the tap and examined the raw burn across the back of his wife's hand. 'Ouch. Con said he writes for one of the broadsheets. Great PR, to get the restaurant reviewed on New Year's Eve.'

'Well. Yes. Provided he gives her a good one.' She wanted to ask Mark if Constance had arranged the review or Steven had suggested it. Lucy had ignored seven phone calls from Steven over the last week. After hanging up on him the first time, she had resorted to switching off the answerphone and sitting like a stone when it rang. Amy had accused Lucy of trying to avoid her mother-in-law. 'Mark, are we going to drink those wines or just admire the labels?'

At nine twenty the following morning, Lucy knocked at Constance's front door.

'Hello, stranger! Have you come to get your puddings?'

'Forget the puddings. I've come to talk to you.' Lucy strode into the house without an invitation and headed for the kitchen, Constance following after. 'So?' she demanded. 'What gives you and Julian,' she spat his name, 'the right to do this?'

'To do what?'

'To interfere in my life and my marriage?'

Constance's eyes softened in sympathy. 'Oh, Lucy. Let me get some coffee. You know, I was hoping you'd come. I've been longing to talk to you about all this.'

'Julian did quite enough talking for both of you. You didn't have to stick your oar in too.'

'What on earth are you talking about? I haven't breathed a word.'

'No? So what made you extend your New Year's Eve guest list?'

'Mark. He begged me to, he said it was your idea.'

The colour left Lucy's face. 'Mark asked you?'

'Of course. He said Samantha was at a loose end, you were both worried and would I –'

'Not *Sam*, Connie,' Lucy said furiously. 'Not Sam. *Steven*.'

For a couple of seconds Constance stared back uncomprehendingly before she released her breath slowly. 'Oh. OK. I understand now. My God, Lucy, it never crossed my mind.'

'Oh, really?' Lucy asked sarcastically, trying to control the tremor in her voice. She folded a paper napkin into a concertinaed fan, pressing the creases flat, then shredded it. Constance put a hand gingerly on her shoulder and Lucy broke down in tears.

'I never guessed it was Steven – how could I? Christ, I could hardly believe it when Julian told me you were having an affair.'

'So he did tell you? The bastard.'

Constance shook her head. 'It wasn't like that, he didn't want to tell me, I sort of forced him. Julian can't hide things from me. Oh, Lucy, I'm so sorry. Christ, what a mess.'

'Yes, but it's *my* mess, nobody else's, and your bloody husband has stirred everything up so badly I'll never get out of it.' Constance, still trying to digest the shock that Steven had been having an affair with Lucy, sat with her hand covering her mouth as Lucy raged and wept by turn. 'I suppose that's why Mark came down to the flat last week? Julian must have told him, the bloody smug self-satisfied bastard prig, and Mark *knew*, knew about Steven, before he even got there, all the time while I was pretending I'd taken up *smoking*,' Lucy choked on the word, 'and he knew all the time. All the time. What an idiot I am. Oh, God, what am I going to do? Is this some horrible game you're all playing? Did Mark tell you to invite Steven? *Did* he?'

'Of course not. Just calm down and listen to me, Lucy. One, I didn't know there was anything going on between you and Steven Armitage. I didn't know you'd even met him, and Julian had no idea who the man was. Two, Julian told me about walking in on you after Luke's birthday dinner, but I'm certain he didn't say anything to Mark. And I haven't breathed a word to anyone. Three, Steven called me yesterday, out of the blue, and said he wanted to review the Falcon. I suggested, perfectly *innocently*, that he came for New Year's Eve. That's what happened.'

Lucy closed her eyes. 'I don't know how anything happened. I don't know anything at all. I'm so bloody frightened . . .' She put her head on the table, her shoulders heaving.

'It's OK, Lucy, we'll sort everything out, I promise. Don't cry, just tell me what's going on, and let's *think*. I am going to help you, I'll do whatever it takes.'

Those promises of help and commitment that come at the wrong time, or just too late, haunt both the person who offers help and the person who knows it is too late to be helped. Constance listened with intense concentration as Lucy recounted her meetings with Steven Armitage over the preceding months. After she had described Mark's arrival at the flat, and the charade over the bed – not omitting to tell Constance that they had ended up using her bedroom, because now that her guilt was rising to the surface it brought with it all sorts of scum – Lucy looked completely drained of colour and life. 'I'm not the sort of person who can have an affair. I can't handle it at all.'

'And that bastard should have known you can't. Bloody hell, Lucy, of all the people you could have picked, why Steven?'

'Don't, please don't . . .'

Constance could not stop herself. 'He's such a classic womanizer, doesn't give a shit about anyone except himself, a hundred per cent callous . . .' Constance ticked off his crimes on her fingers, but did not mention that when she herself had had dinner with him, she had tagged him as a front-runner in the potential lover stakes. It was more for Lucy's sake than her own that she concealed that Steven Armitage had been the cause of the little white lie she had told Julian months before, the lie that Lucy had reluctantly been persuaded to endorse. Constance had never been close to being seduced by him; she had simply enjoyed the flirtation. Now she scratched him off the card as easily as if he had never appealed to her for the most fleeting moment. 'He's a sham, Lucy. A charlatan through and through.'

'He's not. You don't know him at all. He's incredibly warm, and completely honest. He's a *good* man, I promise you.'

'Oh, give me strength! He's nothing but an ordinary bastard. You have to believe that and walk away.'

'If I did believe that, if I thought he was nothing just for one moment, what would that make me?' Lucy's eyes were dark with misery. 'If he's worthless, then I did all this, risked everything – Mark – for *nothing*? For nothing at all?'

'You don't love him, do you? You haven't fallen in love with him?'

'How could I fall in love with a bastard?' Lucy asked numbly.

'For exactly the same reason that I'd be attracted to a bully: because you get tired of what you've got, and look for the opposite. Are you in love with him?'

'I must be, because if I'm not . . . *If I'm not* . . .' Lucy's voice faded into the smallest of whispers.

'Steven's bloody sexy. Are you sure this isn't just lust?'

'Lust?' Lucy looked up at Constance vacantly. 'I'm crazy about him.'

'I'm going to call him right now.'

'Please just stay out of it, Connie. I've told him it's over, I've told him I can't see him, and I won't. Somehow I have to make things right with Mark. I have to know what Mark thinks. Do you think he knows? Why hasn't he said anything? I just have to think . . .'

'Maybe he believed exactly what you told him.'

'How could he?'

'Because he trusts you, Lucy. And he loves you – oh, no, Luce, don't cry, don't cry . . . If you could only hear how he talks about you when you're not there – Look, I'm going to fix us something to eat.'

'I can't eat – I'll throw up.'

'It's not for you, it's for me.' Constance corrected firmly, taking control. 'I need to cook while I think. Don't distract me.'

She cut four thick slices from a homemade loaf and lightly brushed both sides with soft, creamy butter before laying them on a baking sheet. While the bread was in the oven, she cut Gruyère into paper-thin slices, and minced two shallots by hand. Lucy was mesmerized by the speed and surety with which she handled the knife. She silently watched her rubbing the browned bread with a halved clove of garlic, and sprinkling a few drops of white wine and the tiny shards of shallot over each slice, before layering the cheese artistically on top and sliding the tray back into the oven. By the time Constance had put some cornichons and strong mustard on the table, the cheese had turned bubbly, and the distinctive smelly-sock aroma of melted Gruyère suffused the kitchen. A pinch of paprika, a few strong twists of the pepper-mill, and she placed a plate in front of Lucy. The entire operation had taken less than ten minutes.

'Cheese on toast. Don't think about it, just eat it. It will make you feel like you're way up in the Alps on a crisp February morning.'

'I wish I bloody was.'

'Here's what I think, Lucy, for what it's worth. Assume Mark does know you've been having an affair, and knows it's Steven. He hasn't said anything, he hasn't asked you. Fine. Forget Steven and act as if nothing happened. If Mark hasn't raised it then he doesn't want to.

'But, Connie –'

'Wait a minute. Now let's assume Mark *doesn't* know. Then you must never tell him, do you understand?' Constance's voice rang with certainty. 'If he suspects, just a little, and ever asks you, outright, you deny it absolutely. Believe me, I know what I'm talking about. Never, ever, admit anything. Say nothing at all, and if you absolutely have to, deny it.' Constance frowned. It was hard to say whether she was thinking about Lucy's situation or ways in which the recipe could be improved. 'If you deny it enough, you'll end up convincing even yourself that it never happened.'

'Is that what you've done, Connie? Denied anything? Never admitted anything to Julian? '

'What?' Constance swallowed. 'Of course not. What would I need to admit to Julian?'

'You haven't, have you? He said something about that in the car – he said the two of you had no secrets. You've never told him about your affairs, have you?'

Constance set the half-eaten toast on the plate and patted her lips carefully. 'No, Lucy, you're right, I haven't told Julian.' She twiddled her diamond ring around her finger absent-mindedly. 'I haven't told him, because I haven't ever had an affair.'

'Oh – I get it – this is a demonstration of the art of advanced denial. It wouldn't work for me, I'm not a good enough actress.'

'Lucy, I've never been unfaithful to Julian, not so much as a snog. I've talked about it, and joked about it, but I've never cheated on him.'

'I don't believe you.'

'Because I'm such an utterly amoral cow that I must have had twenty affairs?'

'That's what you imply. You talk about it all the time.'

'People who talk about it never do it.'

'You admitted it – you just said, "Believe me, I know what I'm talking about."'

'And I do. But it wasn't me who had an affair.' Constance stood up. 'It was Julian. I wish he had never told me, that I'd never known. And I'm certain that's best for Mark. Do you want a cappuccino? I bought myself a machine as an early birthday present.'

Chapter Twenty

Love is an irresistible desire to be irresistibly desired.

Robert Frost

'You can't be annoyed I told her.'

'It makes me look such a hypocrite.'

'If I hadn't told her you would have *been* a hypocrite. Isn't that worse?'

'I could hardly tell Lucy I'd had an affair.'

'I don't see why not. I would have. It would have been better than making her feel lower than shit, as you gazed down from your moral mountain-top.'

'Forgive me for being perverse,' Julian said calmly, 'but I thought it might annoy you if I discussed our private life when you had chosen not to tell anyone. I didn't imagine that the result of being considerate to you was Lucy labelling me a hypocritical shit.'

'She doesn't now. I admit she did at first,' Constance smiled slyly at Julian as she sat next to him in the car, 'and I encouraged it, just for a little bit. I rather enjoyed it.'

'You enjoy many things at my expense.'

'No, Lucy thinks better of you now, if anything.'

'Because the fact that I once had an affair means I'm not the pompous arse she thought I was?'

'Plenty of pompous arses have affairs every day, bless them. No, Lucy just understands a little now that you were trying to help her, in your own way. And she understands why I put on such a show of being blasé about it.'

'Is that what you do? Is that what I did to you, made you blasé?'

Constance touched his cheek reassuringly. 'Only on the outside. Being flippant was just a way of coming to terms with it, for myself. Lucy understood that better than I did. Anyway, somehow the habit stuck. You'll have to talk to her, you know.'

'Isn't it better to draw a curtain over the whole thing?'

'That kind of curtain takes years to draw, and *skill*. You're lucky I've got it.' Constance grinned mischievously. 'If you managed to draw it, you'd probably put your great blundering foot through it.'

'Just because it's your birthday you don't have to insult me in every sentence.'

'I intend to insult you until you give me my present.'

'Fire away then. I told you I haven't bought you anything.'

'Not a sausage?'

'Not even a hotdog.'

'Just a *little* present . . .'

'You've already bought yourself about twenty presents on my behalf.'

'But a tiny token of your esteem . . .'

'No. Nothing.'

Constance flipped down the mirror and touched up her make up in silence. A mile further down the road she returned to the subject of Steven Armitage. 'I was all for phoning and telling him what a shit he was, but Lucy wouldn't have it.'

'Is she really involved?'

316

'I have no idea. Worse, nor does she. She said she was crazy about him.' Julian snorted, which made Constance angry. 'Being crazy about someone means plenty – maybe more than loving them. I mean, there's a kind of love when you willingly put yourself at somebody's mercy, when you know that you are completely exposed to them, in all your horrid nakedness, all the little warts and moles are out there – and there's another kind of love when you're just drunk on each other, you don't see any flaws at all. Who knows which one is love, real love? I can't honestly, not hand on heart, not right this very minute, even say I love you like that!'

'Constance, is this still about your bloody birthday present?'

'No, I mean it. I "love" you, hugely. You're my husband and I think you're great, but it pisses me off the way you look at the ceiling before you say something, just to make sure everyone knows it's important, and the way you grind your teeth at night would drive a saint to despair and your stomach . . .' Constance mused.

'What the hell is wrong with my stomach?'

'It's fine, but it's not the stomach it once was. None of those things matter, or change the fact that I love you and I want to spend all my remaining years with you, and nobody else has ever come close to making me feel that, but it isn't the same as being crazy about you, or drunk at the thought of you, is it? How do any of us know that being happy to spend your life with someone is really love?'

'It sounds a perfectly good definition to me.'

'That's because you're a man, and a pragmatist. I guess I am, too. Maybe it's a compromise we reach when we get old, and lose sight of being in love. Lucy just wanted to feel a little bit out of control. Only she got carried away by the current. In a way, I envy her.'

'I don't buy that,' Julian said, feeling quite drunk on Constance as he watched her watching herself in the dashboard mirror, painting her lips.

'You don't buy anything, it seems to me, least of all presents.'

'I can't believe Lucy thought for a moment that she was being carried away by the great love of her life. She would never have given up Mark and the children, never. She simply wanted a fling, and didn't think about the consequences.'

Constance returned her lipstick to her handbag and was silent for a moment. 'Is that what *you* wanted?'

'Constance,' he said earnestly, flicking his eyes between her and the road, 'it was sixteen years ago. I have no idea what I wanted, because even at the time, and ever since, for the past sixteen years, I have wanted nothing but you. Literally, nothing but you. Can't I ever convince you of that?'

'You convinced me years ago. You just left a hostage behind. Keep your eyes on the road, buddy.' Constance patted his left leg. 'You convinced me, but an annual token of your eternal regret, in the form of serious jewellery, wouldn't go amiss.' She let her hand slide slowly and firmly up the inside of his thigh. 'I *said* keep your eyes on the road!'

They drove on towards the restaurant where Francesca and Luke were waiting to surprise their mother. Julian slid his hand into his breast pocket for the third time since leaving home to make sure that the airline tickets, and the ruby earrings that lay within them, were still there. He knew that Constance would not be surprised, but he hoped that she would be genuinely delighted.

The relentless approach of Christmas and having all the children at home as well as Mark's mother Mimi obliged Lucy to try to pull herself together for their sakes, if not her own. Mimi arrived the week before Christmas, and was due to stay until the day after Boxing Day, if she could stand the chaos that long. Lucy loved her mother-in-law and welcomed her visits, but she could not stifle the flicker of resentment that Mark now left his office on the dot of six to join his mother for drinks. If Epstein & Rose was struggling, she reasoned, surely Mark should be working day and night? But he didn't: he played with the children, talked to his mother, and he tried to talk to Lucy. Lucy was beyond talking to anyone. She never answered the phone, and agonized hourly over what Steven might say if he called and Mark answered. Steven didn't call.

'Are we going to see those charming friends of yours, the architect and his wife?' Mimi sat on the sofa, sorting out piles of holly and ivy for a wreath.

'Julian and Connie? Yes, we'll get them over. Ma, I want to know what you think of this.' Mark poured a glass of white wine, and gave it to his mother.

'Oh, darling, I like everything you like.' Mimi took a sip. 'It's very pleasant indeed. Slides down easily.'

'Luce? What do you think?' Mark asked as Lucy was leaving the room.

'I don't feel like drinking at the moment, OK? I want to check the dinner.'

In the kitchen Lucy leaned her head briefly against the fridge. Everything was going to pieces: she couldn't handle the children, she couldn't talk to Mimi; she'd ignored Constance's birthday; she was watching her marriage slide downhill without even being able to hold up her hand and say, Hey! Stop! If only she could just get through Christmas, get through one day without thinking about Steven, and wondering what he was doing, one day without the feeling that she was slipping beneath the surface of the water, and slipping quite willingly, because she was so weary she couldn't stay afloat any longer. As she heard Mark at the kitchen door she stepped quickly over to the range.

'Luce?' Mark put his hand on her shoulder. 'You go and sit down with Ma and I'll finish dinner – just tell me what to do.'

Lucy shook her head. 'There's nothing to do, it will be ready in ten minutes.' Mark kissed the back of her neck, felt her shoulders stiffen and pulled back automatically. Lucy laid her hand against his cheek. 'I'm sorry, Mark. I'll go and talk to Mimi.'

Mimi patted the sofa next to her. 'Lucy, do you know I haven't laid eyes on you since you bought your London flat? It sounds so exciting – and so sensible to buy it with friends. When the boys were growing up, I remember longing for a bolthole, somewhere to escape to. Everyone, especially mothers, needs a little corner they can call their own. There were days when one simply wanted to hide in the garden shed.'

'I don't believe you ever did that, Mimi.'

'I did. Once I took the sherry bottle with me . . .' Mimi winked conspiratorially. 'Although I must say that David and Josh were very good boys, and Mark was always an angel.'

'Didn't they ever fight?'

'I suppose they did, but I can't remember a single incident. That's one advantage of growing old: one forgets all the bad things that have happened. Unfortunately, I'm beginning to forget the good ones too.'

'You are outrageous, Mimi. You make such a fuss about being old, and you're what, seventy? You look younger than I do.'

Mimi gave her daughter-in-law a sweeping top-to-toe glance, and said thoughtfully, 'I was actually just saying to Mark how very well you look, Lucy dear. You've lost a little weight, just the right amount, the surplus from Abigail, and you have the most wonderful radiance about you. I even wondered . . .'

Lucy raised her eyebrows questioningly then laughed, holding her hands up in denial. 'Oh, no, Mimi, I'm not pregnant. I think I've done my bit, don't you?'

Mimi's deft fingers twiddled the stems of ivy into place and secured them with florists' wire. 'Of course you have. That's exactly what I thought too, after my three boys. It took another three years for me to understand that I was never going to hold a baby, my own baby in my arms again, and by then it was too late.'

'Mimi, let me make something perfectly clear: I am absolutely *certain* that I do not want more children. It's hard enough finding time for the three of them as it is, and my God, the cost of it all – if we had four, we'd have to spend twenty-five per cent more at Christmas.'

'No, you would simply divide what you have now between them.'

'I'll put it to Charlie, OK? I'll ask him if he'd rather have a baby brother or sister than a Nintendo 64. I have a pretty good idea what he'll answer.'

'I suppose you're right, my dear. It's simply that you and Mark put out such excellent models, it seems a shame to halt production. And now you have all the experience you need. It's so hard for new parents when they're just beginning.'

'Does it ever get easier? I'm always meeting mothers who say, "just you wait – I thought it was hard when mine were that age, but it's much tougher now . . ." I already feel too old and too tired to cope; how am I going to handle it if it gets worse?'

'It doesn't get worse, it gets better. And these *are* the oldest years of your life, far more than when you reach my age. That's precisely how God planned it, that you would have most energy exactly when you needed it. It's not surprising you feel sapped. The most difficult thing is for parents to make time for each other.' Mimi waited in case Lucy took up her offer to talk about Mark, but her daughter-in-law was bending over the wreath, tweaking leaves into position. 'Whatever you do, Lucy, don't worry about your children. You cannot always protect them, or spare them hurt.

Sometimes mothers can't even help hurting their children themselves.'

'I'd be shot through the head rather than hurt them.'

'I know that, my dear. Just follow your own heart. Your instincts will be right.'

'I wish I had your confidence.'

'You will, when you're my age, and you don't need it.'

'Ladies?' Mark bowed low in the doorway. 'Dinner is served.'

Mimi continued her theme at the kitchen table. 'All parents make mistakes, but as long as they keep trying, that's as much as children can legitimately ask.'

'What were your mistakes, Ma?' Mark asked humorously, and winked at Lucy. 'I've spent thirty-seven years under the impression you were blameless.'

'That was precisely the problem. I wanted you three to think I was perfect, and wasted a great deal of valuable time covering up my mistakes. I should have just said sorry and moved on to the next thing.'

'That wasn't your big mistake,' Lucy interjected. 'Your *big* mistake was not teaching Mark how to look for anything by himself. He still can't – nor can Charlie. I spend hours every day looking for things they've put down. They don't even try. Do you think that's because they're boys, or is it something genetic?'

'I imagine that is my fault,' Mimi admitted, while Mark scoffed. 'I probably did rush around looking for things, because it made me feel essential, if my boys needed to rely on me every day.'

'It makes me feel like a skivvy, not essential. They're just lazy. They take no responsibility for their possessions at all.'

'Lord, yet another calumny against the male race.'

'It's perfectly true. You should get glasses.' Lucy snapped back at Mark. 'Except that you'd never be able to find them.'

Mimi was embarrassed by her daughter-in-law's sharpness.

322

'Perhaps men *are* worse at looking for things. Perhaps they have never needed to develop those skills.'

'You mean, in their role as hunter-gatherers?' Lucy said ironically. 'I would have thought eyesight was an essential skill.'

'Don't even try to persuade her, Ma. When Lucy gets a bee in her bonnet about the male species, it's much easier to agree and let her thwack it into oblivion. Charlie and I have learned to lie low.'

'While I rush around finding all your stuff.'

'Do turn off the record, Luce,' Mark retorted sharply, while Mimi studied her plate.

The more she tried to pull herself together and have a normal conversation, the more Lucy found herself slipping into bouts of complaint. As solitude was the only way she approached decency, Lucy left Mark and his mother having coffee and went to bed. The earlier she went to bed, the less soundly she slept. She lay in bed making mental lists of things she had to do: check the tree lights, bake the muffins, find some ready-peeled chestnuts, make dental appointments for Grace and Charlie before the holidays were over, wrap the presents, buy the presents she hadn't yet bought, get stamps for the cards she had written and write those she hadn't, phone each of her godchildren, make sure Charlie really mastered his eight times table, find out when she had to register Abigail for nursery school . . . The more mundane the task, the more it bothered her. Life had turned her into a bore, as well as a nag. Far from seeing herself as a beacon of warmth and maternal tolerance, she had become a ranting recorded message, a Tannoy gone mad: 'Did you brush your teeth? Have you done your homework? Pick the towels up off the floor. I *said* it's bedtime, don't make me tell you again. No telly till you've finished your homework. Put your plate in the dishwasher when you've finished. Did you brush your teeth *properly*? Lights out now. Hurry up, you'll be late. How should I know where your shoes are? Where did you leave them?

323

Brush your teeth this minute!' This relentless, tedious litany could drive anyone quite mad, Lucy thought, the person obliged to recite it quite as much as those subjected to hearing it. All the time she felt herself wanting to leap to her feet and wail, 'But I'm not like this, I'm not this sort of person, it isn't meant to be like this at all . . .'

If Steven could hear her, if he could see her at home, he would have no interest in her: he would know her precisely for what she was, a selfish, silly woman who lived in a mindless blur of trivialities. When she was with him she could believe that she was a person who felt intensely about the situation in East Timor, and was absorbed by the latest Alan Hollingsworth. Without him, she became someone who preferred to read a Hairy McClary story because she knew it backwards and didn't have to concentrate to read it, someone whose primary purpose in life was to rub out the scribblings in her son's comprehension notebook and make him do it again, in the hope that the second time around it wouldn't look like a spider in the advanced stages of St Vitus' Dance. If Steven knew what she was like, saw what Mark saw, he would not want her; and if Mark saw what Steven saw, he would despise her. She turned her face to the wall, and recognized miserably that Steven would never see her again – or, rather, the only time he would see her was at New Year's Eve with Mark, when he would see the woman she was in real life, and he would not want her after that. The days when Lucy had guiltily acknowledged the sins of avarice and envy, when she had coveted no more than Constance's linen sheets, seemed long past. She gazed at the book on her lap without reading a word. Lust, undeniably, whatever she had said to Constance. And pride. And sloth. And most certainly wrath.

'I made a rather foolish *faux pas* this evening,' Mimi confessed to her son, setting the completed wreath carefully on the table. 'I asked Lucy if she was expecting another baby.'

'Whatever made you think that?' Mark asked, with amusement.

'I don't quite know. Something about her face, a certain glow, and she seems rather distracted in that way that pregnant women often have. Perhaps it's just me.'

'No, Ma, she's just a little angry with me at the moment. That's what puts the glow in her cheeks.'

'She did seem a touch irritable.'

'She'll be all right once Christmas is over.'

Mimi wanted to ask if her son and his wife were happy together, but she was too discreet. 'Are you managing to find any time to paint, dear?'

'Here and there. I paint enough, enough for me. Charlie has talent.'

'I always thought you did too, that it was something you should have pursued.'

'I do pursue it, Mother, for my own pleasure. I am too old to pursue anything for any other reason.'

'You and Lucy have all your lives ahead of you,' his mother corrected, 'and you still have a great deal to learn.'

'Oh, Ma, you still make me feel ten years old. How many times have I heard you say, "You still have a great deal to learn"?'

'I haven't finished saying it yet, Mark. One never stops needing to learn. It's simply unfortunate that one's ability to learn from experience declines with age. I suppose that memory serves less purpose as we grow older, and that's why I find myself able to recall the events of my childhood so much more clearly than the events of last week. Young people like you –' Mark smiled, 'don't look at me like that, you're still a young man – are so confident that they've already learned all the lessons they need.'

'Not me, Mother. I promise to stay at school providing you promise to stick around to teach me.'

'That's the dreadful thing about growing old, dear. You end up with nothing at all but weary legs, poor eyesight and experience, and nobody seems to want that any more. Whenever I try to tell some young person, you, or Josh, or Hazel,' Mimi included her other daughter-in-law, 'what I have seen and what I have learned, you children look at me as if I have arrived from another planet, as if what I have seen can't possibly be relevant these days. When you're my age you will realize that nothing ever changes at all. We all go through nearly identical experiences, you, your father, myself, and Charlie and Grace and dear little Abby will go through them too, just the same. Nothing changes.'

'You know what they say, Ma, when you're young you believe everything, when you're middle-aged you suspect everything, and you know you're old when you know everything.' She did not return his grin, and Mark looked at his mother with loving concern. 'Is something up, Ma?' He hoped Mimi would not raise anything that required his urgent care or attention: he was simply too tired.

'Everything is perfectly all right.' Mimi smiled reassuringly and held her tongue. She had been raised in an age when introspection was considered a sure sign of nervous collapse, and it was not an indulgence that she had ever encouraged in herself or in her children. 'Contraception has done the world a great deal more good than introspection ever will,' she used to snort when one of her children dabbled in it. 'Face forward and socks up.' She had many things yet to teach her children, important lessons, not the least being how to grow old and how to die. Unlike most lessons parents find themselves, almost accidentally, teaching, these were not ones she could revise with hindsight, or get a second crack at. She had to be right first time. Even as she said goodnight, she lingered for a moment, with an intuition of concern. There was something about her son's manner, about the tight yet self-effacing smile he wore when Lucy grumbled about his poor eyesight, that concerned Mimi but, like Mark, she was weary.

Ever since he was a child, Mark had struggled to control his composure when he feared he might give himself away. He mastered his expression even when he was left alone in the drawing room. Only those who knew him most intimately, perhaps only his wife, would have taken one look at his face that night and said with dread, 'My God, Mark, what on earth has happened?' After he had heard his mother's footsteps cross from the guest bedroom to the bathroom and back again to bed he went upstairs. Mark looked in on each of the children, tucking Grace's bear back into her arms, and lastly on Lucy. She had fallen asleep sitting up against the headboard, her brows pulled together and a small frown on her lips, with a cookbook on her knees. He closed the book, marking the page, and went out to the garage.

The studio, as he called it only to himself, suffered from poor natural light during the day and worse artificial light at night. Mark knew that no real artist would tolerate working in the conditions to which he had gradually become accustomed, but he did not consider himself a genuine artist for one moment. He lit the Calor gas heater and rubbed his hands before it. He could see his breath in the room as he exhaled, yet he stood in the open doorway for some time, looking at the stars. He treasured the times when he was alone late at night, when the eerie, powerful silence of the deep countryside absorbed him and stopped him thinking about the business, and how he would settle his accounts when there was no money in the bank and he could not bring himself to put pressure on his debtors. Money, or the lack of it, provided one possible reason why Lucy might be so dissatisfied with him, but it was one he sadly rejected, sadly, because any reason at all would have been a comfort to him. He knew that Lucy had never cared about money, and had never craved it: the only reason she clung to the flat was because she had grown accustomed to having it, and he recognized acutely that the willingness to give up what one has is considerably harder than denying oneself what one has never had. That morning he had again tried to talk to Lucy about having to tighten their belts, a phrase that had come uneasily from his lips, and she had looked at his and her own reflections in her mirror with an almost indiscernible shrug. He had wanted simultaneously to slap her and to ravish her, anything to knock her out of herself. He found her deliberate refusal to let him into her thoughts both infuriating and erotic, and his own reaction had frightened him.

Mark had taken pride in the knowledge that he had always given Lucy everything she desired, the home she wanted, the nuclear-family life, enough money to lead a comparatively easy life, his time, his complete commitment to the children as well as to Lucy herself, and the more he thought about it and looked for ways in which he had gone wrong, the more he was forced to accept that he simply did not know why she was now so remote. It seemed only days ago that she had talked him through every moment of her emotional life, every tiny up and down, to the point when he sometimes wished he knew rather less about the workings of her heart and mind. The spring of her intimacy that he had taken for granted had suddenly dried up. That she was unhappy, Mark did not doubt; she demonstrated it every day by moving further away from him. Mark was close to wearily giving up the fight, and throwing away the laurels he had taken for granted as the reward for love. If he had not done enough, he did not see how he could now do more. He had been faithful both trivially and absolutely, and it had not been enough. He loved her, and it was not enough.

He closed the door and locked it behind him without thinking.

He pulled the dust sheet off the portrait he had been working on for the past three months. He did not need Lucy to model for him, as he had in the early years of their marriage. The haunting expression he had painted, the half-smile on her lips, her face in contemplative repose, he knew well. Mark studied the large canvas intensely, inch by inch, before composing his palette. There was something wrong with the eyes, a vacancy about them. He had lent everything else about her too much definition, the cheekbones in particular needed softening. Mark hoped that the knowledge that his wife was having an affair with Steven Armitage had not destroyed his ability to capture her finally on canvas, and he set to work determinedly. He doubted if Lucy would like his Christmas present. All he knew for certain was that he had to cement himself in what he stood for, or betray himself once and for all.

Chapter Twenty-one

Be not faint hearted, as you must kill . . .

Jeremy Lee

Lucy went to London at the eleventh hour, four days before Christmas. She did not want to set foot in the city, but she could not find a copy of a computer game that Charlie desired above all things, and she had not, as she had intended, been efficient enough to order by mail. It was a simulation game she had read about in the newspaper in November, which allowed the player to design an island, create its flora and fauna as well as human inhabitants, and impose all sorts of other events – invasion by hostile neighbours, freak weather conditions, even a volcano. It allowed the child to play God. Charlie had been entranced. Lucy had put the article in a safe place, but she kept many newspapers safely, and spent 19 December leafing through a pile of twelve papers and seven supplements before she found the item. It was a Tuesday; Constance was in the flat, and had suggested that they met later for dinner. Waiting on the platform, huddled against the sleet, Lucy tried not to think about Steven: as far as she knew, he had fallen off the face of the earth. Once on the train she wondered how he would spend

Christmas and with whom. On a sudden impulse she called him.

'This is,' the brittle woman intoned, 'Steven Armitage,' she heard him say, and Lucy's heart fluttered and sank. Of course he wouldn't be there, not just before Christmas, not at nine a.m. 'I am afraid that,' 'Steven Armitage,' he interjected brightly, 'is unable to take your call. However, if you would like to leave a message for,' 'Steven Armitage . . .' Lucy had no message to leave. She could not wish him a merry Christmas or say that she was looking forward to seeing him at New Year; on the contrary, she prayed that he would not come to the Falcon. She could not say goodbye, when nothing had really happened, only the sum total of two afternoons in bed, two times that probably meant nothing to him. But she held on to the phone, just to hear his voice.

'Hello? It's Steven.' His real voice was flatter than the recorded one he interrupted.

Lucy's grip on the mobile tightened. 'Hello? Who is it? This is Steven Armitage.' A pause. 'Look, I've got a great deal of work to do here, so if you're that sod from Conran's outfit, you can tell him from me –'

'It's me,' Lucy breathed. He didn't acknowledge her. 'Steven? It's Lucy.'

'I heard you. I'm just trying to recover from the shock. Christ. Why haven't you called, you bloody, bloody woman?'

'I couldn't.'

'What? Were you going to be thrown out on the streets if you so much as picked up the phone? Have you been handcuffed to the marital bed?'

'Steven . . . Don't be bitter.'

'Don't be *bitter*? Fuck! What do you want me to do, Lucy? How do you bloody well expect me to feel?' His voice rose louder and louder. 'What do you think I am? A fucking pet rock? Have you

332

had any idea, in that self-centred, complacent, screwed-up little head of yours, how I've felt the past three weeks, hmm? Have you thought about that? No, because I'm just the idiot who fell in love with you, till you decided to trot home to hubby. I suppose you've spent the past three weeks cosied up in Dorset trying to decide whether you can really spare the time to take some stupid position on the bloody school bloody board!'

Lucy closed her eyes, but she could not envisage Steven's setting. After all, she had never been to his office, or to his flat; she knew nothing about him. She did not see the startled look that Marcella directed at him, or the way the lips of the Features temp twitched in amusement at his outburst, or the flash of disapproval that crossed the face of Steven's editor, or the way Steven, oblivious to all of them, tipped his chair back with one hand flat on top of his copper hair as he yelled at her.

'I thought it was for the best,' she whispered.

'For me to do the noble thing, and you to do nothing at all? Where are you?'

'On the train.'

Steven covered his eyes. 'On the train. Right. Coming or going?'

Three minutes later Lucy heard herself promise to meet him at the Meridien bar at four that afternoon.

She bought the children five times as much as she had set out to buy them, but managed to find Charlie's game. She stood in the drizzle outside Hamley's, under the garish Christmas lights. She could go to the station at once; she could run to the flat and cry her heart out on Constance's strong shoulder, except that Steven might guess she would hide there and dig her out like a fox gone to earth. She walked slowly to the hotel bar and dropped her bags in a heap at Steven's feet. He barely looked at her as a waiter appeared to take her order. Their entire relationship had circled around waiters, or waiters had at least circled around them.

'My friend will have a glass of champagne – no, she'll have an Old-fashioned. She's an old-fashioned girl, after all.'

'Of course, sir. Right away.'

'That's what you are, aren't you, Lucy?' Lucy's jaw clenched. 'So why the impromptu call?'

'Why did you call Connie?'

'Why not? People have been talking about the Lonely Falcon, it's not often I get out of town, and there's a strong case for reviewing country restaurants that are trying to take the message to the masses.' He looked at her properly. 'Jesus, Lucy, why do you think I called her? Do you think I would have if I had found any other way of making you call me?'

'Promise me you won't come.'

Steven stared at her until she looked away. 'Tell you what, I promise I won't come, I won't call, I won't make any attempt to see you again. All you have to do is tell me that you don't love me. That you never loved me.'

'I don't love you.'

'I don't believe you.'

'Then that's something you're going to have to live with.' Lucy stuck her chin out, her face turned away from him. 'I can't control what you do.'

'Oh, yes, you can,' he said softly. 'Yes, you can. You can make me angry, and you can make me happier than I've ever been in my life, and you *can* make me walk away. You know it. I will love you whatever you do.' As Lucy shook her head, at first slowly, and then more vehemently, he grabbed her hand. 'I will, you know I will. You can tell me to get out of your life, or you can let me love you, and love your children.'

'No!' By referring to her children Steven had unintentionally flung her the rope that might just save her and hang him. She swung round to face him full on. 'You can't love my children.'

334

Steven moved his hands in a vague, sweeping movement, a gesture Lucy had seen long ago from business clients when she raised the need for cutbacks and divestments, a gesture that indicated they had come up against a deal-breaker. The familiarity of the palms-down signal allowed her to recover a little more. 'I have too much invested, *too much invested*, Steven. I can't pull up, and I can't throw it in. It's easy for you. What do you have at stake? At the very worst, you're just left with another relationship that didn't work out.'

Steven covered his eyes briefly, then said. 'All right, Lucy, I believe you. I didn't until now, but now I believe you don't love me. That's settled, then. Look, I ought to be going . . .' He stood up, but as Lucy made a small movement to detain him, a gesture she did not know she had made, he halted and groaned. 'Oh, Lucy. I do love you so.'

'And I love you.' Lucy flinched at the expectation in his eyes. 'I thought I did. But that doesn't change anything.'

'D'you think your marriage is the first or the last to fail? Sometimes marriages don't work. It's no one's fault.'

'Not mine,' Lucy breathed. 'Not mine.'

'And we can't continue as we are?' Steven had intended it as a statement, but his voice, and his heart, tipped up at the last moment, making it a still a possibility.

'As we *are*? Do you really want to do that?' Lucy asked him fiercely. 'We might have carried on as we *were*. If we'd never made love, never had sex,' she corrected herself, avoiding his eyes, 'if Julian hadn't walked in, if so many things . . . But all that happened, and it changed everything, and how can you sit there wanting to carry on as we *are*? Do you have any idea how horrific that would be, how monstrous? Do you have any idea who I am, beyond thinking that there's something novel and quaint about sleeping with a woman who has drool on her shirt? Can you really believe that we have any future together? What do you imagine I would say to Charlie, to Grace? That I grew tired of their father, and traded him in for another model? When it's not true? What do you suggest I say to Mark? Life isn't about sex in the afternoon, not for me, Steven. Having a whole pattern, who pays the phone bill, and who manages the diary, and who's responsible for ordering the milk, all that *matters*. Knowing that when I'm not there, there's somebody else to put the children to bed, and that's their father, somebody they love? Do you know what it is like to lie in bed with a child burning up with fever in your arms? You could never mean more to me than that. Do you think it matters a jot that you are willing to try to love them, when they have no reason at all to love you? What would I become if the children looked at you and cried for Mark, and told me they hated you? How much would I blame you, and hate myself? Do you know what I'm like when I'm tired and angry with them just because they've broken a glass, or left something out in the rain? Do you, Steven? Mark does. I can never take the decision to give that up, never. What do you think, that I can just take Mark's children away from him,' Lucy snapped her fingers, 'and spend my days and nights in restaurants with you? Jet off to Mexico City? Ask Mark to look after the kids for me on Valentine's night?'

'No. I don't think that.' Steven had turned ashen listening to her. He wanted to enfold her, but she had become immovable, granite.

'Do you think,' she whispered, 'that after all this time I don't love Mark? That I'm incapable of loving Mark, just because I fancied you?'

'I don't believe you love Mark. I know you love me.' He spoke with rising anger. 'I think you are pretending very hard that you're a good girl, a devoted little stay-at-home wife. You're fooling yourself, you're a coward. Watch it, Lucy, because if you try too hard you are going to become exactly what you're pretending to be.'

'You don't know what I feel,' Lucy whispered in shock.

'Do you?'

'If you really loved me, and I mean *loved* me, then you'd understand.'

'That's all I want, Lucy, the chance to.'

'But you can't, don't you see that? You can't have any trial runs. We can't be together and see if it "works out". It's too late for that.'

'So there are no good second marriages, good stepfathers or stepmothers in your world? You're going to sit there and dig your heels in and say it can't happen, without even giving it a shot?'

'Giving it a shot?' Lucy echoed blankly. 'Giving it a *shot*? Do you know what I've already done to my children? How I've stopped thinking about them just to make enough space in my head for you?'

Steven sat clasping and unclasping his hands. 'Lucy, you've gone quite mad. I don't want your children to disappear –'

'Just Mark?'

'All right, yes, God damn it, I do want Mark to fucking disappear!'

'He's not going to, not if I can help it. Listen, Steven, you don't know what marriage is like – you think you do, but you don't.'

'Tell me, then.'

Lucy swallowed several times to control the sobs rising in her throat. 'The only way I can put it is that if I had to go to a desert island with one person it would still be Mark. Always. Do you see?' Steven raised an eyebrow ironically, but Lucy dismissed his look with impatience. 'He knows what I look like when I puke, and that when no one's watching I can eat three bowls of porridge with brown sugar and *cream*, and he's the only person in the world I've been to bed with without brushing my teeth, because I can't be shagged and I know he won't mind . . . I don't have to pretend to be anything else when I'm with him. I don't have to hide anything I do.'

'Do you with me? Do I make you pretend?'

Steven had never made her pretend: he had let her become somebody else altogether, the other Lucy. For a brief time she had honestly believed that her two worlds could exist on different trajectories; now she had seen that they were bound to collide and blow each other up. Lucy chewed her lip, yearning to reassure him of her love but determined to get him off course. 'When I feel rotten, or sick, or alone, or frightened, and Mark's not there, I curl up in bed in *his* pyjamas.'

'Have you done that since you met me, curled up in his pyjamas?'

Lucy stared fixedly at the low table, turning a coaster over and over in her hands. 'He's not going to disappear.'

'And I am?'

'I'm sorry. I'm so sorry it has to be like this.'

'But because he met you first, that is the way it has to be?'

'Yes.'

'Tell me you love me.'

'I love you,' Lucy said simply. 'But I can't see you again.'

'Let me come at New Year just to see if you are happy – at all happy – with him.'

'That's your decision, I can't stop you. I have to go now.'

'Are you going home?'

'Yes.'

'To Charlotte Street? Can't I walk you home?'

'I'm going *home*. Goodbye, Steven.' Lucy collected the Christmas bags that had tumbled around their chair legs and left without looking back. It was raining again, and Piccadilly was awash with shoppers buying anything that could be shoved in a box under a tree, and the diffused orange glow of the car lights and street-lights and Christmas lights made the regular greyness of London more oppressive than ever. Lucy did not attempt the futility of trying to fight for a cab. She tucked her chin into the collar of her coat, head ducked against the rain, and walked back to Charlotte Street.

Constance was lying on the sofa in Chinese pyjamas with a greenish-white face pack, painted thickly from hairline to neck, over which she wore her glasses. 'Attractive, no? The glasses add the finishing touch.'

'If you ever write a cookbook, Connie, that's the look to use for the jacket photo.' Lucy smiled wearily.

Constance stretched and put the magazine down. 'Now there's a thought: a cookbook . . .' She eyed the assortment of huge carrier-bags that Lucy dumped on the table. 'No need to ask if you had a successful day.'

'I've got a birthday present for you somewhere in here.'

'For me? From Hamley's?' Constance tore the tissue off the small flat package and caressed the slim silver cigarette case her friend had chosen. 'Oh, Luce, how lovely! That's that, then. I can't ever give up smoking. It's gorgeous.'

'I'm glad you like it. It was either that or Soopah Slime GooWorks,' she began to unpack her purchases, holding them up for Constance's inspection, 'although I was tempted to get both you and Grace your very own *Baywatch* Barbies.'

'You looked wiped out.'

'I am. Hamley's started the job and Steven finished it off.'

'Uh-oh. You saw him today?'

'I just left him. I didn't mean to see him but, then, I seem to be doing plenty of things that weren't part of my Great Plan.'

'How about if we stay in and get a Thai takeaway?'

'Sounds great. Let me have a bath and get warmed up.'

'I'll get it delivered. Shall I choose for you?'

Lucy halted on the way to the bathroom. 'Why not? I've made enough decisions to last a lifetime.'

An hour later Constance picked a lime leaf out of her bowl of *tom yam gung*, held it disdainfully between finger and thumb and exclaimed, with disgust, 'Asian restaurants in England think they can get away with murder. They *can* get away with murder. You know, the best meal I ever had was at the Oriental in Bangkok, a crab soup I'd willingly trade ten years of my life for. Did I tell you –'

'Connie,' Lucy interrupted, in a steady voice, 'I want to talk to you about Steven.'

Constance nodded quickly. 'I was afraid to ask.'

'I said it was up to him if he came to the Falcon, but that we wouldn't meet alone again.'

'Good. How did he react?'

'I barely let him speak. I think, I don't know, I think he wanted me to leave Mark.'

'He wants to marry you?'

'He never said that. He said he wanted a chance to love me, and love my children.'

'Oh, for fuck's sake! I tell you, Lucy, he's so low that when they bury him they're going to have to dig *up*.' Constance waited in vain for a smile. 'OK, that's not original. And not very funny, right?'

Lucy spoke softly. 'I don't think I'm ever going to be able to laugh about it, Connie. Anyway, it isn't as if he were some Victorian villainous seducer, and it doesn't make it any easier pretending it was like that.'

'I thought it might. I'm sorry.'

'When we were together Steven made me feel that I was the

most extraordinary creature on earth, beautiful, witty, talented, everything. I knew at once – I knew all the time that there was no future in it. It was so overwhelming to feel like that, that he was willing to sacrifice everything . . . Until I realized I was the one who was going to sacrifice everything. I've been so vile, to Mark, to the children . . . I've even been vile to *him*. Now I feel empty. Now every time I look in the mirror I'm going to look at myself and think, There's a bitch who cheated on her husband for nothing. I don't know who I am any more, Connie.'

'Oh, Lucy, you won't feel like that for long, I promise you. It doesn't have to be like that. And it wasn't for nothing, was it? He made you feel wonderful. That's not nothing.'

'It's worse than nothing. Now I know what wonderful feels like.'

'Poor lamb. You really are in a mess, aren't you? I can't imagine what falling in love feels like. I can't even remember what it's meant to be like.'

'I thought I was in love with him. It seemed so blissful and sort of *innocent* until we went to bed. It was only then that I saw all the problems I'd made for myself. I know what love's meant to be like . . .' Lucy said softly, almost to herself. *I know what it is like because I have felt it, and felt it with Mark.* All the time she had been chasing the elusive experience of sudden and complete happiness that she found with Steven, she had believed that she was recovering herself, the woman she had been before she married. Yet it was Mark who had first given her the sensation of wild happiness, and that was why it had felt so strangely familiar. 'Connie, do you and Julian stay up after midnight, just talking?'

'Only if I prop his eyes open with bamboo skewers.'

'Mark and I used to all the time, we couldn't stop talking. We'd look up and it would be three in the morning.'

'Julian likes to talk in daylight. Anyway, no one talks till three when they have small children.'

341

'Maybe we've lost the knack.'

'Nah, it's like riding a bicycle. You and Mark will be there again. Have some duck curry.'

'Why did Julian tell you about his affair?'

'He didn't, not exactly. I mean, he didn't pour his heart out in a guilty confession.'

'So how did you find out?'

'I just knew. I felt it. He changed, and I knew why.'

'You guessed?'

'No, Lucy, I knew. I simply asked him to tell me about it.'

'Then Mark knows. He must.'

'If he does you'll find out soon enough. Personally I'm sorry I asked Julian. I regretted it for years. Once I knew I had to know more, and all at once I knew too much. Julian never exactly lied to me – neither of us is a natural liar, we just don't tell. By making him talk about it I made him tell me everything, and the details made me very unhappy.'

'What happened?'

'I don't believe there are ever parallels in these things.' Constance paused. 'I would explain if I thought it could help you at all, but I don't. We agreed at the time that we'd never discuss it with other people, and somehow that let it belong to us, rather than Julian and the other woman. I felt I had to claim the affair somehow in order to get Julian back. All couples have stuff that goes on just between the two of them, and people, in a couple or not, have their own private corners. They should stay private.'

'It's a bit late for me to think that now. Half the world knows.'

'You and Steven do, that's all. As far as Julian and I are concerned I've already forgotten about it. Julian will never breathe a word unless you bring it up.'

'So I spend another twenty years nursing my dark little secret?'

'It's up to you, Lucy. My advice is try to forget all about it.

Confession may help you, but what does knowing for certain do for Mark?'

'If he found out later, and then discovered that you and Julian had known all along, wouldn't that be even worse for him? Make him feel a fool?'

Constance was sitting cross-legged on the floor beside the low sofa table. She held her ankles with one hand, a cigarette in the other, and tipped her head back to blow smoke straight up at the high ceiling. 'It doesn't matter what other people know or think because other people don't know anything, and what they think is almost always wrong. Why should being innocent mean being a fool? You think he'd feel humiliated?'

'I would. Didn't you?'

'Not for a minute. Loving someone isn't about your own pride, for God's sake. It's about loving them whatever they do, and knowing they love you, whatever you've done. All Mark has to decide is whether he loves you, and whether he still believes you love him.'

'But I do love him – I love him desperately.'

'Just love him normally, and make sure he knows it. Don't lose Mark, Lucy. Don't do anything that risks losing him.'

'And what if he knows, like you did, and asks me?'

'So long as you don't put him in a position where he has to know anything he doesn't want to know.'

'What if he's stopped loving me already?'

'Stop borrowing trouble. He thinks Steven's a friend of mine. When he sees him at New Year, I'll make sure that's all he thinks. Get on with your life, Lucy, put all this behind you.'

Chapter Twenty-two

I must qualify all this by saying that occasionally marriage is undoubtedly the happy state . . . which it was intended to be. There must, of necessity, be great purity in the mind of the man, joined with magnanimity, and justice, and where, or rather, how often are these qualities to be found combined?

Emma Hardy

Christmas Eve arrived so abruptly it caught Lucy like a sudden thunderstorm. Constance had generously written out all the recipes needed for Christmas lunch several weeks in advance, even listing the ingredients on a separate shopping list, but on the morning of the twenty-fourth half the store cupboard was still bare and Mimi had nobly undertaken the perilous last-minute foray to the supermarket. Mark and the children struggled to erect the tree, resulting in many swallowed curses as Mark discovered that the fairy-lights didn't work and set Charlie to twiddling each tiny bulb. Amy took Abigail out to visit friends, and Lucy searched the house for the presents she had bought and hidden so successfully that she couldn't find them herself. An hour before they were due to take the children to the Blessing of the Crib service, Lucy ran out of Father Christmas's wrapping paper, and dashed to the shops to find an alternative that would not look in any way similar to the 'family' paper. This left only fifteen minutes to chop some apples, shred red cabbage that she suspected the children would regard with disgust and no time at all to measure the balsamic vinegar, red wine, brown sugar and spices before throwing them all into a pot and into the bottom oven. Amy had the children perfectly dressed for church, but Lucy went in a pair of torn jeans and a sweater of Mark's, a far cry from the long skirt and chenille sweater she had put out that morning. She resolved to get herself to Midnight Mass decently dressed.

Had Lucy made it to Midnight Mass at St Michael's, she would have seen the Purcells sitting four pews from the front, Constance in a swirling greatcoat that made her look like a female highwayman, Francesca in an aubergine velvet dress buttoned all the way up to her delicate chin, Luke looking uncomfortable in what was probably his school suit, and Julian sitting bolt upright, waiting to read the first lesson. Lucy did not see the Purcells, because at eleven thirty that night she was in the kitchen repeating the red cabbage recipe, this time following Constance's instructions to the letter. After seven hours in the oven the first batch had dissolved into a soggy, faintly purple but predominantly grey mass, barring the crusty caramel edges. Mark was stuffing the stockings, following Lucy's instructions as strictly as she obeyed Constance's. When he joined her in the kitchen he opened a bottle of champagne. 'All done. Thank God. And it will all be undone within precisely fifteen minutes tomorrow morning. Here, darling, happy Christmas.' They touched glasses. 'To next year, when I suggest we opt for a Buddhist celebration and gather round a bowl of water.'

'It sounds *wonderful*.'

'You wouldn't do it in a million years.'

She smiled in agreement. 'Was there enough for Abby's stocking?'

'Lucy, she's only a year old. She doesn't know one end of a stocking from the other, or what to do with it except suck it.'

'She doesn't, but Charlie and Grace do. If Abby doesn't have a full stocking, or if it's less than theirs, Charlie will smell a rat.'

'Charlie won't even glance at his sisters' stockings, I promise you.'

'I must remember to put some coal in yours.'

It was an English Christmas tradition – meaning a tradition of Lucy's family rather than the entire nation's – that the adult males of the family should have a lump of coal in the toe of their sock as a warning from Father Christmas that their conduct over the preceding twelve months had not been entirely up to scratch. Lucy's father played his role dutifully year after year, looking increasingly relieved as he neared the bottom, telling his daughters that perhaps that year, for once, Father Christmas had let him off the hook. Fumbling in the toe, his face would collapse into crestfallen disappointment as he retrieved the black lump.

'When does Charlie come of age and get the coal treatment?'

Lucy looked at Mark over her shoulder with a smile. 'God – I never thought about that, not having a brother. It was always just Dad.'

'I was hoping for a little male solidarity. What were my crimes, specifically, this year? Just so I know, if anyone asks.'

'It's only a joke, darling. You are blameless.'

'Am I? I was under the impression you rather wanted to punish me for something.'

Mark waited for a response; Lucy looked deep into the pot, her hair swinging forward in a sheet, which she held back at her ear. She had a habit of holding it there rather than tucking it behind the ear. 'You look lovely, Luce.'

She laughed. 'Only you could say that – I look like a dog. Would you mind making the brandy butter while you're sitting there? I put everything out.'

'Ma, Maaa – Mumm-eee!' Grace's cry came from half-way down the stairs and Mark was there in an instant, carrying her back to the kitchen.

'Grace! What are you doing awake? Father Christmas won't come if you're still awake, you know that, and he'll be here *any minute . . .*'

'We have to do the reindeer, I forgot their food.' Lucy and Mark's gaze met over the little girl's head as she sobbed, rubbing her eyes. 'Charlie says if we don't leave them any food, they won't bring our presents . . .'

'We'll leave something on the doorstep, shall we?' Mark rubbed his hands together cheerily.

'No, it has to be by the chimney. He comes down the *chimney*,' Grace whimpered.

'It's all right, Gracie, Daddy will take you back to bed and I'll put their food out –'

'No!' she shrieked. 'I have to put it out, Charlie *said* I have to put it out or I won't get any presents!'

'OK, OK, you can.' The dire implications of Lucy's capitulation dawned on both parents at once. Lucy drew a few deep breaths. 'Let's just think what we need. Grace, you go into the pantry and fetch the bag of carrots, while I look for the biscuits.' As Grace stumbled sleepily off on her mission, Lucy whispered urgently to Mark. 'You'll have to go and hide everything. Get all the presents out of the room. And empty the stockings – she was there when we hung them up, so tip everything behind the curtains and leave the empty stockings up.'

'Oh, *Christ*. This is insane.'

'Just hurry!'

Lucy bought Mark time by meticulously peeling four carrots before she chopped them up. Grace began to count the biscuits, laying them in a line on the table. 'That one's for Dasher, and that one's for Dancer, and *that* one's for Comet and that's for . . .?'

'Cupid.'

'Cupid. And that's for Prancer, and that's for Vixen . . .'

'And Donder and Blitzen. That's it, my darling, all done.' Lucy looked nervously at the door, hearing banging and clumping. 'We'd better hurry, Grace, and get you back to bed. I think I can hear sleigh bells already. Can you?'

'I hear Christmas,' Grace said gravely, cupping her hand dramatically around her ear. 'I can hear it thumpeting all over the house.'

Lucy hugged her. 'Me too. Now we'd better get a mince pie for Father Christmas.'

'And something to drink!' Grace chirruped.

'Oh, yes, a *great* deal to drink, I'd say.'

'Mummy, what about Rudolph?'

'We mustn't forget Rudolph, he's the most important of all.'

'Rudolph is a *girl*.'

'If you say so, Grace.' When Mark appeared, looking distinctively unfestive and gave the all-clear, mother and daughter trooped into the drawing room and laid the plates on the floor in front of the fire. Grace was bundled back into bed and threatened with the direst of all consequences if she moved an inch.

'Happy Christmas, sweetheart,' Lucy whispered over her head, 'and a hundred more to come,' before she raced back downstairs to help Mark refill the stockings.

On the other side of the valley Francesca helped herself to the bowl of her mother's homemade chocolate toffee almonds, individually wrapped in tiny scraps of silver tissue.

'You'll wake up with an enormous zit on the end of your nose,' Luke commented smugly.

'It can't possibly be larger than the pustulating one on your chin,' Francesca replied loftily and took another to prove her point.

'Children, children, let's have a little more peace and goodwill. We've just come from church.'

'Lucy and Mark weren't there, were they, Mum?'

'Midnight Mass is hard to manage when you have small children, Chess. We stopped going when you were two or three. I was holding you on my lap, and during the sermon you projectile-vomited so violently it nearly hit the vicar.' Constance smiled and stretched her toes out to the fire. 'Anyway, it's time you two headed to bed.'

'Oh, Mu-um!' they intoned together in perfect harmony.

'Bed,' Julian said firmly. 'Or Father Christmas won't come.' His daughter eyed him with disdain. 'OK, if you don't buy that, then bed, or the two of you have to cook lunch tomorrow, and that would punish all of us. And don't emerge before nine!' he admonished, as his children left the room.

Constance rested her head on his shoulder in the glow of the fire, fingering her new ruby earrings. 'I can't wait for New Year's Day.'

'You haven't told the children?'

'No.'

'Let's not, shall we? Keep it a surprise.'

'I bet they'll be more excited about having an extra week off school than they are about two weeks in Thailand.'

'Are you sure you wouldn't rather we went alone, without them?'

'No, darling, it's the most perfect present, to take all of us. I keep dreaming about the Oriental's crab soup . . .'

'You can have it every night.'

'I want to have it every breakfast too.'

'And so you shall. Merry Christmas, my love.'

Mark and Lucy were also sitting in front of the fireplace, although the flames had long since died down and only a few coals glowed in the darkened room. They had finished the bottle of champagne while replacing the presents and refilling the stockings, and turned to the whisky bottle that Grace had carried proudly, with both hands, and set on the floor by the hearth. The dog disdained the carrots but had already wolfed the mince pie and all the biscuits except for a few crumbs that Lucy had saved as evidence. Reindeer, unlike Mungo, did not lick plates clean enough to put back in the cupboard.

'Lucy, what do you think we should do about the flat?'

'You think we have to sell it.'

'It isn't a unilateral decision,' he said gently, 'it's something we should be able to discuss together.'

'I hate the idea of giving it up, but if we have to sell, then we have to sell. I can live with that. I suppose Julian and Connie will be able to keep it on without us, if they want to.'

'I wish I could give you everything *you* want.' Mark stroked her hair, and she leaned in to his side, closing her eyes. She didn't know whether she could cope with the scale of the conversation; whether she could even handle the next few days. She wondered where Steven was and who he was with. He was probably at a party, something very grown-up. She was certain his thoughts did not turn to her the way hers turned to him. 'You were right about the flat, I suspected it even as we bought it. I'm too slapdash about things like that, things that are important, and take time . . .'

'The business, you mean?'

Mark scratched his head. 'I mean everything. Maybe I don't pay enough attention, or I take things for granted.' He was watching her and trying to conceal it.

Lucy slipped her arms around his waist under his shirt. 'You and me too. How can anyone spend so much time getting ready for Christmas and achieve so little?'

'You've done everything, Lucy. The children will believe everything. That's a kind of magic.'

'It won't last much longer.'

'Yes it will, it will last for ever. The children will never forget what these years were like.' After a moment's hesitation Mark kissed the top of her head.

'What about you and me, Mark, when they've all left home? What will we do at Christmas?'

'Meditate on a bowl of water? Drink martinis? Eat blood oranges in bed, and get the juice all over the sheets? We'll be able to do anything we goddamn feel like.'

'You'll be bored when it's just me, and the house is empty.' Lucy's voice wobbled: she felt close to tears and in need of absolution.

'You will never bore me, Lucy. You may try my patience, and you may quite easily provoke me, even when you're not trying to, but you won't bore me. I will always be wondering what it is that you are looking for, and always looking for you, and always listening for the sound of your footstep. Sometimes I forget to tell you.' Lucy turned her head into his sweater to hide the tears that flowed silently down her cheeks, as a cold chill ran down her spine.

All choices lay before her, all possibilities. She did not know who she was inside, but she knew she could choose which cloak to put on, and that she could not keep changing from one to the other. Perhaps the cloak was always waiting, and however long one resists putting it on, it was there, waiting, ready-made since

352

childhood, and it was simply a question of deciding when to accept it. She could not wear two different cloaks at once.

'How can I help loving you, Mark, when you say things like that?'

'Have you been trying not to love me?'

'No, but I've been incredibly wrong. Selfish and thoughtless . . .'

'You are insulting the woman I love!'

'I'm not joking. I've been awful.'

'I don't want to hear another word, not one. All you've done is burn the cabbage, and forgotten the reindeer. And forgotten to ring those blasted sleigh bells.'

She pulled back to look at him. 'Where the hell did I hide the sleigh bells?'

Mark felt behind him and pulled them out from the sofa cushion. 'Let's go outside and shake them together, OK?'

The grass was frosted enough to crunch beneath their feet as they moved away from the house. Mark blew on his fingers, elbows pulled tight to his sides, as he watched Lucy step from one side to the other, lightly ringing the bells that no one but he would hear. He put his arm around her shoulders and pulled her close, forcing her to walk in step with him.

'What? Where are we going?'

'We're going to the garage. I want to give you your Christmas present.'

'Oh, Mark, what if the children wake up?'

'It won't take long. You won't want to play with it. I want you to open it alone. Besides, I can't bring it into the house.'

'It's something horrible, isn't it?' Lucy said, with amused suspicion. 'It's some horrible joke. Remember that Christmas when Julian gave Connie two tons of garden manure as a present? That's what you've done, isn't it? Ordered a bloody great heap of well-rotted cow dung for me.'

Mark smiled secretively as he unlocked the door. 'I promise you it's not manure. It may be a crap present, and it may even end up on the bonfire, but it's not manure.' He switched on the lights.

'It's freezing – even colder in here than it is outside.' Lucy's heart thumped when she saw the painting draped in a dust sheet adorned with multi-coloured bows. Mark's paintings had never left the garage, and never been offered as gifts; Mark's paintings had always belonged to him alone, and she did not know how she would react. Whether she liked it or not, she was touched that Mark had spent his time on a gift for her. She shivered and looked around her at the bleak space that was Mark's refuge, pretending not to notice the painting propped up against the wall. 'Well?' she asked expectantly. 'So where's my present?'

'Open it, Lucy. I'm going to wait outside.'

For a few moments, Lucy delayed looking at the painting while she paced, mentally rehearsing her reaction. *It's lovely Mark, it's absolutely lovely. Did you really paint it especially for me? We'll have to put it in our bedroom so I can see it all the time. I'll move that crappy old print Dad gave me . . .* Then she tentatively tweaked the top edge of the dust sheet and it slithered to her feet.

The painting was a portrait of Lucy. In the immediate foreground was a table on which a few white lilies had been casually tossed. The woman herself sat slightly to the right of centre, her left knee thrown over the arm of an upholstered chair, a book held loosely, about to slip, in her right hand, with her thumb marking the half-way place between the pages. Her face was turned towards the viewer, but not fully; she did not look out of the painting, but rather seemed to be looking outside, through a window, half watching something the viewer was left to imagine. She was wearing a black dress of some dark, woollen fabric, a soft mohair sheath. The fingers of her left hand lifted her hair back, just above her ear. On the other side her hair fell in a dead straight drop. The colours of the painting were stark; the white lilies, black dress, pale hair; only a hint of red in her lips, and otherwise shades of bleach and shadow, and sunlight catching her face and streaking against the table where the lilies lay. These things were all a matter of record, absorbed without conscious thought. The expression in her eyes, the half smile on her lips, were a different matter.

Lucy gazed at herself spellbound, as her portrait looked back. She looked pensive yet contented. There was a warmth and wisdom in the eyes of the woman Mark had painted that Lucy never saw in the mirror, a certainty of her position that Lucy had never felt. It was a haunting image of an alluring woman, who was both the guardian of her world and slightly detached from it, who would never tell the secrets that lay behind her knowing expression or what it was she observed through the window that had brought that enigmatic smile to her lips.

'Well?' Mark said finally, unable to wait. 'Do you hate it?'

Lucy swung back to see him leaning in the doorway. 'Is this what you've been doing all this time?'

Mark shrugged. 'On and off. Why? You think it's crap, don't you?' They stood facing each other, twenty feet apart, each hugging themselves, Lucy shaking her head.

'I think it's incredible. I've never been given anything I loved more. It's too flattering,' she waved vaguely behind her, 'I've never been that, that –'

'What?'

'Oh, God, that gentle, that,' she swung back to face the portrait, 'that thoughtful, or, well, *lovely* . . .'

Mark drove his hands deep into his pockets. 'You are to me. That's how I see you. It was the only way I could paint you. Sam thought it was you exactly.'

'My God, Mark, if only . . .' She walked slowly towards him, and wrapped her arms about his head, pulling it down against her breast, and whispered, 'If I can become that woman before I die, I'll die happy . . . Thank you. I've never dreamed of anything like that.'

'Merry Christmas, my dearest Luce . . .'

There was no fireplace in Steven Armitage's flat. There was a bizarre white marble hearth, with a mantel, but nothing inside; it was a blank. The architect who had lived there previously had described it to Steven as a futuristic, emblematic, symbolic fire; effective *because* of its coldness. He had sold the flat to Steven and thrown in a slim, irregular Japanese porcelain vase that still sat on the marble slab and had never had so much as a stalk in it since Steven had moved in. Steven now sat slumped, near prostrate, in the solitary armchair before his vacant hearth. A cigarette dangled from his fingers, an ashtray and a half-full bottle of whisky sat at his feet. He had been to a drinks party that evening, full of singles with nowhere to go on Christmas Eve, with their loneliness and hope written wide on their faces. At eight he had come home, eaten an apple, which was all he had in his fridge, and thought of Lucy. At nine he had called his elderly aunt in Newbury, who had responded to his Christmas greetings by saying, 'Steven? But Steven *who*?' It had taken a good five minutes to remind her that she had a nephew, after which she had grumbled, justifiably, 'Well, Steven, it's hardly surprising. I haven't even spoken to you since your father died . . .' When Steven had suggested that he visit Newbury to exchange festive greetings, she had said it would be very pleasant to see him in the New Year, but she was spending Christmas with her second husband's niece's family, and would be away for the week. 'Did you ever meet Geoffrey? I can't remember if he came to the funeral . . .' she had said, in a querulous voice. Steven promised to call her in January, then relegated chasing his few remaining strands of family to the what's-the-use pile.

He had felt like religious music, any religion, anything that might have put him in the right spirit, even an Ave Maria would have done the job, but he had no appropriate CDs. He put on *La Bohème* at near full volume, mindless of the occupants of the flat below, and returned to his chair. Now he sat drinking whisky and thinking of Lucy, perversely wishing that she was dying and he had a place at her bedside, then dismissing himself as a fool. He imagined her happy in the bosom of her family, blind to every opportunity life held out. Quite blind, and all the more lovable for that. He had known it would be like this. It was the great reason for never loving a married woman: their marriage certificates and the birth certificates that followed permitted them to be ruthless. He raised his glass and said aloud, 'Merry Christmas, Lucy. Merry Christmas, darling, and may your gods go with you.'

Chapter Twenty-three

. . . the life of a wine has often been compared to that of a human being, not only in the expected progression from coquettish childhood innocence through exuberant youth to the measured balance of maturity, the serenity of age, and the senility of very old age, but in the surprising turns of unpromising children who blossom into long-lived, gentle philosophers or of a brilliant and boisterous child who discovers, in adulthood, the virtues of discretion.

Richard Olney

As instructed, the Epsteins and Samantha arrived early at the Lonely Falcon; Julian was there to greet them with champagne. 'My wife has been possessed by demons,' he confided with a smile. 'She has already sacked Lewis twice, and is making Gordon Ramsay look like a reincarnation of Mother Teresa. How are you, Lucy? You look stunning.'

'Will she bite my head off if I go in the kitchen?'

'On your own head be it. Mark, Constance wanted you to have a word with Philip about the wine as soon as you arrived . . .'

'Oh, I'll let Samantha handle that. She's been eyeing Philip up since we got here.'

Lucy always loved seeing Constance in her working environment, extended to the full length of her leash, with the sinews in her neck taut, her hair slicked savagely behind her ears, and her eyes sharpened to steel. She was wearing her white chef's jacket, and her easy brutality put Lucy in mind of the most cold-blooded surgeon.

'Hi, Lucy, just stand over there for a minute, and keep out of the way, OK? Lewis, I'm telling you, if you screw this up, if you put so much as a single finger wrong, you're dead, do you understand that? Alice, take that steamer off, it's far too early – and get the bloody polenta out of the fridge. Now. *Now!*' Lucy pressed herself flat to the wall and listened to the non-stop barrage that rattled from Constance's mouth. 'Why do I bother? Why? You're all a bunch of useless wankers, you ought to be pushing trolleys up and down trains, because that's the closest you're ever going to get to serious catering – Jesus Christ, Lewis, what the hell do you think you're doing? I said triangles, not fucking tranches, you berk!'

Lewis rolled his eyes at Lucy. Constance put her hands on her hips. 'So you've got enough time on your hands to pull stupid faces? I'm so glad. In that case I can leave it all in your capable hands and greet my guests.' She grabbed Lucy's elbow and dragged her out of the kitchen. 'I swear this is the last time. Tomorrow we close for good.'

'Connie, you know it's all going to be great.'

'Of course I do, but I can't let them know that. Hell. I shouldn't've given the punters a choice at each course – it puts far too much pressure on the kitchen. Why should they have any choice anyway?'

Lucy set her arms akimbo. 'Yes, why should they? Bloody ungrateful arseholes. They should just cough up the fifty quid a head and eat what they're bloody given! And be bloody grateful for it!' She wagged her head in disbelief.

Constance smiled and slipped her hand through Lucy's arm. 'I *knew* you'd understand . . .'

Outside the kitchen she was charm personified. Three long tables for ten had been laid in the main room. She had originally planned to have a table for teenagers, her children and their friends, but Francesca and Luke had begged and pleaded for a small party, 'Not even a party really, just a couple of friends,' at home, and Constance Julian had eventually given in, and written a list of strict commandments: 'Thou shalt not smoke, thou shalt not allow thy friends to smoke, thou shalt not even think about any form of drugs at all, thou shalt not go beyond snogging, nor permit friends to go beyond snogging . . .' It was the first time the children had been left unsupervised. Constance called home before her own guests arrived and Francesca picked up the phone on the first ring.

'Hi, Mum.'

'How did you know it was me?'

'Everyone's here. It had to be you checking up, right?'

'Is everything OK?'

'Everything's fine.'

'Did you put the pies in the oven?'

'Yes, Mum,' Francesca said patiently. 'You enjoy *your* party, and we'll see you later.'

Constance replaced the receiver, by no means reassured, but then her former boss arrived with his wife, and she threw herself into his arms. 'Chef, I'm so glad to see you!' she hugged the old man.

'How many times, hen,' he spoke in a brusque Scottish growl, hugging her back ferociously, 'did I tell you not to call me Chef? You call me Malcolm, like you always did.'

'I'm sorry, Malcolm,' she said meekly. She beckoned to her

361

waitress. 'Have a canapé and some champagne, and tell me what you think of the menu.'

Malcolm Hay took the menu and snapped his fingers at his wife, who at once retrieved his glasses from her handbag.

Truffle Custard

Salt Cod Purée on Fried Polenta Triangles
or
Ragoût de Crêtes de Coq et Sot l'y-laisse

Fillet of Sea Bass in Broth under a Parmesan Roof
or
Tiger Prawns with Pesto, Cannellini Beans and Tomato Confit

Beef Fillet Roasted in a Herb-Infused Salt Crust
or
*Lamb Shanks braised with Shallots,
Portobello Mushrooms and Celery*

Parfait of Raspberries with Mango Vinegar and Mascarpone
or
*Compôte of Macerated Winter Fruits with
Brandy Alexander Ice Cream*
or
Warm Chocolate Tart with Coffee Nougatine

Selection of Cheeses with House Breads
or
Angels on Horseback

'Constance, Constance.' Malcolm wagged his head and peered

at her critically over the top of his glasses. 'Och, Connie. First, the wording's too fussy. Keep it to roast fillet of beef, braised lamb shanks. Don't tell them how you're going to cook it. Second, why slip into French up there at the top?'

'How could I say coxcomb stew, Malcolm? No one would order it.'

'They won't order it anyway if they don't know what it is, and they certainly won't if they can't pronounce it. Have the courage of your convictions, girl! And raspberries. Raspberries belong to the summer. They have no place on a winter menu. Not of someone I've taught.'

Constance gazed back at him with conviction in her eyes. 'You're absolutely right. I'm a fool.'

'You're no fool, hen, you've always had the gift, but there's always more to learn. Go on – get back to your kitchen. I came here to eat your food, not read about it.'

Constance squeezed his arm. 'You're a mean, miserable pig, Chef. I don't know how I stood it for so long.'

'Because you wanted to become a mean, miserable pig yourself, Constance. If I didn't know you were a star in the heavenly firmament, I wouldn't care what your menu said.'

Lucy had heard the beginning of this exchange, but her eyes were fixed on the door while she pretended interest in a discussion on whether the turn of the century would have any impact on their lives.

'In ten days' time we'll look back and agree it was meaningless,' a tall man said smugly. Lucy hadn't caught his name.

'But what about the millennium bug?' his wife reminded him. 'It's going to ruin everything, throw everything upside down. We might not even have electricity tomorrow.'

'I think the danger's been rather exaggerated,' Mark replied politely, 'Personally I adopt the philosophy of living for the moment, each day as it comes, isn't that right?'

Lucy smiled, turned her head from one to the other and appeared to follow the conversation. *This is so boring, boring, boring. Why does any of it matter?* She was conscious of Mark's hand cupped supportively beneath her elbow and wished they were back at home with the children. 'What do you think, Lucy?'

'Excuse me?'

'Your husband was just explaining why he's a burgundy man.'

'Oh. Well, Mark knows much more than I do. I like . . .' Steven came into the restaurant with a woman as she spoke, and Lucy halted.

'You must have a favourite tipple.'

'No. I don't know. Maybe Italian whites.'

'*Italian?* How fascinating . . .'

Steven worked the room in an ever-decreasing circle that brought him closer to Lucy at its centre. 'Hello, hello, what a lovely occasion, my first time here, actually, Steven, that's right, Steven Armitage, so good to meet you, and this is Marcella Irwin, hello, no, I'm not local, wish I was, from what I've seen of the countryside, no, London in fact, good evening, a friend of Constance, absolutely, yes, delighted, looking forward to dinner *enormously* . . . Hello, Mark, good to see you again.' He bent his head to kiss Lucy on either cheek. 'Let me introduce my friend and colleague, Marcella Irwin.'

Lucy smiled at the young dark-haired woman who held Steven's arm but did not move. Mark shook Marcella's hand, then kissed her cheek. 'It seems absurd to be so formal when we'll all be kissing each other in four hours' time.'

'I couldn't agree more.' Marcella turned impulsively to Lucy. 'God, I hate New Year, don't you? Especially this New Year. All those bloody parties. When Steven asked me to come with him tonight, I leaped at it. I thought, At least it's a decent restaurant and I'll get more than a sausage roll, a bowlful of crisps and a hangover.' Lucy smiled as Marcella chatted nervously. 'Have you always lived down here?'

'I grew up in London actually . . .' Lucy searched the room for someone she wanted to talk to '. . . but it's very pleasant here, a wonderful place to raise a family, you know, unspoiled and everything . . .'

'I'd love to get out of London. Being a journalist, I don't see how I could.'

'No. Well, perhaps you'll find a way. Would you excuse me for a moment? There's someone I've been meaning to catch . . .'

Constance's staff passed discreetly among the guests. 'Have you seen the menu? If I could just take your order . . .' while Lucy wove through the bodies and out of the front door. She sat on the doorstep, staring at the stars.

'What are you wishing for?' Steven asked softly from the doorway.

'Oh, world peace, that kind of thing.'

'The waitresses are missing one rogue order.' Steven held a menu out to her. 'I offered to choose for you, but they insisted you were found.'

Lucy held firmly on to the step either side of her. 'OK, I'll go tell them.'

'Have you seen where you're sitting?'

'No' she lied. The seating plan was the first thing she'd looked at, relieved that Constance had put Steven two tables away from her.

'Ah, well. It will be a surprise, then.'

Lucy ignored the hand he offered to help her up. 'Why did you come?'

'How could I stay away when there was a chance of seeing you again?'

Lucy walked back into the restaurant ahead of him.

Constance had planned the seating so that she could perch at one end of the main table, in the brief moments when she could sit down and was not flying back and forth to the kitchen. Malcolm Hay would be to her right, with Lucy beside him, and a lawyer she had known since childhood on Lucy's right hand. Mark would sit on Constance's left, next to a food and wine PR agent whom Constance had been longing to involve in Mark's business. She asked them to take their places and not wait for her. In the slow fumbling as people looked for their seats, Lucy found herself between Malcolm and Steven. She glanced across the table at Mark, but he gave no sign of noticing the change.

'What a fluke . . .' Steven said pulling her chair out for her.

Lucy looked straight into his eyes with a direct, honest gaze and a polite smile. 'I hate you,' she said, very softly.

'Did you choose the *crêtes de coq*? I hope so . . . If not you can try mine. I was tempted by the salt cod, but I doubt there's a single establishment outside London offering coxcombs. Strange, that. They sound as if they ought to be traditional Dorset fare. I must mention that in my review.'

Lucy turned to her left. 'You're Malcolm Hay, aren't you? My name is Lucy. Connie has talked so much about you. She says you have always been a complete inspiration.'

When Constance finally joined them she gave no sign that she was surprised to find Steven next to Lucy, or Steven's guest next to Mark. Malcolm's wife and the PR were on another table altogether. She greeted Steven affectionately, introducing him to her other guests.

'You've met Lucy, of course, I introduced you before, but have you ever met Lucy's husband Mark?'

'I had that pleasure, yes.'

'Mark knows more about wine than anyone in the world —'

'Connie, please,' Mark remonstrated, 'there are probably ten people in this *room* who know more than I do.'

'You have a better feel for wine than anyone I've ever met,' Constance asserted. 'Malcolm, what did you think of the custard?' She bent her head to her mentor and listened like a disciple to the Sermon on the Mount.

The one advantage of many courses, Lucy thought, was that she could rely on most of the conversation being taken up by discussion of what they had just eaten, or eager anticipation of what they were about to be served. She tried to include herself in the culinary debate to her left, but other than craning her neck and smiling idiotically she could not penetrate the discussion. Mark and Marcella had drawn friendly swords over the relative merits of the *Carry On* films.

'May I?' Steven held his fork above Lucy's plate. 'It must be exceptionally good. I've never seen you so intensely preoccupied with your food.' Lucy stiffly drew back to let him fork up a section of deep-fried polenta. 'Superb. Brandade can be chalky, but that's like silk. What a cracking cook she is, wasted in Dorset . . . So, Lucy, made any New Year resolutions?'

Mark caught Steven's question and stabbed his knife towards his wife. 'She certainly has. She's going to stop smoking, aren't you, darling?'

Steven looked amused. 'You've hidden that very well. I didn't know you'd ever been tempted.'

Lucy tugged at her bottom lip with her teeth. 'It's only Mark's resolution for me. Mine is to spend more time at home.'

'Ah! The old cabinet-minister excuse.'

'True, in my case. What about you?'

'I rather think I might travel more . . . Mexico, perhaps. Or Morocco. I fear my tastebuds are getting a little jaded.'

'That sounds very nice.'

'Nice.' Steven stressed the word. 'Yes, I like nice things.

'Luce, help me out here,' Mark urged. 'Marcella insists that *Carry On Up the Khyber* is the best of the *Carry On* stable.'

'It is, isn't it?'

Marcella hooted triumphantly. 'See? Your own wife agrees with me.'

'You're all so bloody orthodox, you women, so conventional. Too scared to stick your necks out. *Carry On Follow That Camel* is *infinitely* superior . . .'

Marcella shook her head until her long jet earrings jangled. 'Steven? What do you think?'

'I'm not a fan of the genre myself.'

'Fair enough. Let's broaden it,' Mark offered. 'Greatest film ever, then.'

Marcella shuddered. 'I've spent the past twelve months writing my own top ten, and contributing to other people's lists. I'm sick of the whole business.'

'Bet you didn't put any *Carry On* films in there.'

'No,' Marcella conceded. 'Critics aren't allowed to give comedy the same weight as serious drama.'

'I find them rather closely connected.' Steven turned to Lucy. 'Don't you? Sometimes the impulse to laugh prevents us from weeping.'

'If not the reverse.' Mark answered, before his wife could.

'Is this the best-of-the-century game?' Constance joined the conversation. 'Malcolm? Greatest ever cook. Present company excepted.'

'I'm a traditionalist,' he growled. 'Auguste Escoffier.'

Constance folded her hands together in reverence. 'I'd go for a living legend. Joël Robuchon. Your turn, Steven.'

Steven shook his head. 'I can't except present company, Constance, not after that custard and the crêtes . . .' He kissed his fingertips gallantly. 'But if you twisted my arm perhaps I'd go for Thomas Keller.'

'In Napa? That's a thought. Greatest ever dish?'

'Impossible.'

'Greatest ever thinker?'

They all laughed without attempting a suggestion.

'I know.' Steven leaned across Lucy, addressing Constance. 'Greatest ever mother?'

'Eve!' someone volunteered.

Mark disagreed. 'Mother Teresa, got to be.'

'What about that Russian woman, the one who had sixty-nine children?' Marcella suggested, and was roundly rebuked for confusing quantity with quality. 'Fair cop. What do I know about motherhood, anyway? How about . . .' Her eyes widened, and she licked her lips suggestively, keeping them waiting. 'How about greatest ever lover?'

'Lucy, you're being very quiet.' Malcolm remarked. 'You start.'

'I don't like party games . . . I always draw a complete blank and wake up in the middle of the night knowing the perfect answer. I pass.' She fiddled with the menu, longing for midnight to strike, but there were four courses still to be endured. 'You lot go ahead, I don't want to spoil your fun.'

'Lucy's right. It's bloody boring doing this routine.' Constance rose to her feet. 'Excuse me for a minute.'

Julian slid smoothly into her place. 'I was rather hoping my wife might award *me* the accolade of greatest ever lover,' he murmured, with chagrin, bringing the subject to a merciful and humorous conclusion. Lucy glanced up to see Mark's eyes on her, mischievous yet loving, and felt a surge of strength. She smiled back with gratitude, touching her fingers to her lips. Steven witnessed the exchange as if he were watching them through a hidden telescope, with great magnification yet artificial proximity, and it wrenched him. Outwardly he looked composed and turned his lazy, equivocal smile, a smile that left women dangerously uncertain whether he was flirting outrageously or mocking them, on the visibly delighted Samantha.

After the fish course Constance instructed each man to move four places to his right. As Steven stood he touched Lucy's arm, and murmured, 'I do hope we get a moment to speak later.'

'So do I,' she replied politely.

'Do you?' He looked desolate. 'I thought you hated me.'

'I can still wish you a happy new year. I do.'

Before dessert was served Constance excused herself from the table, and made no attempt to conceal that she was going out for a smoke; several guests rose with her. 'Doesn't that prove how old we are? The last dinosaurs.'

'Go on, Lucy,' Mark called. 'Go join them, and say goodbye – so you know it's your last.'

With a wan smile Lucy trooped after the sinners. The light from the restaurant spilled softly over the first twenty feet, but the night was too dark to see faces clearly. Lucy withdrew to the furthest end of the garden terrace where Steven immediately joined her. He shook a few cigarettes from his pack and held it out to her. 'What made you take up smoking?'

'I didn't. You left your cigarettes in my bed that night.'

'Christ – of course, I must have.' Lucy nodded mutely. 'Mark found them, and you suddenly developed a secret habit.'

'Yes.'

'I'm sorry, that must have been very difficult for you. My fault.'

'It doesn't matter now.'

Steven spoke in a low urgent voice. 'It doesn't have to be this way, Lucy, it doesn't have to end.'

Lucy continued, in a cool, level tone, 'It was always going to end, we both knew that. I may not know much, but all the time, somewhere in the back of my mind, I knew the consequences, and there were only ever two possible results: either you and I stopped, or Mark and I stopped. The only thing I didn't anticipate was that it would all be over so quickly. But that's a blessing, isn't it? God, it's cold tonight!' Steven at once removed his jacket and draped it over her shoulders.

Constance, watching them from the other end of the terrace and pretending she wasn't, stiffened. 'Steven – Steven, just come up here for a second, would you? I need you to settle a bet.' She saw him bend again towards Lucy, shrug slightly, and then he joined her. She slipped her arm through his in a manner that seemed intimate; only Steven felt her vice-like grip as she marched him towards the french windows, leaning into his side. 'Listen to me, you bastard, I was all for telling you to fuck off but Lucy didn't want me involved. Tough. I *am* involved. I'm so involved I nearly put phenolphthalein in your wine when you had the gall to turn up.'

'Sounds interesting. Some sort of poison?'

'I wish. I don't keep poison in my kitchen, but I do keep a very potent and nasty laxative. I would have done it too, if I hadn't thought you might die of renal failure and I'd end up in prison.' All the time she spoke, Constance's hands flitted like moths in the light, and she smiled and fluttered her lashes, as if she was telling him a particularly risqué joke. 'You're on my turf, my territory, and if you make one more move towards that woman I swear to God I'll have your bollocks off and in a casserole before you can blink.' Steven looked startled, but continued to smile. 'I am absolutely serious. Leave Lucy alone. She loves Mark, and he adores her, and there's no room for you at all. Do you understand that?'

'I can't imagine how you might have made it any clearer, Constance. Thank you for your customary precision.' He jumped clumsily off the low wall, white shirtsleeves luminous in the dark, and he whistled lightly as strolled across the grass to where Lucy had retreated. 'There's been a mix-up about beds at Connie's – no room at the inn after all, I'm afraid.'

'You're not asking me to put you up, are you Steven? I won't do it.'

'Wouldn't dream of it, flower. Constance has shown me the red card, but I don't give a stuff about that. I just can't face looking at you any longer. No, we'll make our way back to London.'

'You can't drive. You'll get stopped and done. Or have an accident.'

'Ah.' Steven laid a hand over his heart. 'I'm touched by your concern for my well-being. Don't think about me, Lucy, there's no need to worry. Now, I believe we are being summoned back to the table.' He took her arm and patted her hand absent-mindedly.

Once in the restaurant, he bent down and whispered quickly to Marcella, then spent the rest of the dinner telling raucous stories of appalling meals he had been subjected to, and great ones during which he had disgraced himself. At eleven thirty he nodded to his colleague, slapped Julian on the back, and kissed Constance four times, each one more exuberant than the last. 'Quite the most splendid and *informative* meal I have had, dear Constance. You possess the one essential ingredient that turns a good chef into a great one – curiosity. I am already struggling to come up with the precise *bons mots* to capture the evening: The splendour of the *crêtes de coq*, and the tantalizing taster you gave me on the terrace of your recipe for *casserole des animelles* . . . I will have to return for that one another time.'

Constance could not control a fleeting smile. 'I'll wait for your review with bated breath, Steven.'

'The review. Yes. I shall enjoy writing it.'

Steven scanned the room for Mark, then pumped his hand vigorously. 'Sorry we didn't have more of a chance to talk about wines, old man. I'll keep an eye open for news of you in the press. Good luck, not that you need it.' Mark looked after him, a strange expression in his eyes.

Finally Steven returned to Lucy, hunkered down on his heels so that his face was inches from hers and took her hand between both of his. 'Goodbye, dear heart. I won't forget you, not a word, not a look, not a moment of you.' He brought her hand briefly to his lips, but did not touch it.

'It isn't even midnight.'

'I don't want to start the year with you knowing you are not going to be part of it.' He grinned suddenly. 'And now I have to work out quite how to get up from this idiotic position without drawing attention to the fact that I'm far too ancient to be squatting at a lady's feet.'

'Steven?' Lucy gripped his hand. 'Thank you. You've been very . . .' She could not finish the sentence. She did not watch him walk away, but she knew absolutely that one of them had to, and she was grateful he had taken it upon himself as a last gesture.

'Goodbye, Constance's flatmate.'

Striding towards the door he nearly collided with Samantha, who had been planning a longer and more intimate conversation in the hope that Steven's companion was simply a colleague. 'Steven! Oh, you're not leaving, are you? So early?'

He jerked his thumb to Marcella, who leaned in the doorway with a finger tapping her wristwatch and a sulky expression on her face, rolled his eyes to heaven and said, in a stage whisper, 'It's the girlfriend, I'm afraid. You should see what happens to her at midnight.'

Marcella waited impatiently for Steven to speak. He sat next to her in his car, rubbing his chin and staring out of the windscreen without seeing anything.

'Well? Are you going to explain why we had to leave like that?'

'No.'

'Can I hazard a guess?'

'No, flower, I'd rather you didn't.'

Marcella folded her arms across her chest. 'Fine. So we're going to sit here in your bloody car. I'm never going to forget that this was how I passed the most significant night of the past thousand years.' She punched him affectionately on the shoulder. 'So what did you think of the dinner, then? Thumbs up or down?'

'Definitely up.'

'I thought it was bloody amazing. By the way, what is *sot l'y-laisse*? I felt too much of a twit to ask.'

'It's a prime bit of chicken. A great delicacy that fools leave behind, the sort of fool you're looking at right this minute.' Steven turned the key in the ignition. 'Let's see if we can find a pub open that will sell us a bottle of whisky.'

Chapter Twenty-four

Come mothers and fathers throughout the land,
And don't criticize what you don't understand . . .
> Bob Dylan, 'The Times They Are A-Changin''

The first official sitting of the 53B Charlotte Street Management Committee did not convene until early February. The Purcells had spent most of January in Thailand, and the Epsteins felt as if they had spent most of it in the land of serious budgetary discussion. The two couples met for supper at Manor Farm and Constance spent the first hour recounting Thai tales and showing photographs; some were conventional holiday snaps, but a handful, of the kitchens of the Oriental Hotel, were more esoteric. Everything was back to normal as she chattered.

'Julian took the children off to Chiang Mai and I spent three days "observing" in the kitchens. It was an incredible experience – religious. It was like reaching Shangri-la. And I learned two great lessons. I had never understood before how important it is to be able to rescue things, do you know what I mean? That being able to undo something that's gone wrong is far more skilful than being able to do it right in the first place. On the third day they let me do some cooking myself, and I completely fucked it up. I was about to chuck it away and start again when a little old lady, Mrs Pen, one of the greatest cooks on earth, stopped my hand and showed me how to rescue it. It was like suddenly coming face to face with God.'

Mark, his head cocked to one side, asked, 'What was the other lesson?'

'Oh, it was more just facing up to a mistake I've been making for years. I make things too complicated. I've always been attracted to recipes that have seventeen different stages, and ninety-four ingredients. It was only showing off. Simplicity, that's my new rule.'

'I wish we'd never gone to Thailand,' Julian said mournfully. 'I'm facing a future of perfectly simple omelettes and boiled chicken.'

Constance ruffled his thinning hair. 'Oh, I'll still indulge you, darling, don't panic.'

As Lucy watched the gentle teasing between them, and saw how Mark laid the table without being prompted, filled their glasses, moved from her side to their guests to their children, she wished that marriage was as simple to understand as cooking. It appeared so from the outside, but she felt that her own had followed an enormously complicated recipe that she could only just keep ahead of, where the omission of any one ingredient might jettison the lot into the waste disposal.

'Being in Thailand made me rethink everything. I went out there thinking we were rounding things off in our life – you know, that Julian and I should just sit back and wait to be mail-shotted by Saga Holidays. I'd just about decided to take up basket weaving.'

'I thought you were going to open a deli? I was banking on it as a retail outlet.'

'Don't worry, Mark, I still am, and keeping the restaurant too.

You know how I'm always banging on about the stages of a meal? The selection of the ingredients, the preparation, the cooking, and then the eating? I thought we were well into the eating stage, me and Julian, in our working lives, our marriage, our kids, everything. Now I think we're still solidly in the prep.'

'You look born-again, Con. A real believer. What was this, some kind of second honeymoon?' Mark asked her, with an easy smile.

'You could say that. Not that I realized we needed one. You two should try it.' After the words left her mouth she glanced at Lucy and looked faintly embarrassed. 'Not that you need it either.'

'I'm booking tickets first thing . . . As soon as we can afford them.' Mark cleared his throat. 'Which brings me on to the flat. I'm terribly sorry to say this but Lucy and I have decided that we simply have to pull out of Charlotte Street. We can limp along for another six months or so without too much pain, but unless my sales have a dramatic expansion . . . Well, it's an awful admission, and a failure on my part. Poor Lucy loves the flat so.' He looked miserable, too miserable for Lucy to bear.

'That's not true at all, I want to sell as much as Mark does. It isn't just the money,' she explained loyally, 'it's a question of time. I've barely used the flat, and Mark has to concentrate on local clients for the time being, especially as he turned down the Scottish offer. You do understand, don't you? It just doesn't make sense for us.'

'We thought you might say something like that, and we have a proposal. You mustn't feel any obligation at all –'

'Constance, why don't you just tell them what it is rather than waffling like an old windbag?' Julian reprimanded her. 'Or perhaps I should explain . . .' Lucy and Mark hid their smiles, but Constance did not: if she had had a road-to-Damascus experience in Thailand, Julian certainly hadn't. 'Without in any way wishing to impose our views, or give the impression that we have

377

improperly leaped to conclusions about your financial situation, which is something I would seek to avoid at all costs –'

'Julian,' Constance prodded gently, 'spit it out.'

'The fact of the matter is, our own circumstances and capital have altered. Malcolm Hay has offered to take a fifty per cent stake in the Falcon, and that will enable us both to explore the idea of a retail outlet and take over all obligations for the flat.'

'We don't want to sell,' Constance concluded, 'because in a couple of years' Chessie and Luke may be in London, and they'll need somewhere – if they can ever manage to live together. And if they don't, we'll sell then and buy a student flat wherever they end up.'

'Assuming either of them manages to get into a university,' Julian warned gloomily.

'So in the meantime, we'll buy you out and leave things exactly as they are, and you can carry on using the flat when you like. What do you think?'

Mark sighed with relief. 'That's an enormously generous offer . . . And I'm going to accept before you have a chance to change your minds.'

'Oh, I feel marvellous!' Constance flung her arms out. 'Suddenly I feel reasonable, and calm, and mature. Isn't that wonderful? I'm thrilled I'm forty. Forty and proud.'

Lucy laughed at the sight of her – Constance looked as excited as a five-year-old at Christmas. 'I'll just make sure Charlie's turned his light off, OK? Then we'll eat.'

When Lucy was upstairs, Constance said abruptly, 'Julian, I forgot to tell you the gossip I heard at the farm when I went over to order. Mark, did you know that William Dawlish and his wife are breaking up?'

'General Sir William and Lady Dawlish?' Julian said, with mock horror. 'Good God! What is the world coming to? They must have been married for thirty years. If it can happen to them, of all people . . .'

'I'm intrigued by the semantics of that,' Mark mused, in a manner reminiscent of Julian. '*Does* a marriage break up, or does it break *down?*'

Constance laid her hand affectionately against his cheek. 'In my limited experience,' she said firmly, 'it does neither. It breaks *out*. Like acne.'

Lucy, who might have been comforted by Constance's comment, was not there to hear it: she was tucking Charlie into bed, and listening to his passionate diatribe against the injustice that had made David Harkham, a talented forward but a notorious bad sport, captain of the under-13s. 'Sometimes life seems unfair,' she soothed him with all the normal platitudes, 'but it all works out in the end. All these things happen for a reason, and you just have to carry on playing and believing in yourself.' Lucy could not imagine how Constance could profess such delight in her own maturity. It seemed to Lucy that she herself never spoke or behaved like a mature woman, but was simply tearing around inside like a lost teenager, a lamb dressed up as mutton. She feared it was all a question of confidence: Constance had it; she did not. She had always assumed that the older she became, the wiser she would be, but life had become more frightening, not less. Far from restoring confidence in herself, the affair with Steven had cast her adrift from her moorings. Mark appeared not to know and, taking Constance's advice to heart, Lucy had held her tongue, but the problem hadn't gone away. Looking back, Lucy could not see precisely where she had lost her footing in that mellow summer. She knew that she had revolted against the most mild form of conjugal neglect and turned herself into an adolescent thrill-seeker and of that she was profoundly ashamed. Somehow she had lost her balance and fallen headlong, but she did not understand why it had happened to her; it could be explained only as a fit of vertigo, a temporary insanity. It had taken her less than a month to convince herself that she had never been in love with Steven Armitage.

Things would never be exactly as they were, whatever Constance promised. The flat belonged, from that evening, to Constance and Julian, as if it had never been hers, as if her hand had never touched it. The flat was gone, Lucy knew that. It was simply another inanimate possession that could be thrown off as easily and impulsively as it had been acquired. She had clung to the idea of it long after Julian had walked in unexpectedly, weeks after it had ceased to signify anything for her. Now she felt a sense of relief, as if a person had walked out, closing the door gently behind them, as if Charlotte Street had chosen, quite of its own volition, to move on and play a role in some other person's life and leave her to restore her own. Every time she had left home for the flat, she had taken the same route out of her front door, passing the garage by inches, without a second thought in her hurry to get to Charlotte Street and find her life. In this way many people, good, kind, interesting people, pass by, missing their lives by inches, even by millimetres.

Marriage was not a straightforward package at all: it was very complicated, laced with all sorts of flavourings and levels of undertaking and negotiation, each following its own separate rules. Mark and Lucy had operated under a different set of rules: they had in their own ways taken marriage for granted and assumed it would flourish as effortlessly as a Yorkshire pudding rises, but they had not paid enough attention to the preparation. The rules that each gave priority, the ones they assumed the other would not tolerate being abused, had never been fully discussed or understood. In bed that night Lucy decided to make a new start as she lay in Mark's arms with her head on his chest.

'I'm glad we've resolved the flat, that it's settled and behind us.' He hugged her closer in agreement. 'There are so many things I regret about the whole thing.'

'Replastering the living room?'

'No . . . I'm being serious. I'm sorry it was such a drain on you. You didn't need that, not with everything going on here.'

'I was the one who pushed you into it.' Mark was determined to take responsibility.

'Mark, if you wanted to pack in the wine trade altogether, if you just wanted to paint, you *would* tell me, wouldn't you? I have this horrible feeling that somehow you're nobly throwing it away, throwing yourself away for me, for the idea of being secure and like the Purcells.'

Mark smiled in the gloom. 'I have never wanted to be like the Purcells. I want to be like us.'

'But you should paint more. All this time I've been living with you, and I never realized how talented you are —'

'Shut up, Luce. I am not talented. You only think so because I finally managed something that was worth showing. I've painted hundreds that would have proven how little talent I have.'

'Why didn't you ever show me?'

'They were mistakes. You didn't need to know about them.'

'You should paint full time.'

'Oh, darling, I'm a Sunday painter, that's all I've ever wanted to be. It would ruin it for me if I did it every day, or had to make it my living. I'm happy.'

'Are you?'

'Truly.'

If she had believed him she might have left it there, but she did not. 'We have to talk about the flat . . .'

'It's late.'

'I know. I have to tell you about Charlotte Street. There are things that happened that you should know.'

'Nothing happened.'

Lucy persisted, swallowing nervously. 'There's something I have to tell you about Steven, that night . . .'

'No, there isn't.' Mark kissed her. 'There's a whole world of things we will never know about each other. If I knew everything about you I couldn't paint you, and I want to go on painting you. It will take time, a good forty years or so, but you never know, I might even get the hang of it at last.'

'But, Mark —'

He laid his hand gently over her mouth. 'Hush, darling. There's no more to be said. The only thing to be said about Steven Armitage is that he's a bastard for not bothering to give Connie a good write-up. And that's *it*.' He spoke with finality. 'I love you, Lucy. Go to sleep now.'

So he knows, Lucy thought, he knows everything. She lay quietly on Mark's chest with her eyes open, her head gently rising and falling in time with his breath, and wondered what Charlie, Grace and Abigail would make of her fall from grace, or Francesca and Luke of their father's. Unless they were told, they could only ever guess at the characters of their parents, trying to piece together fragments of their histories, but never seeing the whole. As Lucy worried what her children would think of her if they knew the truth, she overlooked that children hide just as much as their parents do. All sorts of things must be hidden, the whispered cloakroom conversations, the snatched glimpses of pornography, the petty cruelties that occur in the changing rooms or on the sports field, the carelessly discarded banana skins . . . All these things had to be hidden from parents or partners in case it took them to a point at which they were not permitted to love.

There was a reciprocal agreement to hide the unpleasant, and present the pleasant front, which justified the sin of tinkering, mildly, with the truth. Charlie on his computer simulation game, Constance in her kitchen, Julian, sitting alone at the window looking down on Charlotte Street, Mark in his garage: they all needed to pretend that they were in control. They all needed to play God.

No, they would not tell. In time, Constance and Julian might look back, ever more reflectively as time stretched away, and regret they had not talked more openly to each other and to their friends. Lucy and Mark might turn to each other, years later, with a steady gaze, and admit, 'Ah, yes, that was a sticky patch, but we came through . . .' But they would not tell.

A week after the future of the Charlotte Street flat was finally resolved, Steven Armitage stood restlessly in the snaking immigration queue at Benito Juarez International Airport. It was five days before St Valentine's Day, when he planned to return to the arrivals hall and watch from a distance to learn who, if anyone, turned up. Perhaps he would discover at last the identity of the Fourth Man, not that he cared much if any of them turned up. Steven was tired of London and London people and his job. He had been quite incapable of writing a fitting review of the Lonely Falcon, because every attempt he made had degenerated into an essay on the complacent cruelty of the married. Yet he missed Lucy, and he could not help imagining how things might have been, and how it would be to have her standing beside him, bright-eyed, impatient to see what the world had to offer. He would not forget her, however resolute his determination to look forward. He could not see it, he barely knew it yet, but Lucy had marked him as permanently as if he had been raw clay and she had pressed her thumb, lightly but firmly, on his centre, approved the hollow indentation and set him out to bake in the hot sun. All Steven knew when he flung his bag into the back of the battered taxi, which took off screeching for the city, was that some essential part was missing from the mosaic of his life.